On Loving Josiah

On Loving Josiah

ON LOVING JOSIAH

MAIA

Arcadia Books Ltd
15–16 Nassau Street
London W1W 7AB

www.arcadiabooks.co.uk

First published in Great Britain by The Maia Press,
an imprint of Arcadia Books 2011

ISBN 978-1-906413-79-8

Typeset in Garamond by MacGuru Ltd
Printed and bound in the United Kingdom by CPI Cox & Wyman, RG1 8EX

Arcadia Books gratefully acknowledges the financial support of Arts Council England.

Arcadia Books supports English PEN, the fellowship of writers who work together to promote literature
and its understanding. English PEN upholds writers' freedoms in Britain and around the world,
challenging political and cultural limits on free expression. To find out more, visit
www.englishpen.org or contact
English PEN, Free Word Centre, 60 Farringdon Road, London EC1R 3GA

Arcadia Books distributors are as follows:

in the UK and elsewhere in Europe:
Turnaround Publishers Services
Unit 3, Olympia Trading Estate
Coburg Road
London N22 6TZ

in the US and Canada:
Dufour Editions
PO Box 7
Chester Springs
PA, 19425

in Australia:
The GHR Press
PO Box 7109
McMahons Point
Sydney 2060

in New Zealand:
Addenda
PO Box 78224
Grey Lynn
Auckland

in South Africa:
Jacana Media (Pty) Ltd
PO Box 291784
Melville 2109
Johannesburg

Arcadia Books is the *Sunday Times* Small Publisher of the Year

For all those teachers I have ever loved.

Chapter One

THE INTERVIEW WAS NOT GOING WELL. The man, a young psychiatrist of about thirty, was cowering at a large desk littered with discarded mugs of coffee, while the woman was standing on the other side of it, railing down at him inches from his face.

'So, you diagnose love, do you? Ten years at medical school and that's all they can teach you, you ass!'

'I won't be spoken to like this,' managed the psychiatrist, attempting to meet his adversary in the eye. 'Eve is my patient.'

'"My patient"!' the woman scoffed. 'A more accurate description, young man, would be "my prisoner" or perhaps even "my poodle".'

'Stop it!' The psychiatrist stood up abruptly, eyes ablaze. 'Mrs de Selincourt,' he said, and took some deep breaths, 'the next time you come here to discuss your daughter's progress I suggest you make an appointment. Now, if you'll excuse me, I have work to be getting on with.'

But Mrs de Selincourt wasn't finished with him yet. 'Work? Work? Is that what you call it? Look at the state of you! Look at the state of this room! In my day, secretaries used filing cabinets. Bins were emptied at night!'

The psychiatrist took another deep breath and said, 'Just go, please.'

Mrs de Selincourt, stout and immaculate in tight tweed, surveyed her victim coldly. 'Very well, Dr Fothering. I shall see you at the case conference at two.'

Dr Fothering visibly shrank. 'The case conference? You received an invitation?'

'I wouldn't have driven all the way up from Harrow had I not, Dr Fothering.'

The psychiatrist winced. 'I'm afraid,' he began (and those two words contained the whole truth of the matter). 'I'm afraid your daughter has specifically requested that you shouldn't attend this afternoon.'

'Then damn my daughter's request!' Mrs de Selincourt thrust her hand into her handbag and produced a letter. 'Dr Goodman invited me. Now, could you be so kind as to direct me to his office? Please, don't look quite so idiotic. He is, after all, the consultant directly responsible for my daughter's welfare.'

And then Dr Fothering forgot his deep breaths, and indeed, forgot to behave like a doctor at all, but began pacing the room and muttering, 'It's not his case! It's not his case!'

'I think you'll find that it is,' insisted the woman, victoriously. 'Read this.'

Dr Fothering swept the letter aside with the back of his hand, and, utterly impassioned, he cried out, 'This has nothing to do with him! Leave him out of this! You're right, the buck stops at me, I know Eve! And I know she has every chance of happiness. So blame me if things go wrong. But they haven't yet, Mrs de Selincourt. I beg you, don't jeopardize her chances now! Let her be!'

At that moment a pale girl in a pink, much-washed wincyette dressing-gown appeared in the doorway. Mrs de Selincourt's back was turned towards her, and she waved at Dr Fothering, alternately smiling and making faces.

'Mother! What a nice surprise!' she said, when the joke had gone on too long and Dr Fothering's expression had begun to betray her presence. 'I didn't expect you. You should have written. Oh Doctor Fothering, I blame you – why didn't you tell me? You know how I like to dress up for an occasion.'

'Eve', said Dr Fothering gently. 'I thought you wanted your

mother not to be present.' But Eve resisted his tone and looked at her mother.

Mrs de Selincourt was used to smoothing over many a diplomatic embarrassment and said, 'I hear you're quite well now, my dear girl. Perhaps it's time you came home.'

'I've never been better,' said Eve.

'But you need fresh air, I can see that.'

'You're quite right there. But Mummy, they must have told you, I'm going to marry a gardener. Not quite our class, I know, but quite wholesome. He's a good, solid man. But I can't say you'd like him because you probably wouldn't.'

'Darling, you're twenty! You know nothing of life!'

'But more than you, mother dear. They should turn Fulbright hospital into a finishing school. For the human condition is fairly dire. We spend our lives hiding from that fact, but I feel privileged to have discovered it.'

'Dear God! Oh Eve! Oh Eve! She shouldn't be here, you idiot, Fothering. How dare you keep her in this place? She's saner than you are!' And then, witness this, the last maternal feeling the woman ever felt for Eve: 'Please, darling, come home with us, leave this place, we'll take a holiday the three of us, anywhere you choose….'

❧

It was the last maternal feeling Patricia de Selincourt ever felt for her daughter, but it would be just as true to say it was the first. Nor would it be fair to blame her. It was just one of those gross mismatches between parent and offspring that occur from time to time; for her elder child, George, had adored his mother, and she, him – indeed, their first seven years together, before George's dispatch to a first-rate English prep school, had been a text-book case of excellent mothering: boundaries drawn on the one hand, observed on the other. Eve did not like boundaries, and had railed against them since her first breath. And disobedience was not only intolerable to Mrs de Selincourt, it was incomprehensible.

So when Eve was two, her mother decided she must be deaf and took her to a specialist on Harley Street.

'Eve, look at the doctor when he's talking to you,' she'd commanded, but the pretty blonde moppet had continued to jump on and off a pair of scales and seemed to register nothing. But all the paraphernalia of temptation, the watches and the toy parrots, lured Eve out of herself, and the doctor had said, 'No need to worry there, Mrs de Selincourt.' In fact, he was wrong: a diagnosis would have been a relief.

Mother and daughter continued to drive each other to extreme versions of themselves. Mrs de Selincourt, the perfect wife to a man who needed one – always a gracious hostess to his business clients, always at the ready with a dozen ironed shirts and a peck on the cheek when he came home from work – never imagined that being a perfect mother would be any more demanding. She had happily sacrificed any vision of the modern ideal – that of self-fulfilment – to old-fashioned duty: to her husband, her family, the village church; and duty, besides, to the society whose values she respected and found true. For her, love was an almost biblical concept, interwoven with the idea of charity, not the sentimental, emotion-sodden version we have of it nowadays.

As Eve grew older, her mother became more and more intolerant of her behaviour. In short, Eve humiliated her. It was one thing to have Eve refuse point blank to go to bed when the family was alone; it was quite another when she sabotaged important dinner parties by coming downstairs at midnight to sing to the assembled guests. No one who saw her will ever forget her rendition of *Life is a Cabaret* at the age of ten, dressed in fuchsia pink and diamante, one of her mother's cocktail creations, and now dragging across the floor. The trouble was, she was sufficiently good at it that people were unsure whether to congratulate her mother or commiserate with her. Mrs de Selincourt looked at her husband for some sound, silent advice; and he nodded at her and smiled as if to say, relax, it's quite funny, it's all right. But when Eve picked up her skirts and revealed eighty pounds' worth of brand new silver stilettos, Mrs de Selincourt leapt up from her seat. Eve didn't even notice her, and only saw in the newly vacant chair a convenient way of getting up onto the table. 'Come taste the wine,' she sang, 'come hear the band,' and the guests began moving aside their plates and glasses to make room for her; 'Come blow the horn, start celebrating,' she bellowed out, her skinny arms flailing about in the air. There followed a general cacophony, led by Sir Ralph Holland, managing director of British Aerospace, who had flown over from the Isle of Man specially for the party, and was rumoured to be on the point of large, private investment in Mr de Selincourt's fledgling company. He had begun enthusiastically banging his wine glass with his fork, and was shouting across to him, 'What a wonderful girl! My daughter won't say boo to a goose.'

Not an eye, not an ear was directed towards Mrs de Selincourt, who was whispering to herself, 'May God strike her down.' At every dance step she watched the silver heels embedding themselves into eighteenth century mahogany. What barbarians were these to clap for her? Do decent folk turn into a hideous, belching mass as easily as this? Eve shot her a look of victory, and began lifting up the pink skirts and swaying her child's hips. She was wearing her mother's peach cami-knickers held up by the belt of her school tunic; and kicking her legs up high, she sang to her,

'No use permitting some prophet of doom
To wipe ev'ry smile away,
Life is a cabaret, old chum,
Come to the cabaret.'

Her mother left the room, but no one noticed. Everyone's eyes were on the girl. They were laughing, cheering, raising their glasses to her. Mrs de Selincourt sat at the dressing-table in her bedroom, listening to their cries of 'encore!'

Eve's teachers were to fare somewhat better with her; twenty other children in the class made one to one confrontations the exception rather than the rule. And anyway, Eve was not wilfully destructive; rather, she was willfully absent, refusing to commit herself to what was going on around her. After a few weeks of vainly persuading Eve to co-operate, they saw no reason why they should bother. Every year in September, as Eve moved up through the classes, there was a surge of enthusiasm to 'crack' her; but already by November whoever was the latest of Eve's teachers became tired and gave up.

What infuriated them most was the fact that Eve was so fearfully bright, and couldn't be relegated to the 'slow' stream and left to moulder. She made them suspicious of their ability to teach. If she wasn't gazing into space she would watch her teachers with a terrifying alertness, not out of eagerness to learn but in an attitude of judgment and criticism. No one could claim they had ever *taught* Eve a thing, and yet if she ever condescended to fill in an exam script she was generally first in the class.

Finally a September did arrive, however, in Eve's lower sixth year, when a teacher managed to strike a chord in her. His name was Gilbert Fitzpatrick and he taught her English. Gilbert had, of course, already been briefed about Eve by his colleagues; but he was new to the school and wanted to be open-minded. Perhaps the technique he used to win her was the one Eve had been craving for all these years: namely, he fell in love with her. While she sat judging him at the back of the class, his eyes met hers and softened. There was no retreat, no defence, no refuge, just a look of utter appreciation and love. And Gilbert reaped his reward.

One day Eve was lagging behind the others during the general exodus at break-time, and as she passed his desk, she brushed her mouth against his ear and whispered, 'I love you too, Mr Fitzpatrick.' How could we blame Gilbert for not exhibiting what the headmaster was later to call 'some sense of adult authority and responsibility towards the young'? Because Gilbert knew, as soon as he saw Eve, that she wasn't young at all, and most likely she had never been young in the way that so many adult idealists conceive the word. Mere bodily innocence doesn't imply spiritual innocence. So Gilbert kissed her; and the affair began.

Gilbert invited Eve home with him after school (you did *what?* the headmaster was to exclaim) and recited passages from Byron's *The Bride of Abydos* to her, while she lay with her head in his lap:

Such was Zuleika, (he murmured, stroking her hair)
such around her shone
The nameless charms unmarked by her alone –
The light of love, the purity of grace,
The mind, the Music breathing from her face,
The heart whose softness harmonized the whole,
And oh, that eye was in itself a Soul.

'My darling,' responded Eve, 'Take me.'

And quite soon, the radiant autumn light pouring in through the windows of Gilbert Fitzpatrick's sitting-room, took on a seedy lustre while those two fucked and fucked and fucked, and their little love-nest was no longer the place 'where the virgins are soft as the rose they twine, and all save the spirit of man is divine,' but became, to put it frankly, a little squalid.

They got away with it quite satisfactorily the first term, but as their dependence on each other increased it became more and more obvious to the world at large. When Mrs de Selincourt went to see the Headmaster to question the advisability of Eve taking on a second musical instrument when she seemed to be making so little progress with her first, the Headmaster asked simply, 'What time does Eve get home?' and went a deep red.

Gilbert Fitzpatrick was unceremoniously sacked later that day, and Eve was instructed to remain under the strict supervision of her parents for the next three weeks. Not strict enough, however: she ran away after a day, and was to spend the next year and a half with Gilbert in his cottage. Neither washed much, neither ate much; they spent days upon days in bed together until the sheets were crispy with dried semen.

In the September of 1980, in a state of high conscience, Gilbert persuaded Eve to sit the entrance exam for Cambridge. He sent her up to London to stay with a friend of his who taught English at Westminster Tutors, and paid out of his own pocket (by now her parents had disowned her) for his protégée to take her A Levels within the year. Eve felt happy and worked well, even taking up Greek and immersing herself in the tragedies of Aeschylus. But when she returned to Gilbert at the end of November, a bottle of champagne tucked away in her overnight bag to celebrate the end of her exams, he was dead. 'I love you, Eve,' he wrote, 'but I'm drowning you with my own need. Be brave, but above all, be good.' By the time she found his over-drugged body it was a week old and it smelt.

Eve's grief quietened her. She returned to London numb and serious. She stopped reading love poetry, put aside the tragedies and took refuge in the dry-as-sawdust histories of Livy, Tacitus and Thucydides. Her family, rejoicing in the demise of the man who had robbed them of their daughter, made every effort to persuade her to come home. Mrs de Selincourt even went to London to fetch her, arguing that she was now old enough to commute to West-minster Tutors and she wasn't looking as well fed as she might. Eve surveyed her mother with wonder, as a palaeoethnologist might a new genus of ape. Mrs de Selincourt was understandably hurt, and began saying things her husband and friends had warned her against saying: namely, that the world was better off without filthy men like Fitzpatrick inhabiting it. That didn't go down at all well. For while Eve was sitting demurely, eyes downcast, on the sofa, her landlord (Gilbert's friend) had put himself on guard outside the room where the ill-fated meeting took place, and now swept in to send the 'Old Witch!' packing.

There was one further and final sally from the de Selincourt camp: Eve's older brother George invited her to tea. George, strid-ing the room, hands in pockets and with the attitude of a feisty young barrister (which he was) had tried to persuade his sister to at least go home at weekends, as their parents were terribly upset, and needed her, at least as much as she, in her heart of hearts, must need them. He was quite persuaded by his own pretty speech, and within minutes of her departure was on the phone to his mother to report back that she'd 'distinctly softened.' It was only later, sitting among cronies in a cramped wine bar in Chelsea, that he realised Eve had stolen £40 from his wallet.

Eve only began to be herself again the following year, in her first term at Cambridge. Despite passing her entrance exam in English she soon switched to Classics, and the faculty welcomed her with open arms. Yes, I believe there were a few weeks in which she truly excelled, delighting in her subject as much as the dons delighted in her. But what is it 'to be oneself'? For sometimes it might just be better not to be oneself, or rather, a more perfect version of oneself. Someone who listens to others and follows their suggestions, for example. But by the end of the Michaelmas term, Eve was already fancying she knew better about almost everything than anyone. She wrote a paper on the pre-Socratic philosopher, Heraclitus, which she immediately submitted to *Mind*, and when they didn't publish it declared the magazine to be too 'timorous' for her. She began translations of the *Iliad* and *Aeneid* simultaneously, because the Penguin editions were not sufficiently passionate. She auditioned for the part of Medea in a Greek play, and despite not getting it, learnt the part anyway and would hover at the back of the theatre when the rehearsals took place, politely suggesting alternative renditions of particular speeches. When the director asked her to leave, she simply apologized and promised to be quiet, and seemed quite immune to the shouting and the threats which her mere presence provoked.

There are, quite probably, some very sensible, scientific words for Eve's character: 'bipolar personality', 'manic depressive', perhaps, a box for her with a label on it and a shelf number. Some hope! Nothing could contain Eve. Rather, she was as noble and as carefree as the weather; she was like the wind changing mid-flight, she was the thunder rolling and the hot air rising, she was a wonder of nature and a natural disaster.

And it was this latter manifestation, I'm afraid, which set her on the road to a madhouse, the box of all boxes, to have and to hold until deemed more wonder than disaster. What happened was this.

It was May Week, 1982. A picnic in the meadows of Granchester, Eve and half a dozen friends swimming naked in the Cam, and then an argument. There had been a short item in the paper that morning about a prostitute who, on her deathbed, told her only son to give her 'immoral earnings' to a Christian charity; the son had dutifully done so, only to have the cheque refused.

'That's ridiculous,' said Eve, 'it might have been a story of redemption, yet it's been thwarted by the bloody Christian Church.'

They all agreed with her, all except one called Bill who supposed in a rather dry, old fogeyish way that the charity might have been accused of money laundering.

'Why did the son tell the charity where the money had come from?' put in one of the girls.

'Because he wanted to tell the truth,' said Eve. 'To share in his mother's deathbed confession purified him, too. After all, he was probably the son of one of her clients.'

'I'm not persuaded,' said Bill. 'Stories of redemption are *passé*. And isn't it worth making a stand against corruption?'

So far so good. The little party was warm and well-wined, the girls still topless after their swim, Bill lying stark naked on the grass proving once and for all to his girlfriend what a free spirit he could be.

Eve rolled over on top of him, 'Do you think I'm corrupt, Bill?'

'Get off him, Eve,' said the girl whose boyfriend he was. The boyfriend was having an erection.

'If I did a sponsored fuck for charity, would the charity accept it, do you think? Would that meet with your moral approval?'

'Get off me,' said Bill.

'If by making love to me, you knew you would save the lives of ten starving children in Africa, couldn't I tempt you?'

Then she wet her forefinger with her tongue, and slowly stroked his lips with it. 'How much would you pay me, Bill?'

There was a pause. Interestingly, the others put on their clothes before physically pushing Eve off him.

'Challenge me,' she said. 'Go on, challenge me.'

'We challenge you,' said Bill's girlfriend, because she wanted Eve to be treated like the whore she was.

It wasn't difficult. It took three days and three nights; 148 lovers, paying on average £18–00 each, raised a spectacular £2664. And as she explained to Mr Frederick Upton, that fine, longstanding commissar of Christian Aid in the Cambridge district, as she thrust both cash and cheques into his hands, each and every act was one of love: for they did not choose her, but she, them, and indeed, the entire operation was conducted with the utmost propriety, and, said Eve, blowing the word into Mr Upton's unhappy ear, 'whispering'.

'Whispering?' repeated the incredulous Mr Upton.

'Yes,' proclaimed Eve, proudly. 'I would whisper, "I'm making love for charity, and I would like to make love to you." And I told them the truth, Mr Upton. Let me assure you that I'd never dream of using my body as a mere vehicle for men's lust. I certainly don't know what you use your body for, sir, but I use mine to express love. And when my sponsors asked me to tell them more, I would explain that the Greek root of the word 'charity' was love, the very highest form of love, and I was merely enjoying the lowest form of love to reach the echelons of the highest. And I would whisper in the dear boys' ears, "Socrates himself would have understood where I was coming from. Come with me!"'

Mr Upton was trying to put a generous angle on things; the girl, perhaps, had merely missed out on a sound Christian upbringing; and he began gathering up the money which had spilled out onto the floor while he muttered, 'Goodness me! Goodness me!'

'I do so admire men like you!' gushed Eve, suddenly. 'I've always liked older men, all my life I have, I swear I like their constancy!'

'Constancy?' Mr Upton queried.

'I suppose because I am thoroughly inconstant.'

'Surely…' began Mr Upton. The 'not' stayed put.

'You don't mind me asking if you're married?'

'Now, now, dear,' Mr Upton managed.

'Are you?' Eve persisted.

'Indeed, I'm a widower.' Mr Upton looked distinctly uneasy, and cast a look towards his secretary's door.

Eve kicked off her shoes and planted herself on Mr Upton's desk, dangling her legs in front of him.

'I'm not sure this is money we should accept. You understand, we are a Christian charity. Now, here, here,' (quaked the poor man as he gathered up the money and put it in a plastic bag from which he'd previously shaken sandwich crumbs) 'take it back. Thank you for your good will but you must go.'

Eve wasn't listening to him. She picked up one of the letters on his desk and exclaimed, 'Frederick! What a wonderful name you have! Do you mind if I call you "Frederick"? I want you to know I understand where you're coming from. It's a difficult decision you have to make. But Frederick, I've earned you over two thousand pounds for the poor and needy of the world. And if you don't accept it what would I do with it? For my sponsors gave the money to me, no, entrusted it to me so that I should give it to you. Therefore imagine my guilt if I simply put it all in an account in my name. And look here, some of these cheques have already been made out to "Christian Aid". Now, I insist you dispose of them, not I, for in each one I see a "Thank you" and a human life changed for the better.'

Mr Upton's head was in overdrive; she had a point, he thought. Perhaps he should keep the cheques and she the cash… but that was inconsistent. If it had all been given in good faith, perhaps he really should keep the whole lot. For the Cambridge district branch of Christian Aid had had a lean year, his fundraising abilities questioned, and worse, his impending retirement looked forward to by several young evangelists.

'You look worried, Frederick,' said Eve, gently. 'I tell you what you must do. Come lay your head here on my lap. The velvet of my skirt is so soft. Feel it, Frederick. You'll look just like John the Baptist's head on Salome's pillow. My heart's contracting at the very thought. What love she had for him, that poor woman.'

And even in the second that followed, the way was not clear for poor Mr Upton, not clear at all. For to his shock and horror a part of him yearned to lay his head on the beautiful Eve's lap, and be stroked softly by her, for the years had treated him harshly, and even his dead wife had never looked so tenderly at him.

But his better part suddenly stood to attention.

'Mavis' he called, barging into her office, 'Mavis, there's a woman in here and she's not welcome.'

Eve indignantly jumped off the desk and said, 'Who's Mavis? What's she doing here?'

Mavis was equally indignant, but was used to defending Mr Upton from predators. She was a short, dumpy woman with a great chest like a buttress and stood between him and the velveteen spectacle before her.

'Mr Upton, do you wish me to call the police?'

'Not yet, Mavis. She does seem to have calmed down a little.' Mr Upton instinctively brushed down his suit and resumed a serious air. He looked at Eve and said, 'If you go of your own accord, and take the money with you, we can forget this ever happened.'

But Eve would have none of it. 'How could you betray me like that, Frederick? How could you just turn me in like that? Just when I felt the stirrings... Oh, oh Frederick, just when I was beginning to love you, for what is love but the spirited and unconditional acceptance of another human being?'

'She's a mad woman,' said Mavis.

'And she's a jealous one,' retorted Eve. 'I can spot a rival a mile off. She loves you, too, doesn't she?'

(And indeed Mavis did, and had for many years, even before the death of his wife.)

'We insist that you go! The door! Go!' reiterated Mavis.

'"Insist?"' laughed Eve. 'I've always thought it so funny the way people say, "I demand" and "I insist" when what they mean is, "I feel my power slipping away and I don't like it." And today's your unlucky day, Mavis, today I have the power. I'm limitlessly sexy; what greater power is there? But we need privacy, don't we, Frederick? Our kind of love doesn't come in threes. Now, Mavis, there's a dear, you couldn't leave us, could you?'

'You whore! You whore!' whimpered Mavis. 'And you look like one! Mr Upton, I'm calling the police!' And the fretting, tutting Mavis left the two together.

Mr Upton, who was all heart when it came to it, found himself quite confused. He even found himself feeling faint pricklings of desire for the young girl as she took his hand in hers.

'Eve, you must go, go now before it's too late,' he said, anxiously, withdrawing his hand a few seconds later than he might have.

Then Eve stood on her toes and planted a wet kiss on Mr Upton's mouth.

'I like you,' she said. 'We have about twenty minutes. Then they can carry me out.'

But Mr Upton resisted her (though not her money, as it transpired), as did the policeman, even when Eve told him she wouldn't budge an inch unless he put handcuffs on her, and proffered him her fine wrists. The policeman's colleagues down at the station resisted her too, despite her requests to be strip-searched; and the duty social worker resisted her, despite being a lesbian, and the duty psychiatrist resisted her, because it was his daughter's school play that evening and he wanted to get back in time to see it. So what alternative was there than to admit her to Fulbright Hospital with the full intention of sorting it out in the morning? Only the duty psychiatrist hadn't reckoned on Dr Fothering doing a ward round that Tuesday, and Dr Fothering couldn't resist her. No, for Eve de Selincourt captivated Dr Fothering from the very first moment they met. Dr Fothering, you see, was a closet postmodern Freudian analyst, and had spent two years in the U.S. studying the primacy of the female orgasm under the celebrated Weichian psychiatrist, Dr. Anselm Bott.

For there was something so *fluid* about Eve, something so innocent, something so unscathed by the demands of living in a society, that intrigued Dr Fothering. There was one way in which she was the most mentally healthy person he had ever met; and yet another in which she was a sociopath, who needed to understand that the values of others were worth considering, even if she did not hold them herself.

'Are you suggesting that I be duplicitous?' the winsome Eve asked him, on his suggestion that she might be more aware of others' sensitivities.

'Perhaps human beings are supposed to be, to a certain extent, duplicitous. A self without others can't exist. You need others to forge your very identity. You either beat 'em or you join 'em.'

'I've always beaten them!' said Eve with some pride. 'But look where it's got me. Look where integrity gets you nowadays. Now, I do so hate this sterile room. Can't we go to a pub or something?'

'Stick to the point, Eve!'

'But what is the point?' asked Eve, listlessly. 'Isn't the very point that there is no point?'

'Has there ever been a point, Eve? Has there ever been a time in your life when there's been meaning in it?'

During the eighteen months of Dr Fothering's in-depth therapy, Eve never referred to the one decent and wonderful thing, or rather, dreadful and most terrible thing, which had ever happened to her. She never even breathed the name of Gilbert Fitzpatrick. Though this did not mean she didn't think of him, particularly when Dr. Fothering would begin, 'I want you to remember something that made you sad. You are not connecting to your ability to be sad.'

'I thought your job was to make me happy.'

'Don't you wish to be out of here?'

'I never made any friends at University. Everyone hated me in the end. Why would I want to go back to a place where everyone hates me? You at least don't hate me, do you?'

'No, of course I don't hate you.'

'Then,' purred Eve, 'It's in my interests to stay here.'

'Have you ever wondered why people hate you?'

'No.'

'Not ever?'

'It's none of my business,' said Eve, demurely.

Dr Fothering's relationship with his boss proved rather more testing. Eve's consultant, Dr Goodman, was more amused than alarmed by Eve's early morning ritual, in which she would sneak round the wards and lay her hand on the brow of each and every patient, murmuring, 'May you receive my love.' (Indeed, it was Gibson Nelson's assurances that he had received it that brought him to her attention.) Dr Goodman understood that she fascinated his young registrar, and he also understood that she was proving good fodder for Dr Fothering's MSc dissertation; but Eve's reluctance to leave and Dr Fothering's reluctance to see her go were in themselves not sufficient causes to keep her as a patient in Fulbright hospital: her bed was needed for more pressing cases. This was as much the truth now as it had been six months previously, the last time Dr Fothering had invited Dr Goodman to read his files on the case, with all the trepidation and possessiveness of a young writer with his first novel.

The working title of Dr Fothering's thesis was, *The Self and Society: A Case History*. To give him his credit, he was most excited by the fact of Eve's turning on its head much of what he had held dear. Eve was a radical, a megalomaniac: not in the realm of politics, where we might begin to identify with her, but in the realm of *Self*. She demanded absolute power, and achieved it by behaving in exactly the way she chose when she chose. But the most enthralling and gratifying thing about Eve was that all Dr Fothering had to do was massage her eyelids, and she was in command of the maximum orgasmic tilt, the Weichian definition of supreme mental health. No wonder the beleaguered registrar found it quite impossible to discharge her.

Dr Goodman, however, was a drugs-orientated man and was by nature suspicious of therapy. He held that people *qua* people could be talked into and out of everything, and it was certainly not the business of a mere doctor to claim to know what his patient should be talked into or out of: rather he should seek to find a physical malfunction in that most complicated of organs, the brain, and attempt to alleviate the symptoms accordingly. Psychiatrists were not demigods, he reminded his students: and they would do well to stick to the finer points of chemistry, for it was the correct dosage of a drug, and not the *mot juste*, which would, in the end, cure them.

So Dr Goodman had scanned his registrar's much-loved files on the subject of Eve right there, right in front of his nose. Eve's description of the sexual act as 'a beautiful integration of the self' afforded Dr Fothering material for an entire chapter: Eve, he suggested, had achieved an extraordinary short-circuit to genital primacy, which he had spent several sessions exploring with her. He discovered that she had no envy of the penis; and even, as a child, had been quite conscious of wanting her father to make love to her, but was also aware of the time when that desire was displaced onto other objects.

'No child can be conscious of the displacement of desire,' said Dr Goodman.

'You should question her yourself. I've never witnessed anything like it,' insisted the registrar.

'You know I don't like this approach, Michael.'

'I've found a supervisor in Peterborough, Graham Peterson. He's more sympathetic to Freudian analysis.'

'I want that in writing if you please,' said Dr Goodman curtly.

'But understand what an extraordinary case this is! It's her very state of consciousness which sets Eve apart, she's not shrouded her natural instincts as the rest of us do, in layer upon layer of socialization...'

'Then why is she the patient and we, us poor socialized sods, her doctors?'

'Don't you see? Early Freud would have agreed with you, the sense of power her body had given her is quite remarkable, but later Freud developed the idea of the super-ego, which is akin to the conscience, and results from the introjection of parental authority. But Eve's never done that, don't you see? She's never introjected her parents' authority, and therefore can't regulate her own moral behaviour. In a nutshell, Eve's mother was too strict with her, and never provided the space in which Eve's super-ego could grow, but made it superfluous by doing all the regulating on its behalf. That's the kernel of it: there's been little or no internalisation of parental values!'

'You are too taken by the girl, Michael. I wish you well with your thesis. It seems well-written with enough footnotes to publish in a book on their own. But Eve shouldn't be in this hospital. She doesn't seem to me to be either particularly unhappy or particularly damaged. She suffers from neither visual nor auditory hallucinations; she certainly doesn't suffer from psychosis, schizophrenia or even a mild neurosis. I'll grant you, she borders on what some might consider a personality disorder, though the term is so vague as to be faintly irritating. She is manipulative, has a marked lack of self-criticism, and is abominably fickle. However, to compensate for such failings, she's pretty and has a good share of social skills. I doubt she has little idea about constancy and the maintaining of a sustained sexual relationship, but I'm a doctor, Michael, I'm not a judge. The only thing I feel quite certain of is that she shouldn't stay in this hospital. It's the world that should be taking Eve on, not you, Michael.'

Dr Fothering had snatched his beloved files from the consultant's desk and cried, 'Are you saying there's no truth in this? Are you saying I've been wasting my time this past year? Are you giving me no credit at all?' And even his super-ego couldn't prevent him from storming out and slamming the door.

This was the summer of 1983; Eve had been at Fulbright a full year, and at this time, surely, the guard and his pretty prisoner might have called a truce and gone their separate ways. But Dr Fothering's rage and sense of umbrage would have none of it. When another consultant, a Dr Aggs, professed an interest in the case over lunch in the cafeteria, and even read and approved of the abstract for his thesis, Dr Fothering introduced them, and an informal arrangement was set up in which Dr Aggs became Eve's consultant, and Dr Goodman was barely aware that Eve was still in the hospital. But this new arrangement was never set up as it should have been; the literature on the case never re-filed under 'A', nor the case closed under 'G'. Hence, on this particular day, the 15th March 1984, the day when Mrs de Selincourt felt both her first and last maternal feelings towards her daughter, it was towards Dr Goodman's office that the impregnable woman strode, her invitation to her daughter's case conference held tightly in her fist.

Barely had Mrs de Selincourt begun her onslaught than Dr Goodman realised she had the grounds to sue both him and the hospital. Indeed, it was cases like Eve's that were to force the closure of so many mental hospitals a few years later. For Mrs de Selincourt was right: the hospital was filthy, Eve had been 'allowed to languish in this dire place'; she, her mother, had been kept entirely in the dark as to what was going on, and what was all this about Eve having a liaison with a gardener? And above all, how dare that man Fothering try and keep her away from the case conference that afternoon, as though its outcome didn't concern her?

And it's true, if the dynamics of their meeting had been ever so slightly different, if Mrs de Selincourt had not registered, deep, deep within her psyche that Dr Goodman's Harris tweed suit was bespoke, then her fury and her threats might have been such as to make Dr Goodman postpone his game of golf at two and actually attend the meeting in question. But this annual game of golf with a good school-friend was a fixture he was very loath to give up, and anyway, he knew the susceptibility of women such as Mrs de Selincourt to both charm and breeding, in addition to which he had a whole hour to placate her, to apologize unreservedly, to explain that Dr Fothering's methods were not his own but psychiatry was not an area in which there was a right and a wrong, and whatever the outcome with the gardener he would personally see to it that Eve was discharged within the week, and if she chose not to return home with her, would make it a priority to find her suitable accommodation. Half way through their meeting he summoned tea and biscuits, and they sat on the lower, more comfortable chairs. Soon after, they discovered that they had both holidayed in Provence, and by the end of their jolly meeting they realised that Mr de Selincourt was a good friend of a good friend of Dr Goodman's. Extraordinary co-incidence! What a small, small world! So they said good-bye on the best of terms, with the assurance that he would personally look into any conclusions reached at the case conference. 'And one final piece of advice,' he said in a charmingly conspiratorial voice, as Mrs de Selincourt stood up to go, 'Don't talk too much. Just observe. Mark my words, to observe is to have power. And be my spy. I'd like to know what they talk about.'

'I'll do that, Dr Goodman. Thank you,' she smiled. 'I'll let you know just what I think.'

☙

Hospitals are places of great drama, the fodder of every screenwriter. Mrs de Selincourt, Dr Fothering, Eve herself, are about to take their bow, as well as various others assigned to the case. Events can no longer be controlled by any of them.

Conference room BH8: at first, semi-darkness, till a nurse releases a dust-laden blind to reveal ten low-slung orange chairs haphazardly arranged around two coffee tables. Without comment, the same nurse picks up two old coffee cups from the table and says, 'Laura, could you rinse these out, please?'

Laura is a student social worker who's on a placement for six weeks; a pretty thing in a fashionable denim pinafore and a flowery shirt. She's presently shadowing Alison, who walks in now, senior social worker in the Branston team. She's thin and spiky but efficient; she looks about her for Dr Aggs, Gibson Nelson's consultant psychiatrist, and Fothering's ally, but he's not arrived yet, nor has June Briggs, who is going to be Eve de Selincourt's senior field social worker once she's discharged. Instead, she notices Eve's mother, or at least, an alien force, someone who ought not to be there at such sensitive proceedings. She walks up to her and introduces herself. Mrs de Selincourt is on best behaviour and nods courteously. Alison relaxes. She can stay if she's quiet, she thinks. Dr Fothering makes a joke about the bad coffee, and suggests to Mrs de Selincourt that when asked it might prove a safer bet to choose the tea. She ignores his remarks; Dr Fothering begins to sweat.

Dr Aggs walks in: he's fifty, tall, with a wiry nest of black hair. He's the most powerful man in the room, and he knows it; but it's Alison who'll be chairing the meeting. While Laura's counting mugs in the adjacent kitchen, Alison is counting heads. 'Now, where is June?' she thinks, and June pitches up, slightly breathless, right on cue. It's not in June's nature to be late, and she's reeling off excuses, the roadworks in Burleigh Street, the traffic lights on Cherry Hinton Road. 'Coffee or tea?' Laura calls out from the kitchen door.

Dr Fothering is watching Mrs de Selincourt as though his life depends on how she answers her. 'Tea,' she says. 'Two sugars.'

'Wise choice!' he exclaims, smiling ridiculously. But she doesn't notice because she doesn't look at him.

A couple more nurses arrive, including Eve's key-worker, Janet. Eve has Janet wrapped round her little finger, because, to put it bluntly, Eve is cleverer than she is. But she's a good sort, and will have Eve's best interests at heart. Then Dr Fothering leaps up and introduces Mrs de Selincourt to the assembled party; everyone nods politely and Mrs de Selincourt acknowledges them. There are, by now, cups of tea and coffee in front of everyone, and some bulky files are beginning to appear: some are opened on the low tables, other propped up on knees. Alison is ready to begin. Nothing untoward so far. The chatter subsides.

'Now', says Alison, 'Thank you, Dr Fothering and Dr Aggs, for your reports. Both Eve and Gibson have made substantial progress over the last few months, as I think everyone in this room would agree. I think we would also agree that they are ready to move on. As we know, their attachment to each other is a romantic one, and although as a rule we discourage such affairs of the heart as being detrimental to a patient's recovery, in this case it does seem that Eve's behaviour has plateaued out and Gibson's long-standing depression is finally beginning to lift. If anyone has any objections to their both being discharged as soon as possible, please make them known now. Mrs de Selincourt, I trust Dr Fothering has kept you informed of such a development?'

'No, he hasn't,' says Mrs de Selincourt, politely. 'And I have to confess, it would have been useful to have been kept informed.'

Everyone looks rather shocked, in particular Dr Aggs. Dr Fothering stands up and apologises unreservedly.

Alison continues, trying to keep up the momentum of the proceedings. 'I'm so sorry, Mrs de Selincourt,' she says, 'if you would like to add your own feelings to this debate, please feel free...'

'Thank you', Mrs de Selincourt says, still quite calm. 'I would like to know more about my daughter's fiancé. How do they propose to live?' Only Dr Fothering notices the crescendo.

Dr Aggs is embarrassed. He stands up to speak to her, but sits down again when he realises how tall he is and how low the chairs are. 'His name is Gibson Nelson. His wife died over a year ago and twice he has attempted to take his own life. He was a gardener in one of the colleges, let me see, Corpus. An excellent record. But your

daughter seems to have given him a great will to live, Mrs de Selincourt. He's off all the pills now...'

'Ah,' says Mrs de Selincourt, as cool as a cucumber. 'Excellent.
He's off his anti-depressants.'

'Yes, yes, and you have your daughter to thank for that!' enthuses
Dr Aggs, less perceptive than he might have been.

'Now,' interrupts Alison, 'what we propose, Mrs de Selincourt, is
protected housing, and June here is going to be Eve's social worker,
and she'll be responsible for Eve during her pregnancy ...'

Well, she does say a little more about the house Eve will be living
in, about how it's only five years old and newly decorated. But no
one is listening to her. For they are all wrapt by the face of Mrs de
Selincourt, a face so taut and red and ugly, a mouth so hideous in its
deformity, they are rendered speechless.

Mrs de Selincourt gets up; Dr Fothering follows suit. For a
moment, everyone is on tenterhooks; she looks as though she might
slap him. But she saves the slap for her daughter, who is waiting on
a chair beside Gibson outside Room BH8. They are holding hands.

Mrs de Selincourt slaps her daughter with all the hope and frustra-
tion she has harboured for twenty years. 'I am not its grandmother,'
she utters, under her breath. Gibson looks up, a good face, a kind
face, and holds Eve's hand all the tighter.

As Mrs de Selincourt drives back down to Harrow, one solitary
tear escapes her. She brushes it away with the back of her hand, and
puts her foot down on the accelerator.

Chapter Two

JOSIAH HORATIO NELSON was born on 1st June 1984, in the Rosie Maternity Hospital, Cambridge. He was pretty from the first, and his father doted on him, and his mother felt rather pleased with herself for making him so well.

The Gideons had placed a copy of the Bible in Eve's bedside locker, and no sooner had the midwife handed Eve her son and left the happy parents to coo over their baby in peace, than Eve, in turn, handed her son to Gibson so she could consult it and find a name for him.

She propped herself up against the pillows, held the Bible tight shut on her lap and closed her eyes. 'Now, Gibby darling, this always works. Sometimes it's best to let God make the most important decisions for you, and a name is very, very important, don't you think?'

Gibson looked nervous.

'Here, you put your hand on the Bible too.'

Gibson did as he was told.

'Say 'Om' with me,' and Eve began to resound an 'Om'.

'Om', said Gibson's anxious, lower voice.

Then suddenly, with no warning at all, Eve snatched the Bible and opened it.

'There! Perfect!' she exclaimed. 'Our boy's name is Josiah!' She read on a little and explained, 'Josiah, the greatest of all the Jewish Kings, and only a little boy of eight when he ruled over the entire kingdom of Judaea. That will do nicely. My God, Gibson, do you think we should bring him up as a Jew?'

Gibson shook his head.

'But there should at least be a Jewish theme running through his baptism ceremony. You're not Catholic, are you?'

'The Christian Church doesn't like Jews', said Gibson, ponderously.

'Poodle and poof-cake! The Christian Church doesn't know what's good for them. Jesus was a Jew, after all, yet I've never spotted a single Jewish nose on a single crucifix. We shall begin our ceremony with 'Shalom! Shalom!' And of course we need champagne. And I think we should proceed as soon as we have some.'

'They won't like drink in the hospital. They just won't.' Gibson spoke slowly and anxiously, like the last whines of a devoted Labrador before his mistress sets off to work.

'How can you call 'champagne' a 'drink'? Champagne is a libation which we offer to the Gods! Champagne is about giving thanks for this happy, happy day! I bet you they have some in the foyer, Gibson. There's a love, at least you could go and have a look for me.'

'I don't think they'll have champagne in the foyer,' said Gibson.

'Money! Here, let me give you money!' insisted Eve, and she began rummaging around in the locker drawer.

'I don't think they've got any in the foyer, Eve.' Gibson looked close to tears.

'My dearest Gibson, my sweetheart, don't cry on me again! Here, come, Josiah's sleeping now. Put him in the crib and lie your head here on my breast and let me stroke your hair. That's better! What a silly-billy you are, you great sausage!'

Gibson lay still some moments in his wife's arms; but no sooner had his equanimity been restored, than the great solace of his life jumped out of bed and merrily informed him, 'I tell you what, I'll get the champagne myself. If anyone wonders where I am tell them I've gone to the bathroom.'

And with that, Eve quickly dressed herself, unperturbed by an eight-hour labour and an episiotomy. 'This is for us,' she whispered in Gibson's ear. 'For us and Josiah.' And she strode off down the corridors of the hospital, while the nurses made way for her.

Meanwhile Gibson drew the curtains tightly around Eve's bed and sat hunched in a chair, intent only on her return. A domestic popped her head round the curtain, and he immediately began fumbling for the excuse Eve had given him, but before he could get it out she'd switched the water jugs and was gone. For forty minutes Gibson willed his wife back to his side, holding her image tightly between his temples, and when she came back he was so overjoyed that he couldn't find the words to greet her.

'The bloody anaesthetic's beginning to wear off,' she said, taking four aspirin from the drawer and gobbling them down. But then she lay down on the bed again in full majesty, and the great stalwart Gibson put his arm around her shoulders in relief and pride.

'Gibby, my dear,' said Eve, 'I've done awfully well. Better than champagne by a mile. I bought a bottle of Polish vodka, forty-two percent proof, from the Italian delicatessen just over the bridge. Such a dear Italian boy sold it to me. Did you know there's a Polish Jewish community living in Cherry Hinton? So of course I had to tell him about Josiah. They rip through this stuff, apparently. What more fitting tribute could we make to our dear one? I'll tell him when he's sixteen so can spend a day in a synagogue in remembrance of himself.'

Eve emptied a mug of water into a pot plant and filled it to the brim with vodka. She took a large swig from it before handing it over to Gibson. 'To the three of us,' she said.

'I don't like it,' said Gibson, apologetically.

'But it's delicious, you silly, taste it.'

'I don't think I ought.'

'Go on, Gibby.'

'I love you, Eve,' he said, as he dipped his finger in the mug and licked the end of it, and he might well have leant over to kiss his wife had not Josiah began to whimper a little, and he pulled his bulk (for Gibson was a large, well-built man) off the bed to see if there was anything he might do for his son.

'Look at his lips, Eve, he's feeding from you in his sleep.'

'But he can't be hungry again!' exclaimed Eve, suddenly looking weary.

'It's OK, love, I've given him my finger, he likes that.'

'Bless you, Gibson!' and she took hold of his other hand and held it in hers. 'I can tell, you'll be a much better father than I will a mother. Perhaps we should bottle-feed him.'

'No, no, that won't do, you feed him yourself, Eve. Little Jo, he's a dear'un. He's sucking so hard, Eve.'

But even Gibson's little finger was a large, alien object; a lined, dirt-filled, unsterilized, frightening thing which made a nurse cry out in horror.

'No! No! Take that out! That's a new-born baby! ' she cried. And when Eve looked indignant she went on, 'Your husband's hands are filthy!'

'My husband is a gardener, thank you very much,' declared Eve, quite calm, 'and Josiah is a gardener's son. Earth was coursing through his veins *in utero*, so a little in his mouth certainly won't harm him.'

The other mothers in the ward momentarily looked up in shock or admiration; but the poor nurse blushed angrily and left. She went to see the ward sister, and the ward sister wrote a note down in Eve's file.

'Now, about Josiah's baptism, darling. We must really try to get it right. The first thing we must establish is whom we should pray to, and the second, what we should pray for. Does that seem about right, Gibson?'

Eve began to think, smiling benevolently at anyone who had overheard her. She didn't notice her husband who was stirring uneasily.

'Now, you've already said "no" to Judaism, which I respect, Gibson, I respect! But you can't go wrong with the Holy Spirit, can you? He should be dedicated absolutely and one hundred percent to the Holy Spirit! Hand him over, Gib. Now, where's that vodka? We'll baptise him in Spirit itself.'

'But we don't have a priest,' said Gibson, plaintively.

'A priest?' Eve was contemptuous.

'You need a priest for baptism rites. I know you do.'

'A priest is the archetypal middleman, creaming off a disproportionate amount of the profits. We certainly don't need a priest. Even Luther would back me on that point.'

'He's so hungry, Eve. Don't you think you'd best feed him?'

'Oh, hand him over then, goddammit.'

It was the second feed of Josiah's short life, and Eve grudgingly gave him her breast.

'It's not natural at all,' she said. 'If it didn't have milk in it, I'd think it was a male conspiracy to make us women behave like this. I feel like a cow.'

'A cow's a noble creature,' said Gibson, 'and Jo's happy.'

'You, Gibson, are a noble creature,' and Eve leant over and kissed him on the forehead. 'So you won't mind taking over from me quite soon, will you darling?'

Gibson looked anxious.

'Now,' continued Eve, 'We have to think of three virtues to give Josiah at his baptism. Or do we want him to have any virtues at all? Gibson, do we want him to be good?'

'He's good already,' said Gibson, stroking Josiah's head.

'A good, solid romantic, that's why I love you. The goodness of the innocent, versus the corrupting forces of our so called civilization. I do so think you're right. So, allowing that he's good, we must pray for three special gifts. I suggest beauty. What do you think?'

'He's beautiful already,' said Gibson.

'Beautiful, do you think?' Eve promptly removed Josiah from her breast so she could take a good look at him. 'You're right again, Gibson, we made him beautifully, didn't we, you and I?'

'You go on feeding him, Eve,' said Gibson, and Eve did as she was told.

'Well, if he's good and beautiful in his fourth hour of life, what has he got to strive for? Now, Gibson, should we have him as the object or subject of sexual desire?'

'Poor little mite,' said Gibson.

'Or do you think it's preferable to be neither? Would he be more virtuous, do you think, if he was castrated? Or do you think virtue is a struggle against our natural inclinations?'

'Our Jo will do what he has to do, won't you, Jo?' and Gibson lay his large hand over his son's head.

Then all of a sudden Eve threw her baby into her father's arms and buttoned up her nightdress.

'Oh my *God*!' she exclaimed to her lily-bearing visitor. 'Shouldn't you be in Hull?'

Indeed, that's exactly where Dr Fothering should have been. Even as Gibson and Eve were being dispatched to their new life together, Fothering was applying for his first consultant's post in Hull. His thesis on Eve, subject to a few alterations, had found its way to a sympathetic examiner at London University and passed well. In fact, the future was looking bright, very bright, for the young psychiatrist eager to make a name for himself in the softer therapies.

It is a well-documented fact that some patients become dependent on their doctors; it is less well-known, but equally true, that some doctors become dependent on their patients. Let the fate of poor Dr Fothering be a lesson to all of them.

☙

Eve and Gibson moved into their new home early in April 1984, in a cul de sac off Wolfson Drive on the Arbury Estate. Their house was only five years old, and some young offenders had redecorated it shortly before they moved in. It's status as 'sheltered housing' didn't mean much: the previous occupants, a family of five sons, had one by one found their way to prison, and the mother had finally given up on the lot of them and gone to live with her elderly parents in Scotland. But it did mean the Council was obliged to provide brand new carpets and curtains, and Gibson and Eve were both happy and grateful to have such a fine new home. Gibson was particularly happy, because the house backed onto fields and had a large, if hitherto neglected, garden. And as a wedding present (they were married on the first of May), Eve had bought Gibson a greenhouse.

As can be imagined, the community was happy to have new neighbours and welcomed them. Even the vicar called on them; a man they far preferred to their new social worker, Roger Bolt, a Northerner who was suspicious of all things Southern, always deeming them to be 'not what they seemed'. He looked first at the sexy, blonde Eve, and then at the lumpen, slow Gibson, and he knew that he had to get to the bottom of things. He had read through both Eve and Gibson's files vigorously, yet never bought Dr Fothering's grandiose theories for a moment, and when Dr Fothering dared to suggest that Mr Bolt's approach to the couple was rather heavy-handed, and that in front of his senior too, a grudge was born.

Perhaps if Bolt had been more sympathetic to Fothering's approach, and been happier to take the baton from him regarding the care of his beloved Eve, Dr Fothering would have been happier to have deserted his post at Fulbright and set off to pastures new in Hull. But Eve had become for him his own wayward, teenage daughter – no, more than that, for the good father knows instinctively when to let go – Fothering's ego was bound up there too, his past, present, and alas, future were inveigled in Eve's merest utterance. He could not find it within himself to trust that bloody Northerner, Bolt, or that control freak senior of his, June Briggs. What if Eve became manic again? Would they drug her up, because they couldn't cope? Would they take away her baby? There's not one person I can trust in the entire Social Services Department, he thought, not one. They know nothing of the human spirit. Good God, what will happen to her?

It's true, a wife or even a girlfriend would have compelled Dr Fothering to re-centre himself; even a decent hobby might have distracted him. But if Roger Bolt with his long, nasal Northern vowels irritated him, Dr Fothering in Hull was about as happy as a squid in a goldfish bowl. The comparative straightforwardness of his colleagues he dismissed as one-dimensionality; they were too ready to call a spade a spade and under-estimated the vast and complex energies which define the life-force of a human being. In a nutshell, he yearned for Eve, and wondered for the very first time whether he might have been in love with her, and as for her baby, he felt an odd inclination to bring the child up as his own. After all, any other psychiatrist would have recommended abortion or at the very least adoption, but he had been enthusiastic all the way. Eve's baby was, in a very vicarious sense, his.

At the time of Josiah's birth Dr Fothering had been languishing in Hull for six weeks. Recently he had seemed increasingly distracted, phoning the maternity hospital daily and asking for news of Eve Nelson. When finally they told her she was in labour, he was away, only remembering to explain his absence to his colleagues ('possibly a life or death situation' involving 'someone close to him') from a phone box half way down the A1.

Dr Fothering was in the hospital car park at three pm, and ran, sweet man, all the way into the foyer where he filled his arms with huge lilies. He was too impatient to take the lift and skipped up the stairs; too impatient to ask anyone which ward she was on, and barged into all of them before he found her. He stood for a moment at the door, watching her. She looked wonderful, he thought, glowing, happy. Sheepishly he walked up to her bed.

'Please don't stop feeding your baby because of me!' pleaded Dr Fothering.

Eve did up the top button of her nightdress and looked at him quizzically.

'But I don't understand, what's brought you to Cambridge? Are you visiting friends? Are you attending some conference or other? Of course I'm delighted to see you, Dr Fothering, but you see, you've completely caught me off my guard.'

The poor man threw his flowers into Eve's arms, so appalled was he by Eve's reception of him, and Eve was touched and said the lilies were lovely. She took no care of them, nonetheless, and a couple of them dropped to the floor. Gibson winced as though he himself had been dropped, but could do nothing to save them, what with Josiah in his arms.

'I wanted to see how you've taken to motherhood, Eve! And I came to see you not as an off-duty doctor but as a friend. From now on, you must call me 'Michael'.

'Gosh, Michael. Here, look, you look so uncomfortable. Sit down next to me. I'm so flattered that you've come! Did you really come all the way down from Hull to see *me*?'

Dr Fothering did as he was told, squashing a couple more lilies as he did so. Gibson could hardly bear it.

'Well, I was so happy for you both,' he said, and noted how wretched Gibson was looking. 'Or should I say, happy for the three of you? My goodness, what a beautiful baby he is!' For some reason he couldn't quite fathom, Dr Fothering was rather thrilled by that fact. 'What are you going to call him? He is a boy, isn't he?'

'Isn't he just the most beautiful baby you've ever seen?' cooed Eve, 'Oh Dr Fothering... Michael, have you ever seen a baby quite as beautiful as Josiah?'

'Is that what you're calling him, "Josiah"?'

'Yes, that's his name!' declared Eve, eagerly. 'We're calling him "Josiah" after the great Jewish child king. Oh Gibson, are you thinking what I'm thinking?'

Gibson was not.

'We were just about to perform a baptism ceremony, weren't we? We were trying to work out what religion to bring him up in, nothing strange, no funny cult or anything, but I want him to have virtues and know how to pray, for you must know as a psychiatrist how important it is to pray!'

'I didn't know you were religious, Eve.'

'I don't think you ever asked me.'

'But you don't pray, do you?'

'Dr Fothering, Michael, surely after two years you realise I live a life of unceasing prayer, which is, according to the Russian Orthodox Church, the very best kind of prayer.'

'But who do you pray to, Eve?'

'A good question. Gibson and I were just discussing that very point. But when anyone prays, do they know who it is they are praying to? I would call that very presumptuous. Gibson, do you know who you pray to when you pray? One prays to creation, to good will, to benevolence, destiny, I *bow down* to destiny, I *surrender*, I am flotsam and jetsam being tossed on the sea, O Michael, can't you see how wholly religious I am? And my point is this. Would you like to be a godfather? O Gibson, wouldn't he make a wonderful godfather? You are, indeed, an answer to a prayer I made earlier, and you, without me knowing it, were the very person I was praying to… O Dr Fothering, Michael, don't you see how important it was that you came?'

'I don't know whether I wish it to be important, Eve,' said Dr Fothering, from the heart. 'I was hoping I would be unimportant. Or at least, not relevant. I'm not making myself clear. I came as a friend Eve, not as your doctor. Because you don't need a doctor. You're a woman, and a mother. You're strong. You seem so strong!'

'My dear Michael!' exclaimed Eve, equally from the heart, 'I honestly don't know what you're on about. If you remember, I asked you if you'd be a godfather!'

'I will,' said Dr Fothering, wishing to make progress.

'The right answer! We'll have the ceremony straightaway. We're going to baptize him in Holy Spirit, we were just saying that whatever you believe and whoever you pray to you can't go wrong with the Holy Spirit and look what I've got!'

Eve proudly presented him with a mug of vodka, and mouthed the magic word. 'The three of us shall have a sip, then we'll make the sign of the cross on Josiah's forehead, and then we'll make a wish for him, how does that sound?'

'Blasphemous, I think.'

'Oh nothing is blasphemous if you don't intend it to be!' pronounced Eve. 'Perhaps we should call him Josiah Michael after you? On second thoughts, "Michael" is a bit weak, a bit Mummy's boy, no offence meant, Dr Fothering. I've got it! We shall call him "Horatio"! Josiah Horatio Nelson. Now, did a finer name exist than that, I ask you?'

'No,' said Dr Fothering, 'That's a very fine name. Very fine.' He was sipping thankfully at the vodka.

'And we need your advice Dr Fothering! We hadn't decided on the virtues Josiah was going to be blessed with – no, I lie, we decided that Josiah wasn't to have any virtues, didn't we Gibson, though I can't for the life of me remember why.'

Gibson looked at her pleadingly.

'You're right!' she said, 'because he's both beautiful and good already! What more in life could one possibly want?'

Then Eve began to stroke the baby as he slept in his father's arms, and really quite affectionately too, and there was a moment's relief for the poor doctor, before she sat bolt upright and exclaimed, 'I remember! Dr Fothering, do you think it's better to be the object or subject of sexual desire?'

And Dr Fothering, in sudden despair, retorted, 'I think it's better not to have any at all.'

'Dr Fothering,' cried Eve in disbelief, 'you're not yourself!'

'Call me Michael, Goddammit! So what if it is a namby-pamby name, call me Michael.'

'Oh Michael!' cried Eve, taking up his hand in her own. 'You must have had a terrible journey, and I'm so grateful to you for making it!'

'Yes, it's true,' mumbled Dr Fothering, 'the traffic was bad.'

'There is nothing more soul-destroying than a traffic jam. Tell me, is your soul quite destroyed, Michael?'

'Yes,' he said, because 'yes' was the path of least resistance.

'So all the time I was creating a new, living, vital soul, yours was being destroyed! How are we to re-distribute ourselves? By you becoming Josiah's godfather, of course. And the difference in our ceremony will be that he will provide for you, rather than you for him.'

'Sounds good to me,' said Dr Fothering, sipping at the mug of vodka. His last sober thought was that he should go and visit Eve and Gibson at their home in a couple of days, when he was feeling a little better. He tried to remember when it was exactly that he had lost control of the conversation, but he felt confident that if he had an opportunity of beginning again, all would somehow right itself. Meanwhile he was enjoying a free-floating, rather pleasant sensation of nothing being either important or relevant; and when he heard Eve suddenly exclaim, 'Ave Maria, Ave Maria!' he even managed to rejoin, with surprising gusto, 'Hallelujah!'

'Yes, yes, I have it! I know exactly what our baptism needs: Latin. No proper ceremony is complete without it. Now, what Latin do you know? As godfather you have a particular duty to supply some.'

'Cave canem,' suggested Dr Fothering. 'I'm afraid it's all I know. You can take it or leave it.'

'Well, you never know, we might be able to incorporate it somewhere,' said Eve, graciously. 'Gibson, you don't know any Latin, do you?'

But if Gibson did, he'd long since passed the speech barrier and wasn't going to divulge it.

'Now, now, wait, wait, the Latin is coming, I can feel it coming,' and Eve closed her eyes like a medium in a trance. 'Give me the baby! Give me Josiah!'

'Asleep,' was Gibson's only word, as he cradled his son.

'This is important, Gibson, the words are coming.'

Gibson relented, and the pretty baby was handed over to his mother. Eve dabbed her finger in the mug of vodka which Dr Fothering was still enjoying, and tenderly placed it just above the bridge of Josiah's nose. Her voice was solemn:

Sis sine macula
Sis sine metu
Sis sica inimicis
Ama quantum bonorum
Odia quantum malorum
Cave canem.

Dr Fothering and Gibson looked blankly at her.

'I shall translate, you uncultured pair,' pronounced Eve, and did so.

'May you be without stain,
May you be without fear,
May you be a dagger to your enemies,
Love whomsoever is good

Hate whomsoever is bad
Beware the dog.'

'Oh alas, there's always a dog to beware, *sic vita humana*. Who has been the dog in your life, Dr Fothering?'

'Must Josiah be a dagger to his enemies?'

'How jolly Christian you are! I've always preferred the Old Testament myself. I think my little ode is quite like a psalm, don't you?'

'I'm very impressed,' said Dr Fothering, which he was.

'I'm going to teach Josiah Latin. He's going to imbibe it with his mother's milk, aren't you darling? What a future's in store for you, my dear one.'

At which news Josiah, appropriately enough, began to cry.

'Oh it won't be as bad as all that! God, stop that! Shhhh, shhh,' and while another mother might have offered her baby a breast, Eve was having none of that, certainly not in company, and proceeded to lift up his vest to tickle his tummy. But there was a clamp attached to the bloody stump of the umbilicus, and Eve let out a squeal when she saw it, a squeal quite worthy of Sarah Bernhardt herself confronted with a dead body.

A nurse, then two, ran over to see what had happened, followed seconds later by the ward sister herself, who'd already written a note in her book about Gibson putting an unwashed finger in the baby's mouth; and hot on her heels of her was Roger Bolt, who'd already been discussing Gibson's unwashed finger in earnest for at least ten minutes, and they'd been saying what a shame it was that the courts were powerless to make some kind of Parenting Order, by which parents could be forced to go somewhere and learn about germs and so forth, and they had both agreed that parents were very ignorant nowadays.

What met them were two men sitting on the bed, one drunk, the other dirty, while the mother was holding out her new-born baby at arm's length.

'Take him Gibson! Take him!' she was saying, but Gibson couldn't move for fear.

One of the nurses said, 'I'll take him', and put out her arms.

'You certainly won't!' exclaimed Eve. 'Michael, you're the godfather, you take him.'

'No, sir, you certainly won't take him!' said the ward sister, picking up the empty mug from the bedside locker and smelling inside it. You've been drinking! Let me smell your breath!'

Dr Fothering kept his mouth tight shut and looked defiant. The sister found the bottle of Polish vodka, three-quarters empty by now, and said to him, 'Get out of here! And never, ever come back!'

'But he's the godfather!' cried Eve, indignantly.

'He's also Eve's psychiatrist', said Roger Bolt, triumphantly.

Everyone looked at Dr Fothering.

'What are you doing here?' asked Roger. 'I thought you were in Hull nowadays.' Trained social worker that he was, it wasn't beyond his powers of observation to notice that the man before him was desperate, caught, humiliated. The thrill of schadenfreude made him positively shiver, and the realization – O heavenly realization! – that the baby belonged to none other than this arrogant arsehole was like a meal to savour for days, if not weeks. Godfather, my foot! The man was no more than a pathetic, sex-obsessed upstart, who probably had sex with Eve in the name of therapy.

And trained psychiatrist that he was, and drunk though he was, it was not beyond Dr Fothering to apprehend the exact moment Roger Bolt made his ridiculous assumption. Yet he was sufficiently drunk to say this, and aggressively, too: 'I know what you're thinking, Bolt, and it's obscene of you to think it.'

Two nurses and the ward sister stood to attention, antennae positively swinging. Even as Dr Fothering spat out the word 'obscene' they knew that whatever it was the man was purported to have done, he had done it; and a quick inspection of the scene before them confirmed them in their worse suspicions. That large, mute hulk with the filthy hands had never been this woman's lover, and had been no more than an obliging front for all manner of immoral behaviour. Oh yes, that psychiatrist was a villain of the first order, incapable of coming to terms with his crimes. Only guilt could have reduced him to this hunched, haunted spectre of a man, his eyes raging, bloodshot.

'What is it I'm thinking of, Dr Fothering? I don't know that I catch your meaning.' As Roger Bolt spoke he smiled at the ward sister, and the two nurses smiled at each other.

But the glorious Eve would have none of it. 'Then you're rather more obtuse than I thought you were, Bolt. And you're a meddler. But you're not meddling here. Sister, could you show him out? He's not welcome. He'll dry up my milk.'

Then they all made as if to go, Dr Fothering too, until Eve took hold of his hand and said, 'No, Michael, not you! You stay here with us! You're Josiah's godfather!'

Dr Fothering sat back down on the bed, defeated, bent double. Eve took his hand in hers.

'Don't take any notice of them,' she said, kindly.

'There'll be an inquiry,' mumbled Dr Fothering.

'Let them inquire all they like! Nosey Parkers. If the worst comes to the worst, you can move in with us.'

Dr Fothering looked at her. Utterly ravishing, and quite, quite mad.

'Thank you,' he said, 'I'd like that.'

Chapter Three

ROGER BOLT was a man who held his head high among our nation's foot-soldiers, whose shoulders bore many a burden and whose mind shunned chaos. He had a beard, which he clipped twice a day, and a trouser-press in his bedroom. He'd deserted his wife and children five years ago when he'd taken up the post in Cambridge: or at least, they had refused to follow him there, for everyone in Darlington knew that everyone in Cambridge was stuck-up, and stories were rife of nice, bright kids who'd gone to University there and were too lofty nowadays even to speak to their parents. 'It's not for the likes of us,' his wife had insisted. 'There are people even in Cambridge who need help,' Roger had told her. 'It's good for my career, you're not holding me back.' And she didn't.

Roger found it surprisingly easy to live alone. Of course, he missed his two small children, but he went back home at least once a month and what with bank holidays and such-like he was with them at least six weeks a year. But Roger's real love was his work. He wanted to get to the very top. He wanted to prove himself.

Being a good social worker is rather like being a good housewife. It's about cleaning up mess, efficiently and without fuss. It is about compartmentalizing, making lists and putting things in boxes. But as I have already made clear, Eve was always going to refuse to step into her box, or indeed anyone else's. Roger understood this implicitly and knew he was going to do battle with her, and it was a battle he was going to win. After all, there was a new-born baby to consider. And his greatest fantasy was this: letting Dr Michael Fothering know, in a very professional letter, of course, that Eve's baby had been placed with foster parents. Let the true father step forward! So much more subtle, he considered, (chuckling to himself) than any insinuating communications to his superiors. He would win this battle, as surely as night follows day, and win it with honours.

After Bolt's visit to the hospital, he decided to lie low for a while. After all, Eve would be inundated with other visitors: the midwife would be calling in every day, the health visitor, the psychiatric nurse. Newborn babies were very precious commodities, after all.

Then, after about ten days, Bolt received an alarming letter from the midwife. She had called by at the Nelson's house every day since the family returned home after the birth, but had found no one there. Neither Fulbright Hospital nor the health visitor had heard from Mr or Mrs Nelson, but did he happen to know whether the family were staying with Eve's parents or another relative? Could he, perhaps, throw any light on the matter? Bolt had Eve's parental address on his files, but no phone number, and when he discovered it wasn't listed, he decided to take the matter into his own hands. Eve would never have chosen to go back to the parental home anyway, she loathed her mother. Far more likely they had gone up to Hull to stay with Fothering! But this was for the police to infer, not him. A professional distance from such a sordid matter as this was the key, no finger would ever, ever be pointed at him. Nonetheless he might just allow himself the pleasure of a good old-fashioned snoop, and dangle any clues he might find under their slow-witted noses. He determined to go to their house that very afternoon.

He veritably jumped into his Morris Minor at two o'clock, patting his briefcase on the seat beside him and stroking his newly-clipped beard. It was going to be difficult to resist the temptation to break in; but walking round to the back of the house seemed a legitimate intrusion. In fact, as he drove along he hit upon a rather good plan: just in case the family was hiding inside, he was going to spring upon them unawares. He would park a couple of hundred yards up the road, and see if he could find a route through the fields running along the back of the houses of Woolfson Drive. No, neither cowpat nor gorse bush could deter Bolt now: he was on the warpath.

But man of the world though he was, or considered himself to be, nothing could have prepared him for the sight which greeted him. The baby, or so it seemed to him at a distance of thirty yards, was dead. It had been discarded on the top of a heap of grass-cuttings, completely naked, its little hands set in rigor mortis like starfish. He let out a cry in spite of himself (he rarely let his emotions get the better of him): 'The baby! The baby!' and he realised at once that there would be a lengthy and miserable inquiry and that his job would be on the line.

When the baby actually began to move Roger Bolt became almost hysterical; and when Gibson came out of his greenhouse and scooped up the baby in one large hand, he started shouting at him, even calling him a murderer though somewhere in his psyche he was entirely cognizant of the fact that no, the baby was not dead, because dead babies do not move. Thereupon Josiah began to cry, and Gibson was tense with anguish – not anger, for Gibson was too humble ever to feel angry, and when Bolt had calmed down a little, and had even (to his credit) managed to apologize, he explained that the midwife, the health visitor and various others had been most concerned about his family, particularly the baby, because newborn babies needed caring for, and being left on a heap of grass-cuttings was negligent to say the least. When Gibson said nothing in reply, Bolt suggested that he hand the baby over to him, but Gibson was now rocking Josiah on his large forearm, and the baby, if not asleep, was calm and looking about him quite happily.

Bolt tried another tack. 'You've not been in this fortnight,' he said. 'Have you been staying with relations?'

Gibson didn't answer him. The men were still about ten yards apart from each other, but when Bolt moved a step forward, Gibson involuntarily took a step back.

'Where's Eve?' asked Bolt. 'Is she here?'

Gibson shook his head.

'Will she be long?'

Gibson shrugged his shoulders.

'Is everything going well? She's still living with you?'

Gibson just stared at him.

'I really should take a look at the baby,' said Roger.

Gibson didn't move.

'Do you often leave your baby on a pile of compost?' And when Gibson didn't answer him, he tried again, 'No doubt it's difficult having a new baby in the house.'

The two men drifted into a mutual, mute deadlock. The silence was broken by a cry from Josiah, as welcome as summer thunder, though the rains in this instance consisted of pee running down his father's fingers. But Gibson was no less uncomfortable with pee than he was with manure, and when Bolt suggested he might like to dress the baby and put him in a nappy, he merely surveyed Bolt quizzically.

'The baby's nappy,' Bolt reiterated, mentally taking notes.

Gibson stayed exactly where he was, for he was a man used to standing still, and he might have stayed there all day had Josiah himself not wailed rather more vociferously. Without a word, Gibson turned towards his kitchen door. Bolt followed him, as welcome as a cockroach.

'So where's Eve?' Bolt asked his back, for Gibson's back could scarcely be any less forthcoming than his front. Once in the narrow galley kitchen, Gibson rinsed a dirty bottle in the sink and made up his son's milk formula, all the while magically cradling the lad in the crook of his left arm.

'I can see you're quite adept at this sort of thing', proffered Bolt, 'but has anyone ever told you how to sterilize bottles? And shouldn't you be washing your hands?'

Gibson filled the washing-up bowl with warm water. Now, if he had been alone, he would have talked to his son, because even the presence of Bolt in his kitchen did not quite drown out the song of the nightingale in his garden. He would have said, 'Hark that, Jo, there's a nightingale for you,' and he would have laid his child in the bowl and splashed the water over his belly, and he would have told him how the nightingale was a bird of paradise flown down from heaven to greet him this June morning.

But Josiah's bath was perfunctory that morning, no tender coos, no nursery rhymes; Josiah cried the more and the water darkened, for Gibson had been gardening that morning, and, as Bolt all too eagerly observed, scored few marks for hygiene.

Josiah's tears and Bolt's smugness made Gibson anxious. He fumbled with the bottle, unable to remove the teat with one hand; he lost the measuring spoon which came with the formula and took the one in the sugar bowl, and despite boiling the kettle he used cold water from the tap. He tried walking up and down the kitchen, baby in one hand, bottle in the other, but Bolt was forever getting in his way, and he was saying, 'No, Gibson, no, this isn't good enough, haven't you been told that you have to use previously boiled water? And you can't give babies cold milk!'

Gibson looked at him furiously and took off with Josiah and bottle into the sitting-room. Bolt followed, and sat himself down in the first armchair he saw. Yes, Bolt prided himself on being able to feel at home in any of his client's houses, however inhospitable they might be. It was Gibson's armchair. Had he not already been both red and speechless before such an act of encroachment, Gibson would have most certainly become so, but his repertory was limited, and he sat on the sofa as stiff as a soldier, wrapped his son in a blanket and tried to persuade him to suck at some cold milk.

'Nice pad you've got here,' said Bolt, surveying the pictures of country mice which came with the house. 'Very nice.'

And then, after a pause, he went on, 'I want us to be friends, you know. I want us to get along. Trust. That's what it's called, trust. Too little of it about nowadays. It's like we've all of us got to learn about it all over again. A small word, a big idea. Trust.'

Gibson ignored him, grateful to his son for sipping at the cold milk.

'Doesn't Eve breastfeed, then?'

Gibson closed his eyes and shook his head.

Bolt took this as progress.

'I don't know whether you could tell me where Eve is? Has she gone shopping?'

Gibson shrugged his shoulders.

'Has she been long?'

No reply.

'Does she often go away like this?'

Gibson seemed distressed. Bolt felt momentarily guilty that this eking out of the truth should be so painful for him; whom Eve was with, he had no doubt; he was just curious to know whether Fothering had made another visit down to Cambridge to see Eve or whether Eve had gone up to Hull.

Gibson would have felt more comfortable had a boil been growing on his neck. His body began to tremble (as Bolt dutifully observed) and he swept up his baby and took him straight out of that room and back into the garden. Bolt heard the kitchen door slam. He thought to himself, 'Poor man! But I won't follow him. He needs to be alone. I'll wait a while till he calms down. I'm in no hurry.'

Bolt sat back in the armchair and waited. An hour went by: an hour, Bolt observed, when in most ordinary families an evening meal might be served, when the curtains were closed and the TV switched on. The noise of any approaching car made him jump. Eve would probably be coming home at any moment. What sort of a mother could leave her two-week old baby in the care of a father as inadequate as Gibson? He hadn't noticed any food in the kitchen, he hadn't even been offered a cup of tea. The sides of the leatherette armchair were beginning to stick to his arms, and he got up to walk around the room. Instinctively he ran his finger along the top of the pictures on the walls to look for dust, and found it. His practised eye then sought out the skirting boards: was it possible they hadn't even been wiped down once in the four months of their tenancy? He sighed magnanimously. What else could he expect? Eve wasn't exactly the type to take her domestic responsibilities seriously. And as for poor old Gibson, he certainly wasn't going to lay the blame at that old codger's door. Anyone could see he was doing his best.

How long would he wait? As long as it took, he decided. He'd take the Wednesday morning off in lieu: that would solve the problem of when to take his car in for a service. What if Eve didn't turn up? Then he'd finally have his heart-to-heart with Gibson: he'd crack, and a good thing, too. Finally, Gibson would confide in him, and he was sure to tell a rum tale.

Suddenly he heard a car drawing up outside the house. Bolt thought quickly: Eve didn't have a car, yet this sound of a car door slamming had been the very one he had been waiting for. He stood up and waited near the curtain, smiling to himself. Patience rewarded. He glimpsed Fothering's anxious face, his slump over the steering wheel; he smiled again, maliciously. He hid, waiting for the couple to enter. The doorbell rang. Gibson didn't answer it. The doorbell rang again. Why didn't they go round the back, if Eve had forgotten her key? He watched while Fothering made his way back to the car. Then Bolt stopped guessing and ran out of the house to stop him driving away.

'Dr Fothering, wait!' he cried.

Fothering got out of his car immediately, instinctively adjusting his tie when he saw who it was. 'What are you doing here? What's going on? Is the baby all right?'

'The baby's fine,' said Bolt. 'He's in the garden with Gibson. Come in. Take a look for yourself.'

'Where's Eve?'

'No-one seems to know.' Bolt raised his eyebrows. 'Have you heard from her?'

'Not a word. No-one's been answering the telephone. The health visitor…'

'Yes, I know. She's disappeared. It seems I'm here for much the same reason. Come in.'

Bolt took Fothering back into the sitting-room, and offered him the sofa.

'Don't you think I ought to make myself known to Gibson?' he asked nervously as he sat down.

'I don't think he'd appreciate that,' said Bolt. 'I've been watching him from the toilet. He's taken the baby into the greenhouse with him.'

'But he's looking after the baby?'

'After a fashion.'

'Where does Gibson say Eve is?'

'He won't tell me. But I think he will,' said Bolt mysteriously. 'He's not exactly the chatty type, is he?'

'Gibson is Gibson. He's a good man, and Eve knows that.' Fothering began biting his nails.

'And the baby's not dead yet!' Bolt laughed.

Fothering winced at Bolt's humour. 'Have you seen Eve with the baby at all? How is she with him?'

'Today's the first day I've seen either of them. They've been listed as missing persons by the health services. But all the while, it seems, Gibson has been in his greenhouse.'

Fothering stood up. 'So where's the toilet?' was his question.

'Before the kitchen on the left,' said Bolt.

Fothering slipped out of the door and closed it behind him. But no, it was not relief that the fates afforded him: rather, its very opposite, a feeling of constriction, of tightening, not only within the temples but rushing down through his body, compressing his lungs, stiffening his penis, cramping his feet. At that exact moment, Eve slipped into the hall, dressed from top to toe in an orange sarong like some exotic goddess.

'Oh my darling Dr Fothering!' she cried, 'You noble, loyal, wonderful creature, godfather to my child, no less! Have you come all the way down from Hull again?'

She dropped a large sack which went *thud* and flung her arms around him, covering him in kisses. Nor did Fothering stand like a statue, but received them gratefully, and almost lay his head on her shoulder.

Suddenly the door to the sitting-room was flung open and the Great Eavesdropper Himself was standing within the frame of it like a curse. The three looked at each other.

'Am I interrupting something?' asked Bolt.

'No', said Fothering.

'Yes,' said Eve, simultaneously. 'What are you doing here? We never invited you.'

'We wanted to make sure you were coping, Eve, with your new responsibilities. We wanted to help you!'

'Help!' laughed Eve, 'You couldn't help a flea do a circus trick. But I forgive you! Today, I am all forgiveness, I am Mercy herself, enthroned. Here, let me give you one of these.' And Eve delved into her sack and produced two copies of the *Bhagavad-gita*. 'One for you, too, Dr Fothering.'

Eve gave them each a book and they mumbled their thanks. 'Now, I know that spiritually neither of you is as far advanced as I am. Oh, what are we doing cramped up in this little hall, we must expand ourselves! Follow me into the garden! Breathe in, breathe out! These last days I can't tell you how I've been shined on by all that is divine! I understand all, I understand the very mechanisms of the universe. Why I should be the one chosen for enlightenment God alone knows. But there we have it!'

Eve gathered up the train of her orange sarong in the crook of her arm and merrily pirouetted towards the kitchen. 'Today I have broken through the chains of desire! I am the Ground of Being, I am Mother Earth. Embrace me, my sons! Embrace me, Dr Fothering' – which he dutifully did – 'and embrace me, Roger' – which he dutifully didn't – 'and come both of you to meet my young babe!'

'I should like that very much,' said Dr Fothering.

'Your son and I are already acquainted,' said Bolt.

♣

Gibson and Josiah had been hiding all afternoon in the greenhouse. They were warm and conspiratorial together, Gibson like a great big bear, Josiah, his cub. Fortunately, only Eve could fit in there with him. She shut the door behind her and crouched down with them.

'Gibson darling' she whispered, and kissed him, giving him her hand to hold, as she customarily did. 'Josiah, dearest,' she said, gazing at him tenderly. 'There are these men in our garden, did you know?'

Gibson nodded, squeezing his wife's hand.

'I'm going to get rid of them, don't you worry. You stay here just ten minutes longer, that's all it will take.'

Eve emerged from the greenhouse as elegant as a duchess.

'I'm afraid the baby's sleeping,' she said, matter-of-factly. 'I don't think it's fair to disturb babies when they're asleep, do you?'

'Does he normally sleep in the greenhouse, Eve?'

'Don't be silly, Dr Fothering! He quite often sleeps in his crib! Oh damn, damn, damn!'

Both men followed her sheepishly back into the hall.

'Now, I'm afraid you'll both have to go,' insisted Eve, as she opened the front door.

'But I've only just arrived!' exclaimed Dr Fothering indignantly. 'I've driven all this way to see… my godson!'

'You're right. Roger, you can go at least,' said Eve, flatly.

'But we've not had a chance to chat!'

'Yes, we have. I tell you what. Do you have a card or something? I could pop by if I have any problems.'

Bolt handed Eve a card with the Social Services address on it.

'That won't do,' said Eve, dismissively. 'I want to visit you at home. It's a chat you wanted, not an interview. If I'm not mistaken?'

'I'll be seeing you, Eve,' Bolt said, nodding politely at her, and he saw himself out. The door clicked behind him.

'That idiot is out of here at last,' declared Eve, 'Thank God for that! Let's drink to it. Beer or claret, Dr Fothering?'

'Please call me Michael,' pleaded Fothering.

'A drink for St Michael, what can I get you?'

Fothering followed her into the kitchen and caught sight of Gibson still crouching in the greenhouse.

'What about Gibson? Won't he want a drink?' he said.

'Gibson is as patient as an ox', said Eve, dismissively. 'I want a few moments alone with you, like the old times. I miss the time we spent together, don't you?'

'That would be nice,' said Fothering, anxiously.

The two of them went back into the sitting-room with a bottle of wine. Eve patted the empty space beside her on the sofa. 'Sit next to me,' she said.

Dr Fothering took off his tie and did so.

'So Eve, how are you doing?' he asked her, as she poured him a glass.

'I'm very, very happy,' she said, but there was something glassy about the way she said it, as though her statement had no roots.

'So everything in your life is completely as it should be? You have no regrets about anything?'

'I have one regret,' said Eve solemnly.

'Yes?' enquired Dr Fothering, grateful to feel he still had a role in her life.

'Look at this. I'm just so stupid. I'm lop-sided. I have one brown arm and one white, one brown shoulder and one white.'

'What are you trying to say?' said Fothering, desperately trying to eke out the metaphorical meaning.

'Use your eyes, Michael! Look at me!'

Eve unpinned her orange sarong so that it fell to her waist. She looked like a Greek goddess in a cypress grove, a shaft of white light falling diagonally across her fine form.

'You look all right to me.' Fothering finished his glass of wine.

'Josiah is punishing me for not breast-feeding him. I still have incredibly tender breasts,' said Eve, by the by.

'Please put your dress back on,' said Fothering, coolly.

'How can you call it a *dress*, Michael? These saffron robes are of deep religious significance. And they set me back a thousand pounds. In fact, all my worldly riches. But the widow's mite and all that. You reap what you sow, etcetera, etcetera.'

'A thousand pounds?'

'Money is such a fearful responsibility, don't you find? Anyway, the lad was raising money for his community. There now, godliness with the frock thrown in for good measure. And he was quite happy. And so was I till I realised I was lopsided.'

'Oh Eve!' sighed the long-suffering Dr Fothering. 'I despair of you! Think of your baby! Your future! What will become of you all?'

Eve was suddenly very serious. 'I love my baby, Michael. And it's true, he won't receive the most conventional of educations, but you should see dear Gibson with him. He's taught him the names of at least thirty flowers. He sticks his nose into the petals, and he says, 'mint, jasmine, rose, carnation' – you've never seen anything so touching. To teach by smell! Isn't that a perfect, holistic approach to the teaching of the young? Now, Michael, how shall I persuade you? Here, let me take your hands in mine like so. I love my husband, Gibson. I love my son, Josiah. Us three, we're all good for each other. I once had a teacher called Gilbert who told me the definition of love. He said it's when two and two equals five. Michael, darling, in this family two and two equals five. Let other families go plod plod plod and fill themselves with childcare logistics. But I'm not into that. I'm not into routines and sticking to the book. But I'm good at playing. Josiah and I shall dress up together as St George and the dragon, and I shall be the best of all mothers. I shall utterly commit myself. A dragon is what I shall be.'

'I believe you,' said Michael.

Then something happened in spite of himself. A mechanism snapped, something gave way, the claret got to his head. For Dr Fothering and his patient kissed, deeply and tenderly, for the first time. They knew each other and were, in an important sense, indebted to each other. It was a kiss which signified not a beginning but an end, a seal between them rather than the precursor of more to come.

Such nuances, of course, were missed by one particular observer. Not Gibson, who was still patiently waiting in the greenhouse, but Roger Bolt, the unchosen one, who was waiting malevolently on the other side of the hedge in front of the house.

Chapter Four

SEVEN YEARS ON EVE AND GIBSON were still in possession of their son, and indeed, each other. Less surprisingly, Roger Bolt had long since been taken off the case; for he found the information he had gleaned that early summer evening in 1984 to be too good to keep to himself. His senior, June Briggs, had been as eager to learn what the psychiatrist had been doing to his patient, as Bolt had been to divulge it; and June's senior in turn, Head of Social Services in Cambridgeshire, no less, had demanded more and more detail 'to make a case against him'.

There were various inquiries set up to establish whether this was a *bona fide* case of professional misconduct (after all, the misdemeanour occurred when Eve was no longer his patient). Roger Bolt made numerous pleas for a paternity test (unanswered, thanks to the intervention of the British Medical Council), but the net result was that Dr Michael Fothering resigned his post as a consultant psychiatrist in Hull even before the case had been made against him, and retrained as a General Practitioner. Two years on, he attached himself to a surgery in a suburb of Leeds, where it was his destiny never to find another Eve, either as a patient or a wife.

But while Roger Bolt occupied his sleepless nights plotting against Dr Fothering, the indefatigable Eve spent hers scheming against the carbuncle himself. And so it came to be that Bolt's downfall swiftly followed that of Fothering's: she accused him of trespass, to begin with; of looking at her lustfully, of being a peeping Tom. At first he was simply taken off her case; but when the letters continued, when she threatened to take her complaint to the police as the Social Services were so slow to respond to it, and when, finally, Bolt confessed to climbing over their garden fence to gain access to their property (and June Briggs told him he was a 'moron'), everyone realised his time had come to move on. So his wife and children welcomed him back in Darlington, and his prospects drew to a close: a residential worker in a home for the mentally handicapped was his ignominious fate, for which he was paid little more than four pounds an hour.

Meanwhile, there were other social workers to fill Roger Bolt's shoes: a series of women, coming one after another in merciless succession. Just as Eve thought she might be left in peace, there would be another introductory letter, in which another hopeful would say how much she was 'looking forward to meeting her.'

Of course, it would have been easy for Eve to be out, to have simply avoided contact with 'the termites' as she called them. (Gibson enjoyed it when she railed against 'the termites' – it made him laugh nervously.) But the truth was, there was a way in which she enjoyed venting her resentment at their intrusion. She would smile, inviting each of them into her home, give them cups of tea. Then she would sit them down and ask them what seemed to be the problem.

'Now, tell me everything that's on your mind,' she would say, pleasantly. 'Don't leave a stone unturned. ' And when the poor woman hesitated, she pressed,

'I'm all ears. Now, don't be embarrassed.'

And when the social worker tried to put the record straight, with some inane comment such as, 'We're here to help you,' Eve would lean forward, smiling pleasantly, and ask, 'Could you explain? Who is "we" in this instance? Are you married? Do you mean your husband and you?'

'No, I mean, "our team"'.

'I'm sorry to sound so dense,' said Eve, disingenuously, 'but does that mean you play a sport? In which case, which sport?'

'You know what I mean by "team",' huffed the social worker.

'Well, no, no I don't actually. Tell me about your team and I might get the idea.'

'Now, Eve. I have come to talk about you, not me. We're concerned about you.'

'Oh yes?' Eve would reply vaguely.

'And your baby. Now, where is your baby?'

How vainly these women tried to take the reins! How vainly, indeed, did they write 'unco-operative' in their files, always forgetting to add the ways in which she did not co-operate: if they had done, they might have discovered some pattern in the way Eve manipulated them. So one by one, these women would ask Eve where her baby was, and Eve would try, try ever so hard, to remember.

'Now, where did I see him last?' she liked to muse.

'Might he be in his cot?' the social worker suggested, helpfully.

'Good idea! Let's take a look, shall we?'

And when the bedroom was empty, Eve would open the linen cupboard door, and express surprise that he wasn't there either.

'Oh where, where, did I put him?'

'This isn't necessary, you know, Eve.'

'You're right. But it's fun, don't you think? Wait, the last time I saw him he was in his highchair eating breakfast!'

And the pair would race back down the stairs into the kitchen only to find the highchair quite empty.

'Damn,' Eve exclaimed, good-humouredly.

At this point the social worker might catch sight of the baby in the garden with his father, because, come fine weather or foul, morning or dusk, that is where they would always be. Or Eve, both bored and irritated, and desiring this alien female to be out of her house, would clap her hands and declare she had just spotted him near the greenhouse.

But each social worker was too humiliated to report back Eve's little ruse, doubtless because they would also have to cast themselves as the butt of it; rather, after two or three visits, they would complain of a 'lack of trust between us' or simply 'lack of progress'. Were they ever worried about a 'lack of care', on the other hand? They all agreed they'd seen worse, far worse. Yet they couldn't leave the case alone. In the same way as Eve had managed to remain a patient at Fulbright for twenty months, she also managed to remain a 'client' of the Social Services, and the games went on through the seasons, through the years, with only the slightest modifications, until Josiah reached the age of seven. There was something about her which made the challenge: quagmire I might seem, but stay with me and one day you'll reach solid ground. And to that extent, Eve was irresistible to them.

⚜

Josiah grew into a good-looking boy, and seemed in robust health. He had wavy blond hair down to his collar, and deep blue eyes, which would confront his interlocutors with a brazen stare. His clothes were old-fashioned, button-up shirts and corduroy trousers, his shoes Start-Rite sandals. Yet this was barely the stuff of childcare proceedings, despite the fact (as those women inevitably observed) that his hands were always dirty and there was mud under his fingernails.

'There is something not quite right about the boy,' wrote a social worker. For Josiah didn't like it when the social workers leaned over to pat him on the head, and he didn't like the look of their large smiling faces when they squatted down 'to have a chat'. Nor did Josiah ever give them the relief of one ordinary child-like sentence to prove that his personality was unscathed, that it had somehow survived his parents.

Neither Eve nor Gibson had ever bought him toys, not as a

deliberate strategy, nor even as an economy, but rather because it simply didn't occur to them that Josiah would want toys. And probably they were right: when Josiah was four a social worker took pity on him and produced a sack-load of puzzles, bricks, dinky cars and even an old garage, stuff that her own children had grown out of; but each time she visited (and this particular woman lasted a full six months), she found the toys untouched in a corner of Josiah's bedroom. She wrote a report describing such behaviour as 'disturbing' and 'unnatural'. To be four and never to have said 'brum brum' to a car! The boy wasn't thriving, it was all she could conclude; but frustratingly, there was no positive evidence of abuse.

Josiah was by nature as silent as his father, and as alert and suspicious as his mother, so it should be of no surprise that he never bothered to answer these women. 'What do you *really* like doing?' they would ask him, but why on earth should he tell them? What would they know about gardening? For by the age of four, Josiah had a passion for growing seedlings.

Josiah and Gibson used to go in search of good earth, by bus. Neither of them was too interested in the views through the filthy windows; rather they waited, eyes locked ahead, in mute anticipation of what was to come. At the stop beyond Wilbraham, they would begin an hour's walk deep into the fen. On the way out Josiah would sit on his father's shoulders until they were well out of sight from the road, and then Josiah would help him fill two large sacks of the richest fen soil, chosen by the feel of it sticking to their fingers. Gibson showed his son how to feel the soil, and understand the consistency of it. 'A good wetness', he used to say, when satisfied.

That a seed should contain so much within it and yet be so small and tight and dry, and that he, Josiah, should be the medium by which it might receive life, lovingly separating the seed from its brothers and laying it in its own private bed, filled him with a sense of gratitude and mystery. How his assessors were to mis-diagnose the contempt on his six-year-old face when they showed him how sand runs through the spokes of a plastic windmill! And how those same assessors, with their eye solely on Eve's spectacular performances, were to miss the one true centre of Josiah's existence.

For how *dull* they all found Gibson! And how *extraordinary* that Eve should have married him! Amongst each other (but not in their reports) they discussed the possible sex-life these two might have, and those who bothered to read up on the beginnings of the case found themselves hugely drawn to Roger Bolt's thesis that Eve's psychiatrist had used Gibson to cover an illicit affair, and indeed Gibson wasn't Josiah's father at all. How sympathetic they felt towards Bolt when they learnt of his demise, how angry they felt on his behalf when they read how the BMA had refused a paternity test, how aggrieved they were that the courts had never been involved… though of course, even if they had been, these kind of people always closed rank when it mattered. Even if Fothering had been proved to be the father, some paternalistic law of some bygone age would have been summoned to protect him. The *injustice* of it all, the *unprofessionalism*!

And meanwhile, poor, poor Gibson. 'Heavy-going' wrote one; 'never says a word' wrote another; 'kind' wrote a Mrs Bird, who was a kind woman herself. But Mrs Bird took herself off the case after she'd foolishly consented to Eve reading tarot cards for her; inevitably, Mrs Bird discovered that she was soon to meet death after strangulation by a snake, which didn't do her *joie de vivre* much good a week before setting out on safari to Kenya to celebrate her silver wedding.

No-one was ever sure whether to offer help or deliver threats to the Nelson family; no-one was ever sure whether Eve was mad or pretending to be mad. Manipulative, yes; provocative, yes; uncooperative, a million times yes: but the social work 'team' could never agree upon a strategy to pull the Nelson family into line. The senior who considered it her duty to do so was Miss June Briggs; 'Miss' despite being married and 'June', despite being unmitigatedly frosty. And if Eve was determined not to be defeated, Miss June Briggs was triply determined to defeat her. For she had solemnly watched a veritable army of her 'team' marching into the Gibson household, only to withdraw, shaken and bowed, within a few months. So hers was the fury, the determination, the unfinished business; and at last she had observed a breach in the Nelsons' battle-line: they had repeatedly refused to send their son to school. In other words, they were breaking the law.

Now, there is also a law of the land which allows parents to deliver an education of their own, and what a great and privileged freedom it is that we should be able to mould and shape our children in our own image; or, more pragmatically put, teach our children to read and write ourselves. But the fly in the ointment is that we have to prove it, we have to prove that our children are actually learning as much as they would have been at school, and that means more than knowing how to plant a seedling or two. And Josiah was quite as hopeless as his parents. On being asked to read a passage from a book, his pretty mouth set into a grimace. On being asked to count up to twenty, he positively scowled. It was quite reasonable, therefore, that the powers-that-be assumed the poor boy knew nothing.

When Eve herself was confronted, she replied in riddles. When asked whether Josiah could read, she replied, 'Yes, and he can read your minds too. Take care.' On being asked whether he could count and calculate, Eve told them, 'Why, even a cow can count, even a sheep and a pig, too. Of course he can count, dammit.'

'But can he add, can he subtract?' they persisted.

'Show me a seven-year-old who can't!'

'Well then, could he give us a demonstration of his skills?'

'He's in the garden dividing plants so that they might multiply. You can watch him, if you like.'

What happened to this young family was bad. Whether it's

excusable, you, the reader, be the judge. The baseline was, all the social workers who ever came into contact with Eve disliked her. They loathed her airy arrogance. If only she had cried, perhaps, or better still, if she had ever admitted that she was in need of 'help,' they would have come running to her side. Then the dreadful things which befell them might never have happened.

‡

The idea of a foster placement was June Briggs's. 'Just a very temporary thing' she insisted at the case conference in October 1991. 'He's a very solitary child, it's not good for him. We can't have him missing yet another year at school. If he starts on Monday, then he'll only have missed a month of this academic year. He'll catch up: there's already an assistant in place at Arbury primary school who can help him. If the Nelsons won't send him of their own accord, if the boy's not learning anything at home, then it's up to us to step in. That's what we here for, is everyone agreed? Or do we just sit back and watch the kid fail in life?'

'Do we know for certain he's not getting an education at home?' piped up one of the social workers.

'Has anyone ever noticed a reading book in their house?'

'Or a maths book, for that matter?'

'Anyone ever noticed a Latin text book?'

(Laughter.)

'Seriously, Eve insists her son's a fine Latin scholar.'

(More laughter.)

'Has anyone here ever read with the child?'

'He won't co-operate.'

'Do you think that means he can't?'

'Probably. But it also means that even if he can read, he's in need of help. He's too withdrawn.'

'Not just shy?'

'No, he's more than shy.'

'Is everyone here agreed on that?' said Miss June Briggs, taking the helm. 'Listen, this is only going to be for a few days, until Eve sees sense and encourages him to go to school herself. What that woman needs is a short, sharp, shock, to make her wake up to the real world.'

And so Josiah's fate was agreed: at seven in the morning, June herself, along with the Nelsons' latest social worker, a young woman of twenty-three called Tracy, set off from the Social Services Department in a VW beetle to claim him. They took a policeman, just in case, who sat in the back.

Tracy was nervous, but was pretending she wasn't. It was her first job since graduating, and this was the hardest thing she'd ever had to do.

June was tired. She didn't like the way Tracy never stopped talking. It was a fiery dawn that morning and Tracy said, 'Red sky in the morning, shepherd's warning.'

June said 'Humph' and tried to demist her windscreen. The policeman, too, was bleary-eyed and sat, stiff as a rod.

'Do you think it's possible that Josiah is educationally sub-normal, and that Eve's refusing to send him to school because she's in denial?'

'I don't know,' said June, in a tone which tried to draw the conversation to a close.

'But it's just possible, isn't it?' said Tracy, chirpily, trying to recall which psychologist might have agreed with her.

'Frankly,' said June, 'I wouldn't credit that woman with as much feeling. She wouldn't notice if her son ate coal for breakfast.'

'He seems well-enough fed to me.'

'I don't know what goes on in that house,' admitted June, but disapprovingly, nonetheless.

'So you think this really is the right course of action to be taking, do you, June?'

'Of course it's the right thing. Unless you can think of anything better.'

'It just seems so extreme. The closer we get the more… violent it seems.'

June stopped the car and sighed. 'Tracy, are you up to this?'

Tracy said, 'What I mean is, is Eve really that bad a mother to deserve…'

June's voice was unexpectedly sweet. 'Tracy, she has a history. She has a mental disorder, a file on her as fat as the Bible. We're protecting the child, Tracy. Have you got it?'

They drove on.

♣

Mad or bad: a mere grey wash spills between them. In this final stage of the theft of Josiah, Briggs did not invoke Eve's bad behaviour but the fact that she was crazy. And for those of us mortals who yearn to draw clear black lines where there are none, the truth is that June Briggs in this instance was right: Eve did have a screw or two loose, which loosened even further the morning they took her son away.

Even as a child Eve's mother hadn't managed to make her understand, 'If you do this, I'll do that.' To link actions with their consequences was a mental feat that she simply couldn't manage; Eve didn't live so much for the day as for the minute. When they took her son she couldn't conceive of the notion of 'punishment'; she couldn't understand that they were playing a game and had given her a role to play and a feeling to feel, namely that of remorse. When Eve looked back and tried to piece together what had happened, she could remember a second in which the house was full, yes, she could distinctly see Gibson giving Josiah a bowl of cereal and Josiah chattering away, they were making plans for the day, they were off to the fen again... and then she remembered a further second. The house was empty this time. She called for Gibson but Gibson was gone.

She tried to put into some sort of order the intervening seconds. No, she hadn't heard the social workers coming in. Perhaps Gibson had answered the door. She remembered Josiah saying to her, 'See you soon, Mummy,' and he was holding Gibson's hand. He could have been off on a trip, for the lightness with which he had said it. Then he was gone, and Gibson was gone.

So perhaps that's what had happened, perhaps they'd all gone to the fen together. But if that was the case, why was she looking in the garden for him? And she had kept with her this image, this dreadful image, of Gibson kneeling in a corner, burying his head deep into it, as though only two walls had strength enough to support its weight. So why hadn't she gone up to him then, while she could? Why had she left the walls to hold his head for him? Where had she gone?

Nowhere far, geographically speaking. For the whole of her life she was to imagine that it was Gibson who had run away from her, who was found at the end of that week in a ditch of damp, black earth and taken back to Fulbright hospital. But the truth was, it was she who had run away from him.

She had lain between Josiah's bed and the wall, squashing herself in between them as if in a coffin. And not a thought did she have for anyone in that little family. She was neither angry nor resentful, and was thinking as clearly as she had ever thought. Her mind was ruthlessly engaged on a track which had hitherto been virtually untrodden: namely that of looking for the *causes* of things. For Eve had lived her life timelessly, she had existed with no thought for past nor future. Already, Josiah seemed like a mirage to her, for he had been there, sweet thing! But now he was gone somewhere else.

And in the vacuum that ensued many images fought to be seen, and the one which came upon her with the greatest force was the ghost of Gilbert Fitzpatrick, so physical she could have touched him, a velvet waistcoat and dark wavy hair, smelling of wood smoke. He was kissing her toes, stroking her soft, supple, girl's feet, her smooth shins, her plump knees. He told her she had much to learn, and he much to teach, that they had a complementary mission in this life, and death, and eternity. 'Gilbert', she said to him, (and she spoke out loud to the room) 'Did I ever tell you that I have a son, Josiah? Did I ever tell you that? Will you teach him for me? I'm so ignorant myself. Sometimes I'm just not up to it myself. I can't do it anymore. I've no strength left. I want to crawl into your pocket, my love.'

Was it minutes, was it hours later? Up Eve sat to write Gilbert a letter. She looked for paper, envelopes. She went back into the sitting-room and wondered why she was curious at the sight of an empty corner there, and shook herself out of her reverie. She found paper and sat at the table to write to him; the mood she was in was scary, and the handwriting was too big for the page. Finally she was finished, satisfied. But then she tried to remember the name of the cottage where she was so happy with him, where he read to her while she lay her restless busy head on his lap to be stroked, and with words so beautiful shooed out the words so ugly from her brain. She couldn't even remember the name of the county. The place had become a myth.

As Eve slumped in the chair, her cheek resting on the table, she recognised that other place as freedom, where her mind could simultaneously flit yet be contained by her lover, her body surrendered yet utterly true. Then for a fleeting moment she dared to sink into another reality. She cried out Gibson's name. The good, kind, solid Gibson, father of her child! How ironic it was that this great act of freedom of hers, this running against the grain, should leave her so trapped: the dutiful wife and mother of suburbia!

Suddenly a nausea held her in its sticky, sickly clamp; the air itself became reified: an unbreathable substance choking her lungs. She began to count to herself, one for every inhalation, one for every exhalation, as though she were beginning at the beginning of things, could start afresh and know for certain, this time, that two follows one and three follows two. Calmer now, she considered the seconds following each other in an indefatigable sequence, and it reassured her to know that time was hurtling heedless towards certainty and would carry her along for the ride. In the larger scale of things, there was nothing she could do about anything.

That knowledge began to exhaust her. How odd, she thought, that she ever thought her will might resist her fate. We are not players of the game but part of it. Even spectators are part of the game. No one can escape, no one can reach solid ground. We are all floating, gravity deceives us and makes us believe we have some hold on things, but we are like chess pieces in someone else's space capsule, our weight is a random thing with no truth in it.

'I am a drop of petrol in an ocean,' she spoke out loud and laughed. She got up from the kitchen chair, swaying, as though conscious of her essential lightness, and found herself moving upstairs in an unspecified search for the horizontal, or the path of least resistance. She looked first in her own bedroom, but it smelt of Gibson, not that she minded the smell but that's not what she was looking for; the bathroom was too cold and Josiah's bedroom didn't merit even a glimpse. She drew the curtains on the landing and lay down on the carpet. She didn't sleep and she rarely closed her eyes, but the nothingness was sweet in itself.

♣

At two in the afternoon, June Briggs was in bargaining mood. The morning had been a great success: the lure of school and other children, the first trip in a car in his entire life had made Josiah's first journey without his father an easy one. Even Tracy said she was surprised at how quickly Josiah had trusted them. And then, when Briggs had rung the school at lunchtime, the headmistress was full of enthusiasm, and astonishment that Josiah had never seen a television before. So, Briggs, in full possession of her moral victory, was off to put Josiah's mother in the picture, to inform her that the school bus stopped in the Arbury estate at ten past eight for five minutes, and that if Josiah was not on that bus the following morning he would be taken into care.

She parked the car immediately outside the house. The curtains were closed. Good! Eve must be feeling suitably cowed. But Briggs was too professional to gloat, and she straightened her face in the car mirror. The doorbell made a sing-song chime. No one answered it, but nor did she expect them to.

'Eve,' she called through the letter-box. 'I've got good news for you! Josiah likes school! He's mixing with the other children very well! Let me in and I'll tell you more!' Her voice had the same tone as the doorbell. 'Eve! Gibson!' she called again. When there was still no reply, she shouted, 'Look, I need you to open the door!'

Eve, meanwhile, was calmly filling a bucket with water in the bathroom. This was a first for her, she needed the light relief of it. She was pleased to notice through the crack in the curtains that Briggs had dressed herself up, and had a proper hairdo, which suddenly reminded her of her mother.

'Hello June!' called Eve from the landing window, all smiles. 'I'm so sorry, I was in the bathroom and I didn't hear you. Is there anything you want?'

Briggs craned her neck to look at her. 'Yes,' she said, 'I want to tell you about Josiah's progress today.'

'Josiah's progress?' Eve mulled over the word. 'Progress?' she repeated.

'Eve, I'm getting neck-ache. It would be good to speak to you face to face, you know. Could you be a love and let me in?'

'Love? You've never called me "love" before? Does that mean that *I'm* making progress? Or does it mean that *you're* making progress?'

'Open this door!'

'Hold on a second!' said Eve, disappearing from the window.

Briggs looked down, satisfied, and waited for the front door to open.

Eve fetched the bucket, and spat in it for good measure. Gleefully she surveyed Briggs' coiffured hair. The moment before is always more delightful than the moment after, she thought to herself. The bucket was heavy; it took all her strength to balance it on the sill. Eve was as icy-calm as a ferret. She watched Briggs looking at her watch.

'I hope that's expensive,' thought Eve.

She tilted the bucket, surely and steadily, and the water fell, fast and furious, a perfect hit.

'Bad weather we've been having!' Eve shouted down.

The woman walked, wet but professional, back to her car.

Eve never learnt of Briggs's strategies for revenge, for within twelve hours she had left the country.

♣

Wars happen when language runs out, and that is how it was with Eve that night. Not that she did not rant first, hour after hour, striding from room to room, declaiming that schools were breeding grounds for stupidity and cowardice, places where fear begot fear and like begot like, where homogeneity stifled every living soul.

'That's what they want to do to him!' she cried out. 'That's what they want to do to my son! They want to kill his soul, and when it's dead we can only pray his body will follow suit. I shall ask the doctors to release him from the machine, and I shall say, let him die now, and let us pray that he finds God in the hereafter because he was never given a chance on earth, he was only taught fear! You morons! You morons that think you know better than I do! You dried up, shrivelled up, life-forms, the word 'human-being' is too big for you! And how dare you ridicule my husband! He has more spirit and understanding in his little toe than the whole lot of you wankers put together! You ignorant, empty worms, you pen-pushing, arrogant, stale idiots! You've never had an original thought in your lives, and in your trudging blindness you make a bloody sloth look alert!

'But I shall kill you all before you kill Josiah! You've taken away my chance to breathe life into him, so I shall take away your chance to breathe death into him. I shall take away your evil schools, I shall burn the whole lot of them to the ground! I shall tackle the cog factories themselves, for that is all they are, manufacturing cogs to keep the world turning in its dire course, mindless cogs with less humanity than a cat!'

That was more or less the gist of it. Then Eve stormed out of the house at 5.45 only to return a few minutes later. She took a good look at herself in the mirror. 'My God, I look quite mad,' she said, flattening down her hair and trying to look serious. She went upstairs to change into smarter clothes. The only thing Eve found which was suitable was her wedding dress, a Laura Ashley floral number she'd picked up in a charity shop especially for the occasion.

'I never thought I'd be wearing this again,' she thought, as she stretched her arm behind her back to do up the zip. 'And I'm sure I bought shoes to go with it!' She rummaged around on the floor of her fitted wardrobe and found a pair of pink stilettos. Eve brushed her teeth, combed her hair and smiled at herself in the bathroom mirror. 'Just a little lipstick', she thought to herself, and applied some, though the only colour she could find was red. 'This will be some party', she said to her reflection.

Eve's first stop was the petrol station. She opted for the leaded petrol, deciding it would be the more flammable, and bought two full gallon containers. She smiled happily at all the people in the queue, remarking that it was a warm night for the time of year.

As she frankly didn't know where any of the schools of Cambridge were, not even the primary school where they had sent Josiah, she had to ask directions. And who better to ask than the gangs of drunken, smoking teenagers hanging around the street corners, all of whom, she was quite sure, would love to see their schools burnt down. Teetering on her pink heels, she swayed her petrol cans as happily as if they had been fancy bags from a boutique.

'Excuse me,' she said, a picture of innocent enthusiasm, 'Can anyone direct me to the nearest school?'

'You look like you're about to burn it down!' laughed one, who was handsome and wore a Breton cap at an angle on his head.

'Oh but I am!' she said, meeting his eye. 'Only I've forgotten matches. Has anyone got a box of matches going spare?'

A box landed at her feet. She picked it up and tucked it into her cleavage.

'Thanks boys,' she said.

They laughed, and gave her directions to Chesterton Comprehensive. On Eve tottered, and they waved at her.

Eve might have been a lady of leisure, watering-can in hand, enjoying an evening stroll in her garden. She flitted about the town with her petrol, sprinkling a little over a community college here, a primary school there. She would make a pile of dry leaves on a window-sill, scatter a few drops of petrol, and then set them alight; or eagerly throw lighted matches through any letter boxes she found, only to lose interest even before they had hit the floor. But what a fine sunset there was that evening! How warm and glorious the shades of purple and pink! It was God's handwriting sprawled across the sky, and was she not the saviour of all disaffected youth? And indeed, there wasn't a lad who beheld the vision of her that night who remained unaffected, and they all concluded she was pretty hot.

When Eve got home she made herself a cup of tea. There was a letter on the mat but she left it there, probably from that twat Briggs, she thought. But it was enough to stir her mood; for she was a little more contemplative now. She envisaged nine schools reduced to a few charred splinters, and then the ensuing police investigation. Oh dear, she had witnesses of course. Why had she never learnt to *take care*? But then she relaxed. In fact, there was a moment when she was quite the heroine: she was waving to the crowds outside the Old Bailey in white kid gloves up to her elbows; they did a feature on her for *Blue Peter* in which the various children interviewed were beside themselves with gratitude for Eve's initiative. And then she suddenly understood that she was an arsonist and she would be sent to prison.

Her initial response to this revelation was anger. Freedom was not just a right (rights were like sweets handed out by toadying politicians); freedom was given by God. Freedom was honest, natural and true. She had burned down the schools of Cambridge to fight on Freedom's behalf, and now they were going to lock her up for what was only in the end (because of course they would build more schools) a mere suggestion. There were paltry, pock-pitted men on God's earth who wanted to stop her from walking among its meadows, sheltering in its copses, breathing in the very air warmed by the sun – so who did they think they were? How dare they have that power over her?

Eve found her passport and it was in date by a month. Wasn't it South America one was supposed to fly to at moments like this? But she had neither visa nor money: hadn't she heard that the Costa del Sol was almost as good? Even at this moment they would be looking for her; she fancied she heard fire engines in the distance – perhaps they would have to call in more from neighbouring forces. And of course the police would even now be preparing her photofit. By morning there would be pictures of her all over town.

She packed a few things and called a taxi. Later, when she was on the plane to Naples, she took off those pink shoes at last, and was shocked to see the state of her feet, the blisters eating into her heels, the caked blood where the dainty straps of the shoes had dug into her. Good God, she thought, I hadn't even realised I was in pain.

♣

Eve caused at most perhaps two hundred pounds worth of damage. A window frame had been badly charred at Hills Road Sixth Form college. Close observers might have noticed a few blackened bricks at Milton Primary and Parkside; but even the early morning cleaners didn't understand the significance of a couple of used matches near the door of several of the schools' entrance halls, and they swept them up with as much indifference as they did the odd cigarette end in the toilets. And when the superintendent arrived at eight to inspect the charred window outside the toilets at Chesterton Comprehensive, he shrugged his shoulders and shook his head and mumbled, 'bloody teenagers'.

Chapter Five

'CALL ME MUM,' said Mrs Sylvia Leatherpot, as she leaned over Josiah's breakfast bowl and poured out his cornflakes, 'and I want you to know, we don't mind the teeniest, teeniest bit about your accident last night, do we George?'

George, who'd even given up smoking so that his childless wife could be a foster parent, smiled fulsomely over his newspaper and said, 'Not one bit, Joe.'

'My name isn't Joe,' said Josiah.

'Well,' said Sylvia, 'we were thinking, weren't we, George?'

'Yes, dear,' said George, encouragingly.

'We were thinking that boys can be cruel. And girls can be. Weren't we, George?'

'Yes, dear.'

'And what with "Jozziah" not being a regular name, and seeing as you're a new boy and all that and want to make the most of your new school, well we thought it best that you called yourself "Joe".'

'I don't understand,' said Josiah.

'You see, "Joe" is an ordinary sort of name.'

'No it isn't,' said Josiah.

'It's more common than "Jozziah",' said Sylvia, gently.

'My name is Josiah.'

'Yes, dear,' said Sylvia, and looked at her husband for moral support.

'You call yourself how you will,' said George. 'We were just trying to help.'

'Yes, that's all we were trying to do,' said his wife, patting the boy on his shoulder.

☙

Tracy arrived to drive Josiah to school. She had wanted to tell him he'd be going home that afternoon, but when she and June Briggs had gone to the Nelsons' house early that morning they'd found the place empty and curiously, unlocked. So they'd taken the liberty of walking around. Yesterday's toast was still on the table: interrupted, half-eaten.

Tracy had sunk down onto a kitchen chair. 'They did know, didn't they, that we'd only taken a temporary measure? We did make that clear, didn't we?'

'You know what?' June had said, smiling, 'That kid's finally going to get a life.'

But that wasn't how it seemed to Tracy when she saw Josiah. He kept staring at her, one moment furious, the next, desperate. And all the while Mrs Leatherpot kept chattering on, as happily as if she'd been given a puppy.

'So how are you settling in, then?' Tracy asked Josiah kindly (and thinking, did I really say 'settling in?' God help him.) And because she couldn't bear to hear his answer, she quickly changed the subject. 'So what did you think of your first day at school, then?'

'School! School! Oh he had such a wondrous day, didn't he, George? There was a slight leg-pulling at first I'm afraid, well that's what the form-teacher observed, about his name, and George and I thought he might be better off to call himself "Joe" just to fit in, but apart from that it was glory all the way! He's already at the top of his class, he is! He adds up faster than anyone, and takes away too! And he reads as well as a fish!'

'Oh God,' said Tracy. Josiah ran out of the room, and Tracy followed him.

'I don't know what's got into him,' said Mrs Leatherpot, 'he's been as good as gold, he honestly has.'

For a good few minutes the boy was completely lost: the three of them scoured the house and not a trace. Then from an upstairs window Tracy noticed a small, crouching figure at the bottom of the garden. She stopped the couple from following her, and as she walked up to him she noticed he was eating earth.

'Oh God!' she sighed, 'I can't take this.'

His back was towards her.

'I'm so sorry,' she said.

Josiah turned round: pale face, morose brown eyes and mud around his mouth.

'What have you been eating?' asked Tracy, gently.

'Minerals,' said Josiah. 'Potassium, calcium, and a little zinc.'

'Josiah!' exclaimed Tracy, with feeling, 'It seems you barely need to go to school! You're a very, very bright little boy! And you'll go home soon! I'll see to it personally, I promise!'

'Do you like children?' asked Josiah.

'Oh yes, I love children! I wouldn't be in this line of work if I didn't love children!'

Then Tracy kissed him on his forehead, she just couldn't help herself.

'Because I don't,' said Josiah. 'I don't like children at all.'

☙

They never thought to phone the ports or the airports: after all, why would they run away? June Briggs said she'd eat her hat if they found Eve and Gibson together. They'd probably find Eve with Michael Fothering, who might finally claim his paternity. But when the police drew a blank with Fothering, Briggs got in contact with Eve's mother: no, Mrs de Selincourt hadn't seen her daughter for seven years, but she cared sufficiently about her to suggest places she might have gone. She even gave them the address of Gilbert Fitzpatrick's cottage, and for weeks afterwards would ring to see whether Eve had turned up. In the end Eve became logged as an Official Missing Person, but after a few weeks of intense searching in London, spurred on by Tracy, the investigation flagged.

Meanwhile they found Gibson after about a week, almost dead with hypothermia in undergrowth on the fen. But even Tracy considered his condition too shocking to re-introduce him to his son: he couldn't speak and he could barely walk, and his arms flailed wildly and indiscriminately at anyone in his path. One social worker even lost a tooth, while the duty psychiatrist had his glasses smashed and a piece of glass had to be extracted from his eye under a general anaesthetic. In short, Gibson Nelson had become dangerous: they deemed him lucky to be sent back to Fulbright.

So Josiah had to stay with the Leatherpots. He wet the bed every night and barely spoke to them. Mrs Leatherpot told Tracy that 'it was evident that he'd had a very sorry life' and asked to be told more about it, so that she might be more of a help to him. 'Particularly as he might be here longer than you said,' she argued. But Tracy was discreet.

Sylvia Leatherpot was very kind and patient with Josiah. When he came back from school she would sit next to him on the settee and tell him all about her adventures when she was a schoolgirl, and the kind of pranks she got up to. Then when she was done with chatting she would take out her set of emery boards and settle down to work on the beautification of her hands.

She would shuffle first towards the left, and then towards the right, as she held her hands up to the light, and more than once told Josiah the great wisdom of her auntie Joyce, who 'always said there was something beautiful in all of us. "It might be your eyes, or it might be your hair, but God never left not one of us out," that's what she used to say, and she was right. And with me, Jozziah, it happens to be my nails. God blessed me with beautiful fingernails and beautiful hands.'

On one occasion, when Josiah had been there about a week, Sylvia Leatherpot said to him, 'Now just stay there a tick and I'll show you something.' She blew the nail-dust from her fingers and levered herself out of an armchair. In the corner of the sitting-room was a book-shelf stuffed full of magazines, hundreds of them. She found a copy of *Woman's Own* and brought it over to show him.

'Now, look here,' she said. 'You have a look through here and keep your eyes peeled. You might just recognize something.'

Josiah scanned the pages of the magazine with dead-pan face.

'No, no, no, Josiah! You've passed it!' exclaimed Mrs Leatherpot. 'I'll give you a clue.' She took the magazine and slowly thumbed through the relevant pages of eyeshadows, lipsticks, and yes, fingernails.

'Do you recognize anything?' she said.

Josiah shook his head.

'Look, look again!' Mrs Leatherpot wasn't going to let him off lightly.

Josiah surveyed her coldly and pointed to an eyelid covered in 'lavender'. Mrs Leatherpot giggled anxiously and was on the point of asking him to have another go but thought the better of it. (What is it? wondered Josiah.)

Tracy was ever the bearer of bad news. Within a fortnight the bad news was even getting to Mrs Leatherpot, who found herself being tetchy with her young charge, and she wanted Josiah's mother to come and take him back.

'He's not grateful,' she would complain. 'He's not grateful for anything. I don't think he's ever been taught to say "Thank you". I say to him, I'll not be giving you supper tomorrow, young man, if you don't learn to say "Thank you" but it makes no difference. It's as though he was completely deaf. Now, what's the news on Mrs Nelson?'

Then one afternoon, after delivering Josiah back from school (which she did whenever she could), and after sitting through twenty minutes' worth of Mrs Leatherpot's complaints about his 'rude behaviour', Tracy was about to get into her car when she was aware of two small arms clasped about her thighs.

'Please don't leave me here,' sobbed Josiah, 'you have to take me to my father'. This was as long a sentence as he had ever uttered.

'Your father?'

'I want my Daddy', he whimpered.

'You want to see your father?' Had they ever seriously considered that old sullen man that hung about in the shadows while Eve performed her circus tricks for them? So even he could inspire love. And why shouldn't he, for God's sake? Tracy turned to Josiah and knelt on the gravel in the drive so that she could take his small hands in hers.

'Josiah,' she said, solemnly, 'I promise you, cross my heart and hope to die, you'll see your father soon.'

However, June Briggs didn't care two hoots about Tracy's promise. She shouted, 'Are you mad, Tracy? What did you say you'd promised him?'

Tracy held her ground. 'Do you understand what we've done? Do you understand that we've just fucked up big-time? It's our moral duty to mend what we've broken.'

'Oh yes, and you think a little trip to Fulbright hospital to visit a man who's so sedated he probably wouldn't even recognize him, you think that's going to do the trick, do you?'

'June, he's his father.'

'We don't even know that, do we?'

'Well, he's been a father to him, and that's what matters. Josiah needs to see him! And even if Eve doesn't come back, it's ten times better to have Gibson and Josiah living together again than the awful, awful situation we have now!'

'Tracy, you know what? You've become too emotionally involved with this case. I've told you before, social work is a profession, and I expect you to behave as a professional.'

Shortly after this, Tracy resigned. And as Tracy could no longer do anything for him, Josiah had to take matters in hand himself. One evening he sidled up to Mrs Leatherpot while she was watching TV. There was a moment, just a moment, when Sylvia fancied he was showing her that much yearned-for affection, and she didn't even resist it when Josiah took her hand in his own. Josiah then proceeded to cut off one of her fingernails with the kitchen scissors he was hiding behind his back. The ensuing drama was their last as a little foster family in Cambridgeshire: he was picked up by Social Services within the hour, 'for his own safety' as Mrs Leatherpot put it.

☙

There were now so many people looking after Josiah that he couldn't remember which was which. There was the magisterial June Briggs herself; there was a friendly old lady in charge of adoptions who gave her opinion; there was a younger lady in charge of foster placements but who was new and who needed the older lady to advise her. June Briggs decided Josiah needed a man, firm and consistent, in fact the most reliable social worker in her team, but the man in question already had a caseload of over eighty, and at least four cases which were equally pressing. None of the above loved Josiah or took up his cause, and his first few placements ended before the first week was out.

His placement after the Leatherpots was, in fact, with one of his teachers, who was a curious woman in both senses: she was both strange and nosy. The teacher had been asked to help out in such emergencies before (she had earned herself the reputation of being a 'safe house'). Josiah would come home from school only to be mercilessly cross-examined over half-moon spectacles about his first memories of his mother et al. Josiah naturally stayed mute.

In his next placement he shared a bedroom with a three-year-old boy who bit him. As the child had never bitten anyone before, his parents naturally blamed the interloper and ten days later he was gone. Two further placements later there was a flurry of activity to find him a relation who might look after him. The first port of call was obviously his grandmother. Mrs de Selincourt said she would think about it, and the foster lady told June Briggs that she was optimistic she could persuade her to take on her grandson. The adoption lady piped in that Mrs de Selincourt might even in the end consider adoption, but June Briggs said, 'I've met the lady. She's like the worst sort of Victorian imperialist, and I don't hesitate to blame her at least in part for Eve's appalling character.' So when Mrs de Selincourt asked to meet the child about a month later (and she was now, to do her credit, working in a soup kitchen for the homeless in London in the vain hope of finding her daughter), they told her he was now happily installed with a family of very good standing and it was better not to visit as it might unsettle him, and, as she put it, 'rock the boat.' For a couple of days Mrs de Selincourt was very set on rocking that boat, but her husband persuaded her against it. He was intent on taking up a post in the US for a couple of years, and if the Social Services deemed Josiah 'quite difficult,' then was she really prepared to repeat those miserable years she'd had with Eve?

Nor were the Social Services lying when they informed the de Selincourts that Josiah had, at last, been placed successfully. Lady Brack had been persuading her husband for years that fostering children was 'a good thing' because 'It was right that they should put back into the community just a little of what they had taken out.'

And there was another reason, too: her favourite Labrador bitch Clover had come to the end of her breeding life, and after that last dear puppy had been sold, and while she was slowly, pensively clearing away the newspaper from the little pen in the hall which she had made for Clover and her nine children, she came across a peed-on advertisement from the Cambridge Evening News. 'Have you ever thought of fostering?' it said, 'Do you have a spare room?' (Lady Brack smiled and thought, 'We have six!') 'Do you have patience and understanding?' (Yes, yes! thought Lady Brack). 'Could you give a child a loving home?' (Yes, yes! thought Lady Brack). 'Then phone Pat on 632148.' And she did.

The Social Services had been delighted with the sound of her. For because by now Josiah had lost his soft Lancashire lilt and enunciated his vowels even more perfectly than Lady Brack herself, they had found a perfect voice match, and it was social services policy to mix like with like as far as was practicable. One of Josiah's previous foster families had complained of his 'holding his chin too high,' but at Fratton Hall, they decided, he could hold it as high as he liked.

But Josiah did not sit, nor stay, nor do as he was told. He didn't eat his meals and he didn't sit on Lady Brack's knee when she asked him to. Lady Brack had been told about Josiah's love of gardening, and she would hover by him when he was weeding, her silk scarf doing little to keep a bitter wind from her ears. On one occasion Josiah asked Lady Brack to tell him the name of a certain flower, but she didn't know it and had to find the gardener. When they came back the boy had gone and all hell was let loose; within five minutes Lady Brack had even called the police. He was found a couple of hours later: he had buried himself in the compost heap.

Lady Brack was so pleased to find him that she wasn't even angry, but ran Josiah a bubble bath with drops of her very own eau de cologne, 'Oh Josiah! You don't know how worried you made us! And now you're back and safe with just a few blades of old hay in your hair, oh how happy I am! Now, I want you to tell us, why did you do such a thing? Is there something making you terribly unhappy?'

Josiah didn't know what to say, but because Lady Brack was so insistent he eventually told her that he hated the wallpaper in his bedroom.

'Josiah, is that all? Is there nothing more serious than that? That can be so easily remedied, you know! Funnily enough, I've always hated that pampas grass design. It'll be such fun to repaper your room!'

Lady Brack told her husband Sir Peter (knighted two years previously for services to the export industry) in bed that night about the latest Josiah saga.

'And *where* do you think we found him, Peter?'

'Mmm,' mumbled Sir Peter, as he struggled with the last three clues of a crossword.

'In the compost heap! Can you believe that?'

'Well, just about,' he said.

'Anyway, I thought it was time we redecorated his room.'

'Darling, he doesn't seem very happy. He might not be with us very long. Is it worth it?'

'Men understand nothing!' said Lady Brack, happily, as she turned off the light.

So Lady Brack became ever more devoted to her charge. She would pore over Osborne and Little's nursery collection, and then make Josiah sit next to her after his tea and insist that he *confide* in her (that was the word she used) how, in an ideal world, he would have his bedroom look.

'For you've grown out of little cars, haven't you? But what about these aeroplanes? Have you ever been in an aeroplane, Josiah? Have you ever been to Paris? Shall I tell you about the trip I made to Paris when I must have been your age?'

And yes, Josiah proved quite good company, an excellent listener, and stared up at Lady Brack with his large melancholy brown eyes and quite stirred the cockles of her heart. He also adored her dog Clover quite as much as she did, and he would get down on his knees to stroke her, and lay his head on her back. And to do Lady Brack credit, it was at her house that he stopped wetting the bed for the first time since leaving home.

A full three months later, with Josiah's bedroom happily wall-papered with a design imported from France, (onion-sellers with striped shirts and moustaches riding bicycles) the Bracks, the Social Services, and Josiah himself were still getting along famously. But then something happened, a bridge too far, an unfordable chasm. Josiah spent his last day with the Bracks on his eighth birthday.

Lady Brack wanted to give him a birthday party; though in fact she wanted to give him something else even more: the clothes to wear at that party. She had inherited in almost pristine condition a child's green velvet suit complete with lace collar and cuffs, circa 1880. Her son Angus had worn them at a wedding when he was about the same age, and in fact, as she explained to her husband much later, when she first set eyes on Josiah she thought, how very, very pretty he would look in just that colour green. All she needed was an excuse to retrieve the entissued garment from the attic, and a birthday was as good as any. 'And he's been with us six months,' she pleaded with her husband, 'It will be a mark of our trust in him!'

On the morning of his birthday she gave him his present, suitably wrapped and bowed, and Josiah's pleasure on opening the parcel was so palpably great that even Sir Peter was rather moved. For as we know, Josiah didn't like ordinary toys, he wasn't an ordinary boy, but he knew instinctively when something was lovely, and this velvet suit assuredly was.

Lady Brack let him wear it straightaway and took him to her bedroom so that he could admire himself in the full-length mirror.

'Josiah,' she said to him, 'You look wonderful! I knew the moment we first met that one day I'd give you these clothes, and now they're yours!'

Josiah even kissed her in gratitude, and kissed Clover too, because he was so pleased. Yes, Josiah was that close to a comfortable life, for that one kiss made Lady Brack quite determined to take Josiah away from his primary school and send him instead to King's College prep school, where both her sons had been so happy. And after that, doubtless, he would follow them to Eton! O lucky boy to have landed on her doorstep!

Lady Brack's mistake was not so much to give Josiah the pretty velvet suit but to give him a party. How she had loved giving parties when her sons were small! She rang up her friends and told them about the wonderful Josiah and that all grandchildren were invited; and she blew the old flour off her Constance Spry cookbook and found that very same recipe for Victoria sponge she had used all those years ago.

Lady Brack baked all morning, and watched Josiah running up and down the garden lawns from the kitchen window. She didn't have the heart to tell him that the clothes were old and delicate, and must be kept clean, as she might have done to her own children.

When the guests arrived at three that afternoon (six middle-aged women, a girl of four and two boys of eleven), Josiah was about as cute as a cuttlefish.

'Patricia,' the women exclaimed, one after another, 'doesn't he look exactly like Angus? When I first saw him I thought I was seeing a ghost.'

'You're not a ghost, are you, Josiah?' said Lady Brack, protectively. She watched him whiten.

'Now just when was it,' asked one, 'when we last saw that darling outfit? Such beautiful lace!'

'I remember the occasion only too well,' said a woman in a navy blue cashmere cardigan. 'Alicia's wedding. Pitlochry Castle. Bitterly cold.'

'Come here, young man! Can I just take a look at that *beauti*ful lace?'

But Josiah stayed as still and stalwart as a soldier. This third woman, who was Lady Brack's first cousin, leant over him to take a closer look, picking up the collar as she did so. 'Quite exquisite!' she enthused.

Lady Brack was watching on, anxiously. The two eleven-year-old boys were both wearing football kit, and were shoving each other off the arm of the sofa. The four-year-old girl was sitting on her Mummy's knee sucking her thumb. There was an unhappy pause in the conversation.

'So, Josiah, what do you think of your new home?' asked one of the guests, innocently.

'I've got a present for you!' said another.

'And so have I!' said the third, rummaging around in her handbag.

Then Josiah suddenly said, 'And I've got a present for you all!' With that, I'm afraid to say, he pulled the lace from the collar and the wrists of that pretty jacket, and tore the lace from the bottom of the britches, and threw it at them. And away he went, running up the stairs to his bedroom, and from the landing shouting down at Lady Brack, 'I am not somebody else!'

All Lady Brack wanted to do was follow him, but her friends held her back and said it was best to let him cool down. The boys gloated happily, and to a certain unforgivable extent, so did the women, who for half an hour capped each other in reLating terrible fostering sagas they had heard about. And down fell the questions on poor Lady Brack, does he steal, well you might not know quite yet, and is he ever violent and has he been cruel to the dog? Then because the children were getting bored and Lady Brack was so faultlessly polite, she invited them all into the dining-room for a birthday tea, when all she actually wanted to do was throw the lot of them out of the house.

If ever there was a moment to pity the boy, pity him now. Josiah had ripped off his green velvet clothes and did his best to tear them, which was hard work except for a sleeve where a moth had given him a head start; then he'd scrumpled them up and thrown them under his bed. But the agony he felt was not anger at those stupid people, for the anger was vented the moment he lay shivering on the bed. Rather, his feelings were of remorse and loss: loss at first of the pretty clothes he'd had on, but then the loss of his old life where he had a proper place, and the way his mother had made him laugh and his father who made him feel king of the world. All he wanted was to find them again, and he couldn't understand why there were so many people looking for them and where they had gone, because he knew they would never, never leave him. And then it occurred to him that perhaps he was the missing one, perhaps that very first day they hadn't realised he was going to school and they were out looking for him even now. And because Josiah was thinking very, very hard he was quite sure he'd heard his father calling him from the garden. 'Jo, Jo,' he heard. So softly, as in a dream, and he ran to the window to open it.

'Daddy, are you there?' he said to the cool breeze. The trunk of his body was shaking and he held on to the sill to steady himself.

'Daddy? Daddy?'

With a sense of urgency he threw on some clothes and slunk out of the back door, even while the others were still enjoying his birthday tea. Again he heard his name, Jo, Jo, and he wandered into the small wood at the bottom of the garden. Every shadow of every tree promised him his father; again and again he ran towards them in a state so heightened that when he heard a twig break he jumped to attention. One minute he was ready to fall into his father's lap; and the next to throw himself into an abyss of despair. And as the minutes wore on, the abyss grew ever deeper and more inevitable, and he began to make preparations to throw himself into it.

He found a spade and began digging under a rose bush, his small hands sliding impatiently over the wooden handle. Then he threw down the spade and began to dig the earth out with his fingers.

Sir Peter Brack was watching him from an upstairs window. He had already seen the torn lace on a table in the drawing room, had put his head round the dining-room door and had an earful about Josiah's antics that afternoon, but the velvet suit wasn't from his branch of the family, while the *Madame Isaac Perere* he'd planted himself.

But the saddest moment was not the slap, nor the threats (all carried out the following morning) that Josiah would be removed from their home, nor the shouting which brought Lady Brack out into the garden in tears, but the very first moment, when Josiah had first seen the shadow running towards him, and was waiting to be scooped up in its arms.

Chapter Six

ON THE 2ND JUNE 1992, Josiah Nelson, aged eight years and one day, was classified as an emergency. His mother had not resurfaced, his father had not spoken a word for nine months, and even a course of ECT hadn't managed to resurrect him. His grandparents were still living in the US, his uncle wasn't even interested in meeting the boy, and he had been deemed a failure by no fewer than five foster families. Lady Brack, it's true, missed him terribly; but when the social worker had picked him up that morning, Josiah was sobbing so convulsively, and Sir Peter had been so disagreeable, that the fostering lady was persuaded to put a little black cross by 'Brack' in her file, for despite having six spare bedrooms, they were incapable of providing a child with a loving home.

Then there was Josiah himself, who had once been so appeaseable, so ready to fall in with a new plan; he was now absolutely resistant to any suggestion put to him. He even refused the temporary lodging with his teacher, whom he 'hated,' and in fact he seemed to hate everyone, and more than anything else in the whole wide world, he said, he hated families.

'If you don't co-operate, we shall have to put you in a Children's Home,' said June Briggs.

'Then put me in a Children's Home! I don't care!' shouted Josiah.

They were lucky to find a vacancy. Usually the Social Services are good at easing a child into a new situation – supervised meetings, key workers, trial days etc. But, as I have said, Josiah was now an emergency. It was a question of dropping him off with a suitcase. *The*

Hollies, a large Edwardian Residential Care Home for Children on the outskirts of Cambridge (Coleridge Road, Cherry Hinton) was to be his home for nine years.

The girl who received Josiah at the brown-painted door of his new home was called Kerry. She was dark and skinny and dressed in skimpy black clothes and looked about fourteen, but in fact she was eighteen and had already been on the care staff for a year.

'Come in,' she said. 'Are you Joe?'

'Josiah', corrected the boy.

'Josiah! What a lovely name! Come in, Josiah,' and she stood to one side and ushered him in, and told the social worker who had brought him that they would be just fine. Josiah was the youngest in Kerry's fold by two years, and her heart went out to him. All she'd been told was that the lad's mother had deserted him and his father lay catatonic in Fulbright hospital, and that foster care hadn't worked out.

'You and me,' said Kerry, bending her knees to meet him in the eye, 'are going to be best mates, you'll see! Fancy a glass of orange squash?'

'No thanks,' said Josiah, politely.

'Well, then, I'll take you to your room,' said Kerry, picking up Josiah's suitcase. 'You follow me. You know what? You've got the best room in the house! Your bedroom is twice the size mine is, and it's got the best view, right over the gardens.'

The stairs were steep, and Josiah found himself having to hold onto the banister. Each step was a climb in itself, and Josiah pulled himself up behind her, because there was no alternative. With a flourish, Kerry opened the door on the other side of the landing.

'Here you are, Josiah. Not bad, is it? But it'll be even better next week because we're giving it a lick of paint and you can choose any colour you like!'

Kerry put the suitcase down on the bed and then sat herself beside it. 'So what d'you think?'

'Who was Rob?' asked Josiah, still standing by the door.

'Rob?' asked Kerry.

'"Fuck you Rob,"' said Josiah. 'Look, there's a message.'

The message was small and in pencil, written neatly under the light switch.

'Ah Rob!' said Kerry, as though she'd only just remembered who he was. 'Rob had this room before you. And now he's gone. You see, young man, he was always in trouble with the police, just for small things, nothing serious. But yes, he went down yesterday. And that was lucky for you, because this is the best room in the house. And you'll get new paint.'

'Where did he go down to? Won't he come back?'

'No, he won't come back, not here he won't.'

'Is he in prison?'

'That sort of thing.'

'Wouldn't he be upset if he found me in his room?'

'He won't find you. He's not coming back, I promise.'

Josiah sighed. 'Promises, promises,' he said morosely, looking at the floor.

'Have you had some bad luck with promises?'

'I'd like to unpack on my own, if you don't mind,' said Josiah.

'You mean you want me to go?' asked Kerry, surprised.

'Yes, I want you to go.'

'Right-o,' said Kerry. 'Just to warn you, they're back from school at half past three, and tea's at five. I'll be in the kitchen if you want anything. And remember, the bell goes three times for afternoon tea. You'll soon get the hang of it.'

♣

Josiah, at this time in the story, was a mere eight years old, but he was not broken. He was brave for his father; he was brave for his mother.

His father was a rock, and his mother a lioness, and he was brave for both of them. And he knew that one day they would find him again, and in fact, even now they might be looking. That knowledge gave him strength, even at the worst of times. So when he went downstairs at five o'clock he held his head high. There were even a few minutes when his companions gave him the benefit of the doubt.

Kerry thought Josiah looked just like Mark Lester in *Oliver*, a film that had set her heart so aflame that it was the chief reason she'd gone into residential social work in the first place. And there was another girl who'd been eyeing him up for mothering, called Maggie, who was ten and wore frosted pink lipstick and stilettos.

'Maggie, you come here a moment,' said Kerry, kindly. 'I want you to meet young Josiah, who's going to be staying with us a while. And I want you to be his special buddy, and make sure he gets everything he wants.'

Maggie tottered over to Josiah and said, 'Hi.'

Josiah looked serious and said 'Hi' back, and when she offered him her hand to shake he took it.

'You come and sit next to me,' she said.

The dining room was large and light with stained carpet tiles and brown floral curtains. Plastic cups and cheap cutlery were piled up on one end of a long, battered table. The children, twelve boys and three girls, were making their way from the kitchen with plates piled high with beef burgers and chips. Each found himself a chair at the table and sank down into a slouch; some of their chins were a mere six inches from the table. Hair unkempt, spots unpicked, sweatshirts sweated in, inhabited by egos simultaneously vast and fragile. Maggie set Josiah down amongst them, whispered him reassuring words about her imminent return, and went into the kitchen to fetch them both supper.

Josiah knew he had to stay very still and look straight ahead till his protector returned.

'So titch, who are you?' asked his neighbour, a lad of eleven called Darren who'd been called 'titch' most of his life. There was faint interest from the others, whose chomping jaws paused briefly to hear titch's reply.

'My name is Josiah,' said Josiah, avoiding their eyes.

Immediate laughter: "My name is Josiah," imitated Darren, enunciating every vowel.

'I'm so sorry,' continued Steve in the same voice, 'I think you've come to the wrong place.' He was tall with bad acne, and had been living at *The Hollies* ever since he'd stolen his mother's car at twelve and she'd signed any paper she could to get rid of him.

'Yes,' said a third boy, Jason, who if he'd been asked to say boo to a goose would have said 'boo' but was asked instead to throw a brick through a jeweller's window. 'You'll find the Queen doesn't visit often.'

A fourth said, 'No, she simply doesn't find the time.' That was John, thirteen, who'd come to *The Hollies* at much the same age as Josiah. He was the youngest of eight, whose father had left home on the day of his birth, and he'd always been one too many.

But then Maggie returned with tea, and shooed them all off him as if they'd been pesky fleas. She put Josiah's burger and chips in front of him and wriggled into her chair. 'They're fucking idiots here,' she said.

Josiah began to gently suck on a chip, as though that might be nourishment enough for a day, while Darren leant over to grab a handful of them.

'Ignore him,' said Maggie, and went on saying it until Josiah's plate was empty.

'Here, help yourself to mine,' she said.

'Oooooo, love!' said the three lads opposite, in unison.

Steve reached over the table with his fork and stabbed it into one of Maggie's chips. Maggie grabbed the ketchup bottle and squirted the stuff over Steve's face.

'Lay off, Steve,' she said.

'Wrong move,' said Steve, coldly, getting up from the table and nodding almost imperceptibly to John and Jason. For the three were gangsters, joined at the hip, and the only friends each had ever known. They were moving round the benches like a single, menacing organism to find their prey. Maggie thought that was her and took a stiletto off her foot to be ready for them. The other children were watching expectantly; Kerry was clearing the kitchen; Josiah was sitting very, very still and only Maggie noticed he was shaking.

It was Josiah they wanted. Moving as a threesome, each prodded a fork into his neck. Now, if Maggie had been a target she would have put up a good fight; twice she'd been expelled from school for putting up rather too good a fight. But her sense of outrage that Josiah was their chosen victim was such that Al Capone himself would have marvelled. Down came the blows on Jason's head with her stiletto, down they came on the smallest of those three villains, and even the first gushes of blood did not satisfy her, but on she went till all the children in the room were screaming and Steve had his hands around her throat.

Kerry, poor thing, herself still a teenager, was just not up to the scene which confronted her. She burst into tears like a baby and was feebly shouting, 'Stop it! Stop it!' At first, she didn't even notice Jason who was unconscious now, blood pouring from his head, but happily surrounded by curious children who were wondering if he was dead. All she saw was Steve, his two thumbs pressing down on Maggie's windpipe, and all she heard was Steve's assertion that 'You will die.' Kerry ran up to him and began pulling at his hands.

'Get off her! Get off her!' she cried. 'Are you mad? Are you going to kill someone? Are you going to prison for the rest of your fucking life?'

Darren said, 'She's the murderer round here!'

And suddenly they were all quiet.

It's so strange the way children move, like birds, like rabbits, like sheep, like animals. Kerry sat slumped on the bench with Maggie, who was fighting for her breath; Jason lay corpse-like on the floor, while the others, even Steve, even Josiah, congregated against the walls of the room.

'You're all fucking useless,' said Kerry. 'You, Steve, call a fucking ambulance.'

It was Maggie who suggested getting towels to wrap round Jason's head, and Kerry took her cue from her, happy in the momentary refuge of her kitchen as she fetched clean tea-towels from the drawer, happy in the dense quiet of the dining room as she took authority once more and knelt beside Jason's body and took his hand in hers to check his pulse, and happy, above all, that his hand was warm and the day would pass like any other day.

How good the children were that night! How they took themselves off to bed without demur! How quiet the house was! The ambulance came and went, and by the time Kerry's co-worker Dave had come at six with the promised electric guitar no one was interested. Kerry said, 'Not tonight, Dave,' and they had a cup of tea instead.

♣

When Josiah brushed his teeth with his new *Mickey Mouse* toothbrush, courtesy of the Social Services, and took his carefully folded pyjamas out of his top drawer, and folded back his bedcovers before slipping inside, he felt better than he had for a long time. Foster homes made him feel claustrophobic: whether he was being watched, criticized or fawned upon, he was always the object of attention. He loathed the feeling of indebtedness, when it was not coupled with the love which turns such a feeling into gratitude. Josiah also instinctively felt that in his case a certain amount of hardship was appropriate. If his parents were suffering on his account – he felt quite certain their disappearance had something to do with him – then he should be suffering on theirs, and he was looking forward to a cleansing of conscience that no amount of molly-coddling or 'understanding' could ever satisfy.

Kerry came in at eight o'clock to say goodnight to him. She found a boy lying in his bed as stiffly as a knight in his bronze coffin, staring up at the ceiling.

'I'm so sorry, Josiah,' she said, sitting down on his bed. 'I'm so sorry about tonight. You know it's not usually as bad as this.'

'That's OK,' said Josiah.

'Jason had a few stitches and he's fine. Dave's cleared it all up downstairs and everyone's going to bed.'

'Who's Dave?' asked Josiah.

'Ah Dave! I've not introduced you yet! You'll like him, we have good fun with him. Sometimes he brings his guitar along. Do you know any good songs, Josiah?'

'No,' said Josiah.

'Then you'll just have to learn them. Here, let me tuck you in.' Kerry knelt down beside him and tucked him up tight. 'There,' she said, 'did your mother used to…?'

'No, she didn't tuck me in,' interrupted Josiah.

'Dear Josiah,' gushed Kerry, feeling overwhelmingly moved, and suddenly kissing him on his forehead. 'You shouldn't be here, you know.'

'Oh yes I should,' said Josiah, confidently.

Kerry sighed and took hold of Josiah's hand.

'No, don't,' said Josiah.

And Kerry, with all the sadness of the day heaped upon her, said goodnight and left him.

♣

Of course, Josiah was bullied right from the start, but he didn't really notice much. He felt all the comfort of the true outsider: he was untouchable. But it would be inaccurate to describe him as 'lonely', because 'lonely' suggests the still-warm memory of a time when you have known something else, and *The Hollies* managed to free such a memory entirely, relegating his past to mere text-book history. Maggie continued to mother him from time to time, telling him he'd catch a chill if he stayed outside so much, insisting that he let her know if any of the boys were giving him a hard time. But the trouble was that Josiah knew that she meant it, and thought it best to keep quiet.

He listened quite happily to the attentions of Kerry, Dave and a new field-worker called Lizzie, all of whom took it in turns to endear themselves to him. He was always polite, and when they asked him whether he was happy at *The Hollies* he always said, 'yes'. 'It's incredible how self-sufficient he is,' was what they said about him behind his back, and each, in their own way, rather loved him.

But after a few months, Dave realised that he wasn't going to be able to initiate Josiah into the mysteries of Motown music, Lizzie was getting a heavier caseload and Josiah was an 'easy' kid who didn't make demands upon her time, and Kerry got herself a boyfriend. By the time Josiah was nine, they were leaving him much to his own devices.

There were two mature trees in the small garden at *The Hollies*: a large majestic beech and a small, fairly stumpy yew. But within Josiah's first month there, the beech had become Heaven, and the yew, Earth, and Josiah had appointed them as his Confessors. It was good, he decided, to have one tree for his heavenly anxieties, and another for his earthly ones. His next task was to attempt to discover their answers to him, and to learn their particular language. There had never been any doubt in him that trees had a language: his father had told him as soon has he was capable of understanding that trees were living, and he had witnessed for himself their acute sensitivity to the seasons and the weather. What he required of them now was that they should apply that same sensitivity to other matters, and he thought that if only he could manage to communicate to them some of what he was feeling, then there could be no wiser nor more constant arbiters than they.

So he set about trying to de-code the trees' peculiar language, and to look for signs (Heaven and Earth must have so much to talk about, he thought), and he decided that it was no mere co-incidence that the words 'three' and 'tree' were like each other. The trunk, the branches and the leaves were each responsible for different kinds of messages, and though he had never been particularly religious before, (despite his mother telling him on several occasions that 'Josiah' was both a famous and a good King in the Bible, and his father taking him to Church at Christmas and Easter), he now considered that either the Father himself, or his Son, or the Holy Ghost, might well wish to communicate with him. God himself was the trunk, and the trunk only swayed when a communication of the highest order had to be delivered; Jesus was the branches, wavering and nodding and always ready to reply; and the Holy Ghost had found his home among the leaves. 'The Holy Ghost is like a wind,' he thought, 'and leaves love wind.'

Josiah preferred the beech tenfold to the yew, and when it lost its leaves that first autumn he gathered up the more beautiful ones and took them to his bedroom. He considered it his solemn duty to keep them safe until the spring, and he kept them in his drawers under his clothes, and when it was too dark to go out into the garden after school, these shrivelling leaves became his soul mates.

Josiah often wondered where the Holy Spirit got to when He left the Heavenly beech for half the year, and until he was fourteen (when his life was to change irrevocably and he had other things to think about), he tried out several theories, none of which could wholly satisfy him. There was a while, even, when he wondered whether his own banal conversation caused the leaves to lose their vivid colour, and then by extension that he was causing the leaves to fall in the first place. But if that was the case then he was also the reason why buds burst forth in April! Josiah's was indeed a year of grief and hope, of wretchedness and joy, but all these emotions were so painful to him that to dare to lie under his Heavenly beech was something he only occasionally had the strength for.

He chose the yew to be his everyday advisor, to whom he complained about tummy aches and homework and the like. For the yew kept its dark green spines all year long, and Josiah knew they could be utterly relied upon. So year in and year out Josiah took the yew into his confidence, lying in an indentation in the moss beneath it. When Kerry left *The Hollies* to go and live in Wales with her boyfriend, the yew was the first to know. When Tracy Fortune, the social worker who had first taken him from his parents, fell upon him one afternoon and in floods of tears apologized for her part in his demise, Josiah told the yew. He also talked about the children in his class at school or at *The Hollies*. He was always careful that no one should ever catch him going outside, and once there he could trust that he'd be left alone. No one else ever bothered to come into the garden. Why would they? It was far too small for football. And anyway, once everyone was home from school, there was a general lunge towards the kitchen for bread and jam, and he could always manage to sneak out.

What was curious, however, was that Josiah rarely bothered the yew with what he considered minor irritations: he didn't bother to mention quite how many times Steve, Jason and John continued to prod him in the back with a corkscrew or a new penknife, or how that boy Darren drew pictures of penises in toothpaste on the mirror above his basin. He was more concerned about the anxieties of newcomers, who were unaccustomed to the chaos of the place, the lack of predictability, the interminable noise, the arguments that seemed to break out constantly about which TV programme to watch or who had taken the last portion of trifle. For each time a new child came to live at *The Hollies*, he saw it all again through that child's eyes, and continued to be anxious on his behalf until bewilderment was replaced by the more reassuring gang mentality.

When Josiah was ten he told the yew that his thirteen-year old protector, Maggie, was pregnant, and was going to leave soon. He felt privileged to have received a private confession from her. One evening at seven o'clock she had knocked at his door, and said, 'There's something I need to tell you, love.' She had sat down on the bed right up close to him and taken his hand in hers and said, 'I'm going to have a baby. Would you like to see my tummy?' Then Maggie had taken up her jumper and let him feel her taut, smooth stomach. 'They wanted me to have an abortion,' she'd told him, 'but I said, "I'll never kill a little baby, never." When she's born I'll bring her to visit you. I'm going to call her Cherry.'

Two months later Maggie was gone, and she never said goodbye. Josiah told the yew all about it. He said he'd like to see her baby very much.

It was a mood rather than a confession which drove Josiah to seek the solace of the Heaven-beech. Here, he never even tried to put anything into words, but rather listened very hard to the creaking, whispering tree, and instinctively knew that its message was this: *there is somewhere else which will one day be yours.* That was all the solace he needed. Well, usually it was. Just occasionally, Josiah's head was too full to listen properly, and there was a bottleneck between his head and his heart. There was a week at the beginning of June 1995, when the eleven-year old Josiah rarely left the beech's protection.

What happened was this. In May, a new residential social worker arrived at *The Hollies*. There was nothing strange in that – during the year after Kerry's departure there had been no fewer than five new young men and women who'd run the gauntlet and promptly resigned. But this one was hip and called Josie, and she had long, fine blonde hair that ended in a perfect line three-quarters of the way down her back. Josie would swing her fair hair back when she laughed, and because she was good-natured and slightly nervous, this happened rather often. Within a few hours of her arrival, all the older boys had to acknowledge that they fancied her rotten. At this time Darren was fifteen and trying to grow a moustache; the older boys had of course left, but there were younger ones whom Darren was happily grooming to be quite the callous shit he was: Dan and Ricky, Kev and Jed.

But Josie only had eyes for Josiah. While the others continually bombarded her with demands for attention, Josiah would eat his meals quietly and take his empty plate to the kitchen without a murmur. While the others would talk until midnight and gather in each other's rooms to smoke cigarettes, Josiah took himself off to bed at eight o'clock as though he barely existed. When Josie learnt from *The Hollies Birthday Book* that there was soon to be a birthday and it was Josiah's, she set to work and made him a huge chocolate cake.

Josiah, of course, wasn't expecting it at all. That tea-time, the first of June, when the last vestiges of ketchup, chips and sausages had been cleared away (Josie had even insisted that the tables be wiped down), a large cake was suddenly produced with the words *Happy Birthday Josiah* written across it in broken flake bars (which alone had taken Josie an hour). Five lustful adolescent boys began nudging each other and gazing furiously at their new object of hate. Josie didn't notice because she was busy closing the curtains.

'I always think,' she was saying, 'a room needs to be dark before we light candles.'

'Oh fuck me,' declaimed Darren, raising his eyes to the ceiling.

Josie's hair was by now swinging at quite a rate, first over her left shoulder, then over her right; but by the time she came to be lighting the candles one by one, her face was suddenly still and glowed angelically.

'Now,' she said, 'Where are you, Josiah? You come here, birthday boy.'

Josiah did as he was told, though sheepishly. He'd had three more years experience of *The Hollies* than Josie, and already he knew he'd have to pay for this. Then Josie put an arm about his shoulder, and he made himself small and retreated into his body.

'OK, so are we going to sing?'

'Sing?' sniggered these streetwise lads in disbelief.

'Come on,' she said, trying to jolly them along. 'Happy Birthday to you…' went Josie's tuneful solo. No one joined in, and she stopped singing.

'You're a useless lot,' she said. And then, as she looked down at the glum Josiah, feeling desperately that she didn't want Josiah to be hurt or feel that his birthday was ruined, she took both of his hands in his and planted a kiss on his forehead.

'Ooooooo,' piped up a couple of the younger boys.

'Fucking disgusting,' reckoned one of the older ones, and stormed out. Four others followed him.

'I don't know what's got into them!' said Josie, anxiously. 'Just ignore them, Josiah. Come on, blow out your candles then!'

Josiah did, to please her, and it seemed very hard work. He then had to be the first to eat the damn cake, but he managed that, too. But the younger children all guzzled it down, and in fact Josie was quite relieved that all that 'bad karma,' as she called it, had left the room.

When Josiah went to his room at seven o'clock that evening he saw that a bit of paper had been glued to his bedhead. At first the message written in thick green felt pen was difficult to decipher, not least for its strange spelling, but after a few minutes he managed to make out the following:

So sorry to have missed singing your birthday song at tea. Here's one we thought you'd like instead. If you behave yourself we'll sing it to you later tonight.

Happy birthday to Josiah
Have you seen your pants on fire?
Just wait a tick
While we suck your dick
Darren wants to swallow it.

Darren's name had then been crossed out and various other names put in its place, even Josie's; it was in fact quite unclear who wanted to swallow Josiah's dick; but for Josiah, who had had sole possession over his dick to that point, the prospect of a nightly visit was terrifying. There was no lock on his bedroom door so Josiah saw no alternative but to spend the night in the bathroom. He got into his pyjamas and dressing-gown, and then smuggled a duffle-coat and blanket into the small bathroom on the second floor, which was hardly ever used (everyone preferring the newly installed showers). He bolted the door and tried hard to stop himself from shaking, and every time he heard a foot on the stair he started. Finally he managed to line the bath with the blanket: even so, his head made a soft thud on the enamel as he lay down on top of it, and he wished he'd brought a pillow, too. He'd left the duffle coat on the floor next to him, but he realised he was incapable of stretching over the side to pull it over him, or indeed of moving at all. So he lay and waited: first, for the night to fall, and then for the dawn to follow.

It had been dark for a couple of hours when Josiah heard them clambering up the stairs.

'Jo-Jo, Jo-Jo,' they called, in fake silvery voices, 'We know you're in there. You mustn't be frightened of us, we just want to sing to you… You just open the door, Jo-Jo.'

Josiah couldn't have answered them even if he had anything to say.

'Jo-Jo, you know we can break this door down by just breathing on it. Anyone would think you didn't want us to sing.'

Josiah heard them laughing and then one of them took a kick at the door.

'A bit harder than that, Kev.' More laughter.

'Come on, Jo-Jo, open up, or we might get angry. Now, you wouldn't want that, would you? We only want to fucking sing to you.'

And then their tone became more serious. 'It's only a flimsy bolt in here, y'know. Come on, let's get it open.' Five shoulders rammed the door, and the bolt broke. The strip light went on.

'Well, what've we here?' sneered Darren, when they found Josiah shivering on his blanket. 'We thought you'd be having a nice hot bath, didn't we? But I trust it wasn't us what stopped you. Poor boy, I think we should give him a bath. Poor little mite.'

'Judging by the state of his feet he fucking needs one,' said Kev.

'Just take a look at his neck and behind his ears! You keep yourself in a disgusting state, arsehole,' said Ricky.

'Fucking disgusting,' agreed Jed.

'I bet his dick's crawling,' suggested Dan.

'We'll soon see whether it is.' Darren was in command. 'Are you going to strip, Jo-Jo, or are we going to do it for you?'

Josiah lay as stiff and passive as a doll. Darren began to untie the cord around his dressing gown; Josiah instinctively held tight onto the knot.

'I'm going to need a little help here. Come on, you lot, hold him down.'

Dan and Ricky held Josiah's wrists against the head of the bath, while Darren summoned Kev's help to strip him.

'Fuck me,' said Darren, 'What sort of pathetic shrivelled little stump is that? You're not exactly going to give the girlies a lot of pleasure with that, are you, Jo-Jo dear?'

'Shall we cut it off?' asked Jed, producing his new gleaming penknife.

'I'll have that,' said Darren, and Jed just handed it to him, with a certain pride.

Josiah flinched. Darren held the knife in front of him and admired the blade. 'Hold him, you idiots. We don't want there to be an accident, do we, Jo-Jo? This is a tricky operation, you know. Jed, you hold his dick so I can just lop it off. It's a good blade. Let's hope I can do it in one swipe, hey?'

Josiah screamed and hands immediately piled over his mouth and nostrils so that he couldn't breathe. Josiah thought, 'Dear God, let me suffocate first,' and shut his eyes. No one thought to make him open them. Josiah was waiting to bleed to death. He was waiting for the pain, and the release from pain.

The five of them saw that in some sense they had lost him. They put cold water in the bath and dunked him; they jabbed the knife into his inner thigh and threatened more, but they saw that he was gone. Even his stiffness had gone, his body was white and small and flaccid. Their game stopped being interesting.

For Josiah was lying under the beech tree and knew one thing only: *there is somewhere better than this.* He was deaf to their leers and their lewdness, and when they threatened to put the knife up his bum, Josiah said, because it suddenly occurred to him, 'You haven't sung to me yet. You promised you'd sing.'

It was midnight, and the boys realised that whatever momentum there'd been was now gone. So they told him not to worry but they'd sing to him the following night. 'Same time, same place,' said Darren. They turned out the light and left the room.

Josiah waited in his bath until he heard the last of their bedroom doors slam shut on the floor below him. He turned the light back on and noticed the bath water was pink, but had neither the spirit nor the curiosity to inspect his wound. Then he put on his duffle-coat and sat with his back against the wall and his head between his trembling knees. And this was the only time, in all the years that Josiah had spent and would spend at *The Hollies*, that he cried.

Chapter Seven

IN THE MIDDLE OF THE AUTUMN TERM 1998, in a large, warm room in Old Court, Corpus Christi College, Dr Thomas Marius was refilling the glasses of three female undergraduates with sherry. There was a fire burning in the grate, around which they all sat hugger-mugger in an array of armchairs, files and essays either spread out on their knees or at their feet. On the mantelpiece were three or four formal invitations to the various college feasts which were held at that time of year, and above these a large, blank space with a picture light above it, for Thomas had never found himself a painting he liked well enough to hang there. He was undeniably handsome, yet oblivious to the fact; his clothes were donnish, all corduroy and wool – though the clothes which would have really suited him were velvet britches, linen and lace, and a glorious frock coat, for there was a look about him of a neurasthenic eighteenth century poet: pale, flawless skin, wavy dark hair and bright blue eyes, and his physique was slight, effete and effeminate.

It was half past six in the evening and Thomas Marius was teaching, an activity which he generally found disappointing. The young Classicists he met tended to be privately educated – he himself had been at one of the last grammar schools – and he quite often found them confident, cocky and clever, but a deeper commitment to a subject that he had loved from the first was too often lacking. His pupils often knew how to write a good essay, how to use primary and secondary sources well, and doubtless would one day be fine lawyers and sassy city traders, but it was a shame, he considered, when a university was considered a mere means to an end, and a sound education not an end in itself. When he was feeling charitable, he would blame the Government (at High Table, he was the first to blame national educational policy not for a decline in standards but in genuine interest); however he felt no charity towards the three New Hall girls before him, and pouring them a second glass of sherry was really an excuse to have another himself.

'Samantha,' he said, 'you've been rather quiet this evening, though at least your book is open on the right page. If you could just translate from line 17…'

Samantha crossed her long, naked legs first in one direction, and then the other. She had thick dyed white-blonde hair and a pouty red mouth. 'I'm so sorry,' she gushed, 'I've not had a chance to look at this. I'm in a play tonight, *Oedipus Rex*, I'm Jocasta. Perhaps you'd like to come and see it?'

'Translate it anyway,' said Dr Marius. 'It's not difficult. Just six lines. If you'd read them out first, please.'

'I find Catullus terribly hard…'

'Go on, read it out. We'll help you if you get stuck.'

And Samantha read out, quite beautifully as it so happened, these words from Catullus 76:

O di, si vestrum est misereri, aut si quibus umquam
Extremam iam ipsa in morte tulistis opem,
Me miserum aspicite et, si vitam puriter egi,
Eripite hanc pestem perniciemque mihi,
Quae mihi subrepens imos ut torpor in artus
Expulit ex omni pectore laetitias.

They then proceeded to attempt a translation, which after a few minutes emerged as something like, 'O Gods, if you know what it is to have pity, or if ever you have brought any help to those facing death itself, see here how wretched I am, and, if ever I have lived a pure life, take this disease and ruin from me, which so crawls through my innermost being that it has driven from my heart all happiness.'

'So then, Samantha, have you led a pure life?' asked Dr Marius.

Samantha tapped her silver-painted fingernails on her black PVC mini-skirt. 'I don't quite get your drift,' said Samantha.

'Well, then, do you think Catullus has lead a pure life? He asks the gods to help him *si vitam puriter egi* – he evidently thinks he has led a good life. But do you? Now, Catullus is suffering badly, and he doesn't feel he deserves to, but do you think he deserves this *pestem*, this *perniciem?*'

'Are you suggesting that I'm not pure?' asked Samantha.

'I'm not suggesting anything of the kind. But I want to know by what standard, if any, you would judge yourself. Now, Catullus considers himself pure despite committing adultery with a Roman matron, something utterly unheard of, something utterly shameful for all parties concerned. And he's asking the Gods for their help! How dare he?'

'Because he thinks he's pious, that's what it says here, in line 2,' said Jane.

'Good,' said Dr Marius, 'but what kind of piety is this? Would a Christian ask for pity for bungling up a burglary?'

'Perhaps the Romans didn't believe in their gods,' said Jane.

'A good point, and the intelligentsia probably didn't. But that didn't mean that invoking the Gods was meaningless. And he uses the word "*sanctus*" to describe their "*fides*" – their bond of trust is *holy*, as Catullus tells us with great feeling. How can adultery be holy?'

All three girls waited to be told.

'This love is different. For the first time in Roman history, we have the complete package. The Roman might eroticize his *meretrix*, his whore, he might write love poetry to her; but his wife demanded his respect, at best, his friendship. To feel lust for your wife, except for the first few weeks of your marriage, was considered rather embarrassing, or rather, simply wrong. Sex with your wife was always about procreation, never pleasure. Now, with Lesbia, Catullus has redefined love. He wants both mind and body. I'd call him the first modern lover, or perhaps even, the first modern husband. And the thing is, he thinks the system he has fallen upon quite by accident is right, right not necessarily in the eyes of the law (because obviously it isn't) but *by nature*. That is why he has *pietas* – which incidentally has a profounder meaning than our English 'piety', in that it is about inner obedience to moral laws rather than outward appearance – that is why he can look into his heart and say he has lived "*puriter*". Catullus is living true to how things are *by nature*, and nature transcends custom.'

Dr Marius paused and was surprised by the vigour with which he delivered his little speech, as were his three students. The sexy Samantha, the sensible Jane and the lanky Henrietta, twenty years a piece, had all known desire and had all known guilt, and they wanted to know what was to be done about it.

'But what do you mean by nature?' asked Jane, putting her edition of *Catullus* on the floor and sitting forward in her chair.

'Nature is everything,' suggested Henrietta. 'Nature is cancer and nits and squidgy bottoms.'

'But perhaps nature itself contains civilization, perhaps it is just "what is". In the animal world, we have bucking reindeer; in the human world, bucking ideologies and hence wars.' Dr Marius stood up and paced the room, which was what he did when he was thinking. 'But you see, it isn't as simple as that. Because the human experience of an ideology is that it is true. Whether it is or not, there is no way of knowing, but man's experience is one of seeking truth. Do the gods exist, or don't they? Is this a truer paradigm, or that one? Or simply, is the theory of relativity true? Yet suddenly with human beings it becomes more difficult. Nothing is clear anymore, all is a muddling through. If we embraced unfettered individualism, we'd all end up as alcoholic existentialists, where nothing would matter ever. If the state was the arbiter of what mattered or not, then look at fascism, at communism. There has to be a truth which transcends nature, state and individual. Well, there doesn't have to be. But it's a nice thought. And when Catullus invokes the Gods he is seeking out a truth which is eternal, like prising an oyster from its shell. It takes precision, but one can also feel one's way to it. '

There was an awed silence, or at least Dr Marius hoped it was 'awed', but then the bell chimed seven in the quad and Samantha said she thought oysters were quite disgusting creatures. Dr Thomas thanked her for her valuable comments, and Samantha said, 'Any time.'

Dr Marius handed out essay titles and book-lists for the following week. For some reason it irked him to watch the girls get up from their chairs and blithely pack their books away, and for some reason it irked him even more when they said, 'See you' rather than 'Thank you'. Henrietta and Jane scuttled away; Samantha lingered just a moment.

'You will come tonight, won't you, Dr Marius? The ADC at eight.'

'We'll see,' said Dr Marius, and forced a smile.

♣

Samantha as Jocasta. He had certainly not been intending to see her, but he did; and he went because he didn't like Samantha, and was curious to see whether she could ever inspire sympathy, and because of the inertia that fell on him when, for the first time that day, he found himself alone.

She was wearing a short red dress, high heels and lots of jewellery. Was it the director who had cast her as a whore? Or did she herself insist that there was not enough colour in the set? How capable she was, he thought, of seducing her own son. He watched her; and when he saw her crying out before her suicide, he thought to himself, 'Why don't I desire this woman? The whole of Cambridge desires her, look at them all salivating on their seats! Yet I've seen her skirt riding up a dozen times in my supervisions, I know it's deliberate, and the more I see of her legs the colder I become.'

But the star of the show was undoubtedly Oedipus himself. His skin had been chalked white, and his blond hair shaved almost to the scalp. He was wearing a simple linen tunic with a knife in his belt, and his calves were strapped in leather bindings, to remind his audience of how he had been found by a shepherd as a baby, feet pinned together: the reason for his name, 'Oedipus' – 'swollen-feet'. When he moved, he stumbled and rocked, inciting those who watched to come and steady him; and then he asked them, he asked Thomas Marius, Am I all impure?

'And is he?' thought Thomas Marius. 'If his intentions are pure but his body is defiled, if he has made love to his own mother but didn't know it, should we blame him? Would God blame him? Surely, if purity means anything, he is purer than Catullus. But is he "*pius*"? No, because "*pietas*" is beyond intention, it's more like "*grace*", something god-given, a disposition to certainty, to knowing; his ignorance, through no fault of his own, has robbed him of it.'

The audience was now moving to go, laughing, joking, gushing enthusiastically, debating the pub to head for; while Thomas was sunk in his seat and his reverie. And then suddenly the magnificent Jocasta herself, restored to life, began making her way towards him. All those she rubbed against congratulated her, and she was like a star, thanking them, waving to friends, self-effacing in her moment of glory.

'Oh Dr Marius!' she exclaimed, 'I'm so pleased you made it, 'I'm so flattered that you came…what did you think? Didn't you think Oedipus was brilliant?'

Dr Marius stood up from his seat and answered her, without feeling, 'I thought you were all very good.'

'Just wait there, I'm sure Oedipus would love to meet you, I've told him all about you, you know.' And off Samantha skipped to get him. When she came back a minute later, Oedipus' arm was about her waist. 'Meet Dr Marius, Simon.'

Simon, now donning a black leather jacket, held out his hand and grinned.

'Hi,' he said, 'Sam's told me a lot about you.'

'I can't think why,' said Dr Marius diffidently.

'She likes you,' said Simon, raising his eyebrows to make the point.

Dr Marius smiled absently and looked at his watch. 'It's late,' he said.

'It's not late!' insisted Samantha, 'Why don't you come to the pub with Simon and me? It would do you good to stay up once in a while.'

Dr Marius surveyed her quizzically. 'I'm going home,' he said, 'and goodbye, Simon. You're a good actor.'

❧

So Simon and Samantha went to The Red Cow without Dr Marius and perched on red velvet stools. It was almost closing time, and the place was packed; but Simon and Samantha had made an island of themselves by facing each other and entwining their knees, and talking loudly into each others' ears

'The trouble is,' Samantha was saying, 'he's so repressed! Do you know that story about the girl who couldn't cry until she was given a bag of onions?'

'So you're a bag of onions now?'

'In a manner of speaking. I might be the catalyst he's been looking for all his life. I'm a damn good lover, you know.' Samantha caught a glimpse of herself in the mirror behind the bar, and smiled. 'I only want to make him happy! I'm a good soul. Sometimes to seduce someone is the kindest thing you can do.'

'I'd call him a very lucky man,' whispered Simon, putting a tongue in her ear.

'How would you know? You're gay!' giggled Samantha.

'Ninety-nine percent gay and one per cent for you.'

'Honestly, Simon, you flatter me!'

'Have you ever considered that Marius might be gay?'

Samantha suddenly sat up and was serious. 'You don't think he is, do you? How can you tell? You can tell, can't you?'

'Relax, Sam. What does "gay" mean, anyway? If you ask me, "gay" is such a weak word. We're all gay, none of us are gay, so fucking what. We all like being rubbed up in the right way, at the right time, by the right person. How do you like being rubbed up?' Simon leant forward and their interlocking knees became interlocking thighs. 'You know what?' he said. 'You are enchantingly naïve.'

Samantha wriggled and jiggled on her stool. The bartender told them to move on, but they ignored him.

'No one has ever called me that before,' she said, rising to the challenge. 'De-naïve me, Simon.'

'I will,' Simon said, obligingly. 'Your place or mine?'

♣

'So what kind of justice was it that Sophocles believed in?' mused Thomas Marius as he bicycled home to Coleridge Road, the wind whistling through his thin jumper. 'Are us moderns right to distinguish conscious from unconscious guilt? A driver who is distracted for a moment as he watches the first swallows of spring, and runs over a child who has darted across the road: what punishment do we give him? Are we any more advanced now in our own system of justice? Would Sophocles have cursed him? Of course he would, and rightly so: the man has no piety, in the classical sense, no god-given grace. Or perhaps the man was already cursed, for sins of another generation and another story.'

Eventually Marius arrived at number eighty-three, and his frozen fingers attempted to un-numb themselves while he fumbled with the lock for his bike and the keys of his front door. He was pleased to see that his lodger, a post-graduate engineering student called Greg, had gone to bed; and in celebration of his privacy he switched on the gas fire in his sitting-room and poured himself a glass of red wine.

He crouched down by the fire and warmed his hands. 'The problem is,' he considered, 'despite forever claiming otherwise, we're all closet dualists. We've divided ourselves up into a mind that's too clever, too ready to make excuses for itself, and a body which never lies, all innocent: it's hungry, so it eats; it wants sex, so it seeks it – how pure, they say, no double-talk here, the body can get away with anything. But it shouldn't be able to. Even in its innocence, in its inability to speak for itself, it is surely capable of being defiled, and of defiling – "am I all impure?" Now when does Oedipus say that? When he suspects the truth about himself... let me see if I can find the words in the original Greek...'

Thomas left the warmth of the fire to go upstairs to his study, the third bedroom on the top floor of his Victorian terraced house. He scanned his bookshelves for the relevant Oxford classical text, and found it with ease, abundant with pencil-written notes he'd written in the margins when he was an undergraduate. It took him barely a minute to find the appropriate line, and then he mulled over the use of the word '*anagnos*' – 'impure' and 'unholy' are the same in Oedipus' mind, and yes, it's true, he is unholy. There's no modern weight given to human responsibility, it doesn't matter that he's unconscious of his guilt. Blessed, unblessed, who are we to say who is or who isn't? It's for the Gods to decide.

Then Thomas hurried to the Chorus to look for more evidence, and found it, even a monotheistic reference to 'Our only father Olympus in Heaven' and the 'laws' which were 'made in Heaven'. Just about the same time as Moses was writing down the Ten Commandments on stone tablets on Mount Sinai, the Greeks understood and paid heed to laws which were never written down, but intuitively apprehended. And isn't that what human beings are always seeking, truths which are universal? And aren't the Greeks right to suggest such laws are agraptos – unwritten and unwritable? For no culture has better understood that truth cannot be categorized, only recognized. Blessed, unblessed, clean, unclean: today we don't want any of that. Holy, unholy: it doesn't make sense to us. Today we have one unwritten law: everything is permitted provided no one gets hurt. But why are we so arrogant that we think we know what 'hurt' means? The Greeks were more subtle than we are. They understood that being moral and simply being didn't present an insoluble philosophical conundrum, but were two sides of the same coin. Their concept of miasma, the seeping pollution which accrues when wrong has been done and hubris festers, where there is nothing blessed and dark shadows lie hidden from the Gods, is an ontological and not a moral thesis.

And while Simon's pulse raced and Samantha was crying 'mercy' into her pillow, so did Thomas Marius' when he found notes he had written in the margins of the Greek text. 'Family curse', he read, 'What about Laius?' Oedipus' father, the innocent victim of his own unblessedness, destined to be murdered by his own son. Sophocles doesn't mention the fact that Laius himself was guilty of kidnapping a beautiful young boy called Chrysippus and taking him to Thebes. Laius set eyes on Chrysippus at Pelops' house and fell in love with him – this was another Zeus and Ganymede story – and Pelops cursed him. Chrysippus ends up killing himself. Would Sophocles' audience have been aware of the story? If they had been, modern order is restored, Oedipus becomes a mere crime and punishment story, albeit not his own. But why do human beings need that sense of order? Why are we always looking for cause and effect, cause and effect, as though that was the only way of looking at the world? Why do we limit our Christian God to the role of meting out justice, to being a shadow of us, rather than admit to ourselves that we are a mere shadow of Him?

We have turned ourselves into a race of terrifying free agents, responsible for everything we do, everything depending on our own free actions; but what about fate? What about providence? Would it not be more religious to say that Oedipus was simply unlucky, than that he was living out a family curse which was deserved?

And on that passionate note (while strawberry gel and bodily fluids were drenching Samantha's thighs, and metal handcuffs were digging into both her wrists and ankles) Thomas Marius looked at his watch and saw it was already almost one in the morning. He went down to the kitchen to make himself a cup of tea and a hot water bottle, and took himself off to bed.

☘

It would be fair to say that Dr Marius didn't like his house; or at least, house-ownership didn't mean a great deal to him, and seemed to bring more bother than pleasure. When he had decided that it was time to move out of college, it had been because college life was beginning to oppress him: being continually cajoled into formal functions in which he had no interest, and being too easily accessible to anyone needing his help, academic or otherwise. But the last straw had been a Girton girl in the Spring term of 1994 who used to come round almost every evening looking all starry-eyed to ask about this or that reference, or an obscure poet she had suddenly learnt the name of. Finally the girl, whose name was Annabel, had

had the courage (or desperation) to ask Dr Marius to have dinner with her, and because Dr Marius was a decent sort who didn't wish to offend, he'd reluctantly agreed.

That fateful night: his cheeks burned whenever he remembered it, the girl sitting opposite him in a dress which seemed to raise her breasts up to her neck, defiant of gravity. And when she confessed her love for him, only huge self-discipline had kept him from leaping up and leaving the restaurant for air.

'It's not right,' he had said meekly.

It did no good. On and on she had whinnied, she had given him her whole life's story, her misspent youth, her parents who had never understood her, and a catalogue of her physical desires: and all the while he could only think how much happier he'd be if he was a beetle lying on its back, or the moth blackening its wings with the soot of the candle on their table – anything, anything would be preferable to sitting here with Annabel, eating zabaglione with a long-handled spoon and watching her licking her own in a hideously suggestive fashion.

He'd left Annabel in the market square and told her he still had some marking to do that night. And in fact, that was the last he ever saw of her: in her humiliation she persuaded her Director of Studies to find her another supervisor in Peterhouse. But her legacy was to make Dr Marius realise that he was becoming claustrophobic living in his college rooms, beautiful though they were, and that the time had come for him to move out.

Number eighty-three Coleridge Road was the first house he had looked round. After all, what could one expect of a house besides its having four strong walls and a roof? He neither noticed the avocado wood-chip wallpaper, nor the brown, nylon carpets or the dingy kitchen; and when he moved in he continued not to notice them, and four years later when the condition of the house was even worse he never understood that it was within his power to do something about it. The best he managed was the self-reproachful question, 'Was I right to move here?'

Then one night during an Autumn storm in 1996, while Marius was in bed with a cup of tea and his copy of Herodotus, he noticed that water was dripping through his ceiling onto his quilt. So he moved his bed by a couple of feet, put a bucket on the floor to catch it, and resumed reading. It wasn't until the morning that he understood the full significance of two pints of rainwater: the plumber he'd called told him he was going to need a new roof.

And now poor Dr Thomas Marius was going to have to re-mortgage his house and find a lodger. He went to the University Lodgings syndicate and was introduced to Greg, a post-graduate student in engineering. He didn't much warm to Greg, who was small, with glasses and mousy, wispy hair, and was deadly, deadly silent; but he had no choice in the matter, and Greg moved into his spare bedroom.

That first breakfast they had together: Thomas had laid the cereals out on the table and put into operation for the first time a cafetiére that his mother had given him for Christmas.

'Would you like a boiled egg, Greg?' he asked him, and in the dreadful realisation that 'egg' rhymed with 'Greg', he turned his back and began fiddling with the toaster.

'No thanks,' said Greg.

'I always like an egg,' mumbled Thomas, which was a lie.

When there's no conversation at breakfast one is perhaps too aware of the noise of food rolling around the mouth. And if on that first morning it was a little embarrassing, to the extent that Thomas tried to modulate the movements of his own mouth (in the vain hope of leading by example), on subsequent mornings Thomas' sensibilities were being tested a full ten minutes before the very first cornflake was being scrunched up against Greg's palate. In addition to which, Greg had taken to eating yoghurt. Within four days of his arrival, he had taken over a shelf of Thomas' fridge with twenty-eight pots of Eden

Vale's natural yoghurt; and when Greg had finished his cornflakes he would put his bowl to one side and begin a ritual which would ruthlessly hold Thomas' attention until its perfect completion.

First, Greg would remove the foil lid in one piece: though never in a thousand breakfasts was Thomas ever to witness it tear, each morning it seemed to present a new challenge to Greg. Then, carefully laying the lid face up on the table, he would take his teaspoon and scrape off the thick layer of yoghurt in exactly five successive strokes, each time his tongue hovering beneath the upturned spoon in piquant ecstasy. Next, he would make a well in the centre of the pot and fill it with two dessert spoons of granulated sugar, and Thomas would watch the sugar mountain subside bit by bit, mixing firstly with the yoghurt in the pot, and then with the yogurt already moving around inside his mouth. Finally, Greg would fold the foil lid into four, put it into the empty pot, and get up from the table.

Even on the sixtieth occasion Thomas was mesmerized by the accuracy of Greg's breakfast performance, even on the hundred and sixtieth occasion, but after Greg had been living with him for nine months there was another distraction. Her name was Cilla.

And, quite fittingly, it was breakfast when he first met her.

'Hello, my name's Cilla. I hope you don't mind me staying sometimes,' she enthused, grinning wildly at Greg. 'Would it be all right if I called you "Tom"?'

Now, no one had ever called Thomas Marius 'Tom', at least, not since he was ten years old. But that wasn't why his jaw dropped now, nor did it drop because she was evidently a pretty, sweet thing somehow lured into Greg's lumbering embrace. No, what astonished him was her name. For in his time he had met two Camillas (both rather aptly named, he thought, fighting Aeneas with Amazonian courage and one breast bared); an Athene (and why not call your daughter after the goddess of wisdom?); a Clio (muse of history, quite inspiring); a Thalia (muse of laughter and good cheer, a blessing, surely); and even a Calypso (whose sexual charms arrested Odysseus for seven years.) But what could Cilla's parents have been thinking of? Perhaps they were thinking of Scylla before Circe cast a spell on her and gave her six heads with three rows of teeth in each. Scylla, beloved of Glaucus, one of the deities of the sea…

'Or I could always call you "Dr Marius"?' Cilla giggled nervously. The expression on her host's face was unfathomable, and he didn't answer her.

'I was thinking,' she said, 'this place could really do with a lick of paint to cheer it up a little. I've had a bit of training in colour, you know, I'm a beautician. I've quite an eye, so they tell me. I'll be bold. I want to paint Greg's bedroom coral blush.'

Dr Marius was still one conversation in arrears. 'No, don't call me "Tom". I wouldn't know who I was.' And then, he added tactfully, 'What would you like me to call you? Have you got a nickname or something?'

Cilla giggled again. 'Greg calls me "Cill",' she said.

'Right then,' said Thomas, 'I'll call you "Sill" too.' He was oblivious to Greg's stony stare, and thought only how much better to be reminded of windows.

'And the spot of decorating?'

'What?'

'What I mentioned, getting this house in a bit of order.'

'Oh yes, yes,' said Thomas, vacantly. 'Go ahead, by all means.'

And before his very eyes Thomas Marius watched his house become coral blush, orange pekoe and lime green: only his bedroom and his study were impervious to Cilla's promiscuous paintbrush, remaining stalwart behind their avocado woodchip wallpaper.

'What a good job you've done, Sill,' Thomas would tell her when he was shown yet another transformed room, and Cilla would grin, chest out, hands behind her back, and say, 'It was nothing, Tom, honestly. You know, I could always do your bedroom, too…'

'No, no, thank you. I'm quite happy.'

And by day, at least, Thomas was quite happy. Cilla was always smiling, always ready to oblige; and sometimes when Greg was at an evening seminar and Cilla was back from her beauty parlour, she would make Thomas a cup of tea and bring it to his study.

'Come in, Sill, haven't you brought a cup of tea for yourself?'

'Well, I thought you'd be working.'

'You get yourself a cup. Come and talk to me.'

And that was, for Thomas, a rather pleasurable twenty minutes of the day, when Cilla would tell him about her father and his father before him who'd both been train drivers, and she promised that one day she'd bring in the family photograph album because the early photos, what with the steam and that, were something else. Occasionally Cilla even tried to regale him with stories from her parlour, about eyebrows and waxing and hairy moles, but she could see from Thomas' grimaces that these didn't go down well, and being a sensitive sort she kept them for Greg. Meanwhile, Thomas was always trying to switch the subject to Greek mythology, telling Cilla all about the voyages of Odysseus, which was as close as he ever got to a direct question about Cilla's peculiar name. She never rose to the bait, of course, but enjoyed the myths and would tell Greg when they were snuggled up in bed together, 'Your landlord is so eccentric, but I do like him.'

Then Cilla began to cook for her man, and the invasion of Thomas' fridge continued apace: hamburgers, sausages and bacon appeared on another shelf, and tins of tuna and sardines were piled high in his kitchen cupboard. Thomas soon got into the habit of going back to college for his supper, and when he returned home at ten o'clock he was greeted with wafts of Greg's fishy breath. But for some reason this only became truly offensive at the thought of that lovely girl suffering it as well.

One night he came in and found them kissing on the sofa in his now iris-blue sitting-room; he'd rushed past them and up the stairs, and Cilla had followed him up to apologise.

'I'm so sorry,' she said, 'we're pushing you out of your own house. We'll stay in the bedroom, Tom. Don't mind us.'

But that was when he really did begin to mind. The walls weren't even particularly thin, but perhaps, Thomas thought, as he lay there listening, I'm too conscious of it. Is there an aural equivalent to a peeping Tom? Should I tell them to be quieter? Is that the more moral thing to do, or is it simply the less liberal?

At first Greg was the one he was angry with. Not being exactly a man of fashion, he'd taken Cilla's rather tight-fitting tunics to be a mark of innocence: he'd even considered that the reason why they were so short was that she'd worn them while she was still at school, and had never had sufficient money to replace them with something a little more modern. The first time he heard Greg say to her, 'You've been a naughty girl, my little one,'; the first time he heard a slap, and then two, why, Thomas was on the point of entering and rescuing the poor girl; but the giggles which ensued confounded him. He lay there in the dark, his heart beat resounding in his chest, alert to every Gregorian grunt and squeak of the old mattress, and so uncomfortably present was he in that little menage that he fancied he could smell salted herring on Greg's breath.

Occasionally it was all he could do to resist running into the room and shouting 'Stop!' Would Cill want him to? he wondered. Was she being raped night after night while he was lying idly by? For the girl would often shout 'No! No!', and vigorously, too. And human beings were sufficiently complicated to shout 'No!', mean 'Yes!', and then, when considering everything in the cold light of day, deeply mean 'no' after all. And if even the participants in a rape didn't know whether 'yes' meant 'no' and 'no' meant 'yes', however was a jury supposed to know it?

And then a most unfortunate thing happened. For while Greg

was guilty and his girlfriend innocent, things were at least bearable. But overnight there was a sea-change: her noes turned to yeses. The timbre of her voice changed: initial alarm at Greg's violent advances turned to greed for them. And Cilla suddenly became Scylla in all her terrible glory. Thomas could bear it no more. He got out of bed, tightened his pyjama cord and put on his dressing-gown. Upstairs he went to his study at four in the morning, scanning the shelves until he found what he was looking for. Ovid's Metamorphoses, Book XIII: here you are, Scylla, bathing in the fountain up to your waist, but look down, Scylla! You think you're so pretty, don't you? You look happily for your reflection. But all you find in the water are three monstrous, barking dogs, and you thrash about trying to escape them, but you can't, dear Scylla, because don't you understand they're part of you?

Cilla didn't come down to breakfast the following morning, and Thomas was relieved. He felt he could never look her in the eye again. Greg ate his yoghurt with his customary precision, and for some reason Thomas said to him,

'I always think how tasty those yoghurts look. Do you mind if I try one?'

'Go ahead,' said Greg, surprised, and looking up only briefly from his own, in case he should miss an interesting subsidence of sugar.

In fact, Cilla was only to remain in his house for a further three months. There were no signs of her imminent departure, though Thomas had by now become distinctly less observant and solicitous, and their now occasional *tête à têtes* in the early evening had become stiff and consisted only of the briefest formalities. But when she was gone, Thomas felt in some way responsible for it; or rather that he had misjudged her. He wanted to write her a letter to tell her how sorry he was that she had left so suddenly and without saying goodbye; he wanted to ask Greg for her address, or at least to be given some small clue as to what had happened between them. But Greg was as unforthcoming as ever, and wouldn't have told him about Cilla's pregnancy for the world.

❧

'Well,' said Samantha, who that afternoon had dressed herself up in silk and leather and spent an hour applying her make-up, 'I've come to the conclusion that you're gay. And in this day and age, they're not exactly going to imprison you for it! I'm being no more prying than if I were to ask you your middle name.'

'If I tell you my middle name, will you leave? This is my tutorial hour and I, thank God, am not your tutor.' Thomas sighed and was as bored as he sounded.

'Just tell me this, have you ever lusted for a woman? Tell me that, and I'll go.'

'For God's sake,' said Thomas, looking at his watch.

'For example, have you ever noticed that I was a woman? Has it ever crossed your mind?'

'Unfortunately, yes.'

'There you see, you don't like women.'

'Has it ever occurred to you that it might be you I don't like?'

'But what about desire? Desire is surely a more profound condition than mere liking or disliking.'

Thomas sighed and said nothing.

Samantha laughed easily and sat on the arm of an armchair with her legs astride. 'Do you know, Dr Marius, I don't think I've been to a single supervision without an overwhelming desire to take my shirt off, and I never wear a bra when I know I'll be seeing you, just in case desire finally does overwhelm me.'

'Aristotle, *Nichomachean Ethics Book V*: read it, Samantha, and see how you share your free-flowing qualities with the animals. There is nothing profound about desire, nothing at all. Desire is the least human part of us.'

'So, I'm in touch with my inner animal. Is that possibly the nicest thing you've ever said to me?'

'Is love within your range, Samantha? Or are you pure desire?'

'My God, I've traced an incurable romantic. And?'

'And what?'

'Have you ever loved a woman, then?'

It would have been so easy to have told the truth to Samantha, 'I was married, once.' But that would have been sinking to her level, playing her game. The admission would have been a defeat in itself, and he was saved from making it by a knock on the door.

Samantha pleaded, one last time, and Thomas reiterated that he didn't have to tell her anything.

'Come in,' he said.

A fresh-faced undergraduate hesitated when he caught sight of Samantha, as the buttons on her shirt were half undone.

'Adrian, sit down,' said Thomas, more effusively than usual. 'Don't worry, she's just going.'

And this was the way he triumphed over Samantha, for the time being, at least.

♣

That night, Thomas took a cup of tea to bed with him. He sat propped up against a wooden headboard, enjoying the slight discomfort of it.

His Bengali wife, Benita, had been a virgin when he'd married her in Warwick in 1986, when he was twenty-seven. Beautiful, pure, unassuming, Benita had been the librarian at the University where he'd had his first teaching post and lectured in Latin Literature. Her simplicity of spirit had enchanted Thomas; and she'd been the first woman in his life who'd looked up to him to provide the right answers, to make him feel manly. In short, he had desired her more than any other woman he had ever met.

What a sorry thing it is when worldly matters intrude on the unworldly! For Benita had underplayed the resistance of her family to their impending marriage.

'They so want to be modern!' Benita had exclaimed. 'They so want to accept you as their own!'

Which was true, though Benita forgot to emphasize the word 'want': for they had indeed wanted to, but could not, accept Thomas, even for their daughter's sake. Only insiders would have understood there was a distinct lack of joy at their wedding, for everyone was on best behaviour and as civil as could be, but even the Hindu celebrations after their marriage in a registry office lacked lustre.

For all his desire, however, this business of the taking of the virginity had become, by its fifth week, more of an engineering than a romantic feat, as Benita (who was a bit older than Thomas, and had years' worth of virginity-related anxiety to dispel) had used brute force to push his slender hips away from hers. And even though their sex-life was non-existent, Thomas had himself an insurmountable rival in the bedroom, namely the telephone and Benita's mother.

Night after night Benita's mother used to call as they were lying in bed together, and it occurred to Thomas that Benita had even asked her mother to phone so late, 'to be saved by the bell', as it were. And then Benita would proceed to talk in Bengali, right there in bed beside him, for twenty or even thirty minutes every single night. When Thomas had complained, Benita had accused him of not recognizing the importance of the family.

'Just because you English ignore your own parents, why should I ignore mine?'

'Can't you get your mother to phone earlier?'

'They eat just as soon as my father gets home.'

'And before that?'

'I'm at the library till half past seven, as well you know!'

And so the lovely Benita, the possession of whom he had yearned for for the best part of a year, continued to elude him forever. By the time Thomas was awarded a fellowship at Corpus three years later, they were divorced.

Thomas sipped at his tea and considered. For six years, now, he had been celibate, assuming an almost monkish existence, his body as separate from himself as if it had been a mere adolescent appendage.

But that night, O blast Samantha, it wasn't his wife he was thinking of. The most important kiss of his life had happened in the Bavarian forest, when he was fifteen and on a German exchange with a boy called Hans. They had been skating together on a small, hidden lake and the sun was setting. And yes, if Hans had been Hannah, the strength and seriousness of that moment would have been lacking. But do moments like that define you? Do they cast you in that role forever?

He was still lost in thought at half past eight the following morning while riding on his bike into college. 'And if I am incapable of love, should I mind? Is it a defect in my character?' And would such a defect, quite happy, quite silent as it was back then in November 1998, have been preferable to the upheavals which were to occur in his soul over the next few years? Thomas Marius was riding his bike too fast. A pale, blond boy with a satchel on his back was on the zebra crossing on his way to the school opposite. There was an accident – Thomas clipped the back of his satchel and the boy fell.

'I'm so sorry,' he said, 'I'm so dreadfully sorry.'

The boy told him not to worry, he'd been quite in a dream himself. His name was Josiah.

Chapter Eight

THOMAS MARIUS had barely noticed that he lived opposite a school. Why should he? During the week he was in college; at weekends, the school was shut. But ever since crashing into one of its schoolboys his curiosity was roused; not least because the boy in question had left behind him a charming drawing of a tall beech tree, probably, as Thomas surmised (owing to its shape and the fact it had been drawn on the back of an old cereal packet), used as a bookmark.

The moral dilemma facing Thomas at that time was whether he ought to return it. The morning of the accident, he had picked up the bookmark from the zebra crossing and had called after the boy, but the boy had disappeared in the general hubbub at the school gate and Thomas had simply put the bookmark in his briefcase and biked on. In fact, no dilemma presented itself until the moment Thomas realised that he liked the bookmark and he wanted to keep it. If, the first time he saw the drawing of the beech tree he had considered it 'well executed', by the end of a week it had become an object of genuine beauty. In which case, its artist might be missing it badly, and it needed to be returned.

So if it had been Thomas' custom to leave his house at about twenty past eight, he now went upstairs to his study at that time where he had a good view of the school and of all those entering and leaving the gates. The first time he saw the boy again, why, he had the bookmark there on his desk ready to give back to him; but something held him back, and if that 'something' had been at first waiting for an appropriate moment, when he wasn't surrounded by other children, that innocent 'something' began to be transformed into something else. For the boy had begun to fascinate him.

He decided that the boy was about fourteen; and that, as he had confessed on the morning of the accident, he lived in a dream. He had never seen him talk to another child, and seemed to have developed a knack of being invisible to them. But he was not exactly an outsider, either; he never set himself apart from the crowd, and was, quite often, in the midst of it. But it occurred to him that he had never seen the boy smile, and the expression on his face was generally one of absence.

Then one morning Thomas opened the door to the postman, who was in the throes of shoving his *Classical Journal* through the letter-box. It was still only eight o'clock, but he noticed the boy walking quickly towards him a full half hour earlier than usual. He was also walking alone. This was his chance.

Up to his office he ran, two steps at a time, squeezing past Greg who was on his way down to his yoghurt-fest, and opened up his briefcase on his desk. Where was the bookmark, for God's sake? From his window he watched the boy coming closer, closer still, but where was the bookmark?

He snapped the briefcase shut and took it down to the hall with him; and his sudden sense of urgency to restore the lovely thing to its rightful owner rid him of his natural timidity. He opened the door and called out, in the nick of time, 'Hello there! I've got something that belongs to you!'

Josiah turned towards him. He was both curious and calm.

'I'm so sorry to spring upon you like this! But not only did I crash into you the other day but I robbed you of a rather lovely... well, I think it's a bookmark, but correct me if I'm wrong.'

Thomas moved back into his hall and said, 'Come in, I'll find it for you.'

Josiah said nothing but was pleased to follow him. He knew

exactly what it was that the man had picked up, he had at least a dozen of them, but he had often wanted to know what it was like in the man's house. For if Thomas had noticed Josiah, Josiah had certainly noticed Thomas, standing at an upstairs window.

Josiah watched while Thomas put the telephone on the floor and put his briefcase on the small hall table. 'Now, where is it?' Thomas was muttering to himself, as he began rummaging through the case.

'Do you like orange, then?' asked Josiah.

Thomas looked up. 'I'm sorry?'

'The walls,' offered Josiah.

'The truth is,' said Thomas, 'I don't really like orange. No, I don't like orange at all.'

'Me neither,' said Josiah.

'Here it is! At last! Is it a bookmark?'

'It is,' said Josiah, taking it back. 'Did you use it?'

'As you can see, I did.' Thomas picked up the book in whose pages it had been nestling.

'Catullus,' said Josiah. 'He spoke Latin, didn't he?'

'Yes, he did speak Latin. And he wrote Latin, too. This is a fine book, and one day…'

'I know it's a fine book.'

'Ah, you're a Latinist already?'

'Odi et amo.'

'Heavens, that's very good!'

'I hate and I love.'

'Do you learn Latin over at your school, then?'

'No. My mother taught me those words. Catullus was her favourite poet. I'm afraid that's all I know.'

'So your mother was a Classicist?'

'I don't know what that means.'

'She studied Latin and Greek.'

'I know she learnt Latin.'

'And does she teach you now?'

'She's dead. It's all right. She died a long time ago.'

'I'm so sorry,' said Thomas, and he meant it.

'I'd better get to school, then.'

'Can I not offer you anything? Like breakfast?'

'I've eaten, thanks. I'd better go.' Josiah smiled awkwardly. Then he turned on his heel and left.

This glimpse into the boy's history only managed to exacerbate things. When Thomas took up his customary position in his study to watch him go into school the following morning, the boy waved at him. And suddenly he felt terribly ashamed. So he stopped looking out for the boy, and tried to get on with his work. And when he couldn't work, he decided to invite the boy for tea.

At first, his feelings about such an invitation seemed relatively simple. There was no law against befriending strangers, after all; and he was no child. He was a kouros, a handsome youth, worthy of any Greek sculptor's attention; yet his good looks were by no means the most pressing reason he was attracted to him. There was a quality in his character, a certain wistfulness, which roused his curiosity, and curiosity had been the driving force in Thomas' life.

Why the passion of Thomas's life, hitherto, had been books, was because he had found books so very much more interesting than people. The character of your average person, he had brutally decided many years previously, could be reduced to a thumbnail sketch: nice/nasty; stupid/clever; wise/obtuse – and the third category didn't even exist until he returned to Cambridge after the demise of his marriage. But the exciting thing about ideas was that they existed over and above the people who happened to have them, and a work of scholarship thrilled him inasmuch as the writer had fallen away, or ought to have. For the self and prejudice were as one – for what was prejudice but the public display of personal desires and aversions? And what was the self but the private catalogue of those same desires and aversions, for one's own personal use?

Which was why his interest in the boy stupefied him. Undergraduates arrived in Cambridge more or less complete – with the personalities they would have for the rest of their lives: he could plot them on his mental graph and they rarely threw up any surprises. But the boy was endearingly imperfect, in the sense that he was not complete. When Thomas looked for the exact expression to describe his peculiar quality, he had to resort to the Latin: *perfecte imperfectus*, for there were two strands in his character which ran parallel to each other and were prima facie contradictory; namely, that he was more self-reliant than most adults, in that he seemingly had no interest in nor derived any self-esteem from his peer group. Yet at the same time there was a hole so large in his life that those few moments with him betrayed (or so it seemed, as he replayed their encounter a hundred times in his head) almost a manic desperation for whatever it was that was missing. And as the days turned to weeks he understood why he was becoming obsessed: because he felt that he, Thomas Marius, could help him find it. And that was why the boy must come to tea, and he must issue that invitation as quickly as possible.

But was it really as simple as that? O, ye Gods, what is ever simple? For by the time Thomas Marius' brain had pulped every version of every event and recast it in every mould, his anxiety about this peculiar and unprecedented situation was taut and dangerous. Thomas decided he was deceiving himself. For in the same way as the sketch of the beech tree had seemed ever more beautiful, Thomas was aware that the boy was also becoming so. One lunchtime (he had never stooped so low!), he found himself spying on the boy (for what else could it be called? Nowadays his study seemed barely more than a crow's nest) admiring the fullness of his mouth, the way he carried his broad but skinny shoulders, his long neck, like a woman's. And what he asked himself was this: 'Was this way of looking at him morally wrong? To admire the beauty of another being, is that always unproblematic? And above all, do I invite him for tea?'

If things had been left to Thomas, the truth is, he would never have invited him to tea. But if Thomas' original and surely virtuous motive had been to save the boy, because he recognized there was something about him worth saving, Josiah's prayer was that the god-like figure who looked out over his world would be his saviour. And it was with this intention that Josiah knocked on his door one Saturday morning in March. 'Will you teach me Latin?' was what he asked the wracked, ruined, unshaven man on his doorstop.

'Of course I will,' said Thomas, 'Won't you come in?'

It was nine o'clock; Greg was still asleep; and Thomas, suddenly woken from days of sleeplessness, saw his house as an outsider might see it. He suggested the boy might like a cup of tea, and as they walked together through the long, thin hall to the kitchen at the back of the house, he apologized for the orange paint, and yearned that his house might be sober and uneventful, clean and forthright. He noticed, as though for the first time, the lime green walls, the mock-pine kitchen units, the dirty electric rings on the cooker. Thomas made the tea – two teabags in two ugly brown mugs – and they sat down momentarily at the kitchen table. But when he fetched the milk from the fridge he saw the yoghurt, and he said, 'I tell you what. I'm taking you upstairs to my study.'

Josiah followed him upstairs and noticed neither the decor, nor lack of cleanliness, nor the fact that the cups of tea had been left behind; for he was bathing in the warm slipstream of the man who was finally going to teach him what it was he wanted to know. And once in the study, with the door shut behind them and the old world safely cordoned off, Josiah was almost immediately aware of an unravelling of himself, a surrendering which was both physical and joyful. This is what it feels like, he said to himself, to absolutely trust another human being; to lay yourself at their mercy.

It was Josiah who had shut the door. The moment they were alone together, Thomas was nauseous. His sense of responsibility was suddenly so acute that for all he knew one wrong move might bring about a plague in Africa. So far, Josiah and Thomas were just standing looking at each other, the former with a large open smile and the latter with a brain on overload and a lined forehead. For there was only one chair in his study, so should he go to fetch another? Would the stool from the bathroom do, or would Greg be there? Would the small armchair in his bedroom be too unwieldy to carry upstairs? Would it be too eccentric to make a stool out of a few volumes of the Oxford English Dictionary? This was the option which he chose, and happily the boy seemed delighted to sit on it, as though sitting on dictionaries was something that scholars ordinarily did. And while Thomas was negotiating his next problem, namely to choose the distance at which to sit from the boy (he was initially too unfriendly, and then, perhaps, too bold), Josiah was thinking how much nicer it was to be here than lying under his yew on these cold, dark, damp days or lying in his over-heated bedroom counting moths on the ceiling and listening to the squabbling next door.

At last, with the seating arranged to their mutual satisfaction, and the tea thoroughly forgotten by both of them, Thomas asked his young companion his name.

'Josiah,' said Josiah.

'Aha,' said Thomas, 'A king in the Old Testament.'

'That's right,' enthused Josiah, 'and he was a good king, a good and just king.'

'I'm sure your parents wouldn't have named you after a bad king,' laughed Thomas, nervously, as a dreadful image of Scylla shoved itself into his head. 'So then, Josiah, you want to learn Latin.'

'I do,' said Josiah. 'Before she died, my mother used to teach me, and I remember quite a lot. The five declensions, the four conjugations, amo, moneo, rego, and audio. Is that right?'

'How long ago did you learn all of that? That's very impressive.'

'Seven or eight years ago now. But I made myself remember it. For years I would repeat what she taught me night after night. She made me feel like I was learning a secret code. But I only know a part of it, and probably after repeating it so much I've got it wrong, like Chinese whispers. I want you to teach me what I don't know.'

'I'm sure I could do that. Incidentally my name is Thomas Marius.'

'I know,' said Josiah, coolly. 'It was written on a folder I caught sight of in your briefcase the other day. And you teach at Corpus Christi College.'

'That's right. What else do you know about me?'

'That you live with a creep. I don't know what his name is, but I've watched him go in and out of your house.'

'And do you watch me go in and out of my house, too?'

'Oh yes! Of course! And I watch you standing by your window, right here!' Josiah got up and walked over to the exact spot. Then he leant on the sill and looked out towards the school. 'You have a great view. You can see everything.'

'I'm lucky,' Thomas said, his cheeks reddening.

'So will you teach me?' asked Josiah, without looking round.

'Of course I will,' said Thomas, too ebulliently.

♣

They agreed to meet at nine o'clock every Saturday morning. For the seven days and nights Thomas had to fill before they met again it was as though every synapse was on red alert. When he opened the window to return Josiah's wave that first morning, the shot of fresh, cold air which blasted through his study was the first fresh, cold air he'd ever noticed. And long after Josiah was out of sight, Thomas stood there leaning over the sill and letting his head feel the full force of it. Even the colours of the car roofs seemed rather splendid that morning, and he felt he understood their purring engines while they waited patiently at the traffic lights, and their sense of anticipation as they revved like greyhounds in the stalls. He remembered something his father had told him about birds not being afraid of cars because they knew that they weren't animals, and caught sight of a robin remaining grave and undeceived in the branch of a poplar tree opposite him.

And in the same mood he saw a neighbour of his struggling home with some heavy shopping bags, and sprinted down the stairs to rescue her.

'I've lived here four years,' he said to the woman in a hairnet with incipient beard, 'and I'm afraid I don't even know your name. Imagine that, I don't even know your name…'

'Call me Marjory, duck,' she grinned, revealing a row of immaculate white teeth.

Thomas briefly considered what a rare sight it was to see a woman so old with teeth in such good condition, and almost complimented her, but suddenly remembered his mission.

'Marjory, here, give me those bags!'

'Well, all right then. I won't complain,' said Marjory with alacrity, as she handed them over to him.

'They're very heavy,' observed Thomas.

'It's good quality coal in there.'

'Does that mean you've got a real fireplace in your house?'

'Well, I'm not putting coal out for the birds, am I?'

'But are you allowed to use real coal in Cambridge?'

'Whatever makes you think you can't?'

'There's no law against it?'

'You can't stop people being warm, I say.'

'No, you can't,' mused Thomas, as he left the bags by Marjory's front door.

So within the hour he was ready for Josiah's return visit. It had never occurred to him that the small Victorian mantelpiece in his study could be unblocked quite so easily, revealing a small grate; and the pleasure of moving around furniture to get the best possible effect was quite new to him. Up came two small armchairs from the sitting room, and a small coffee table. If they needed to use his desk, he would bring up a chair from the kitchen, but in his mind's eye this is where the two of them would sit together, and he would teach him everything he knew.

But there were a further 166 hours to dispose of. He sat in one of the armchairs to consider textbooks. A book he'd enjoyed as a boy was by one F. Ritchie, old-fashioned, yes, but which would give Josiah a solid grounding in grammar, far surpassing the new-fangled Cambridge course which he'd always been faintly suspicious of. And look! There was his old *Kennedy's Latin Primer*, perfect! If his mind had been less restless, he would even have been happy.

But Thomas couldn't be still. Because for every generous concern about the boy, there was an opposing one, one which he tried hard to fathom. For why, O why, was he so absurdly pleased? What was it that he felt the boy could give him? What was it, exactly, that he had already given? Here was no educated equal, offering him food for thought on a topic that interested him. Yet the boy himself was that topic: he wasn't a means to an end, he himself was that end… No, it was even more than that, for the boy wasn't a mere trinket which he wished to put in his pocket and possess, somehow. It was true that his physicality excited him, not in any sexual way, but in the way one might be excited by a fine tree in the Botanical Gardens. Yes, Thomas, who had never been in the slightest bit observant before, and who had lumped humanity together under the report card, 'has talent, but works well below par', found himself intrigued by the boy's fringe, which tended to fall into his eyes, and the way when he was sitting he would hold onto his knees with outstretched palms, and the pretty shape his lips assumed when he was thinking. His trousers were too long for him, and his coat too large, but he held himself proudly and he had more dynamism in him than any undergraduate. No, not 'dynamism', which suggested activity; rather *dunamis*, the Greek word: he had power, an inner strength, a potentiality. No, smiled Thomas to himself, I don't know a child like him. And then, reluctantly, he acknowledged that he had never known a child.

He took solace in the fact that the Greeks would encourage him; he trusted their judgment in most things, and remembered that his copy of Plato's *Symposium* was among the pile of books on his bedside table. He fetched it, and saw that his hands were trembling; and when he settled back in the armchair to consult it he closed his eyes and questioned why the book should alarm him so.

As an undergraduate he'd read the dialogue through with a couple of friends. And true to the spirit of a *symposium*, they had lain sprawled over pillows on the floor, drinking wine together. For God's sake, what had happened to philosophy, that it had become as dry as dust and dull as ditchwater! For those Greeks were lovers of life as well as truth. And they didn't categorize, analyse, cut, squeeze and push for meaning, they felt it in their hearts, they recognized it. *In vino veritas*: those were the days, when to surrender was to receive the truth, and wine was considered a help rather than a hindrance.

Even Catullus, claiming to be *pius* when he was committing adultery with a married woman, sought a truth over and above the *mores* of their time. For any living culture will have customs and angles on life which define it, and set them apart from other cultures. And some cultures, and this is the point, are better than others, in that they have a better understanding of *how things are by nature* and a greater aspiration to seek and achieve *how things might be even better*; and *truth* is ever their criterion. Without truth, all dissipates, all is equal and nothing is of value.

Thomas lay back, eyes closed. Calmer now, he even smiled, while he brought to mind Plato's recommendation than an army should be made up entirely of pairs of lovers, men and their boyfriends. Back in 1980, Thomas and his friends had been beside themselves with laughter – was the laughter uneasy? No! No! No! All these gay Greeks, what a joke, bet they could teach the Green Jackets a thing or two. He opened his *Symposium* and the book fell open on a well-worn page:

So if there were some way of arranging that a state, or an army, could be made up entirely of pairs of lovers, it is impossible to imagine a finer population. They would avoid all dishonour, and compete with one another for glory: in battle, this kind of army, though small, fighting side by side could conquer virtually the whole world. After all, a lover would sooner be seen by anyone deserting his post or throwing away his weapons, rather than by his boyfriend. He would normally choose to die many times over instead. And as for abandoning the boy, or not trying to save him if he is in danger – no one is such a coward as not to be inspired with courage by Eros, making him the equal of the naturally brave man. Homer says, and rightly, that God breathes fire into some of his heroes. And it is just this quality, whose origin is to be found within himself, that Eros imparts to lovers.'

Sixteen years later, and the passage made perfect sense to him. Of course, Kenneth Dover had a lot to answer for, with his book on Greek homosexuality, who had done for the Classics what Freud had done for psychology, a massive reduction of all that is human and interesting to a description of mere animal drives. The mistranslation of *eros* caused our minds to take a wrong turn, our use of the word *erotic* was simply mistaken. Whatever happened to love, pure and simple? And whence the random, modern decision that a love which is passionate is necessarily sexual? Dover would have us imagine that Plato's ideal of an army was a vulgar, homosexual orgy – except, of course, he's too academic, too unbiased, to admit to the word 'vulgar'. *Let us all enjoy our bodies, like the Greeks*! he seems to be singing in his turgid text.

Thomas in his anger leapt up and began urgently seeking instances of the Greek word *erastes*, 'lover'. Here we are, Pericles, urging his citizens to be 'lovers' of Athens – for God's sake, would Dover suggest the Parthenon was a Freudian masterpiece? What has happened to us all? What has happened to our minds, to our spirits, when all we see are bodies? For ten thousand years the greatest civilizations have been making the same point, that the human spirit is greater than the body, that an obsession with the body diminishes the spirit, and then for a mere eighty we turn our backs on such an obvious truth and make the bizarre claim that human beings are all about bodies after all, like it or not. And the worst of it is, perhaps in the end we malleable humans will actually fulfil such an abysmal description of ourselves, and we'll call it *truth*.

But the paradox was, the more Thomas enthused about the human spirit over the weekend, the more connected to his body he became. He suddenly noticed the smoothness of a particular shirt against his skin, or found himself standing closer to a friendly face in the queue in the corner shop; he was suddenly aware of the minutiae of the weather: a cool breeze invigorated him, the sun on his face warmed him, whereas previously Thomas had even been unaware of the changing seasons. And on the Sunday, when he made a rare excursion to the Botanical Gardens, he found himself particularly entranced by the patterns he saw amongst the bare branches of fruit trees, and the softness and colour of a rare Alpine moss. Then, on the Monday, he was back in his college rooms, and a supervision with the Noxious Newnham Three, as he thought of them.

Unfortunately for him, the subject of their supervision was to be the second century C.E. Greek novel by Longus, *Daphnis and Chloe*. Personally he didn't like the novel: the story of a simple goatherd and a nubile shepherdess falling in love and never *quite* having sex because no one had told them what to do was rather trite and irritating. In fact, it was even a set text for that summer's exams – he personally had put in a vote for good old-fashioned Thucydides, a magnificent stylist, as he had tried to convince the examiners – but the mood of the times was one of 'discourses', sexual discourses in particular, and the progressives had won the day. That sex should be Samantha's favourite subject also irritated him, because he wanted to bore her into submission with accounts of phalanxes and battle-lines.

So the three assumed their own particular battle-line before him, and Samantha, as usual, was dressed for business: leather trousers and a tiny pink t-shirt.

'You look cold, Samantha,' he said to her, ready for the fray.

'I've always found coldness a mental thing, myself,' she retorted.

'How did you get on with the essay, then? Any joy?' Thomas addressed the three of them.

'I've never heard you use the word "joy" before!' exclaimed Samantha.

Jane and Henrietta shot her a look and a sigh and she momentarily shut up. Henrietta had her essay on her knee, and she said, 'Shall I read it out, Dr Marius?'

'Yes, thank you Henrietta,' said Dr Marius.

Henrietta read out the title: 'Purity and Innocence in the story of Daphnis and Chloe: are they necessary bedfellows?' and then began: 'Very little is known about the author of the book, Longus, except that he lived in the second century C.E.. We have, however, extensive knowledge of the milieu in which he wrote: namely that virginity was highly prized, and, if unmarried, the loss of it meant an end to any marriage prospects. Indeed, a guardian would have the right to sell his 'impure' ward into slavery. We also know that the only sure way for a woman to be treated respectfully by society was that she should be of aristocratic birth. Therefore in Longus' novel, as was *de rigueur* in the New Comedy of the time, it was important that its heroine be proved to be of good birth. This was surprisingly easy, as rich families would regularly expose superfluous daughters so that the family wealth should not be dissipated by paying out large dowries to their future husbands. The baby would be left with trinkets, which, in drama and fiction at least, would be recognized many years later by a highly respectable family only too happy to reclaim their lost daughter. So Chloe is pure on two counts: blood and chastity, as Longus' readers require her to be. But she herself is ignorant of the meaning of either 'good family' or 'chastity', which has the effect of doubling her purity (as her natural character has not been corrupted by knowledge, Garden-of-Eden-style) and also reinforcing the social *mores* of the time – namely, that such a charming and happy story *could not have happened* if Chloe had not been of good birth and had not been a virgin.'

'That's very good, Henrietta, thank you. If you could just stop there a moment,' said Dr Marius. 'Jane, Samantha, would either of you like to comment on what you've heard?'

'It just proves the rich have always been wicked. Just killing your baby like that,' said Jane.

'It was an ancient form of abortion, that's all,' suggested Samantha and in fact, rather kinder. The baby can fight back, well, sort of. Be rescued, anyway.'

'Yes, rescued by a pimp, great life. I'd prefer to have died of exposure myself,' argued Jane.

'Why,' asked Dr Marius, and it was really a question to himself, 'are we beguiled by innocence?'

'Are we?' asked Samantha. 'Speak for yourself. Innocence doesn't move me.'

'Come on, Sam,' said Jane, 'name me a book or a film that's any good which doesn't have an innocent protagonist. If the hero knows everything on day one, there's no movement, no story.'

'Why do we like stories about innocent people becoming less innocent? *Liaisons Dangereuses*: we are appalled by the behaviour of the Marquise de Merteuil and Valmont, yet simultaneously drawn to the story, as though in the end everyone must be corrupted like us. Now wait, I have here the account of how Daphnis loses his virginity…' Henrietta found the appropriate page of her essay. 'Now, the two would-be lovers don't know what to do. They have all these sexual feelings and they don't know what to do with them, so the nymph Lycainon does the handsome Daphnis a favour and seduces him. Longus writes, "She ordered him to sit as near to her as he could and to kiss her with the sort and number of kisses he was accustomed to, and, as he was kissing, to embrace her and to lie on the ground. When he had sat down and kissed her and lain down, she discovered he was ready for action and erect. First, she raised him from this position lying on his side; then she skilfully spread herself underneath; and led him to the road he had long sought. Then she did nothing strange. Nature herself taught what else had to be done."'

'That gets my vote,' said Samantha.

Jane said, apropos of nothing, 'Someone's written on the back of the loo door in our corridor, 'Cancer is nature's way of saying "no".'

'And sex is nature's way of saying "yes",' said Samantha.

'Only if there are babies,' said Henrietta.

'Are you saying,' asked Thomas, 'that if there's no possibility of pregnancy the sex isn't natural?'

'That's exactly what I'm saying,' insisted Henrietta. 'I'm a Catholic, and though I don't agree with the infallibility of the Pope, I happen to think on this point he's right.'

'That is so stupid,' said Samantha.

'At school we were taught that sex had to do with gametes and zygotes and the like, in other words *making babies*. Everything else is about human beings rubbing each other up for pleasure, an entirely different occupation, which has nothing to do with sex at all.'

'What about homosexuals?' asked Samantha, intrigued.

'That's exactly my point.' Henrietta was getting up steam. 'They're just human beings who like rubbing up against people the same sex as they are. And they shouldn't be called 'homosexuals', they should be called something like 'quasi-sexuals', because they behave as though they're having sex, when scientifically speaking, they are absolutely not. Is there a biology text-book in the land which had a picture of two male organs engaging in mutual arousal? Of course not! Homosexuality is about culture, nothing more, nothing less.'

'But they've found a gene,' said Samantha, 'I know they've found a gene!'

'And one day they'll find a gene that'll prove once and for all why some people prefer spinach to asparagus. So what? And perhaps they'll find some people who have memories of being force-fed spinach in their high-chairs. So what? Except they might not like spinach when they grow up. How can we even begin to differentiate between our genetic predispositions and reactions to childhood experiences? And my argument is, so what? Nature, nurture, culture, who cares? I've got a fact for you. Of the eight Ptolemys who ruled Egypt, four married their full sisters.'

'And do you say, "so what?" to that as well?' asked Samantha.

'I've been brought up in the West. I have a natural aversion to incest. But if I had been brought up to imagine one could do no better than sleeping with one's brother... well, who knows? I was brought up a Catholic, and it worked on me. I never rebelled. Perhaps I am just... not rebellious, and would have found my brother perfectly attractive in second century Egypt. Who knows? Who cares?'

'How can you say "Who cares?" when it's all we do care about. Aren't you interested in twin studies and stuff?'

'They're a load of crap. Expose identical twins to two middle class families in the same country and of course they like the same clothes, films etc. But who's done a twin study that leaves one child in Acton and takes the other to some Amazonian tribe? My point is this, nature without nurture doesn't exist for us humans. It's the wrong question.'

'And what is the right question?' asked Jane.

'It's human nature to want to be taught. We have big brains, that's what they're for. And that's the point; Daphnis and Chloe don't even know how to have sex if they're not explicitly taught what to do. Nature gets us nowhere. Nature is a false God.'

'Of course they would know. This is fiction, right? Their bodies would just tell them.'

'You know, I don't think they would,' said Henrietta.

Jane objected. 'What about the bit where Chloe keeps saying she wishes that she were Daphnis's pipe so she could lie in his mouth all day long and be played by his fingers? That's fairly explicit, isn't it?'

'I liked that bit, very sexy,' agreed Samantha.

'That's not nature, it's art, Longus's art. A charming metaphor, to titillate his readers. What we've been reading is second century pornography. And all the rules are in place, the rules of that particular culture at that particular time. If the story were a play rather than a novel, it would be a pantomime, and the audience would be shouting graphic instructions on what the innocent couple should be doing next. It's a knowing, clever piece of literature. So if you ask, Dr Marius, whether purity and innocence are necessary bedfellows, the answer is yes, and Longus knew it, but he never got there, he never persuades us, because he himself was neither.'

Suddenly the three of them looked at Dr Marius, and it was clear that he hadn't been listening to a word. He looked at his watch and said, 'Goodness, is that the time?'

The hour was up. The three looked at each other and, without saying a word, packed up their bags and left him in peace.

Though, of course, peace it wasn't. Thomas was wondering exactly when it was that *eros* had changed its meaning, from passionate and particular love to sexual desire. For Plato had used the word in its former sense, and Longus in its latter. Both, supposedly, reflected social realities, in the same way as 'making love' in the nineteenth century meant something different to 'making love' in the twentieth. And our minds fall in with these different meanings, which determine our ways of thinking, so that those who use the words 'make love' believe that love and sex are necessarily part of the same package. But are they, in truth? What is the reality out there when we take away the words to express it? I desired my wife, I never loved her. I never even knew her, but like a sleepwalker I thought that love must be the name for the feeling, because modern language hints that that's the case. We all live in doublespeak; it's not the case that there are rulers who know the truth and who lie in order to rule. We are all in thrall to a language which does not necessarily reflect what is really out there, and we are obedient to it.

That is why innocence is beguiling. The innocent aren't steeped in hackneyed words and hackneyed thought. For them, everything is fresh and new and possible, before society socializes them and holds them in its vice. That's why I like the boy. That's why I need him. He's still on the outside. In a way, he's like me. A teenager, my soul-mate. It's truly pathetic. But have I ever found a friend at school, or kept one? Or from my undergraduate days? Or from Warwick? Was I even friends with my wife? The truth is, at thirty-five years old, I'm lonely. There is no one in whom I can confide, not a soul. I've wasted every second of this life. I used to think I was so clever, but the last laugh is on me.

§

It wasn't true that Thomas Marius didn't have friends; he was both esteemed and liked by several of the Fellows in Corpus, and they'd noticed he'd been 'out of sorts' for some weeks. And in fact it was the Master, of all people, a benign and gentle man who treated his Fellows as an extended family, who suggested to the Chaplain and reader in Theology, the Reverend Dr. Justin Phipps, that he approach Dr Marius and discover why he seemed so 'heavy laden'.

The Reverend Phipps was a gentle, wise and approachable man, a clergyman of the old school who wore both his weight (substantial) and his dog collar with pride, and he dutifully contrived to be sitting next to Thomas the following evening at High Table. Seventy undergraduates dressed in black scholars' gowns stood to attention while a Latin *benedictio* was said; seventeen portraits of previous masters gazed down upon them from oak-panelled walls. The atmosphere was solemn, even devout, but at High Table at least, broken by the conversation.

'Aren't you fed up,' asked a Dr Peter Campbell, specialist in medieval history and plainsong, 'with the M11?' Dr Campbell was sitting to the other side of Dr Marius, and had been sitting in traffic jams all day. 'It claims it takes you to London but it leaves you in a backwater in God knows where, is it Walthamstow?'

Thomas looked up from his quail stuffed with apricot and said, 'I can't say I get up to London much.'

'"Get up" or "go down", why is it that we never know which to say?'

'I'm sorry?' Thomas asked his neighbour, politely.

But though Thomas had little interest in the matter, a sociology don sitting opposite overheard Dr Peter Campbell and had sat up to attention.

'Are you going to suggest, Peter, there is a right answer? Then I refute you.'

'Of course there is a right answer.'

'And would the upstanding people of Cambridge be aware of this right answer, and put it to good use?'

'That's irrelevant,' insisted Dr Campbell. 'Ignorance is no excuse.'

'Sometimes,' dared the sociology don, 'I use the one phrase, and sometimes the other.'

Dr Campbell rose to the bait; the don might have hit him for how shocked he looked. 'So how do you determine which one to use, if you don't know the truth of the matter?'

'It's a question of mood,' continued the sociology don. 'There's more power behind the phrase, "go down". If I'm feeling *more* than London, if I'm feeling *London needs me*, i.e. if I've been invited to speak at some function or other, or as an adviser on some inner city problem, then in those circumstances I tend to say, "I'm *going down* to London". If, on the other hand, the occasion is more whimsical, when London remains the big city and I, merely the small visitor, I might say – *might*, mind you, there's no rule I follow – I might say "get up" or "go up" or even simply "go".'

Dr Campbell was too dumbfounded to reply, and muttered to himself, 'The arrogance of it!'

But a Dr Gareth Pettigrew, who, as Director of Studies in Modern Languages, was working on a linguistic history of the romance languages, entered the fray at full throttle. 'Guy!' he exclaimed, 'How can you use language so disrespectfully? The only phrasal verb which is grammatically correct in this instance is "to go up". There are precisely three towns in England to which one "goes up", Oxford, Cambridge and London, regardless of one's original geographical point of departure.' Dr Pettigrew's expression said, 'Take that!'; Dr Campbell, who was sitting next to him, nodded happily.

'Does a rule continue to be a rule when so few people know it?' asked Guy. 'Language is use, and all that. Wittgenstein was right.'

'Ah, Wittgenstein,' said another Fellow, further up the table, and the conversation shifted. Thomas rose to none of it, but sighed over the little bones that were congregating on the side of his plate.

'How did you find the quail?' asked the good, gentle chaplain of his neighbour.

'Was it quail?' asked Thomas, ingenuously, suddenly remembering the stoical robin who lived in the poplar tree outside his house.

'The meat was a bit tough, you're right, but a good wine, don't you think? '93 was a good year for Chablis.' The Reverend Dr Justin Phipps put on his glasses to survey the wine label. 'I don't think I know that particular vineyard. Good wine, though.'

'Yes, it is good,' said Thomas, absent-mindedly.

'So how's the term been going so far? How's the lecture course?' inquired Dr Phipps, kindly.

'I'm not giving a lecture course,' said Thomas.

'It's been abysmal weather, hasn't it? Do you think that's why there are now only six undergraduates in the whole of Cambridge who wish to learn about the first hundred years of Christianity? I began the course with a healthy twenty-five, but I've convinced myself that it's the rain and cold that's been keeping them from pounding on the doors.' It was evident from Dr Phipps' drawn eyebrows that he hadn't quite convinced himself.

'You're probably right,' said Thomas diplomatically.

Two slim, pretty Brazilian girls in pencil black skirts and white blouses took their plates away and smiled deferentially. Some moments later Thomas and Justin Phipps were confronted by bowls of crème brulée. Justin visibly relaxed. 'Ah, my favourite!' he exclaimed happily.

'I've never been much of a pudding man, myself,' said Thomas, 'Here, the portions are terribly small, you have mine.'

'No, no! I resist! Quite delicious, but too many calories!' There was a pause, while Thomas tapped the caramel crust with his spoon, and Justin savoured every spoonful as though it were the most delectable pleasure he knew.

'So, Thomas, what is the equivalent of a good pudding to you?'

'I'm sorry?'

'What earthly pleasure do you enjoy?'

'What are you getting at?' asked Thomas, for the question seemed to require the answer 'sex' and yet he knew the chaplain well enough to know this wasn't the answer he wanted.

'Thomas,' sighed Justin, 'We all need earthly pleasures, you know.'

Thomas looked astonished; and in exasperation at his lack of progress, Justin suddenly blurted out, 'I notice you seem to be a little under the weather, recently, Thomas, not your usual, cheery self…'

'Have I really ever seemed cheery to you, Justin? So odd, I've never thought of myself as cheery.'

'Perhaps "cheery" is the wrong word. What I mean is,' said Justin, surprised at feeling his cheeks burn, 'you seem a little, how should I say, burdened by something. You know, I'm a good listener. If you ever feel you need to get something off your chest…'

'It's a strange expression, isn't it, "getting something off your chest."'

'I think it's quite an accurate one, don't you?'

'There's a good line in Virgil,' said Thomas, '*Mitte hanc de pectore curam*, literally, "Send this care from your chest". In your experience, Justin, as the college Chaplain and counsellor, do the cares of the soul gather in the chest or the forehead?'

'I believe that the cares of the soul lie very much in the chest. Virgil is right, and God can meet those cares. But the cares of the body, an anxiety about an illness, for example, or even financial concerns, these seem to lie in the forehead. It's strange, but of course in my profession, and particularly when I was a young curate at St Pauls', I was often called out to see to the needs of the ill and the dying, and while it was still possible to survive, all that person's energies were centred on "Who shall I see? Where shall I go? Who will know the right medicine?" God never had a look in. But as the illness progressed, yes, a few would be angry, very angry… But most of us, I assure you, become strangely calm, their cares desert their minds and enter their hearts, and the heart is the ante-room to God, and the heart's prayer is the truer and is always heard.'

'It must be wonderful to have faith,' sighed Thomas.

'I think our hearts always have faith, even if our minds don't know it.'

'And our bodies?'

'Our bodies hold us altogether. Do you know the wonderful definition of "life" in Samuel Johnson's original dictionary? "The temporary, mutual co-operation between body and soul." That's rather wonderful, don't you think? And also true.'

'Dualists like you are rare, nowadays.'

'Don't think that dualists devalue the body. The body is a miracle. Even Augustine, whose body was always getting the better of him – "make me good, Lord, but not yet" – concedes the body is a miracle, as indeed are all created things. They are created by God, hence their beauty…'

'You know, Justin, I think you can help me.' Thomas suddenly looked up so eagerly that Justin was quite ready for the confession he'd been hoping for.

'Anything! I'll do anything I can!'

'You would, of course, be acquainted with Augustinian and medieval Latin?' Thomas' excitement was in perfect synchronicity with Justin's disappointment.

'"Acquainted" is the right word, I'm afraid, I'm no Latinist.'

'But you know the works of Augustine in English? You know them well?'

'Fire me a question,' said Justin, anxiously.

'I need to know if there's any virtue in loving beauty.'

Justin laughed in relief, and suddenly understood all. The man was in love. 'Then you must borrow my *Confessions*', he said. 'Come to my rooms after dinner.'

As they walked towards Old Court in the dark, Justin was smiling to himself, hoping and expecting to put his entire range of pastoral skills to good use. He felt mellow, generous and thoroughly good-natured. On reaching his rooms, he offered Thomas a fine malt whisky. Thomas declined, but Justin helped himself, and began to prod the coals in his grate and bring them back to life.

'Sit down, Thomas,' he said. 'Make yourself warm.'

But Thomas said, 'No, thank you', and continued to stand awkwardly by the door.

For a moment Justin forgot why he was there, but then he said, 'Ah yes, of course, *The Confessions*!' He went over to his bookshelves and murmured something about a good recent translation.

'Translation? Oh no, I need the Latin,' insisted Thomas.

'How stupid of me, how very stupid of me...' Justin's voice petered out into a sliver of non-comprehension.

He found a text from 1927 and surreptitiously wiped away a layer of dust with his handkerchief. 'Here,' he said, simply. 'Keep it as long as you like.'

'Thanks, Justin,' said Thomas, 'This is just what I need at the moment,' and he took the large burgundy volume and held it in both hands like a prize.

'Good luck with it,' laughed Justin, uneasily, as he held the door open for him.

What Thomas was wanting was permission, and that night Augustine gave it to him. He read the Latin hungrily:

Hoc est quod amo, cum deum meum amo.

Et quid est hoc? Interrogavi terram, et dicit, 'non sum'; et quaecumque in eadem sunt, idem confessa sunt. Interrogavi mare et abyssos et reptilia animarum vivarum, et responderunt: 'non sumus deus tuus; quaere super nos.' Interrogavi auras flabiles, et inquit universus aer cum incolis suis: 'fallitur Anaximenes: non sum deus.' Interrogavi caelum, solem, lunam, stellas: necque non sumus deus, quem quaeris,' inquiunt. Et dixi omnibus, quae circumstant fores carnis meae: 'dicite mihi de deo meo, quod vos non estis, dicite mihi de illo aliquid.' et exclamaverurnt voce magna: 'ipse fecit nos.' Interrogatio mea intentio mea et responsio eorum species eorum.

Which, for those less literate amongst us means:

This is what I love, when I love my God.

And what is this? I asked the earth, and it answered: 'It is not I.' Whatever things are in it uttered the same confession. I asked the sea, the depths, the creeping things among living animals, and they replied: 'We are not thy God; look above us.' I asked the airy breezes, and the whole atmosphere with its inhabitants said, 'Anaximenes is mistaken; I am not God.' I asked the sky, the sun, the moon, the stars: 'Nor are we the God whom you seek,' they said. And I said to all these things which surround the entryways to my flesh: 'Tell me about my God, since you are not He; tell me something about him.' With a loud voice, they cried out: 'He made us.' My interrogation was my looking upon them, and their reply was their beauty.

'In every looking, there is a seeking. And Josiah, you answer me, your beauty answers me. Who made you? For the world didn't. The pure are made by God and left naked. That is why I love you.'

Thomas went back to the *Symposium* that night: 'Love, more than anything (more than family, or position, or wealth) implants in men the thing which must be their guide if they are to live a good life. And what is that? It is a horror of what is degrading, and a passionate desire of what is good.'

That's the answer, thought Thomas, the Greeks believed that to love beauty is to love goodness. Nowadays, we love neither; we love sex. There are no ideals anymore; nothing to transcend our appetites. But I'll prove to Josiah that I can love well, I know I can do that.

That night he dreamt of Hans. They were on a bobsleigh together, shooting down icy channels; his arms were hugging Hans' waist, finding their natural home under his jumper: the pleasure of warm skin in a cold place.

Chapter Nine

JOSIAH ARRIVED FIVE MINUTES EARLY. Five minutes before that, Thomas was wondering whether the honourable thing to do was to renege on his promise to teach the boy Latin at all; but luckily that was after he'd laid out a few text books and made a fire, which he was stoking when the doorbell went. He jumped up and looked in the mirror; his face did not belie his mood – skin wan, but clear; eyes bright, but not manically so – and that fact alone gave him the strength to go downstairs and answer the door.

'Josiah, you're keen!' exclaimed Thomas, making a show of looking at his watch.

'Well, I am,' said Josiah, unapologetically. '*Iterum nos videmus*' – is that right?'

'*Ita vero, puer. Sed ubi didicisti illud?*'

'I'm sorry?'

'Where did you learn that? I'm impressed.'

'*Ex bibliotheca librum cepi* – is that right?' Josiah was still standing on the doorstep, grinning happily, wearing a striped jumper two sizes two big for him.

'Here is an angel dropping by,' thought Thomas, 'here is fresh water from a clear spring!' But he said, rather more sensibly, 'Come on upstairs, Josiah. It's warmer there.'

So the two of them sat on armchairs by the fire, every bit as comfortably as Thomas had imagined they might, and perused each others' textbooks like old hands.

'The library was quite good,' explained Josiah, 'despite not letting me take the dictionary away. They had about four different courses and I chose the Oxford one for the pictures, and you see, I want to be able to *speak* Latin.'

'That's a rare ambition, Josiah, and can I ask you why?'

'My mother used to say to me, "When you grow up, people will try and persuade you that Latin is dead. But Latin is the most living language there is."'

'She's a wise woman, she's right.'

'So can you tell me *why* she's right?' asked Josiah, looking up at Thomas expectantly.

'You really want to learn Latin, don't you?' There was something about Josiah's manner which made Thomas feel he was shielding himself against sunlight.

'Apart from… apart from seeing my parents again I've never wanted anything more.' Josiah looked hard at Thomas, in a manner which forbade him to look away.

'I'm not sure where to begin,' muttered Thomas. He didn't want the boy to have a dead mother. He needed him to have brothers and sisters and play football on Saturdays.

'But begin, Mr Marius, begin, begin, begin!' Josiah was sitting on the edge of his chair, more childlike than ever.

'And you must begin by calling me "Thomas".'

'Why aren't you called "Tom"?'

'Because no one's ever called me "Tom".'

'Then I shall be the first, Tom. And you can call me "Jo". Just my Dad calls me "Jo". I don't let anyone else.'

'I'm flattered, Jo – without an "e"?'

'Yes.' Just J O,' Josiah said slowly. He looked very solemn indeed.

Thomas shifted in his chair, and anxiously shuffled the textbooks around on the table between them. 'I don't see why we can't follow the Oxford course,' he said.

'You never answered my question,' said Josiah.

'Which was?'

'Why is Latin the most living language there is?'

'I think I can answer you that,' said Thomas, his own enthusiasm suddenly rising up to meet Josiah's. 'Because Latin is made in such a way that each word is pregnant with meaning. In other languages a word takes you from A to B with barely a detour – but in Latin, how shall I explain this? Take the gerund, or even better, the gerundive. The gerundive is a verbal adjective which contains within it a sense of 'ought', a sense of moral duty. Now in philosophy no one knows how to get from *is* to *ought*; it's hard to find the bridge which leads us to universal principles. But in Latin the sense of *ought* is built into the word. The girl's name *Amanda*, for example, means *woman to be loved*, there's no two ways about it, there's no dilemma, the *ought* is an *is*. You are a *puer docendus*, a boy who ought to be taught, there are things which ought to be done, *agenda*, that ought to be said, *loquenda*.'

'Why is there no *Amandus* then? Do you think than men need to be loved less than women do?'

'I think we men need to be loved, don't we?'

O, but the question was far too serious! Whether it was true or not was irrelevant.

'Well, if I ever have a son I shall call him *Amandus*, the boy who ought to be loved! Have you got a son? Or a daughter?'

'No!' said Thomas, and he tried to add to that 'no', to soften it, but couldn't think how he might.

'Have you ever wanted to have children?' continued Josiah, full steam ahead.

'I can't say I've ever thought about it.' Thomas wanted to say that he'd never been married, but that, of course, wasn't true.

'If you were to think about it now, what would you say?'

'I think I would say I wasn't ready to have children. What about your father? Is he a good father to you? Was he ready to have children, do you think?' An old tactic, turning the question on the questioner. Was that fair on a boy so young?

But Josiah seemed unperturbed. 'Yes, he was. He was a very good father.' Josiah suddenly became very serious and thought hard. 'He *is* a very good father. Of course, since my mother's death, it's been quite difficult.'

'That was how many years ago?'

'Seven and a half,' said Josiah.

'Does he work?'

'He retired early. He used to be a gardener at one of the Cambridge colleges. I can't remember which one.'

'And is he pleased you're learning Latin? He knows you're here now?'

'Yes, of course he does,' said Josiah, meeting Thomas' eye and looking deadly earnest.

'Do you have brothers and sisters?'

'No.'

'Do you like football?'

Josiah shook his head.

'I see,' said Thomas, and sank back into his chair.

'So are we going to begin the lesson?' asked Josiah.

'Of course we are, Jo.'

The hour and a half of industry which followed – armchairs locked together now to share the textbook – were all that either could have hoped for; Josiah hungrily sped through the chapters, his inexhaustible eagerness to learn matched only by Thomas' eagerness to teach him. Jo's farewell; their determination to continue same time next week, perhaps for longer, perhaps they should make a day of it if Jo's father had no objections: their arrangements were made with such ease and straightforwardness that the moment the door was closed behind his young pupil, Thomas' anxieties fell away and he knew that everything that had happened and would happen between them was an unconditional good. And such was his confidence, that he went straight back to his study and found a book that he had last read when writing his PhD on Marcus Aurelius: namely the correspondence between him and his teacher Fronto, written while he 'burned with love' for his teacher and his teacher 'burned with love for him.' Then he blew away the dust and dared open it; only to remember that Fronto was even willing to give up his consulship in order to put his arms around the young Marcus once more. He put the book back, and sighed deeply.

Meanwhile, such was Josiah's exuberance that day that he found his way to Corpus. He went into the Porter's Lodge and told the amiable, elderly porter that he was meeting his uncle for lunch that day, and where were Thomas Marius' rooms, please?

'He never told us he had a nephew,' said the porter.

'Oh, lots of people have nephews,' said Josiah enthusiastically, and he noticed that the porter had a toupee and wondered why someone so old and so kind could be bothered with covering his baldness. Perhaps it was the cold. Do bald people complain about the cold ever?

'And your name is?' asked the porter.

'My name is Josiah Nelson. My father is married to his sister.'

'I didn't know Dr Marius had a sister,' muttered the porter.

'Well, why should you know it? Lots of people have sisters.'

'So they do, sir.'

'So could you direct me to his rooms, please?'

'He never comes in on a Saturday,' said the porter.

'But he's expecting me,' said Josiah.

'I'll ring him to make sure he's in,' insisted the dutiful porter

'Don't worry yourself! Don't worry yourself!' said the lad, shrugging, hands under his jumper and walking backwards.

Josiah ran through the courts and skipped over the gardens, he put his head through the chapel doors and read the names painted at the bottom of every staircase. At last he found the name of his teacher, and slowly he licked the tip of his finger and wiped the dust off DR T E MARIUS. Upstairs he went to the first floor and tried the door which was, of course, locked. Unperturbed, he peered through the keyhole, and saw shelves of books and a mantelpiece with three or four chairs in front of it (just like his study at home, he thought, proudly) and the edge of a desk in front of an enormous window with leaded glass which was probably hundreds of years old. Josiah was so ludicrously happy that when he noticed the porter on the warpath he could barely be bothered to hide from him. But hide he did, in a bathroom, in a broom cupboard, and finally, just as he was making a dash for the outside world, he found himself in the college library.

Josiah stopped running after that. He stopped noticing the way people were looking at him, or even feeling out of place. Slowly he ran his fingers along the spines of the books, the leather and the cloth, the soft paperbacks in their cellophane covers; he didn't register their titles or their authors, only the fact that men had thought so hard about things that mattered so much to them, and that in this place they were allowed to exist, all hugger-mugger, together. And if such private lives, hidden from all the world, were allowed a mere inch in such a place as this, didn't it make that life immediately worth living?

In the end Josiah chose a book about Egyptian mummies. He chose it because he liked the white leather binding and the embossed gold lettering. He like the fact it was old and mysterious, and when he opened it on an old oak table by the window, he was smiled at by the lovely girl who was sitting opposite him. The pages were thick and creamy, the typescript clear and dark; and from time to time there were black and white photographs of pyramids, mummies, camels, goblets, jewellery and archaeologists wearing moustaches and hard white hats. The lovely girl had long silky brown hair, and Josiah quite thought he loved her, too; in fact, the love within him was so strong he knew that anything falling in its beam would be swept up in it. And then it occurred to him that when he had first learnt about the Egyptians, at the age of eight or so, the teacher took it for granted that the Egyptians had been wrong to embalm their dead, and that their rituals were an elaborate waste of time: fun to learn about, but fundamentally wrong. But what if, at the very moment of death, when you feel the body slip away, you have a craving to return to it? Perhaps it's the first time you really understand the importance of what you are about to lose. What if the Egyptians were right? Perhaps right now in heaven Pharaohs are sitting in state, bodies, robes and all, with buckets of gems at their side, mocking those simple spirits who flit about weightlessly because they had no faith in life after death.

But then Josiah's friend – yes, surely she counted as a friend by now, for had they not been in Egypt together? Had she not been there at his side in the heat of the desert? – got up to leave, and a man in a leather jacket had swooped in on her with a proprietorial arm around her waist, and the two of them had walked out of the library together. Not even a wave! Dejected, Josiah put the book back and slowly wended his way back to *The Hollies*, the place he called home.

♣

Josiah had a new key-worker called Angela Day who was waiting for him. In fact, he'd had seven 'key-workers' since Kerry had left to live with her boyfriend in Wales, all of whom had had cosy chats with him about their 'special relationship' with him, but none of these special relationships had ever come to much. At thirty, Angela was rather old for a residential social worker, and rather more sensible. She was short, stocky and committed, a real rock, and quite as unimaginative as a rock. So when Josiah was absent at lunchtime and hadn't signed himself out, and what with a stressful morning trying to organize several of the older children into 'painting teams' in the hope that they might 'pull together' to decorate their home, she was understandably angry with him and stood in his way at the bottom of the stairs.

'Not so fast, young man,' she said.

'Hi,' said Josiah.

'Well?'

'Well, what?'

'Have you forgotten what day it is today?'

'The 21st February,' said Josiah, innocently.

'Where have you been, Josiah?'

'Nowhere.'

'Have you eaten?'

Josiah shrugged.

'Please don't look so impertinent. It's not like you.'

'What is like me, then?'

'Eat something and get some overalls on. You knew today was the day.'

'The place doesn't need painting.'

'You just come with me,' Angela insisted, and took him by the arm into the dining-room. 'Doesn't this look so much better? So much brighter? Admit they've done a good job!'

But Josiah just asked where the curtains were, and one of the 'painting teams' walked up to them and told them just what they thought of the matter. 'It fucking took us three hours and we weren't paid a fucking penny for it. It's fucking exploitation. And where were you, mate?'

Josiah's old bullies had long gone, but this new batch stared at him menacingly, like they might just see to him later. But nowadays menace was water off a duck's back; he was nearly fifteen and he didn't give a damn. No one could touch him, no one in this place, anyway.

That evening, though, he went up to Angela and apologized.

He explained there was an old lady he'd met who lived just opposite the school, and he'd been helping her clean up her kitchen and move some furniture around. Angela's face softened immediately, for though Josiah was by now a consummate liar the expression on his face rang true and she believed him.

'Oh Josiah!' Angela sighed happily. 'You're a good boy, you really are!'

Angela gave him an affectionate pat on the shoulder, which Josiah received with good grace.

He looked up at her winsomely and said, 'There's a bit of paint left over. You know what would really thrill her? If I gave her kitchen a whitewash in the morning. Can I have your permission to do that, Angela?'

♣

Josiah was standing outside Thomas' door at eight o'clock the following morning. As he'd been awake since four, planning his assault, the borrowed overalls, tin of Dulux paint and a couple of brushes waiting expectantly in his rucksack at the bottom of his bed, his setting out at seven forty-five seemed positively restrained. He even remembered to sign himself out in the book this time, though he paused under the column which asked him for a destination address/phone number, and wrote down the number of the house next door, where a nice old lady, he smiled to himself, happened to live.

But at eight o'clock that morning Thomas was not expecting him; in fact, just as Josiah was waking at four and did not know what to do with himself, Thomas was finally falling asleep, after a night of anguish, yearning and guilt, a diet, known, I fear, by paedophiles throughout the land. And the man who actually opened the door to Josiah was not a sympathetic one, Greg the lodger no less, who was unhappily interrupted mid-yoghurt.

'Hello,' he said, aggressively looking him up and down, 'What do you want?' Greg was not a man to mince his words.

'I've come to see Dr Thomas Marius,' explained Josiah.

'And you are?'

'I'm his nephew.'

'I never knew he had a nephew,' said Greg, suspiciously.

'If that fact interests you in any way, you might want to know he has three nephews, of which I am one, and two nieces, and three living grand-parents. And, if you're interested in Thomas' family connections, my great uncle Patrick died last year, but the others are in excellent health.'

'A family of great longevity,' remarked Greg, without budging.

'Ah, I see you have your eye on my rucksack. Would you like to take a look inside it? No bomb, just a tin of white paint.'

'Come into the kitchen, then. He's asleep,' said Greg grumpily, unwilling to be kept from his breakfast a moment longer.

'Ah, so they're your yoghurts!' said Josiah, as he sat down beside him to watch.

'So, you've had breakfast here before, then?' asked Greg, down to his last spoonful now, and all ears.

'I might have, what's it to you?'

Greg shrugged malevolently. 'It's none of my business.'

'No it isn't,' said Josiah, and he got up and walked upstairs.

The orange pekoe walls disturbed him, and he instinctively went back to the hall to fetch his rucksack. Armed thus, he felt braver. He found the bathroom, and then Greg's room, which was dirty and gloomy with deep purple walls and a large unmade bed which took up two thirds of it. The third door, then, would be Tom's. He looked at his watch, eight fifteen. That wasn't so early, he decided, even on a Sunday.

Josiah crept in quietly. Josiah had never been into somebody else's bedroom, and he saw immediately it was an intimate thing. Tom's bed was no bigger than his own, though he took up a greater proportion of it. He was so fast asleep that his first thought was to go back to *The Hollies* and come back later, but he couldn't resist walking a few paces closer to him. The window was wide open, though it was only February, and the room was cold; but the closer he got to Thomas's bed the warmer he became. Thomas had a wardrobe in his room, old and stark and brown, and Josiah smiled when he realised Thomas' chest of drawers was rather like his own, and the top drawer was open and filled with socks and old-fashioned y-front pants, which he'd always imagined was the prerogative of the over-sixties.

His eyes were acclimatizing now to the dim light, and Josiah thought it would be interesting to kneel beside him and look very hard into his face. How finely made he was, he decided, like an aristocrat: a delicate nose and chin, unshaven but prettily shaped, though his dark hair seemed fraught and wild this morning, and Josiah could tell from the way his eyes were moving under his lids that he was still dreaming. He would have given anything to be sharing his dream right now and seeing what he was seeing. Then he held his hand an inch or two over Thomas's mouth, the lines of which could have been drawn, so well made it was, and his breath felt humid and excited him. So then Josiah went further still, and leaned right over Thomas' face so that his mouth was hovering over Thomas', and he took Thomas' breath and breathed it into his lungs, and it felt good and precious, as he tried to get the rhythm of it. And once he had mastered this, and felt its eroticism, he breathed his own breath into Thomas and willed, 'Now, dream of me!'

Still Thomas didn't wake up, but suddenly he noticed that his mentor had gone to sleep with a book in his hand, which was now wedged against the wall. Well then, he thought, here was another way of entering Thomas' head, perhaps this is what he was dreaming of after all. He managed to extract the book without waking him and sat down with it in the recess of the window so that he could see what it was about.

The book itself was a handsome one, he thought; it smelt good and was bound in dark blue leather. Its title was *Symposium* which meant nothing to Josiah. The introduction set out its theme, namely that a number of speakers were asked to make a speech in praise of Eros, or erotic love, and when he read that Josiah turned towards the sleeping Tom and wondered at him reading it. The dialogue itself, of course, was written in Greek, and he couldn't understand a word; but for twenty minutes at least Josiah's imagination enjoyed what his linguistic skills could not.

At last, Josiah was woken from his pleasant reverie by some strange noise of Thomas who had spotted him there. Josiah leapt up, book in hand, full of apology and explanation, and said he'd brought some paint with him to whitewash his walls, for hadn't Tom said he didn't like the orange and the green? Hadn't he said that?

Thomas lay very still on his bed and said quietly, 'Josiah, you can't do this, you know.'

Josiah ignored him and went on, 'I was reading your book. Who was Plato?'

'Josiah, you need to go home. I'll see you next Saturday as we planned. You can't do this.'

Josiah then knelt at Thomas's bed, so their faces were less than a foot apart. He said, 'I am so, so sorry.'

Thomas looked up at the ceiling. He said coldly, 'Go home, Josiah.' And then he waited, as though frozen, while he listened to Josiah's tentative steps on the stairs, and the opening and closing of the front door. 'The fool!' he said out loud.

The following day, Thomas said 'The fool!' a second time, as he read a note in his locker left by the elderly but good-natured porter Mr Ron Herrod (who had known Thomas even as an undergraduate) saying that a lad who claimed to be his nephew had been looking for him that Saturday lunchtime. But if Thomas had been angry with him on both counts, the discovery of the tin of paint and two paint-brushes at the end of his bed that evening rather moved him, and he feared he had been too stern with the boy. By the Friday evening he had so softened that he had bought him a *pain au chocolat* as a way of making it up to him. What's more, with a clearer conscience than at any time since he had first set eyes on the boy, he slept well, and happily welcomed him into his house at nine o'clock exactly, ready to resume their Latin lessons.

Josiah's restless energy had been used to master the whole of the first book of the Oxford Latin Course on his own. Thomas remarked on his prodigious memory and solid grasp of grammar. Then after about an hour they paused, and Thomas produced his *pain au chocolat* and apologized for being quite so angry with him. But then he said, 'Josiah, why did you visit my college behind my back?'

Josiah hung his head and said simply, 'I wanted to know where you worked.'

'Why didn't you ask me? I could've taken you round. I would have shown you my rooms, the chapel, the library. It's a strange thing to do to go on your own.'

'I went to the library. I read a book about Egyptian Mummies.'

'But why, Josiah?'

'I wanted to know what it was like to be you.'

'Then ask me. Ask me anything you like.'

'What goes on in your head day after day? Are your thoughts now different to the ones you had as a boy? Or are they more or less the same, just a bit more complicated?'

'Sometimes I think boys see more clearly. When you're young you can see the road ahead. Now I'm distracted by the signs on the left and right. I want to do the right thing. But then I ask myself, who put the signs there, God or Man?'

'Why does it matter to do the right thing?'

'Do you ever play chess with your Dad, or some other game?'

'Not really.'

'Then with friends at school?'

'I know what it means to play a game, if that's what you're getting at.'

'A game has rules, and someone made up those rules, and the players have to obey them in order for the game to be interesting, to have meaning. Because, if you continually broke the rules, the game would be both boring and meaningless.'

'That's true,' said Josiah.

'But you'll never find the name of the writer of the rules on the box. The game is so presented as to suggest that the rules are out there in the universe, and are here being divulged to the lucky few who bought the game in the first place. It's the same in real life. When you tell a child not to lie, it *feels* just like you're divulging a universal truth to the new generation. But what if we knew the name of the first man who said, 'I've got a good idea. In this game of life, let's forbid lying. Then we won't have to waste money in the law-courts, and everyone will know where they stand. It might even make people happier, who knows?''

'I think that sometimes lying might be a good thing,'

'That's a very modern attitude you have, Josiah, no absolutes for you. But what would you think of the new rule, "Sometimes lie, sometimes don't. Do as you see fit." And let's imagine that rule was written in 1974, for the latest version of this game of life, and it was written by the great Joe Bloggs, who now has a statue in Trafalgar Square. And great treatises have been written about his rule, and a few have even dared suggest that when Joe Bloggs suggests that we are to do as we see fit, he is actually saying, "do what you recognize to be right, over and above lying" – in other words, Joe Bloggs is an even greater absolutist than the writer of the Ten Commandments. But other commentators might place *feeling* in first place, and feeling can't be pinned down at all. Tell me, Josiah, when you tell the truth are you obedient to the ideas of a man, if there were one, who commanded everyone to tell the truth, or are you obedient to something within you or without you which seems to be transcendent?'

'How do you know that I tell the truth?'

'Do you?'

'Sort of.'

'You have an honest face, Jo, and that's an honest reply.'

But Josiah turned away his honest face and changed the subject. He asked Thomas, 'Why is your college called Corpus? "Body College." That just seems so weird.'

'It doesn't quite have the *gravitas* of the Latin, does it?' Thomas laughed.

'It's full name is "Corpus Christi", though "Body of Christ College" doesn't sound much better.'

'What does "gravitas" mean?' asked Josiah.

'It means "weight" or "seriousness" or a mixture of both, really.'

'Do you think bodies are important? I mean, they must be, if Christ had one, and if a Cambridge college is named after his body. Are there any colleges which refer to Christ's spirit?'

'You mean, such as *"Anima Christi"* or *"Spiritus Christi"*? I'm not much of a theologican, but the *Spiritus Sanctus* seems to have hogged the *anima* and left Christ with a mere body.'

'Why do you call the body "mere", Tom? Perhaps that's all there is, in the end, our bodies.'

'Do you think you've got a soul, Jo?'

'I don't know. But I do know I've got a body.'

'Have you ever heard of Descartes?'

'No. Perhaps.'

'Descartes would have put it the other way round. He would have said, you might be experiencing the illusion that you have a body. But the important thing is you are the subject of that experience. *Cogito ergo sum.*'

'"I think, therefore I am,"' smiled Josiah happily. 'But I, Tom, I *know* I have a body. I don't care what Descartes or anyone else says. Do you feel the same about your body?'

'Well, obviously I hope I have a body,' said Thomas, tentatively.

'Ah!' exclaimed Josiah. 'You *hope* you have a body! Does that mean you like having one?'

'That's an interesting question, Jo. I don't really know how to answer it. Sometimes I forget I have one altogether, and quite often that suits me. I don't often gets aches and pains. I'm not often ill. That means I don't have to think about having a body.'

'But what about the good things about having one? Here, give me your arm, Tom.' (I'm afraid Thomas kept his arm very close to his side, and his one sensation was one of the stiffening of it.) 'All right, I'll show you what I do to myself, when there's a great racket and commotion outside my bedroom door, and I can't sleep at night, and I need my body to be mine again, far from these… these invaders. I pull up the sleeve of my pyjamas, and I run my finger between the crook of my arm and my wrist, very lightly so that it half tickles. And somehow, because then I remember I have a boundary which they will never infiltrate, I feel better and stronger.'

'Who are these invaders, Jo? Do they exist, or just in your head?'

Then Josiah remembered one lie, at least, and promptly added another to it. 'They exist, all right. We live next to a pub, you see, and at closing time the noise can be awful, right outside my window.' And then, seeing that Thomas wasn't quite persuaded, he continued apace to distract him. 'But worse than that, even, is when the boundary of your body separates you from others, when you wish to be pressed upon so heavily that you're breathless.'

Thomas paused and said, 'I don't understand what you're saying.'

'I was thinking the other day, and perhaps this is the kind of thought you used to have,' began Josiah. 'I was thinking that it was a very good thing to have a body, because bodies don't lie. And I was thinking that bodies that live side by side aren't any good at all, because that's not the point of them. They ought to be pressing against each other. Otherwise we might just as well be ideas or something. We might just as well not exist at all. Do you see what it is I'm trying to say?'

'Well, yes, I do,' said Thomas, co-operatively. 'So tell me, what's the name of the pub you live next to?'

'I like having a *corpus*, Tom, it sounds substantial.'

'Does your father ever drink there?'

'No, he doesn't. The other day, while I was in the library, I looked up the word for "pressing" and found "*insisto*", and I thought, yes, that's what I have, I have a *corpus insistens*, a pressing-upon body, and I quite liked that.

'Good, Josiah, amusing.'

'But then I thought, "No, that's not quite right. I think what I really have is a *corpus insistendum,* a body which ought to be pressed upon." What kind of body do you have, Tom?'

'What is it that you're asking me, exactly?'

'I'm asking a question about boundaries and how we break through them. Boundaries are interesting, aren't they?'

Thomas sat forward in his chair and asked, 'Are they there to contain you or to tempt you?'

Josiah said passionately, 'Nothing, nothing, will ever contain me.'

'That is a dangerous thing to say.'

'I am dangerous,' said Josiah, more to himself than to Tom.

Thomas already knew that. He made some excuse and told Josiah he'd better be going; but when Josiah's eyes had looked up at him so accusingly on his doorstep, when his whole demeanour seemed crushed, Thomas relented and kissed him tenderly on his forehead.

'Next week, we'll whitewash those walls,' he promised.

Chapter Ten

IF EVER THOMAS HAD EVER THOUGHT JOSIAH a fool for taking himself off to Corpus, by the end of February the idea rather moved him. In fact, he even sought out the porter who had left the note – Mr Herrod was a reliable, kind man – and asked about what the boy had said to him and where he had gone; he even dared to ask what kind of mood he was in. The truth is, by now he was interested in retracing Josiah's footprints: for if Josiah had pleaded that he wanted to see the world through Thomas' eyes, Thomas was keener than ever to see the world through Josiah's.

Allowing himself to indulge his love – for by now, that's what Thomas had decided the feeling was, for better or worse – made him happier and more even-tempered. He was even kindly disposed towards Samantha, who seemed more serious nowadays, and was producing good work, at last. She was thoughtful, sad. He preferred her sad. In fact, he even felt sympathetic towards her and some-where, somewhere he understood her wistfulness. For if to be wistful is to look back with sadness at something which might have been, then he too had been in that place all too recently. The difference was, that right now he was optimistic. For he and Josiah were going to be friends forever, and love deeply and truly and hold their heads high before Time itself. The thought steadied him. And the new, steadier Thomas allowed the good Fellows of Corpus to notice his change in spirits and remark upon it to themselves, and in particular the chaplain, Justin, felt it was an appropriate moment to ask how Thomas had got on with the Augustine he'd lent him. That was in the quad, *en passant*, but Thomas took the opportunity to suggest that there was a lot more he wanted to pick his brains about. Might he come to see him again one night after dinner? And this time he would happily drink a whisky.

So Thomas found himself one evening with a glass of whisky in his hand, in the gentle light of Justin's college rooms and enjoying the warmth of his fire, and Justin said to him, 'So what is it you wish to consult me about, Thomas?'

'Well, first,' said Thomas, leaning back in the armchair he'd been given and enjoying the smell of Justin's room – books, wood, warmth and furniture polish –I found Augustine quite wonderful. The beauty of the world demands a God, at the very least. And beauty is a physical thing, or rather beauty is not a thing but the frontier where the physical meets the spiritual. And I think Augustine is right.'

'I think he is too,' said Justin, making a mental note to incorporate such an observation into a sermon. Then Thomas suddenly broke into a smile, and Justin said. 'If you don't mind me saying so, you seem so much happier than you have done for a long time. It seems like you've resolved something.'

'Actually, I was just thinking of a rather good question asked me by a pupil last week, "Why is your college called 'Body' college"? And I'm afraid to say, Justin, that I couldn't really fill him in.'

'Didn't they make you swear an oath of allegiance when you became a fellow?' Justin was genuinely shocked.

'I think you could call it that; and of course I swore it, as an article of faith. But tell me, Justin, did I swear allegiance to the body?' Thomas was whimsical, amused, happy.

But Justin stood up and began pacing by his fireplace, and proceeded to lecture Thomas as he might have a prospective undergraduate. 'The college was founded by the Guilds of Corpus Christi and of the Virgin Mary in 1352, specifically to train priests, as so many had died during the Black Death. It's the only Oxbridge college to be founded by the townspeople, and the phrase *Corpus Christi* is St Paul's, of course, referring to the church, which is the body, and Christ, which is its spirit – though in *Ecclesiastes*, Christ is referred to as the head of the body. Does that ring any bells, Thomas? I want to say, shame on you, as a Corpus man.'

'Shame on me,' agreed Thomas. 'I think I knew some of that at about twenty. But I'm afraid, Justin, I feel rebellious on this point, and perhaps posterity will too. I hear they're doing away with the apostrophes in place names – it confuses people, apparently, too many spelling errors in King's Cross and St John's Wood. Well, as we know, for ages people have been trying to do away with Latin alto-gether, calling it 'elitist' etcetera. So don't you think one day there'll be a popular cry for the removal of these pompous Latin names and a desire to get back to basics? And what could be more basic than a body?'

'You've changed, Thomas, you used to be such a traditionalist!'

'Oh, I am, I am! But the question is, in what period should we steep our traditions? The traditions of ancient Rome, or Greece? Or do we admire Renaissance Man or Late Victorian England? Where are we to get our traditions from, Justin? More than once you've told me you'd like to go back to the spirit of the early Christian fathers, you've told me that those first Christians had the right take on what it meant to be a Christian, and we've been falling foul of that vision ever since. So could you tell me how we've fallen foul of it? This is why I'm here, this is what I want to know about. I want to know about the relationship between the body and the spirit, and I thought that, of all people in Corpus, you would be the one to put me straight.'

'That's a big subject,' muttered Justin, anxiously.

'You could just tell me what your conclusions are, if you like. You have a wife. You have known carnal desire. Or do you think

I've already biased it? I should say, the desire to know the horizon between bodies and souls – would you put it like that?'

'Sexual desire seems pretty biological to me. Without it there would be no human race. But what Christianity does, or any religion for that matter, is that it turns what is a morally neutral thing into a good thing.'

'A lot of people would argue with you there, Justin. They would argue that Christianity turns what is a morally neutral thing into a bad thing.'

'Religion provides sex with boundaries. In Christianity, sex, love and commitment to each other are a perfect triad. Love redeems sex.'

'But why does sex need redeeming?'

'Because sex when it is out of control is wrong. People always suggest that the advent of farming watered the first shoots of civilisation as we know it. But I've always maintained that when people first adopted sexual *mores,* when they began to live as couples and families, long before the family was defined as such, when sexual fidelity was approved of and promoted – that was the moment civilisation began to establish itself. The rules which rein in sexuality are the bedrock of society – and all those books which tell us otherwise, which tell us that monogamy is unnatural etc. etc., I want to shout back and argue against them, "What's so good about what's natural, all of a sudden?" Anger is natural, does that mean we shouldn't try to control it? Human beings deserve their title "human" for the simple reason that they can curb "natural" behaviour for their own good, and for the good of the society they live in.'

'I would argue with you on two points, Justin. You seem to advocate repression of natural desires – well, we all know that repression is absolutely no good for the individual at all, it can cause all manner of nervous diseases. Freud was right on that point, surely, if wrong on so many others. And secondly, you seem to think of society as some kind of organism which is *ipso facto* right in all its requirements, and needs conformity from those who belong to it. But what if a society is somehow *wrong*? For example, the ancient city of Carthage required the sacrifice of babies to propitiate their gods, but what if some mother refused to hand over her baby, and under threat of death ran away to another city? You can't blame her for it! What I'm saying is, if the *mores* which define a particular culture are relative, then so are sexual *mores*. OK, even if they are the first organising principles in a society, are we going to applaud the tribe in some far-flung jungle who holds that the only way to ward off evil spirits is for the father to take his eldest daughter's virginity? In Eskimo communities, it is customary – or has been, anyway – for the host to lend his wife to his guest for the night.'

Justin poured himself a second glass of whisky and began scratching above his ear.

'Why are you here tonight, Thomas? What is it that you want permission for? Are you wanting me to support adultery? Do you want someone to lend you their wife? Or are you already borrowing her?' Though Justin's words were angry, his tone was gentle, for he was eager, now, for a confession.

'I've not come here to discuss a personal matter, Justin. My personal life is squeaky clean, not a body in it. I have a purely academic interest. I want to know what Jesus would say about love, the spirit and the human body. Or even, truth and the body. For God must like his creation – didn't he settle back on the Sabbath and decide he was pleased with his handiwork? To admire the beauty of another human being – wouldn't God think that was a good way of spending Sundays? Even a holy way?'

Justin was a wise man who was out of his depth. He considered giving Thomas another lecture, about how the Old Testament was more into bodies than the New, or at least, was more holistic about them. But there was something about Thomas' manner that alarmed him: yes, he was happier, but also more out of control. Despite

Thomas' protestations, he decided that Thomas was without doubt seeking permission for something which was – for want of a better word – unchristian, and he was certainly not going to give it to him. So Justin apologized, and drew the conversation to a close with a fairly paltry excuse, and Thomas went home, enthusiasm undented.

❧

Decorating the house – or in this case, undecorating it – is a good, earthing thing to do with someone you love. On the following Saturday, immediately after their Latin lesson, Thomas and Josiah vigorously whitewashed walls together in an act of purification. The one germ in their midst was Greg, who made a point of drinking a cup of tea at the kitchen table while Thomas and Josiah were scrubbing down Cilla's lime-green walls, and even clearing out cupboards. When he eventually left, Josiah said, 'How do you put up with that man?' and Thomas replied, 'Better the devil you know… he pays his rent on time.'

Greg didn't succeed, however, in dampening their mood. Thomas told Josiah how much pride the Romans had taken in their cooking, and how they had kitchen implements as sophisticated as those on sale nowadays, spatulas and balloon whisks and clay pots in which they roasted chickens and exotic birds. In fact, some of the tools were so strange-looking that neither cook nor archaeologist had been able to guess what they'd been used for – gouging out a particular bird's brain perhaps, or extracting a boar's brain through its nose. And as the two set to work cleaning out the oven, kneeling side by side on the kitchen floor, Thomas told his young companion about Roman banquets, and how the guests wore wreaths of flowers and rubbed perfumed unguents into their skin. He told him how they lay on couches three sides round a table, resting on their elbows, while the slaves would serve up course after course: sows' udders stuffed with sea urchins, dormouse, flamingo, sugared meat; the stranger and the more exotic, the more the cook would be admired and the host be praised. The different slaves had different names, depending on their duties; there was a slave called a *structor* whose sole purpose in life was to set out the dishes for the next course; another called a *scissor* whose task it was to cut the meat into bite-sized pieces…

'If I were a "*scissor*",' interrupted Josiah, 'and I had a knife, I would probably murder my master.'

'Owning a slave, being a slave, that was the norm, Josiah. Few questioned the system into which they had been born. And slaves even had a few rights – you could run away from a master who had mistreated you, for example. And if you were an educated slave, you might even eat at the same table as your master from time to time, though obviously at his invitation. Cicero – have I told you about the great orator, Cicero? – had a slave who became his most trusted friend and advisor, and relied on him too heavily to ever grant him his freedom. But if you were set free, you were given all the rights of a Roman citizen, and could even own slaves of your own. And the evidence is, slaves were fairly happy. They had a private life outside the home, they could follow their own religion. Though the one thing they couldn't do was marry.'

'I wouldn't care if I were happy or miserable,' insisted Josiah. If I wasn't free, my life would be completely pointless.'

'Freedom is an attitude of mind, Josiah. In fact, all those with an interior life are free, which is why communist regimes have never known quite what to do with artists and composers and the like. You can't own a man, in the same way as you can't own a piece of land. The contracts are cultural, man-made. They aren't true in any impor-tant sense, in any god-given way. So many politically "free" people are not free at all, but tossed about by the merest whim; while some of our greatest writers have done their best work in prison. The secret to freedom, Josiah, is your own mind, nothing more, nothing less.'

'But how can someone be sure that they're free? What if you fall in love with someone, for example? Does that mean that suddenly you're no longer free, because you can't control your own feelings?' Josiah put down his scrubbing brush and looked up at his mentor.

Thomas answered, 'But surely love is a good thing. When would you ever wish to control those feelings?' When Thomas stood up and looked away, Josiah took hold of his hand and pulled him back towards him.

'I would willingly be *your* slave,' he said.

Thomas squeezed his hand but said nothing, either to quash or promote the sentiment. But the painting stopped soon afterwards, and another week went by.

❧

The good, gentle, virtuous Dr Thomas Marius spent the week justifying, normalizing, and occasionally glorifying his relationship with the young Josiah. So he read reams of Greek and Latin literature, quite often spending his evenings in the Corpus library. In the spring term he was giving a series of lectures on Marcus Aurelius and Stoic philosophy, and he saw no reason not to get to grips with Aurelius' love letters to his tutor. To be both wise and capable of love was beginning to seem to Thomas a perfect pathway through this life, for a life without feeling was meaningless. Human beings were born to *feel*, but this did not mean they should be reckless with such a capacity, rather they should learn to feel *correctly* and *within bounds*… and yet, when it came to love, why should there be any bounds? An infinite, boundless, constant love was unconditionally a good thing.

If the boy Marcus Aurelius remained constant in his devotion to his master, the nature of Fronto's appreciation of his pupil shifted with time. At the beginning, Fronto sees their love in strictly Platonic terms; he distinguishes himself from Aurelius' other suitors, whom he disparagingly terms as *erotokoi* – lovers who desire him for themselves, who are possessive and needy and might even 'pay a fee' – while *he* gives money expecting nothing in return, *he* admires Aurelius disinterestedly, and appreciates the boy's beauty as an aesthetic thing, not as something to be bought and used. But later on in his letters Fronto falls from his lofty ideals, he'll give up his consulship to hold the boy in his arms. And whom do we like best, the younger or the older Fronto? Don't we prefer him when he's given up his highfalutin chatter? Isn't being human first and foremost about needing and wanting?

Josiah's progress in Latin was such that they were already beginning to read a few lines here and there from original texts. Thomas found him aphorisms to translate, which they would muse over together: Cicero said about himself that he sought the antidote to pain from philosophy – *Doloris medicinam a philosophia peto.* Is it possible, they discussed, to remove an emotional pain by rational thought alone? Thomas confessed that he had previously thought so but now he wasn't so sure, while Josiah was the polar opposite, saying that so far he hadn't been able to, but one day he thought he might. On Thomas probing into the nature of any *dolor* at his tender age, Josiah was evasive; though less so on the subject of destiny. *Quocumque trahunt Fata, sequamur* – wherever Fate drags us, let us follow, as suggested by Virgil. Josiah shocked Thomas by insisting that Fate would never get the better of him, that he was stronger than Fate itself, that if he wanted he could be in Scotland in twenty-four hours, or, for that matter, in any part of the world, because he had a passport and he knew where it was kept and he could just take it if he felt like it. Thomas limply asked Josiah where he'd been on holiday, anything to shift his strident tone, and Josiah told him he'd been on a school trip to Belgium to check out battlefields, but it had all been rubbish. So Thomas took him to a saying of Seneca, *Quos amor verus tenuit tenebit* – If the love which holds you together is true, it will always hold you – and he asked Josiah if he felt more sympathetic to that particular sentiment.

Josiah shifted his tone completely. 'A *verus amor* will hold people together forever,' he said, sternly.

'And how do you know about such a love?' asked Thomas.

'I know about parents, don't I?' he said.

'Of course,' repeated Thomas, and if there were a word to express being moved and disappointed all in one breath, that was what he felt then.

By the end of term, Josiah and Thomas had not only completed both volumes of the Oxford Latin course, but had applied three coats of white paint to Thomas' walls. Thomas now decided that Josiah was ready to be introduced to Latin Literature proper, and, what with the advent of the Easter holidays and *Sweet Spring, full of sweet days and roses*, he found his old copy of Virgil's *Eclogues* and suggested that a little pastoral poetry might be just the ticket.

Thomas knew from the first what he wanted to show Josiah. They plodded through the first eclogue like schoolmaster and schoolboy, and Josiah was quite frank, he found it both difficult and dull, and he wanted to read Catullus.

But Thomas was determined to read out the first two lines of the second eclogue (it was a bold venture, three sleepless nights' worth) and so keen was he to know Josiah's reaction to them, that his voice was flat and stilted.

Formosum pastor Corydon ardebat Alexin,
Delicias domini, nec quid speraret habebat.

'Do you want to have a crack at translating any of that?' Thomas asked, as if they were just any two lines.

'These aren't Latin names,' observed the clever Josiah.

'You're right, they're Greek. These pastoral idylls are directly modelled on Greek lyric poetry. There's the shepherd Corydon and Alexis.'

Josiah considered the first line. 'Are they both male?' he asked.

'They are,' said Thomas, who didn't even dare look up.

'"The shepherd Corydon burned for the beautiful Alexis."' Josiah translated with equanimity. 'Why "burning"?'

'That's was good, Josiah, well done. "Burning" means "in love with" – aren't there pop songs about "feeling the heat"? The next line's more difficult, but we've just done the subjunctive – which verb is in the subjunctive?'

'Was homosexuality quite mainstream, then?' asked Josiah.

'Corydon would not have called himself homosexual. He would have thought of himself as a man in love. Alexis is *formosus*, he is beautiful. The Greeks and Romans loved beauty wherever they found it. See what you make of the second line, Jo.'

'I can't do it,' said Jo. '"*Domini*" means "of the master".'

'Alexis was the "*delicias*" of his master, his master's darling.'

'So his master was in love with him too?' asked Josiah, incredulous.

'This is a story of unrequited love,' said Thomas, using his sensible voice. 'Now, which is the verb in the subjunctive?'

'"*Speraret*",' said the good pupil.

'And "*spero*" means?'

'"Hope",' said Josiah. 'He did not have a why he might hope, a reason to hope.'

'That's right, Corydon hasn't a hope in hell, because Alexis' employer is also in love with him.'

Josiah paused and said, 'This is really strange, Tom. Is this normal life in Roman times?'

'Among the upper classes it probably was.'

'What, you mean they were all gay?'

'They weren't gay. But the culture was freer than ours, looser. The Romans didn't categorize people like we do. As I said, they delighted in beauty, wherever they found it. See here in line fifty-two, he's in full pastoral flow, picking downy apples and chestnuts, "*mea quas Amaryllis amabat*", which my Amaryllis used to love, because once he might have been picking apples and chestnuts with her and the mood, Josiah, just carries over: boys, girls, narcissus, fragrant dill and marjoram – it's all in the one poem. And here, right at the end: "*me tamen urit amor: quis enim modus adsit amori?*" "Love is consuming me, for can one set bounds to love?" For that is what sets love apart from everything else in this life, don't you think, Jo? For love is limitless, timeless, eternal. Because it's not an act of will, it's a surrendering, it's an act of faith. Love is in the realm of the divine. Can you understand that yet, Jo?'

'I've known that forever,' said Josiah.

❦

That afternoon Thomas had a surprise for Josiah, for the theme of the day was smell, soft bilberries and yellow marigold, laurels and myrtle. And when Thomas said, rather seriously, 'Sometimes man forgets he has a nose', and Josiah laughed at him, Thomas announced with some passion, 'Today, young Jo, I'm taking you to the Botanical Gardens. And then you won't be quite so sniffy about noses.'

The day was the 21st March, when even officialdom recognizes a change in the seasons. And this first day of spring obliged them, the air was warm and sweet, it was a true gate between the seasons, and while they walked together to the gate on Hills Road, Thomas suddenly broke into Latin: "*iam ver egelidos refert tepores*" – there, you wanted Catullus – "Spring brings back warm days from cold" – do you notice the seasons changing, Jo?'

'There's a large beech tree in our garden. It's a great, solid beautiful thing, beautiful in every season, naked and clothed, with or without its leaves.'

'But you drew it naked, as far as I remember.'

'That was the winter version. There's a Summer one too, and an Autumn. Next week I'll bring you the Spring.'

'Do you write as well as draw? Have you ever tried your hand at poetry?'

Josiah shook his head.

'Then I shall introduce you to John Clare,' announced Thomas, and then he began to recite poetry right there on the pavement:

'Come luscious spring come with thy mossy roots
Thy weed strewn banks – young grass – and tender shoots
Of woods new plashed sweet smells of opening blooms
Sweet sunny mornings and right glorious dooms
Of happiness…'

Then Thomas stopped in his tracks and said quite suddenly, 'That is the point, dear boy, I'm happy. I know the quality of it. Catullus was happy too when he wrote that poem. He says he wants to go abroad to distant Asiatic lands. But perhaps we should go to Italy, what do you think? Would your Dad let you?'

'I should think so,' said Josiah.

'I don't see why we can't bring him along with us.'

Josiah paused and said, 'He doesn't like the heat.'

'Well, I shall ask him along anyway. I would want him to know this is all above board and with a view to your education, Jo. I think we should go to Italy, don't you? To the gentle hills of Tuscany, and its rows of cypresses? Have you ever thought what a wonderful thing a future is? To have a future, and not to know the contents of it, but occasionally to glimpse and hope?'

'I would like to go to Italy with you very much,' said Josiah.

'Well, I shall knock out some dates with your Dad,' said Thomas. 'I should very much like to meet him, you know, and tell him what a gifted son he has.'

'He would like to meet you too,' said Josiah, because it seemed like the right thing to say. 'But he's quite ill at the moment.'

'The warmer weather will soon sort him out. Perhaps in a couple of weeks, what do you think? Invite me to tea. I should like to see that beech tree of yours in the flesh, as it were, on the cusp of getting dressed.'

'I'll fix something,' said Josiah, distractedly. As they crossed the threshold between pavement and grass, Josiah said, 'I never knew this place even existed.'

'But your father was a gardener. Did he never try and inspire you?'

'Of course he inspired me,' said Josiah defensively. 'When I was a boy...when I was younger, he would always consult me.'

'*He* would consult *you?*'

'Oh yes. He would say, "So shall we plant geraniums next year?" And he would blindfold me and teach me the different scents, even of leaves. I remember, he would tear them in two and make me smell them very hard.'

'So do you think you could recognize the smell of a beech?'

'We didn't have a beech tree.'

'But...' began Thomas.

'We moved house when I was about seven.'

'But didn't you smell things any more in your new garden?'

Josiah shrugged. 'You know how it is, I felt too old to smell things.'

'What a sophisticated seven-year-old you must have been. Well, I shall unsophisticate you. Here you are, Jo. A beech tree to dwarf even yours, I imagine, and one which existed well before any botanical garden was even conceived of.'

Josiah spontaneously thrust his hand into Thomas' and was as much in awe of its hugeness and majesty as if he'd been a child of three.

'As fine a tree as there is in the whole of Cambridge,' agreed Thomas. 'It's a good metaphor, a tree, I've always thought. It is both moved by wind and storm, but nonetheless holds steadfast. The perfect stoic philosophy. Buddhists would have us stay out of the wind altogether, but how can you know anything of life if you simply hide yourself away? Or at least, hide your mind away, which is almost as cowardly. Some knowledge you can only experience.'

'Well, then,' said Josiah. 'Excuse me while I experience it.'

And immediately Josiah took his hand away and lay down amongst the daffodils and bluebells beneath it. 'Lie down with me,' said Josiah.

And he said it in such a way that Thomas almost did, but he pretended not to have heard him.

'The Romans, of course, loved beech trees. Beech trees featured in both the eclogues we read, of course. "*Tityre, tu patulae recubans sub tegmine fagi,*" Tityrus, lying under the spreading beech…'

'Was Tityrus gay, too?'

'No, Tityrus wasn't gay.'

'Does our word "fag" come from "*fagus*"?'

Thomas laughed anxiously. 'No, it doesn't,' he said.

'Please come and lie next to me,' Josiah pursued.

'This is a *fagus sylvatica*, a woodland beech. Have you noticed how all the names of the plants are in Latin? That some are *fruticans,* others *fragrans* or even *fragrantissima*? Those Victorian botanists must have had a field day.'

'Can't you come here,' yawned Josiah. 'What is grass made for but to lie in? *Herba est iniacenda.* Grass ought to be lain on. Isn't that right?'

So Thomas looked around him nervously and obeyed his pupil. 'You've persuaded me,' he said, sitting down stiffly on the grass about three feet away from Josiah.

But Josiah immediately rolled over the grass towards him and took hold of his hand. 'That's better,' he said. 'Now, lie down and look up through the branches.'

Thomas did as he was told; after all, any passers-by would assume they were father and son.

'Do you know,' said Josiah, 'I used to think I could talk to heaven lying under a tree. I would watch the movements of every branch, and imagined it was some kind of sign language. I just had to crack the code. But then I wondered if it wasn't a language like ours at all, but a language which contained all languages, and was over and above them.'

'I think you might be right,' said Thomas. 'Do you know about Plato?'

'I don't want to know about Plato. Not today,' said the boy. Then he lay, if it was possible, even closer to his *magister*. 'I've often wondered whether buds are even more beautiful than the leaves which they promise. Look how sharp they are! They're as sharp as needles, Tom, and bound so tightly. Then one day they'll just burst and give birth, with leaves so fresh and green you could eat them.'

Thomas, aware that his body felt quite as tight as any bud, moved away, and said, 'There's a herb walk here, you know. I think I'm going to give you a test.'

'A test?' sighed Josiah.

'Yes, I'm going to blindfold you with my scarf, and see whether your olfactory cells are as good as they once were.' Thomas stood up, and part of him wished he hadn't contrived his escape so soon.

'Have you ever been completely in someone else's power?' asked Josiah, while he followed his master obediently whither he led him. Josiah was walking with eyes half closed, the sun warming his cheeks and eyelids. 'I feel so loose today, like I'm all flesh and no bone. Have you ever felt like that?' Thomas was dutifully pointing out the trees and shrubs as they passed them, and Josiah said, 'It's no good, I have no eyes today.'

'Well, you don't need eyes for the scent garden,' said Thomas. 'Now, I want to see how well you can smell – how old were you when your father used to blindfold you?'

'He never did. He just told me to shut my eyes.'

'I'm not sure I can trust you. I want to make absolutely sure you're not sneaking a look at the labels. Here, stand still while I wind my scarf round your head.'

Now there really were onlookers: a mother with three young boys and two old ladies. But Josiah and Thomas were oblivious to them.

'I'm going to steer you into the path. Are you ready, Josiah?'

'I'm ready,' said Josiah, passively.

But Thomas in his eagerness to begin let him trip on a large stone; Josiah fell but, happily, was caught. 'I was right to trust you,' said Josiah quietly.

'Sorry about that,' said Thomas brightly. 'Now, we're coming up to the first scent, are you ready?'

'Jasmine,' said Josiah.

'That's very good, very impressive. And now for some herbs.'

'Rosemary.'

'Well done!'

'Mint.'

'That was an easy one!'

'Thyme.'

'You're very good at this, you know. You really are a gardener's son. Now, thrust your nose into this.' And Thomas took hold of his hand and took him to a tarragon bush. But when he looked round he saw that the boy had shrunk into himself, and his pretty face was all scrunched up; and when Thomas removed the scarf with a sense of urgency, as though it were suffocating him, he saw it was wet with tears.

'Josiah,' he said, gently, 'tell me about your father.'

Josiah wiped his eyes roughly and stood up tall. 'He wanted to come today,' he said.

Thomas considered this, or tried to. But his overwhelming sense was of a man deceived, and he said, coldly, 'No, Josiah, he didn't want to come. He didn't even know we were coming here. You didn't know. I didn't even know.'

Josiah was quiet. Thomas had an expression he hadn't seen before, angry, unforgiving. Finally he said, with a trace of defiance, 'It's time I went home.'

'You know what? I don't even know where your home is. In fact, I don't even know the first thing about you. For all I know, your name's John and you fancied calling yourself after a Jewish King.'

'You do know about me,' said Josiah, the struggle between tears and no tears playing itself out over his face.

'So why don't you take me home with you?'

The boy stood there, sobbing, too vertical, his body begging to be taken hold of. Still, Thomas didn't touch him.

'Follow me, then,' he said, suddenly turning away and running as fast as he could.

But Thomas stayed where he was.

☘

Full term ended for Thomas, but Josiah's was to continue for a further fortnight. Thomas was quite brazen now; every morning and afternoon he waited at his study window, and often didn't get so much as a glimpse of the boy. And when he did, he neither smiled nor waved at him, as he used to do, but looked stern, like a captain on his ship. And when Josiah saw him standing there, he looked away and hid himself amongst throngs of schoolchildren.

But on the Saturday morning, when Josiah didn't turn up for his Latin lesson, Thomas' mood softened. He waited the whole weekend for a knock at the door, and quite often he would randomly walk out onto the street to see if he could see him coming. And by the Monday afternoon, nine days after their confrontation in the Botanical Gardens, Thomas was quite determined to follow him home.

It was a game they were both happy to play, but it was a sad one. Josiah knew that Thomas was following him and let him: he was too listless to resist. Though occasionally, just to add interest, Josiah would pause on his journey to rip leaves from bushes, which he would tear in half and smell; but then, just as Thomas caught up with him and their eyes met, Josiah would accelerate away. When they eventually reached *The Hollies* Josiah neither talked to Thomas nor invited him in, but stood momentarily and tantalizingly in the doorway and shot Thomas a look which said *now you know and are you satisfied?* before turning away.

Thomas was not satisfied. For ten minutes or so he stood staring at the austere Victorian building and at all those who entered and left it. He watched while two thuggish older boys had their hands on the collar of a child about ten years old, pushing him along as though he were a shopping trolley; the child was giggling nervously. He watched as a young girl, plump, ugly and caked in make-up, left the house in a mini-skirt and see-through blouse and made her way to the bus stop. Three boys, all about twelve, left the house with handfuls of jam sandwiches and even seemed happy. He looked up at the large first floor windows, and the smaller windows under the roof, waiting even now for a wave or at least a glimpse of him. Wasn't Josiah even curious to know if he was still waiting there? It seemed that he wasn't.

By the time Thomas was in bed that night, a self-loathing had possessed him such as he had never known. His ignorance, his brutality, his lack of generosity; his lack of faith in a boy who was so good, so sensitive, so unutterably beautiful. He could not imagine how he might begin to make amends. So where were his parents? Were they alive or dead? Was the boy an orphan? If so, since when?

'I am a clambering idiot,' said Thomas, out loud. 'No punishment is bad enough for me.'

There were a hundred scenarios Thomas tried out that night. He decided that Josiah's mother was probably dead, and his father was probably alive. But whether he was mad, bad or simply incapable of looking after the boy, he hadn't a clue. His mother was a classicist, his father, a gardener: he saw no reason why Josiah should lie about that. But then, how strange that they should ever have married! And wasn't there a clue in that? And for a while it seemed perfectly clear to Thomas that Josiah's father was serving life for the murder of his mother.

In the cold light of day Thomas decided to find out. His first instinct was to phone the Cambridge Registry of Births, Marriages and Deaths, but the question he might have put to them, namely, 'Has a man called Nelson, a gardener in a Cambridge college, died in the last fifteen years?', seemed risible. So his next project was to ring up the Social Services Department in Burleigh Street, and the receptionist asked him whom he wished to speak to.

'I have an inquiry,' he began.

'Which area would this be?' asked the receptionist.

'It's about a boy, Josiah Nelson.'

'Where does he live?'

'Cherry Hinton. In a Children's Home, *The Hollies*.'

'One moment. I'll put you through.'

A moment was a minute. Thomas thought he'd been cut off and was about to try again, when a flat voice said:

'June Briggs.'

'Ah, hello,' said Thomas.

'Can I help?'

'I want to make an inquiry concerning Josiah Nelson.'

'And you are?'

'I'm sorry?'

'What's your name?'

'Thomas Marius.'

'In what capacity are you inquiring?'

'I'm sorry?'

'To what organization do you belong?'

'The University.'

June Briggs sighed audibly. 'What exactly is the nature of your inquiry?'

'It's about Josiah's Nelson's father. I want his address.'

'And why exactly is the University wanting to know about Josiah's father?'

'It's my personal inquiry,' said Thomas Marius.

'Then I'm afraid the information is confidential.'

'Would you be able to forward him a letter on my behalf?'

'I'm sorry, we can't help you, Mr Marius.' But then suddenly curiosity got the better of June Briggs, and she asked, 'How do you know Josiah?'

'I'm afraid that information is also confidential,' said Thomas, coldly. He hung up on her. But he was making progress: now he knew for certain that Josiah's father at least had an address.

Thomas's self-recrimination became even harder to bear. So intent had he been on their present pleasures, he had never given Josiah the space to talk about his past. In his brutal categorisation of his fellow-creatures, childhoods, like dreams, were only interesting to the people who had actually had them. He'd never even bothered to ask Josiah what he remembered about his mother; he didn't even know their Christian names, nor whether they'd been kind to him, nor whether they'd been rich or poor. So, had Thomas really expected some sort of confession from his protégé, when it was evident he had so little interest?

In the end Thomas wrote Josiah a note, which he delivered by hand.

'My dear Josiah, how will you ever forgive me? I am a brute, I know. I deserve to be gagged and kicked. But here is an alternative. Would you like to come with me to Siena this summer, a beautiful medieval city in Italy? Would they let you? We could go away together for the whole of August. What do you think? With affection and huge regret, Tom.'

As soon as Josiah read the letter, he set fire to it under the beech tree. But he couldn't get it out of his head. The apology was neither here nor there. The image, rather, that kept returning to him was that of a sun-baked road, narrow, dusty, and of himself walking down it, sometimes alone, sometimes with Tom. And he didn't know or care where it was going but it was of paramount importance that he was on it and it was taking him *somewhere else, somewhere other than this*; and he needed that road so badly that he thought he would go mad if he didn't find it. So on the next Saturday morning, with a strange, layered mood that had no centre to it, he set off for his Latin lesson as though there hadn't been a cross word between them.

Thomas's delight on seeing Josiah was tempered by the realisation that he was not himself. And Thomas was wise enough not to entirely blame himself on this fact, for yes, he might have been the cause of Josiah's introspection, but not for the demise of his parents. Thomas had always considered himself a bad tutor; he was not good at dealing with the emotional problems of undergraduates, he didn't even take them very seriously. But the boy standing before him at that moment he loved. Anything Josiah was enduring, he also endured. And Josiah had a face which made you feel you were looking into his very soul, and even if he were to tell a hundred lies that morning, his face could only tell the truth.

As both were shy and diffident, at first Latin was the theme of the morning. Josiah was almost at the end of Book Three in the Oxford course. How grateful they both were for the exercises which confronted them! There's a true saying that routine takes the place of happiness, that the smaller satisfaction of getting a translation exactly right is all that most of us are capable of. They went on together till they had covered every article of grammar in the book; and suddenly the books were shut and something needed to be said.

'Are you still angry with me?' asked Thomas, after about a minute's silence, during which Josiah didn't even look up.

Josiah shook his head.

'Did you think at all about my proposition?'

'Yes,' said Josiah, and gave Thomas a half-smile, but his attempt (which failed) to make it a larger one was the lasting impression.

'But you haven't made your mind up.'

'I have! I have!' sung Josiah inside himself, but he slunk down in his chair and said nothing.

'You have months to think about it, that's okay. No pressure, Josiah.'

Then Josiah began to pack up his books in his rucksack and made as if to go.

'Look, you don't have to answer me. But you've left me… how do I say this? With unanswered questions. You don't have to answer me.'

'My father's in hospital,' said Josiah, meekly.

Thomas's first thought was 'Broadmoor'. Regular hospitals didn't have long stay cases.

'Do you know where?'

'Fulbright,' answered Josiah. 'He's been there since I was seven.'

'Do you visit him?'

Josiah shook his head. 'They won't let me.'

'Why not?'

'They say that I would be bad for his health, and he would be bad for mine. He can't speak, you see. He's a mute.'

'Have you ever wanted to visit him?'

Josiah was crumpling up before him. Here was the boy of a fort-night ago; here was the boy crying silently into his scarf. But this time Thomas was gentle, and he knelt by Josiah and stroked his hair, and every feeling of remorse he'd had these past few days was suddenly released.

'Josiah, I'm so sorry,' he mumbled, 'I'm such an idiot, please forgive me.'

And then, when Josiah just cried into his chest like a small child, he said, 'Who are these villains, that they won't let you see your father?'

'I don't know,' said Josiah. 'The state. The people in charge.'

'Then the people in charge should be shot, shouldn't they?' said Thomas, with more spirit.

'Oh yes!' exclaimed Josiah, laughing amidst his tears.

'But you and I, we don't take any notice of people in charge, do we? We follow our hearts, we follow what is right, don't we? Nothing will stop us!'

'No!' agreed Josiah, looking up in admiration.

'Right is might! What do you think, Josiah?'

Josiah nodded enthusiastically.

'Fulbright's not far from here, is it? I'm going to order a taxi now, what do you think?'

Josiah looked terrified, but Thomas missed it, so keen was he to pursue justice.

A kind of freedom descended on Thomas: a new power, like breaking through the starting tape of a race. No sooner was the taxi ordered than he wished they were walking to the taxi rank, despite the closest being half a mile away. But the taxi arrived promptly, and the two of them slipped into the back seat.

'To Fulbright Hospital,' he instructed the driver, and to the boy leaning against him, he said, 'Let's go, Jo!'

Josiah had goose pimples and was shivering, and Thomas wanted to put his arm around him, but instead he took off his jacket and put it around Josiah's shoulders.

'It's cold for April,' he said.

As they entered the gates to the hospital, there were a hundred cherry trees in bloom; even the sun was out.

'Where to, sir?' asked the driver.

'The main reception, please,' said Thomas. There was no stopping him.

Josiah knew that his parents had met here. They used to have jokes about it, about their fellow patients, and even the staff. The place had been built as a Victorian asylum, and as Josiah looked up from the taxi window at the huge grey stone structure looming before him, it seemed so sad, lifeless, and sombre that he marvelled at his mother's humour.

'I don't know your father's name,' said Thomas, as they got out of the taxi and braced themselves for what was to come.

'Gibson.'

'Is that his first name?'

'Yes. Gibson Nelson. My grandmother's maiden name was Gibson.'

'Did you know your grandmother?'

'My father was quite old. Both his parents were dead when I was born.'

'Were you close to your father?'

Josiah didn't answer him, but was visibly trying to hold himself together.

'I'm sorry. That was a stupid question,' said Thomas.

Thomas walked up to the reception desk in the main hall. A young, pregnant woman was knitting behind it, and asked them if she could help.

'We've come to visit Gibson Nelson, a patient here. I'm afraid I don't know what ward he's on.'

The woman put down her knitting and typed in his name on her computer.

'Beeson ward,' she said, smiling. 'Down that corridor, first staircase on the right, second floor.'

'Thank you,' said Thomas, and took Josiah by the hand. 'That was alarmingly easy.'

They found the staircase, which was narrow and badly lit. Thomas went first and Josiah a few steps behind him. Thomas made a remark about Victorian hospitals but Josiah didn't hear him and didn't ask him to repeat it. Thomas wanted to look behind him and see the expression on Josiah's face, but he resisted. Sometimes privacy is all we have, he thought.

The ward consisted of one enormous room with four dormitories leading off it. There were three vast arched windows, perhaps eight feet high, and if these were a credit to the Victorian age, their skimpy orange crepe curtains put the late twentieth century to shame. In one corner of the room five residents were watching a quiz show on the television: one was persistent in shouting the answers, four in asking him to shut up. A woman of about sixty with hair the same shade as her plain grey serge dress was sorting out socks in a laundry basket at a large table in the centre of the room. It was difficult to tell whether she was a resident or a nurse. Thomas approached her. Suddenly the boldness of his venture appalled him, and he needed to be insulated from it.

'We're looking for the ward sister,' he said, suddenly wishing he'd managed things more officially. For this particular woman, whoever she was, wouldn't have understood that the boy beside him was about to see his father for the first time in seven years.

'She's having her lunch break. I always say, we're all entitled to a lunch break.' The woman laughed. Her yellow teeth made Thomas think she was mad, but he corrected himself. She was wearing a uniform.

'Of course,' said Thomas, uneasily. 'When are you expecting her back?'

'Do you mean Daphne? She'll be off till quarter past one. Or give her another twenty minutes if she takes tea.'

'Does she usually take tea?'

'Sometimes yes, sometimes no,' said the woman sharply, as she continued to sort out the socks into pairs.

'Would you happen to know where we might find Gibson Nelson?'

'Gibson?' said the woman looking up. 'Yeah. He'll be in that room over there with the blue door.'

'Thank you,' said Thomas.

The woman waited by her basket, smirking, hands on hips. 'There's no need to knock,' she snickered. 'No one ever knocks here.'

Inside the room were three lavatories without doors.

'Isn't he sitting on one of them?' she squealed, suddenly helpless with laughter. 'I would've bet my own baby daughter that that's where you'd have found him. Well p'raps he's over there through that door, with the ladies.'

By now the woman was bent double, her face creased like a premature baby. One of the quiz-watchers told her to shut up and turned up the volume of the TV.

'Gawd, they've got no sense of humour,' she managed, trying to straighten herself up. 'You'll find Gibson in the men's ward. Over there.'

No sooner had she divulged the information, than she was reduced yet again to such hysterics that she could only vaguely gesticulate towards Gibson's dormitory.

❧

Josiah didn't even recognize him. The large bulk of a man in the doorway with expressionless eyes was no-one he knew. He'd remembered his father as strong and well-built, but now his stomach bulged over his belt and an open shirt button revealed white, over-hanging flesh. He'd remembered his father with thick, brown hair, but now it was thin and grey. He didn't make any attempt to speak, but breathed though his nostrils, which made him sound like an old, neglected animal.

But Gibson recognized Josiah, and life began to suffuse his face. He attempted to smile, but his muscles had forgotten what to do, and he nodded instead.

'This is your father, is that right? Is this Gibson?'

Then Gibson said quietly, 'Jo.'

It suddenly occurred to Thomas that no one had ever properly known the boy's name: that he himself was a mere mimic, and when he heard his father speak it, he knew immediately that he was listening to its originator, its rightful owner. The twenty feet between them were like a sea; the voice, a siren; the walk to his father, a journey. Josiah lay his head on his father's chest and waited for the remembered hands to hold him there; and when they didn't come soon enough, he cried. He closed his eyes and felt the tears pouring down his cheeks in a continuous, silent stream, and when the hands eventually came nothing could have stopped their flow.

'Jo,' said Gibson again.

Gibson took hold of his son's hand and took him into his dormitory. He made him sit down on his bed while he began rummaging in his top drawer. Josiah watched his hands, fumbling, uncertain. There was a man asleep on the bed next to him, mouth agape, and another sitting on an upright chair beside the bed opposite, filling in a crossword.

At last Gibson found what he was looking for and he sat down on the bed next to him. He looked as happy as an unsmiling person could, and he began stroking Josiah's cheek. Then he thrust the contents of his hand into Josiah's, eyes ablaze, and for a full minute Gibson's large hands held Josiah's between them. He nodded, and Josiah said, 'Thank you, Dad.'

It was not until they were on the bus home that Josiah understood the significance of his present. It was a crumpled pack of Horringays's lilac seed, dated October 1991, the month they took him away. His father had been going to plant them that very morning.

Chapter Eleven

WHILE THOMAS AND JOSIAH were planting lilac seeds in a neglected bed in his garden, Greg was watching from the window.

'Stay here,' instructed Thomas. 'There's something I should have done a long time ago.'

Greg saw him coming and sat himself down at the kitchen table with Thomas' newspaper. He was ready; in fact, he was surprised he hadn't been driven out weeks ago. After all, grooming a boy for the purposes of having sex with him was an imprisonable offence. He'd even let most of the engineering department know of his suspicions, but no one there was quite sure of Greg himself and hadn't taken his accusations seriously. He'd say, 'I'm thinking of calling the social services about it,' but no-one rose to the bait, and he never did.

Thomas found him and said, 'You know what, Greg. You snoop. I don't like it. I believe I have to give you a month's notice.'

'I don't snoop,' said Greg, defiantly. 'It's you who behave so... obviously.'

'This is my house.'

'And I pay you effing rent,' said Greg. 'I never asked for the effing peep show to be thrown in.'

'The peep show's in your effing head, Greg. So have your little fantasies. I just don't want you to have them under my roof. Do you understand?'

'What I understand,' said Greg, standing up and reddening, 'is you need privacy.'

'Thank you. For a man who understands so little, you're being surprisingly sensitive.'

'I'll pack, then,' said Greg. He walked out of the room, and twenty minutes later Thomas and Josiah heard the front door slam.

Greg's bedroom was badly in need of purification: but those two did it. Within twenty-four hours the purple walls had had three coats of brilliant white and even the carpet had been taken to the dump.

'When I'm sixteen I can legally live with you. I can be your lodger. That's only fifteen months time, you know,' said Josiah, lying on the mattress with arms folded behind his head.

'I'm not sure about that,' said Thomas, looking down at the boy from the doorway.

'What do you mean you're "not sure"? Not sure it'd be legal or not sure you'd want me here all the time?' Josiah sat up to ask his question, and he suddenly looked so sad that what could Thomas do but sit next to him? And nor could he resist putting his arm about the boy's shoulder; today it was an instinct too profound.

'Would you mind what other people thought about that particular arrangement?' Thomas asked him.

'Nope,' said Josiah, simply. 'Would you?'

'I hope I wouldn't,' said Thomas.

'I want to go to Italy with you,' Josiah suddenly exclaimed, nuzzling his head into Thomas' jumper. Thomas took his arm away, but returned it a few seconds later to stroke the boy's hair.

'And I want to go with you,' he said, with feeling.

♣

The summer term began in earnest. Thomas' workload greatly increased: both those he tutored and supervised, Samantha included, were stressed by looming Finals, and a steady stream of them came to see him in his rooms in Corpus. Samantha was humbler, sweeter, and for the first time Thomas noticed she was actually very pretty. She even had a steady boyfriend, or so she claimed. But what was really preoccupying him were his lectures on Marcus Aurelius. There were only four of them; but his spring holiday had been eaten up with well, other considerations, and he had to settle down to work.

As he skimmed notes that he had been writing for years, well beyond the submission of his PhD thesis, he was struck by how dualist an interpretation he had made: always reason was supreme, the body a mere irritation. When Marcus Aurelius wishes death upon himself as the only sure means of ridding himself of all desire, Thomas had argued that he had spoken as a Stoic philosopher: this was his way of drumming his point home. But Thomas' mood in that spring of 1999 was strangely different. When he read, 'Let no emotions of the flesh, be they of pain or pleasure, affect the supreme and sovereign portion of the soul,' Thomas suddenly understood that Aurelius had made this demand upon himself. "See that it never becomes involved with them: it must limit itself to its own domain, and keep the feelings confined to their proper sphere." Yes, Aurelius, resist, resist! And yet, even in the next sentences Aurelius softens, and he can't resist: "If, (through the sympathy which permeates any unified organism) they do spread to the mind, there need be no attempt to resist the physical sensation; only the master-reason must refrain from adding its own assumptions of their goodness or badness." What a U-Turn! And in the same paragraph too! There should be no attempt to resist the physical sensation, for touching, thought Thomas suddenly, was truth, was unadulterated truth.

But while Thomas was happily re-writing his lectures and working well into the evening, Josiah missed him. At first, his father took up his time. But he wasn't to know that when Gibson called his name at their reunion in the spring, they would be the last words he ever uttered. Mute he had been for seven years, and mute he was to be for the remainder of his life. Two or three times a week Josiah took the bus to see him. Daphne Field the ward sister had dutifully informed June Briggs that these meetings were taking place, and to June's credit she did nothing to stop them. In fact, she was momentarily embarrassed that she hadn't suggested the meetings herself, for Josiah, at nearly fifteen years old, would by now have been sufficiently mature to understand what was involved. But even though there was no conversation between them – ah, you see, Marcus Aurelius would have understood this – there was touch, and the father and son became as father and son, a *unified organism*, and a mutual sympathy permeated them, a seamless truth. But after several weeks this seamless truth wasn't enough for Josiah. They would sit together utterly close and secure, Gibson's great arm about Josiah's shoulder. But Josiah needed more than that, and Thomas wasn't there to provide it. A couple of hours on a Saturday morning wasn't enough. And that was why Josiah smuggled himself in to one of Thomas' lectures.

As irony would have it – and this nearly caused Thomas to feign some acute illness and leave the lecture hall – Josiah found himself sitting next to Samantha. Samantha noticed her neighbour first, and wondered whether this pretty boy was one of those precocious geniuses you read about in the newspaper. And even Thomas' wise words at the lectern before her could not push aside a fantasy of seducing him, for his lips belied a ripeness and an innocence which were quite irresistible. So Samantha smiled at him, and a very lovely, warm smile it was, and Josiah, so she fancied, responded to it. In fact, if truth be known, neither of these two were listening to a word Thomas said.

But what Thomas was telling this little audience of twenty-somethings was so important to him that within a few minutes he was even oblivious of Josiah. He might have been talking to himself, pacing up and down his study, his mind and heart in permanent dialogue with one another. For Thomas had always recognized in Marcus Aurelius, who reigned as Emperor one hundred and sixty-one years after the birth of Christ, a veritable soul-mate, who seemed to shift his own ideas at the same rate as he himself.

'If you take one thing away with you this morning,' Thomas was telling those undergraduates, 'it's this. Everything is connected. Nothing stands alone. Bodies, minds, hearts feed into each other, and not just into each other but into the Universe, into God himself. Those justly famous words of Aurelius, which you'll find at the top of the hand-out, I want to read to you:

"All things are woven together, and the common bond is sacred, and scarcely one thing is foreign to another, for they have been arranged together in their places and together make the same ordered universe. For there is one Universe out of all, one God through all, one substance and one law, one common Reason of all intelligent creatures and one Truth.

"Frequently consider the connection of all things in the Universe.

We should not say, 'I am an Athenian' or 'I am a Roman' but 'I am a citizen of the Universe.'"

Thomas spoke these words as though they were his own, but Josiah noticed only the fiery look he shot at him when their eyes briefly met and quickly scuttled away before the end of his lecture.

The following Saturday Josiah braced himself before knocking on his mentor's door. Thomas didn't know until that moment how he would greet him.

He was cold. 'You can't do that,' he said. 'Why weren't you at school, anyway?'

'We had an inset day,' said Josiah, explaining himself on the doorstep.

'What the hell's an "inset" day?'

'It's when teachers learn how to be teachers,' explained the boy. 'I didn't miss school, if that's what you mean.'

Thomas' neighbour was waving at him as she heaved rubbish into her wheelie bin. 'It's a lovely morning,' said Marjorie.

'Here, let me help you,' said Thomas; and Marjorie, who liked Thomas, let him move a little furniture around the front room as well. By the time he was set free his front door was shut and Josiah was waving at him from his bedroom window.

'I'll only let you in if you promise I can live with you,' Josiah shouted down at him.

'Don't be so stupid,' Thomas retorted under his breath. Families out on their Saturday morning jaunts were approaching from the left and the right of him.

'Open the door, Josiah,' he said firmly, like a schoolmaster.

'Only if you promise.'

A mother pushing a double buggy was getting closer.

'This isn't a joke. Let me in,' pleaded the schoolmaster.

Suddenly the door opened, and Thomas missed the wheels of the buggy by inches. Josiah stood in the hallway, smirking. Thomas put his hands on the boy's shoulders and shook him.

'What the hell was that about?' demanded Thomas.

'It was a joke.'

'A singularly unfunny one.'

'You're right, I was being serious,' said Josiah, looking up at him, suddenly earnest.

'Well, you can't. It's not legal. A boy living with a single man. These people have minds like sewers, Josiah. You can forget it.'

'Look at this.' Josiah produced a key from his back pocket.

Thomas momentarily panicked. 'That key has nothing to do with this house.'

'No, but it does have something to do with the prison I live in. I've managed to get a duplicate of the back door key. So late at night, just occasionally, I could… if you gave me a key too…'

'Oh yes, and what if you were ever caught? What if you were ever followed by some over-zealous careworker? Where would that leave us, Josiah? Do you think they'd solemnly let us go to Italy together?

Which reminds me. This morning I write to your key worker – is that what her title is? Come on, come upstairs and fill me in with all this crap. Do you understand? We have to be above board. We've nothing to hide from anyone, we've not done anything wrong and nor will we, but everyone will always suspect the worst of us. Come upstairs. Tell me the woman's name.'

Thomas wrote the letter at the desk in his study; and as he did so he took out a bundle of old postcards of Siena and insisted Josiah sat down in an armchair to enjoy them.

'Now,' said Thomas, musing on how he was to begin, 'She does know you've been learning Latin these last few months? '

'Of course,' lied Josiah.

'And what does she know about me?'

'She knows you're a Fellow of Corpus, that you give lectures.'

'Then I shall give Justin's name as a referee, a friend of mine, Josiah, as a character reference. They want all this stuff, you know.'

'I know,' said Josiah, wisely.

'And I'm going to give them our address in Italy. Now, I shall be giving you an "educational tour" – how does that sound.'

'I hope not too educational,' said Josiah.

'We're going to be sleeping in a medieval chapel I know of. Now where did I put Signor Scroppo's address? Here we are. It's about four kilometres from the nearest house, not that your Miss Angela Day need know that. And there's just a small track from the Scrop-pos' farmhouse which leads there, which means there's no point bothering with a car. I hope you're a good walker. It's about twelve kilometres as the crow flies from Siena.'

'It sounds good to me,' said Josiah.

'Now, I've got some large-scale maps somewhere or other.' Thomas found them in a bottom drawer and laid them out over his desk and over his half-written letter to Angela Day. 'Come and have a look, Josiah. Come and see where we'll be walking.'

Josiah dutifully got up and feigned interest but the truth was he wasn't much interested in maps. He wanted to know whether there was a place they could swim together. He said the word "together" and Thomas flinched.

'There are streams and watering-holes running right through the valley, and there must be a lake somewhere but I've not been there. I warn you, though, the water's cold.'

'Sounds good,' said Josiah.

'There we are, that's where the chapel is, right there.' Thomas was pointing at a small cross drawn in biro. 'You see, Jo, no one knows it even exists. It's on the Scroppos' farm. I found it quite by chance when I fled my wife about six years ago – there's something about me you didn't know, I used to be married.'

Josiah felt strangely unsettled at this piece of information. If he had ever felt this particular feeling before, he would have recognized it as sexual jealousy.

'What was she like?' asked Josiah, biting his lip and sounding cool.

'She was from Bengal. She was very beautiful. Kind, honest, close to her family.'

'So why did you leave her?'

'Marriage is a strange business, Jo. You marry because you want to be really close to someone. I imagine more often than not that closeness never really materializes. You just fall back into the old habits you had when you were single, and I would spend more and more time with my long-dead authors and she with her parents.'

'Was she sexy?'

Thomas was faintly surprised at the question but answered him. 'I certainly thought so. There was a sultry look about her. She had thick black hair, these soulful brown eyes…'

'But why did you marry her if she didn't like books?'

'Funnily enough, she was the librarian in our faculty library. Our

| 207 |

eyes met over piles of books. She would find books for me, reserve them for me, and lend them to me, all with that sultry look of hers. There was a time when I thought she was perfect.'

'Did you have good sex with her?'

'You don't ask someone that question, Jo. It's one of the few forbidden questions.'

'But I don't know anything about sex. I don't know what to expect.'

'Don't you talk about it at school?'

'Not really,' said Josiah. 'Not properly. They all talk about who they fancy and who they've shagged. But we don't get details.'

'What about biology lessons?'

'Of course I know *technically* what happens. I just thought you could tell me something else.' Josiah looked so pleadingly up at Thomas that he did his best to answer him.

'Sex is a way of connecting with someone else. I would actually say it's one of many ways – just communicating honestly with someone is a way of connecting with them, or listening to a piece of music together, that sort of thing. But sex has the potential to be really high up on the list. Or I've always thought it has, but if I'm to be totally honest with you, I've almost always been disappointed. Sex is not much good if you just *do* it to someone else. It might be physically satisfying but otherwise it's dead.'

For some reason, this wasn't the answer Josiah was wanting, and he tried to get the conversation back on track.

'Have you ever had sex with a man?' he asked.

'You don't ask that question either.'

'But I can ask you, can't I?'

'As it so happens, I haven't had sex with a man.'

'Why not? If it's not much good with a woman?'

'Because I'm not gay.'

'I think you are.'

'Well, Josiah, I hate to disappoint you.'

'Why did you show me that poem, then?'

'Which poem was that?' asked Thomas, knowing full well.

'About Corydon and Alexis. That one.'

'There are several poems, many poems, celebrating the love between men.'

'But more which are not,' insisted Josiah, correctly as it so happened. Then suddenly Josiah leant forward and kissed Thomas, slowly, lingeringly, wetly, on his cheek.

Thomas closed his eyes to relive it, and said, 'You shouldn't have done that. You mustn't play dangerously.'

And Josiah understood that if he were to get to Siena, if he were to spend a month with his lover in peace, he had to abide by the rules which separated May from August.

In fact, there were a good number of things which Josiah understood more clearly than Thomas. To begin with, that it didn't matter how many referees Thomas gave Angela Day, or how capable a pupil he was, or how educational the proposed tour might be, there was not a chance in hell that permission would be given. So Josiah simply disposed of Thomas' carefully crafted letter, and equally simply nicked some headed notepaper from Angela's office – in fact, so easy was it that despite finding his passport in an unlocked tin he decided to leave it there until he needed it.

Josiah wrote Ms Day's reply in an ICT class:

Dear Dr Marius,

I see no problem regarding Josiah's holiday in Italy for the month of August. I have written the dates in the diary. Please contact me if I can be of any assistance.

Yours sincerely,

Angela Day

The presentation of this sealed letter! Josiah gave it to him nervously, as though he had no idea of its contents and its verdict, and said, 'Fingers crossed'. The envelope was typed, addressed to Dr Thomas Marius, Corpus Christi College; and then, in the right hand corner were scribbled the words 'By Hand'.

'It looks promising,' said Thomas, as he opened it. 'She would have sent it by post if she hadn't trusted you.'

'There you are!' said Thomas happily. 'What did I tell you? It always pays to be above board.'

And in their relief and delight they allowed themselves a good, solid hug.

In the weeks that followed, even though Thomas could still not give Josiah the attention he wanted, he began lending him his books, not just the Classics – Loeb editions of Lucretius' *De Rerum Natura*, Ovid's *Metamorphoses*, Catullus, of course; but a couple of volumes of poetry, too, Wordsworth and Philip Larkin. Josiah took down from his shelf a copy of Bunyan's *Pilgrim's Progress*, Thomas' fifth form prize from his grammar school back in 1976, and immediately opened it and read out loud, 'As I walked through the wilderness of this world, I lighted upon a certain place...' And Thomas interrupted him, to tell him about the Slough of Despond and the Valley of Humiliation and the town of Vanity-Fair, which was lighter than Vanity.

'Take these books home with you,' he insisted, and Josiah, arms piled high, took the books back to his room, and reverently placed them on his chest of drawers. His favourite book to read in bed was *Pilgrim's Progress*, because it was the largest and the heaviest book and he liked the weight of it.

Josiah also began to commit himself more to his life at school; suddenly he was getting 'A's in his GCSE coursework, and his teachers noticed his 'complete change in attitude'. A couple of evenings a week he even helped the care staff prepare the evening meal, and he resisted the advances of two girls who told him they wanted to sleep with him.

The lilies in Thomas' garden grew strong and tall; and there was a moment at the end of May when Josiah picked his father a great bunch of them, and yes, there was a response when he thrust them into his arms, but there might have been a happier one. Gibson was near to tears and hugged his son, promptly squashing the flowers which were still between them, and on seeing the lilies' demise he completely broke down, as though what he had just witnessed was the most dreadful metaphor. Josiah just laughed, a hysterical, nervous laugh, but that didn't do much for their relationship either. Josiah yearned for something real, something to hold onto. He began to feel thwarted. And then, one day, he dared to ask him the question which had been preying on his mind. 'What happened to my mother? Can you remember?'

The great human bulk which was Gibson lurched forward and held onto his son's shoulders. It occurred to Josiah that all his life he had needed his father's weight to steady him, but that now he had found it, it could only topple him. Gibson said nothing, of course. He was as mute as all his social workers had been over the years on the subject. To all intents and purposes, his mother simply didn't exist. She had less substance than the air.

By the middle of June, however, Thomas's term was over, and he could devote himself once more to his young pupil. They immersed themselves in the works of Virgil, Ovid and Pliny, paying particular attention to their descriptions of rural life. Together they read one of Pliny's letters about the beauty of a Tuscan landscape, and 'some enormous amphitheatre that could only be the work of Nature, the broad plain ringed by mountains, their summits topped by ancient groves'; they dwelt on the pleasure that was to be August, and even learnt a little Italian.

So good was Josiah at living dangerously that he didn't even bother to retrieve his passport till the morning of his departure. The only precaution he had taken was to duplicate the office key when it had been left in the door while Angela had been writing up case notes: a dash to and from Cherry Hinton High Street to the key-cutter had taken him a mere twenty minutes. So Josiah now had in his possession two keys. The power of it! And at 5 a.m. on the first of August he used the first to let himself into the office and the second to let himself out of the back door. It amused him to write Angela a note explaining he'd be away for a month and leaving it on her desk, locking the office door behind him. What a conundrum that'll be for her! O, the power of it!

He was at Thomas' house at 5.15; at the station a half an hour later after a sleepy cup of tea and a taxi ride; at Stansted airport by 6.30. They barely said a word to each other, just half-smiled from time to time. The plane left at 8.15: Josiah took the window seat. They touched down in Florence two-and-a-half hours later. They were free.

Freedom is a heady business, and the heat disoriented them even further. Dear Thomas, the responsible one, tried not to not succumb to it: he was all maps and taxis and logistics. They were waiting in the taxi queue; Thomas was sweating, remembering that he still hasn't warned the Scroppos about Josiah. In his head: a hundred ways of explaining the boy away, the pupil who wants to see Siena, the nephew whose parents are abroad, or perhaps the nephew who wants to see Siena. Tell the truth, goddammit! Have you done anything wrong? Will you do anything you regret?

Thomas turned to Josiah. He was intending to say, 'You keep the place in the queue while I phone the Scroppos to tell them we've landed.' But his eyes were closed, and there was a half-smile upon his lips, as innocent as a babe's. The boy so pure and pale and calm that Thomas was held there for an instant – there was too much beauty here to interrupt it – too much beauty! Then a certain sickness forced him to action, and he shook him quite violently by the arm, and said, 'I'm going to that phone booth over there.'

He got through to Signor Scroppo, and told him he was in the taxi queue and should be with them by lunchtime. There was more he had to tell him, of course, but Signor Scroppo was so pleased to hear from him that he never stopped talking, they'd been painting the walls of the chapel, the weather has been excellent... then the phone went dead, and Thomas had no more change.

The taxi queue moved quickly; the roads were fast. The smiling boy was soon asleep. But his neck was lolling onto one side, and Thomas was anxious that when he woke up his neck would be stiff – oh, he reasoned this and that, and the long and the short of it was that Thomas offered the sleeping head his shoulder, and the sleeping head accepted it, and he slyly stroked the head's hair, or 'slyly' was how it felt to poor Thomas, and when the head suddenly lurched away from him, he guiltily pulled his hand away.

The Scroppos' farmhouse was at the end of a long drive, with an orchard of pears to the left and the right of it, and even as they drove up women and children were gathering them in baskets. The house itself was made of warm Tuscan stone, with fig trees growing up it and small slits for windows, as though no-one in the Scroppo family had seen fit to modernise it in four hundred years. Thomas paid the taxi driver and waited nervously by the front door. No-one answered the dong of the old iron bell. Josiah stood with his face skywards, lit up by the sun.

'Come on, let's go in, they're expecting us.'

The room was awesome in its simplicity. It made Thomas forget, even, to call out and declare his presence. A large table stood on an old brick floor, and from the ceiling were hanging plaits of garlic and onions. But the room was dark and dour and serious. Josiah instinctively sought out Thomas' hand, which Thomas pushed away when Signora Scroppo bounded in like an overweight Labrador with a tail that won't stop wagging.

'Mr Thomas, my English friend! Welcome again!' She planted warm kisses on both of Thomas' cheeks, and Thomas managed to return them, feeling like an Englishman.

'This is my nephew, Josiah,' said Thomas, and almost immediately the signora's tail stopped wagging and there were certainly no spare kisses for him.

'Now you make me worried, Mr Thomas. You see, they are carrying a bed over the hills even now, three, four, kilometres, *allora*, you know how far away is the chapel. But the bed is small. We thought you were coming alone.'

'I was!' exclaimed Thomas. 'But at the last moment I persuaded Josiah to come with me. His parents both work, you know, and it's not much fun being home alone in the holidays.'

Ah, those lies, they came quite tripping off his tongue! Where was the honourable gentleman now?

'But we need another bed!' insisted the signora, looking at Thomas accusingly.

'I just had a bit of rush matting when I was here last. Simplicity suits me, Signora, don't mind me.'

'But you are happier now,' observed the signora, as though luxury was a thing that happier people required.

'I'm sorry?'

'Your marriage was finished, no? You were a sad man.'

Thomas laughed, or tried to, at least. 'Yes, I suppose I was,' he said.

If Thomas was supposedly happier, the signora was sadder than he remembered. Six years ago there had been a houseful of children in their early teens; there would have been a great cauldron of soup on the stove and a smell of home-made bread. But the children had grown and found work elsewhere, and the signora was older and fatter and yes, sadder. The first time Thomas had been to this house the signora had been singing over her sink, washing lettuces; a glass of wine and a bowl of olives had been his within moments. But now there was an awkwardness between them, as if they were made of different stuff.

When Signor Scroppo walked in a few minutes later, Josiah thought him quite ridiculous. He had a large moustachioed pink face, and black, greased-back hair; in fact, a good deal blacker than the last time Thomas had seen him, and his braces were decorated with cartoon characters, which is what he seemed to have become. How many times had they spent the evening together, was it twice? In his mind's eye there were a thousand such evenings, there was food and wine in abundance, they were the refuge from the world; they were, above all, the people who had happily lent him their chapel for a couple of months after coming across it on a solitary walk. But today, who were they, these people?

If the Signora had ignored Josiah, Signor Scroppo more than compensated for her. In fact, for the hour and a half they were together, Signor Scroppo's eyes rarely left him. While they ate home-made pate and bread, a tomato and onion salad and a plate of sliced pears, his wife introduced the boy as 'Mr Thomas's friend', and when the sensitive Thomas reiterated, 'My nephew, Josiah', Signor Scroppo laughed and said, 'Let us call the boy Guiseppe, shall we? He is a fine-looking boy, Thomas.' And Signor Scroppo had shot him a look as if to say, 'Well done!'

Josiah said not a word throughout the meal; Thomas' interjections were limited to 'Not for me!' 'Please don't bother on my behalf!' and several 'No thank you's – for where is an appetite to come from when your host and hostess are bickering, in Italian, about whether one bed will be sufficient for the pair of them? By the end, Thomas and

Josiah were more than happy to accept their gift of a bag of pears and a bottle of wine and be sent on their way.

The weight of their bags and the heat of the sun dried up whatever conversation they might have had. Thomas would have said, because he kept thinking it, that the landscape was as perfect as the backdrop for a Madonna and child: tall dark poplars on the hill ridge, winding streams falling downward amidst outcrops of rock, pale blue in the early evening light; and the grass so green, so untrodden, so fed by the water running through it. But Thomas kept his thoughts to himself, conscious that the sudden sound of his voice would seem harsh and unnecessary when he so wanted Josiah to hear every murmur that the valley could offer him.

'We've arrived,' said Thomas.

'It's good,' said Josiah.

'Simple, but lovely in its way.'

'It's how I imagined it.'

'It would have had a bell once.'

'Perhaps the Scroppos took it.'

Thomas laughed. 'You know you might be right. Make yourself at home, Josiah. There's no lock on the door. Or never used to be.'

The chapel consisted of a single, rectangular room. Its walls were newly whitewashed with lime, and the paint smelt faintly sulphurous; its floor was made of large slabs of stone, surprisingly worn, suggesting that at one time the chapel was well-used. At the head of it, underneath its only window, was a small painting of the Virgin Mary dressed in blue, her eyes questioning, and her head bent slightly to one side as if she were listening to their answers.

The bed was unremittingly single.

'That's where you're sleeping,' said Thomas.

'And you?' There was no matting. There weren't even any extra blankets.

'Don't worry about me, Josiah.'

And Josiah didn't, because he knew there'd be no need.

'Let's unpack,' said Thomas.

Josiah laughed. 'Where do we put our clothes, Tom?'

'I suppose we'll just keep them in our bags. Here look, I've brought our first supper. Light, but nutritious.' Thomas unzipped his rucksack and laid out on the bed a few provisions from Sainsbury's: biscuits, tea-bags, ready-sliced cheese, marmite and a pack of Knorr's vegetable soup.

Josiah was neither surprised nor grateful. 'Isn't it about time we opened that bottle of wine?' he said.

'Unfortunately we don't have a corkscrew,' said Thomas, oddly relieved.

'And fortunately, it has a screw top.'

'Well then, I have tin mugs. We must celebrate!' But Thomas's voice was half-hearted, and tired, too. He couldn't deny a fifteen-year-old boy a glass of wine. Thomas delved once more into his rucksack and found the tin mugs, and a small gas stove, too, and said, 'I hope you're impressed. There's a whole kitchen in here you know.' And while he proceeded to take out tin plates, bowls, cutlery and even a saucepan, Josiah opened the bottle of wine and poured it into the mugs, taking a swig from one of them more or less immediately.

'To the holiday!' toasted Josiah.

'To the holiday!' attempted Thomas, anxiously.

By now it was six in the evening, and the heat of the day had finally receded. They sat with their backs against the still warm chapel walls, watching the reddening sun and aware, at last, of a cooler breeze. A herd of goats with bells round their necks grazed nearby; the rushing of a hill stream broke the silence.

'*Fortunatus est ille deos qui novit agrestis,*' said Thomas. Josiah wasn't interested, so Thomas translated. 'Happy is he who knows the gods of the country.'

'I'm too tired for Latin,' confessed Josiah unapologetically. He was holding his empty cup between his knees.

'Did you notice the green earthenware jug?' asked Thomas.

'No,' said Josiah, 'Should I have?'

'It was here last time I came here. I used it to get water. I imagine we'll be using it again.'

'Well get it, then. And bring out the wine, too,' said Josiah.

Thomas did as he was told, and he filled Josiah's cup half way. Josiah shot him an angry glance. 'More,' he said.

'Do I sound like an uncle if I recommend diluting that wine?'

'Yes, you do,' said Josiah seriously. 'Listen, I've had wine before. I like it, it's good.'

'Well, all right. But then we put the rest away till tomorrow, right?'

'Uncle, I don't like your tone.' Josiah was merciless, and he downed the wine in one.

'I don't like yours,' said Thomas, taking the empty cup from him.

For a minute or two they both sat shocked and silent, backs against the chapel wall, eyes locked on some distant vista.

Then Thomas said, 'It's getting dark. I'm going to get water.' He picked up the jug and set off purposefully down the hill. Josiah ran after him.

'You were going off without me,' he said.

'I was,' said Thomas, without looking back.

'I want to swim.'

'You can't. The water's not deep enough.'

'Surely you found a pool when you were here.'

'It's a mile away.'

'So what's stopping us? I need to be purified. It's still the first of August, Tom. It's still the beginning. That's what rites are for, the shedding of an old skin, living again in a new.'

That was as good an apology as Thomas had ever heard, so he fell into the trap.

Thomas filled the jug at the stream and left it on the bank. Without saying a word, they both walked on upstream into the sunset. Neither even exclaimed at the strange noises in the valley, the scratchings and moans of night animals beginning to stir. Josiah was plotting his performance: or rather, devising his very own purification ceremony. He was going to invite Thomas to join him; but of course Thomas would say no, because he was far too virtuous. And anyway, if they were to swim together, any purification ritual would be made a mockery of. So Josiah was smiling to himself, calm and happy, ready for his nakedness. So ready that he was taking off his clothes before Thomas could say something like 'We've arrived!' or 'Watch out, the water's cold!'

Thomas pretended, even to himself, that he didn't notice. What is a body, after all? A body can be analysed away in a trice: this one was regular, slender and smooth; this one was healthy and young. That's all!

Josiah stood there naked on the shore, with his arms above his head as though he were about to dive in; but no, the pleasure would be over too soon. So he looked back over his shoulder and called out, 'So aren't you going to purify me? Isn't there a god you'd like to dedicate me to?'

'Whom would you like to be dedicated to?'

'To my Uncle Zeus, what do you think?'

'And you are?'

'I'm Ganymede, of course, I'm your cup bearer. And I shall be a better cup bearer than you turned out to be.'

Thomas laughed nervously.

'The gods are all here tonight, can't you feel them, Thomas? Can't you feel them watching us? What should I say to them?'

'You could say, *Euoi! Euoi!* That was how they would summon Dionysus. *Euoi! Euoi!*' And those words began to sweep Thomas along.

So Josiah thrust his arms over his head and looked up into the darkening sky and shouted out, '*Euoi! Euoi!*' Then he put his arms back by his sides and said, seriously, 'Now, I want to make a sacrifice.'

'A sacrifice?'

'Yes, my noble Lord. Because to sacrifice means to give, doesn't it? No, it's more than that. I want to make amends, I want to balance things again, I want everything to be *right*. So I'm going to make a sacrifice.'

'But what of? There are no rams lurking in the thicket, dear Josiah.'

'I'm sacrificing my own body, Uncle Zeus, it's all I have.'

And with those words the water welcomed Josiah into it, all the way up to his chest, rising up to meet his arms splayed over its surface. Then all at once Josiah's body seemed to give way, and he sank down into its cleanness and let it wash him, running over his body and his hair and forcing his eyes shut.

Thomas began calling him from the bank: twenty seconds seemed an eternity as he watched the boy's shadow in the water, looking for movement or evidence of struggle, or some sign which would tell him how to act. Perhaps the cold and the wine had made him pass out. He seemed so serene, so still, it crossed Thomas' mind that he was already dead.

Josiah was no fool, he knew what he was doing. They talk about relief being 'palpable' – which means, literally, 'that which can be explored by touch': and the relief which Thomas felt when he saw Josiah's head emerging from the water lasted well into the night. For the shivering body walking back to the chapel needed an arm about him, there were no two ways about it, and once inside the chapel an arm wasn't enough, by any stretch. They slept, wrapped up in each other, in a bed made for one.

Chapter Twelve

THE NEXT MORNING the fact that the two had slept in one another's arms was never referred to by either of them; both knew better than to turn into language something as innocent and loving, as giving and as needy, as the embrace they fell into that night. And to those of you that wonder, were they naked? Did they touch each other in *that* way – because that's all any of you are interested in; the answer is no on both counts. Nonetheless, touch reigned absolute, touch was what it was all about, skin on skin mattered like two stray souls becoming one.

Thomas was the first to get up; he felt no shame. He pulled the blankets back over Josiah and watched the sunlight flickering over his eyelids, incorporating itself into a dream. A dream of angels, he thought, tenderly.

Once outside, Thomas set to business. The air was cool, invigorating: it was still only seven o'clock; six, English time. He went down to the stream to fetch the jug of water, set up his little camping stove and aluminium kettle on a rock nearby, and found the teabags. They hadn't eaten the night before, and Thomas found himself ravenously hungry, wolfing down slices of cheese and two or three pears to boot. After all, there was no point in waiting for Josiah to wake up – didn't teenagers sleep all morning? There was no hurry! For what pleasure there was to be had in maps, in drinking tea in a sweet-smelling valley in Tuscany with a spread-out large-scale map in front of you, and every square inch brimming with promise?

Josiah was to sleep till eleven that morning; if he hadn't, the country gods might have won, and a rural idyll worthy of Virgilian shepherd-boys might have been the theme of their month together. But after a couple of hours with his map, Thomas sought his Blue Guide to Florence and Siena, and a different kind of excitement overwhelmed him. For yes, in the beginning there was Nature, but what Man does with that beginning is surely even more awe-inspiring, and it was his duty, yes, as his teacher, to lead his pupil into the realms of Culture.

So by the time Josiah was awake, Thomas' mind was made up. That first day they would walk to the nearest village, pick up a bus timetable and shop for food; they might even spend the afternoon swimming in the pool together – for how happy Thomas was, in every aspect of their friendship! – and then, early the next morning, Josiah's cultural education would begin.

That day, Thomas dutifully roused Josiah's interest; on their walk to and from the village, while Josiah kicked rocks and skimmed flat stones across the surface of the widening stream, Thomas told him how Siena had prospered in medieval times, and had more or less ignored the Renaissance altogether.

'I should think,' said Thomas, 'that it's probably the most perfect medieval city on this earth.'

'What's the Renaissance?' asked Josiah.

'Haven't you learnt about the Renaissance at school?'

'Nope,' said Josiah. He was watching a dragon-fly come into land on a rock in the middle of the stream, and was wondering what on earth could have induced it to have landed *there*, in such a precarious place, its wiry legs struggling to attach themselves to the slimy greenness. He told Thomas to hold on a minute while he took the role of rescuer, but it all took more than a minute, and the charming sight of Josiah balancing on rocks in the spray to save a beleaguered dragon-fly, who would probably have managed perfectly well without him, irritated rather than enchanted his educator.

'Now, the Renaissance! This was the period when Western Europe said *yes!* to Civilization.'

'I wish no one had ever said 'yes' to civilization. I don't want to be civilized. I want to stretch out my arms for all I'm worth and have no one tell me *ever* that they're stretched too far. Anyway, luckily Siena was built before civilization got a grip, is that right?'

'Four large volumes could be written on that little speech, Josiah. Human beings are complicated. Man does not live on bread alone. First we are the animal, responding to nature; but we have large brains, and we make life easier for ourselves – we farm, we build houses, we live in communities – and that's why we have to make rules for ourselves, and we have to obey them, for the good of everyone. Socrates was sentenced to death, accused of corrupting youth. His friends begged him to escape, but no, he drank his hemlock. The laws were bigger than he was. He never said, "Hey! I've been unjustly treated, I'm getting out of here!" And even now we're struck by what he did, there's a nobility about it, don't you think?'

'Not really. Some laws are good, some bad. I don't think we should obey bad laws.'

'There is a justice above justice, Josiah, and that justice would have us obey laws which were not perfectly just. I think Socrates was right. What if a poor man stole from a rich man and his defence in court was that he was obeying "a higher justice than the justice of the land?" He might even be right, in an absolute sense, but that's irrelevant. Josiah, there'd be anarchy. Imagine in a court of law: was this man acting out of greed? Or because he had intuited an absolute of right? No one can see inside us, no one knows our motives, quite often we don't even know our own.'

'Do you believe in justice, then?'

'Even you will, after your visit to Siena. Siena believed in justice, Josiah. What's remarkable about Siena is that it seemed to spring from the very souls of the Siennese. In Florence you have a classical idea let loose upon it. It was the vision of an elite, those who had money and power. Siena is more like classical Athens, essentially democratic, whose true ruler was Virtue enthroned, and recognized by all.'

'I'm hot. I'm going to lie down in the stream,' Josiah announced suddenly.

'What, here?'

'Yes, right here. Don't worry, it's only six inches deep here, I won't drown.' Josiah took off his trainers and lay down fully clothed on the sandy bed of the stream. He closed his eyes and felt the cold water gliding over him.

'That feels so good. Come and lie next to me, Thomas.'

And Thomas thought, 'Why the hell shouldn't I?' And he did.

Their clothes were still damp when they reached the village of Buonconto. It was three in the afternoon, hot and dry, the old pale stone dazzling in contrast to the rich dark green of the valleys which surrounded it. Its one shop was still shut, so they sat at a table in the square with the sun on their backs and Thomas ordered two bottles of beer from the local trattoria.

'*Due birre per favore,*' he said in his best Italian to the squat old lady in a black dress and shawl.

'*Bene,*' she muttered and went to fetch them.

They drank their beers; Josiah said he wasn't surprised that there wasn't a god of beer because it was bitter stuff. He, like the, gods preferred wine. Thomas said that when he was fifteen he wouldn't have been seen dead with a glass of wine, it was considered bourgeois and wet. Then a bus on its way to Siena stopped right by them and Thomas found out from its driver that the only other daily bus left at nine in the morning.

'We're going to be getting up early this week,' he said.

The shop was tiny but half of it was devoted to fresh cheeses and dried hams; and the two sat on its steps eating large wedges of gorgonzola before setting off home with two large bags of supplies.

In the evening, which was to become a regular fixture of their day, Thomas read Josiah passages from Dante's *Inferno*, or they translated *The Aeneid* together. Their desire was stilled, even somehow satisfied. They were tired, fulfilled, happy, and they both thought there were no more questions to be asked, now they knew how to share a bed.

By the time they were on the bus the following day Josiah knew these things about Siena: that it was built on three hills, and that farmland still came right up to the city walls, and that its geography was so integral to it that walking down one street you might just glimpse another a half a mile away running up another hill. He knew about the Council of Nine Good Men, men chosen to be 'Defenders of the Commune and the People of Siena' in the fourteenth century, and men chosen, quite literally, on account of their goodness – proved first and foremost by their having been fair and kind employers, whether they were bankers, spice-dealers or goldsmiths. If you were from the nobility or were a judge, you had no chance, too many vested interests, you couldn't even put your name forward as a candidate. Siena's rulers must come *del mezzo* – from the common people – they must be *ordinary*: and with an extraordinary level of trust invested in them, the Nine Good Men were able to transform Siena. They had ideals, they had passion, they really believed they could make things better. They broadened the main streets, they gave instructions to the citizens on how they should build their houses, and above all they commissioned artists, not just for the pleasure of the elite, but for everyone. They built the Palazzo Publico in the main square, and its bell tower, the Torre del Mangia, perhaps the most famous landmark of Siena, and from the top of which the beauty of the city can be held in the palm of a hand.

Thomas proved a good guide, Josiah a good and curious tourist. On that first morning they walked up to the Duomo, the cathedral on the summit of the Castelvecchio, resplendent in dark green, pink and white marble.

'It took nearly two hundred years to build,' said Thomas, 'and every Sienese artist and craftsman of any distinction worked on it. The citizens themselves oversaw the project at first, but when the Nine Good Men were in power, their plans for it grew even more ambitious – the whole of the Duomo would be a mere transept of a cathedral which would outdo in magnificence Brunelleschi's dome in Florence, which funnily enough had been built to rival this Duomo – there was no end of these Tuscans vying with each other. But the Black Death put a stop to those plans, probably rightly so, in my opinion. I've never asked you if you're religious at all?'

Josiah said, 'My mother baptized me in Polish vodka. I was about three when she told me. She told me it was very special stuff for special boys. Of course I didn't have a clue what vodka was, I thought it was a Polish word, I thought it was something very mysterious you could only find far away.'

'How old were you when you knew the truth?'

'I was quite old, eleven or twelve, the residents of *The* Hollies don't go in for vodka much. Even so many years on, I felt hugely betrayed by her, like I was a butt of her joke. My father was the good, consistent, reliable one, he was the grown-up.' Josiah paused. 'You wouldn't think that now, would you? How could they let him get so fat in there? He was never fat like that.'

'He's ill, Josiah.'

'No he's not. He's just sad. Sometimes I think I make him even sadder. Perhaps he felt better when he had forgotten all about me.'

'He wouldn't have forgotten you, ever.'

'Probably not,' mused Josiah.

'Do you know what happened to your mother?'

Josiah shook his head.

'She's not dead then.'

'She might be.'

'Perhaps one day she'll just turn up.'

Josiah shrugged, as though it didn't matter whether she did or not.

On the road up to the Duomo they passed the strange, separate inhabitants of the late twentieth century world. There were middle-aged women in shorts with bulging stomachs under white tee-shirts; there were babies in sunglasses lolling in their high-tech, fat-wheeled pushchairs; whining children complaining in a half a dozen languages; sullen, sweating fathers cajoling them, present in body, and absent in mind. There were Americans buying postcards, photo-shoots when faces momentarily lit up; Siennese shop-keepers looking anxiously for trade. A particular eager one approached Josiah and Thomas with a basketful of flags, and on every one a different animal, perhaps a goose, dragon or giraffe.

'Go on,' said Thomas, 'I'll buy you one.'

'Palio, Palio,' said the shopkeeper.

'Si, si, Palio,' said Thomas wisely, and looking to Josiah, he said, 'On the sixteenth of August we'll be coming to the Palio, the greatest and the oldest horserace in Western Europe.'

'Is there a racecourse round here?'

'The racecourse is the town. Siena is everything,' said Thomas proudly, as though he'd been born there.

Josiah had chosen a flag with a black eagle splayed across it. He was waving it as happily as if he were a boy of six.

'Now,' said Thomas, 'there are, and always have been, seventeen *contradas* in Siena. Think of them as electoral wards. No, don't think of them as something so banal! Each has a different animal and a different colour, and in the Palio every horse is decked out in its *contrada's* insignia, and ridden bareback round the Campo. We can't miss it, Josiah. You'll remember the sight forever.'

'I'm sure I will,' said Josiah absent-mindedly.

They'd nearly reached the Duomo, and they squinted in the sunlight to admire it in its entirety.

'Do you think the people who built this amazing thing were building it for God?' asked Josiah.

'They all believed in God in those days, and they took it as a given that everyone they met would be a fellow-Christian. There was no soul-searching, no new-age stuff, no pick-and-mix religion. When the great Siennese artist Duccio completed his *Maesta*, which means 'majesty', Josiah, and always depicts the Virgin Mary and her worshippers, there was no one who questioned that its rightful place was above the high altar in the Duomo. And the night they carried it there, every single inhabitant of Siena, every man, woman and child carried burning tapers and processed around the Campo, and all the bells of Siena pealed the *Gloria*. They would have walked right up this street, as we are, and they'd be carrying the insignia of their *contrade*, perhaps they would have been waving flags like yours, and all the while they would be offering prayers and giving alms to the poor. Why did we ever have to become *individuals*, Josiah? Did we ever realise it would be such a curse?'

'I don't think it's been a curse. Crowds are dangerous. They all believe the same thing. That's spooky.'

'Believing different things doesn't make us any happier.'

'But you're a truth-seeker, Tom. What has happiness got to do with anything?'

'I'm happy now,' said Thomas, seriously. 'I'd say, quite a lot.'

They entered through the great medieval door of the Duomo della Santa Maria dell'Assunto, as sure in each other's love as a bride and bridegroom, and for a boy who had never even seen inside a church the effect was mesmeric. Josiah was to say that it didn't feel like being in a building at all, there was no sense of prosaic things like walls, floors and ceilings; it was rather like being inside a jewel, where every surface had been cut with only beauty in mind, or perhaps heaven, or perhaps this was the place where the two became one.

'*Marmor lapis deorum est*,' said Thomas, because nowadays the two had taken to speaking in Latin when the spirit moved them.

'*Vere dicis*,' replied his companion.

And if marble is the stone of the gods, not only was the floor paved in it but every wall and column was carved in stripes of black and white, ascending high into the ethereal hexagonal dome, as though it were a work of nature rather than art: and the very highest point of it was studded with stars. Josiah, being only a boy, lay under that dome on the marble without a thought in the world, and because his expression was one of awe rather than mischief, no one disturbed him.

The following days they were more observers of the particular: Pisano's pulpit, with its seven panels depicting scenes from the life of Christ; the frescoes in the Chapel of St John the Baptist, the plaster busts of a hundred and seventy popes made in 1570, and the third century Roman copy of the *Three Graces* in the Libreria Piccolomini, and a hundred other things which enchanted the pair hugely. But perhaps these two felt at their most intimate poring over the illuminated anthems of the fifteenth century, written in Latin, of course, which instinctively made them feel, somehow, conspiratorial: for these songs of praise were written in *their* language, and lived only for them.

The Duomo led them to the Basilica, and St Catherine of Siena's head, stolen by her adorers in 1380 from Rome and smuggled here in a bag along with one of her hands. So her body with one hand was buried in Rome; while her head was mummified along with the other hand in Siena. Which city had the greater prize? St Catherine herself would argue that neither did, that the body should be mortified to reveal the spirit within it, and if it wasn't actively being flagellated by her religious order – both by friars and her fellow sisters – it should at least be being starved.

'She was mad,' insisted Josiah, peering through a thick glass window to survey the thick leathery hide of St Catherine's sunken cheeks.

'She was also charming, apparently. Everyone loved her. And the greater and more acute her physical pain, the greater her spiritual exultation and the closer she felt to Jesus. She had visions lasting three months. And then she would emerge and help the sick and the dying – she was fearless, death was nothing to her. Yet she wasn't mad. Far from it: she was quite at home in the world of church politics and reform, and impressed every Pope who met her. Even on her death bed she was issuing instructions on some aspect of reunification. Denying the fleshly demands of the body was considered part and parcel of the life of any Christian. St Catherine dedicated her virginity to Christ when she was only seven.'

'How did she know what virginity was at that age?'

'She was the twenty-fourth of twenty-five children in a dyer's family. Perhaps she'd overheard her mother nagging her father to keep his hands off her. She would probably have shared a bedroom with them.'

'So what would St Catherine say to me?' asked Josiah, guilelessly. 'About desire.'

'I don't get you,' said Thomas, less guilelessly.

'According to our biology teacher, it's natural for adolescent boys to think about sex almost constantly.'

'Do you? I don't think you do, do you?'

'Sometimes I feel like an industrial electrical cable which has been cut down, and there's a vast current running through me which doesn't know where to go.'

Thomas' lips puckered responsibly. 'I think St Catherine would tell you to fast.'

Josiah looked disappointed.

'The last time I was here you could buy replicas of St Catherine's scourge in the gift shop. Perhaps I should whip you mercilessly.'

'I should like that,' said Josiah.

Thomas couldn't tell if he was joking. He stood back a foot to survey Josiah's beauty. 'You're not serious!'

'I think I see the point of a sound whipping,' said Josiah, flirtatiously.

'Which is?'

'If you're in pain, it's as if you don't exist anymore. You can't plot and plan, you can't say one thing and be another. It's too complicated. You're literally, beside yourself in pain. Doesn't "ecstasy" mean, "standing outside yourself?" The thing about pain, is that you're set free from being you, and sometimes being you is the greater pain.'

'How did you manage to get there, Josiah, at your tender age?'

'Aha, Tom, I still have secrets.'

'As I have from you,' said Thomas, aware of sounding childishly competitive.

'I bet you never had your parents disappear into thin air one day, boom!' Josiah clapped his hands, like a conjuror. 'You've never had to ask, day after day, year after year, "Where are they?" to the only wankers who could possibly help you, and who barely seem to notice you've asked a question.' Josiah was shouting, gesticulating. People were beginning to stare. Thomas put a finger to his mouth and pleaded, 'Shh.'

The boy obliged. He spoke so quietly Thomas could barely hear him. 'Sometimes I just want to lose myself. I just want not to exist.'

Thomas's every instinct was to hug the boy, but they were in the Basilica, the large, empty public space which invited God's presence, not human intimacy. So Thomas patted him – oh a pat isn't very good when you wish to be taken up in someone's arms! – and he said, 'At least you have your father now!' But these words failed equally miserably; Josiah looked at him as if he was some alien who could never understand him, and he said, 'You call Gibson a father?'

Thomas took Josiah out of the Basilica, and out of Siena, and they didn't go back there for a week; the bus left too early, and there was too much lying together to be done. If truth be told, half a single bed would have been ample for them, and in the morning they watched the sun rise in their own chapel, the red, musky glow giving way to a white sharp light. Thomas kissed the boy's hair, often and happily; Josiah held onto Thomas' hand under the blankets as tightly as Michaelangelo's Adam had yearned to take the hand of his God. Then, at eight in the morning, with Josiah lying in the crook of his arm, Thomas said, 'I think Plato was wrong to be so dismissive of shadows.'

'I didn't know that he had been,' said Josiah.

'Then I shall tell you the allegory of the cave,' said Thomas, momentarily turning towards his pupil to kiss him on his temple. 'Plato believed that human beings were like men living in a cave, who never even suspected the existence of another realm of sunlight, and who mistook shadows for real objects.'

'How's that possible?'

'It's quite elaborate, as far as I remember. They're held prisoner, they can't move their heads from left to right, there's a fire at the back of the cave and a low wall somewhere in the middle of it, behind which people crawl up and down holding up a range of objects whose shadows are reflected on the wall of the cave – so that's all the prisoners are capable of seeing, that's their sum reality and they don't question it.'

'I don't get it,' said Josiah.

'Perhaps there's another, truer reality out there which we can't grasp. Some would say, if you can't grasp it, it can't exist. They used to call themselves "logical positivists".'

'And what do you think?'

'Pure arrogance. There are minds in Cambridge, for example, which think in lines so rigid they even manage to reduce infinity to a man-made proposition, useful in mathematics but otherwise defunct. And they have no conception of a truth which is not pure logic, with its meaningless dependence on Aristotelian syllogisms. If all boxes are red, and x is a box, then x is red, that sort of thing. And if your mind is full of that, where do you go next?'

'To a deep pool somewhere?' ventured Josiah, only half-listening.

'You're right! Down to your very bones, you're right!' Thomas was impressed, and kissed Josiah on the top of his head. 'We humans find simplicity hard going,' he said. 'But you're right, we should give it a go.'

So out came the large-scale map; out came the red pen to draw over footpaths they might take and pools they might swim in; out came the trunks (last worn, in Thomas's case, six years previously) and out came (and Thomas remembered the slight unease he felt both in buying and packing it) the suntan lotion. Josiah, meanwhile, had deliberately forgotten to bring his own school swimming trunks, imagining he would rather be naked if push came to shove; but strange to say, the more intimate these two became, the more aware they were of the feelings of the other, and Josiah knew that his nakedness alarmed Thomas and he kept it to himself. Inevitably they lay on the bank in the heat of the day, and yes, they did massage the cream into each other's backs: Thomas on Josiah – perfunctorily, and to the point; Josiah on Thomas – with a little more feeling, a little more awareness of the contours of his back, for this was the first skin he'd been let loose on. They also sat in dappled shade, reading and eating gorgonzola, and Josiah took Thomas's fingers into his mouth and licked them clean, and so easy were they with each other, that Thomas laughed, even in his heart.

'What does sex feel like, Tom? What does it feel like to have sex with a woman?' Josiah asked late one afternoon. The pair had been swimming all morning in a deep pool about seven miles from their chapel. The water was a pale verdigris; Thomas said that was probably because of the high copper content in the soil (Thomas knew everything). Then they'd both fallen fast asleep, lying outstretched by the water, and Josiah had been dreaming erotic dreams that he was trying to place.

Thomas considered. 'It feels secret and dangerous. It's good.'

'You said once that you said it disappointed you.'

'Did I? I meant, I think, not the physical experience itself, which is pleasant, Josiah. The experience as a whole is difficult to get right.'

'I want to know about the physical experience. I want to know what it feels like to be inside a woman. Can you describe it?'

'Of course you've felt… sexually aroused?'

'Oh yes. But by what? By Woman? By Man? What I feel barely has an object. Or at least, everything is its object. If that poplar over there came to life I would desire that tree.'

'I was thinking myself what a handsome tree that poplar is.'

'Do you think desire can just be free-floating?'

'I do, I think you're right. I think it can have any object at all. The desire for God, knowledge, beauty, the desire for possession, the desire to hold onto someone, or something – doesn't desire give us the illusion, at least, that our lives have meaning? Doesn't desire have a necessary journey built within it: here I am, and there I wish to be? Isn't that feeling the very core of what makes life worthwhile?'

'I desire you,' said Josiah quietly, sweetly; Thomas took his hand and kissed it, but was keen to turn desire into something noble.

'I've often wondered whether to introduce you to Plato's *Symposium*. Socrates suggests that all desire is ultimately the desire for Beauty Itself, the Platonic Form of Beauty – we talked about Plato's Forms the other day, they inhabit the realm beyond the shadows. Do you remember the cave allegory?'

'I don't desire you because you're beautiful, Tom.'

Thomas ignored the look Josiah gave him, and launched forth into a further salutary lesson.

'My point exactly! I've often thought there are two kinds of desire, one with a small d and one with a capital D. The small d is barely worth discussing. It's about good health. It's about fitness to procreate. It's about evolutionary biology.'

'What if you're homosexual? What if you desire someone of your own sex?'

'Are you looking for a merely physical experience?'

'You mean, do I desire with a small "d"?'

'Yes, do you?'

Josiah said seriously, 'I do want a physical experience.'

'But as part of something bigger, surely?'

'Not necessarily.' But when Thomas looked crestfallen, he added, tactfully, 'So tell me about desire with a big D.'

'You make it sound ridiculous.'

'Or desire with a big P.'

'Josiah!'

'Come here, Tom.'

'No, no I won't.'

'Then I shall come to you.'

Josiah rolled over and lay his hand over Thomas' stomach, spreading out his fingers over the dark hair above his swimming trunks.

'You've caught the sun,' Josiah said, 'You're looking good.'

And with that Josiah tentatively moved his fingers under the elastic of the trunks.

'You've got an erection,' he said.

Thomas pushed him away and snapped, 'Get off me, you idiot.'

⚜

They slept like a married couple after a row that night, hands by their sides, looking up at the ceiling. At five a.m. Thomas got up because he was hot and anxious and needed to get out of there. He walked for four hours, in a rage at himself, at Josiah, and at the world, and it was with the world he was the first to make his peace with, because Tuscany at dawn placates even the sternest souls.

The dew was heavy and wet, luminous in the soft light, and Thomas walked through seven valleys that morning, pausing only once to drink at a stream. Here were the *valles reductae* of Horace and Virgil, a classical landscape undamaged for two thousand years, and by the time Thomas had reached the top of the seventh hill, the sky was a brilliant, deep, blue, the dense low-lying mists beneath him finally beginning to disperse. Thomas sang out to the beauty of it, 'Salve!' so that anyone who saw him would have though him quite mad, though Thomas felt himself touched by some primordial joy.

As he walked back down the hill towards the chapel, he could make out Josiah fetching water from the stream, but his pleasure at the sight of him was soon pushed aside by the unhappy memory of the day before. So he approached the scene sullen, even angry, and Josiah offering him a cup of tea didn't move him at all.

But Josiah was a clever, perceptive boy, and had spent half the night working out how he might raise himself up in Thomas' estimation once more. He endured the *froideur* between them with grace; he humbly handed him his cup of tea and they sat together in silence while they sipped at it. And then (timing was everything!) he lay down his gauntlet. He'd been preparing the question since Thomas deserted him, and he asked with great earnestness, 'Why did the Romans write such a lot of poetry about farming?'

The question proved quite irresistible.

Thomas' eyes lit up. He didn't reply immediately, but paused to consider it, as a gourmet might enjoy every nuance of a truffle. And finally, what with the loveliness of the *prima luce* and Josiah's pretty, pouting mouth, the Latin quite spilt out of him: *"Salve, magna parens frugum, Saturnia tellus, Magna virum!* Translate, Josiah, translate!'

'Greetings!' translated Josiah dutifully.

'And whom is Virgil greeting?' asked his master.

'Tell me again,' said Josiah, so happy to see Thomas quite himself again.

'Look about you! This early light, how deeply green the land, how blue the sky, and look, over there, acanthus, myrtle, cypress trees! The land of Italy, *Saturnia tellus*, Saturn, the ancient God of the land, and more precisely the land of Italy! Virgil wrote those lines two thousand years ago, and even our little chapel here might have been built over one dedicated to Ceres, Saturn's daughter – that letter of Pliny we read only a month ago...'

'When he's ordering marble columns to embellish his own little temple to Ceres.'

'When he's building her a portico.'

'No, he's building a most beautiful statue for the goddess, and a portico for men!' corrected Josiah, victoriously.

'If you're so clever, why is the land called "*magna parens frugum, magna virum*"?'

'Great parent of fruits, great parent of men. I don't know.'

Thomas was thinking very hard now; he put down his tea and began to pace up and down.

'"Parent", hmm, I'm not sure about the word "parent,"' he said. 'What happened to it? There's something rather managerial about the word, there's no love in it. The Latin word, "*parens*" is a doing word, the present participle of "*pario*". It means, "giving birth to" or 'creating', and you see, it actively goes on all the time, and it's a warm word in the Latin, like "mother". So how about a translation like, "Great mother of the harvest, great mother of men", because that is the point, and it answers your question, too. The earth is the mother of farming, and the mother of civilization. Farming is about creating order out of a wilderness, it's about imposing man's will on chaos and making something good come of it. In fact, you could say that poetry was an attempt to do the same. They are both an act of creation.'

'My father used to say the very opposite. Sometimes he'd take me bird watching in the Fens. He used to say, "These farmers are destroying everything."'

'But in the beginning,' said Thomas passionately, 'the impulse was good and true; if you like, it was "authentic", it came from the heart of man. Over time that authenticity has been taken over. Our minds have taken our hearts and bodies hostage. We believe nothing if it's not couched in terms of acreages and yields and the like. We like facts and figures and measurements, ever since the Enlightenment numbers are the only language we have faith in. One day the world will be like one enormous graph, they'll even find a way of measuring happiness. But a long time ago farming was not so much a business as a way of understanding nature, it was an authentic response to nature, it was living with nature. Tomorrow, Josiah, I shall take you to the Palazzo Pubblico, and there, painted on a few walls and commissioned by the Nine Good Men in medieval Siena, Man's very soul will be revealed to you, not as something divided and categorized into public and private, heart and reason, but something unified and true – something simple, didn't you want simplicity, my dear, darling boy?'

♣

So on the next day they forsook their simple life and went back into Siena. Golden dirt was being spread all over the Campo, and flags were flying from every window; even though there were still four days to go till the Palio, the air was thick with anticipation: there were horses being led round the track, already decked out in the colours of their *contrada* – a horse might lose its rider during the race and still win, but losing its elaborate headdress meant instant disqualification – and each of them had a group of followers dressed in medieval costume, gaudy waistcoats and caps with dyed feathers, or belted doublets and hose. There were musicians, too, lutenists and flautists and children in embroidered smocks and flouncy skirts playing on their recorders – and even the anachronistic throng with their digital cameras and mobile phones pointing at them barely detracted from the possibility that here before them were glimpses of the *real* Siena.

'You see why I love this place,' said Thomas, inadvertently taking hold of Josiah's hand on the steps of the Palazzo Pubblico. 'The Nine Good Men who built this Palace for the People of Siena, instigated the *Palio* as well. Such order! Such passion! All in the one breath. You see the Torre del Mangia, Josiah? The bell it housed was the voice of the Commune. It rang at dawn, to signify the lifting of the night curfew, and then again at midday, when everyone would stop work for lunch and a siesta; in the evening, it used to announce the sunset…'

'It sounds awful,' said Josiah. 'It would be like living in a factory.'

'Ah no, order is a good thing. And they didn't have watches, remember. And order brings with it security, and security, freedom. And the people knew that, they understood it in a way that we've lost sight of. There's a balance to be struck, it's true, but the Siennese struck it. Come, I'm taking you to the Sala dei Nove. If you forget everything else about Siena, what you are about to see you must hold in your heart forever, till you die! Do you promise me that?'

'I promise,' said Josiah obediently.

The Palazzo Pubblico in the Piazza del Campo is one of the most graceful Gothic buildings in all of Tuscany: its ground floor rooms are light and large and gracious, and contain countless treasures, but Thomas was a man with a purpose and he took Josiah by the hand without so much as pausing before any of them, until they had climbed the broad marble staircase and reached the Council Chamber of the Nine Good Men. There was hardly space to stand among the tourists gazing respectfully up at Ambroglio Lorenzetti's frescoes describing the Effects of Good and Bad Government, but Thomas said, 'There would have always been people crammed in here. This room isn't about one to one communing with great art, it's about people, it's about how to live together well.'

Thomas happily closed his eyes for a moment or two, imbibing the communal breath, and talked as though he were the only man in the room.

'Now, imagine it's 1350. We're just regular townspeople, I'm a blacksmith, you're my apprentice. And we've heard about these astonishing frescoes, which are going to tell us everything we need to know about justice. We're illiterate, you and I, but these frescoes have been commissioned by the Nine Good Men for the Commune of Siena, and everyone has been encouraged to come and have a look at them. In fact, let's walk into the room again, let's start right at the beginning.'

Josiah was smiling, not just at Thomas who had drifted onto another plane, but at everyone about him, as though he were apologizing for his eccentric companion, and he said, 'I'm with you, Tom.'

Thomas was transported right back; Josiah followed. The Vices greeted them (the sight was almost shocking): Tyranny enthroned in black, a female demon with horns and fangs, toasted them with a golden cup; and her acolytes are Cruelty, an old woman strangling an innocent child; Betrayal – there's a lamb on his lap with a scorpion's tail; Fraud, a handsome woman till you see her claws; Fury, half-man, half-beast; Division, a lady sawing herself in half; and there's War beside her, head to toe in armour. There are equally vicious women hovering at Tyranny's head: clawed Avarice, holding her coin-press, Vaingloria with her mirror, and horned Superbia rising above them all, Pride herself with sword and crooked yoke, who will never bow down for the good of all, but only looks to herself. Below them all Justice, a pathetic figure being dragged along the ground by children, lies bound and powerless, her scales broken – 'See what

happens, Josiah, when Tyranny usurps the throne of Justice!' cried
Thomas, with as much feeling as a Good Man of Siena. 'The Min-
isters who serve the Tyrant serve only themselves! Yet some of these
vices we pretend are virtues; we pretend that the avaricious create
money, that vanity serves beauty, that pride in oneself makes us
happy, when all it does is separate us from our fellows. Deception is
considered a social nicety, Division the best way of running a Court
of Law. No one knows what virtue is anymore, no one cares about
goodness, whether in others or in themselves. Goodness is *passé.*'

The crowd looked towards the Englishman: some amused, some
irritated, some positively angry. But Josiah enjoyed his outburst, he
even felt rather proud of him, and flicked his fringe in appreciation.

'The thing is, Josiah, that we're born knowing about justice.
Yet somehow it's considered polite to forget. If justice is our first
instinct, that nothing is fair is our first lesson. And then it's a hard
and necessary journey to find her again, because we have to nurture
the goodness in us first. Justice is not justice which puts rights before
duties, which puts the self before the common good. That's Aristotle
for you, and Plato. It's Cicero too, and Thomas Aquinas, in fact it's
everyone, it's all of us, it's a fact, it's out there, it's an absolute.'

'But who's to say what the common good is?'

'Plato's *Republic,* I shall lend you a good translation the moment
we get back to England. Or do you think the time is right for you to
begin Greek? Have you ever thought you would like to learn Greek?
The world is ours, my dear boy. But look, we're not finished yet!'

Thomas put his hands on Josiah's shoulders and steered a path
through his fellow-tourists, of whom he was still quite oblivious.
When Thomas was satisfied with a clear view of the adjacent wall,
he began again at full volume: 'Now take a look at what constitutes
a good Government! How wonderful is that, the private virtues are
all public virtues, when o when did we lose sight of such an obvious
truth?'

An official tour was now congregating around the entrance to the room, and if at first the English guide – a most genteel and well-spoken lady in a cardigan with pearl buttons – was on the point of interrupting Thomas, she suddenly recognized his passion and respected it, and told her dozen or so British charges that he might be worth listening to. So Josiah and Thomas stood side by side, in wonder at the great frescoes of Lorenzetti, and a crowd gathered behind him while he spoke:

'Now, Josiah, look at this Italian framing the border... I shall translate it for you. "This holy virtue, Justice, where she rules leads many spirits to unity. And they, gathered together, make a common good for God." That is the thing about absolutes. Without them, we shall always be divided, there will always be wars.'

'What a load of bunkum!' piped up an English voice behind him. 'Wars happen *because* people believe in absolutes.' The speaker, who was young, bearded and insistent, began muttering about the Middle East, but Thomas barely gave him a second glance, nor the tour guide either, who by now was keen to intervene, and was tactfully trying to catch Thomas's eye.

'Justice is intuited at three years old, but we need another thirty years to understand it. First we must know temperance, fortitude and magnanimity. And look here at the figure of Peace –'

'I love her!' enthused the tour guide,

'She's fat!' denounced Thomas' enemy.

'But she understands a thing or two,' said Thomas. 'And she's stronger than you think. Peace and Concord! We must read Cicero, Josiah!'

Thomas' voice displayed a new crescendo of excitement as he stood back to admire the fruits of Good Government: tall painted houses with balconies and large windows, pot plants and bird-cages, cobblers' shops. 'And a schoolmaster with his pupils! And that man's selling kitchenware and wine-jugs...'

The tour guide stepped forward. 'If you don't mind,' she began, gesturing towards the group of tourists behind her, '*I'll* take over now, thank you very much.'

Thomas, visibly wounded, took a step backwards and said, 'But I still have to show my son the countryside!'

'By all means,' said the guide, as though it were nothing to do with her, and she took her coterie back to the burning city behind her, back to the ruin and destruction ruled over by tyranny, where the only trade was in arms. Her voice was high-pitched and full of historical detail about the wars which would have been confronting Siena at the time; but Thomas took Josiah away from all that, and put his arm about his shoulders and said, *sotto voce,* as though he were telling the boy an intimate secret, 'Take a look at this, Joe, you asked about farming, didn't you? This is why it's a subject for poetry!'

This time they were quiet. They stood together, side by side, an island far away from the crowd about them. In the foreground of the fresco are reapers, and a peasant taking his pig to market; there are noblemen setting out for their castles; donkeys laden with bales of wool, heading for the weaver's shop in the city; a packhorse bridge over a river and a river flowing to a lake; in the background wheat is being gathered in and the hillsides are furrowed; there are prosperous farmsteads, and far in the distance a myriad of palaces with towers and crenellated walls. Then suddenly Josiah spotted a tiny white chapel on the brow of a hill.

'That's our chapel,' he whispered to Thomas.

And Thomas replied, 'Let's go home.'

This time, they didn't bother to take the bus. Somehow, it was too hot. Walking out of the city gates to hit the main Siena bypass wasn't quite the experience those hunters on their noble steeds had promised it would be, but it was good enough for them. And Josiah did say, in appreciation of it, that if you spent your whole life looking at pictures and then walked out into the real world, what a weird and amazing place that world would seem.

'For the thing we have which paintings don't have is air,' he said. 'Air is hot or cool or damp or dry, air can blow over you or stultify you. Not only that, we breathe it in the whole time. And breathe it out. Like we're breathing in the whole world, without realising it.'

'In Latin you breathe out your spirit when you die, *animam exhalare*, or there's a rather good phrase, *exhalare mortiferum spiritum*, to exhale your death-bearing spirit.'

'Then can you do the opposite? *Animam inhalare volo, inhalare vitaferum spiritum*. I hope you got that. I want to inhale life-bringing spirit.'

'You do that already, Josiah. Any more and you'd be dangerous.'

'Have you ever lived dangerously?'

Thomas took the question seriously. They were negotiating a short cut over barbed wire to get out into the open countryside. 'The truth is, not dangerously enough. I've been living in a flat-paged book. This air business is good for me.'

Thomas hadn't bought a map with him; things hadn't turned out quite how he'd thought they would, not that he was in the mood for caring. It was really too hot to care about anything.

'Northern climes make people live too much in their heads,' he said.

'What?' asked Josiah.

'It's not important,' Thomas said to himself, and then to Josiah, 'Wait.'

Josiah stood patiently, looking up at his mentor, Siena and her traffic murmuring beneath them. Thomas brushed the boy's fringe aside with his hand and said, 'You've caught the sun. You look well.'

Even Josiah was abashed and turned away.

'No, look at me, Josiah. You are exquisitely beautiful. You are the pulse of life, not just mine, but all life. One day you're going to make someone supremely happy.'

'What about you?'

Thomas laughed. 'I don't count,' he said.

They walked on. Thomas was leading, though he didn't know it. For a while they followed a path, but when the path petered out they followed a line of cypresses over a hill and walked down into the valley. A stream took them to a small lake, and they both swam naked, shamelessly, and lay on the bank to dry like washing.

'I don't think we'll go back to Siena,' said Thomas.

'I thought we were going to the Palio.'

'There's no need. It's just a horse race. We won't be missed.'

'I don't get it,' said Josiah.

Thomas rolled over to kiss Josiah and sighed. 'One day you will.'

⚜

They didn't get back to the chapel for three days. It was as though they were both under a spell which neither of them wished to break; there were no 'oughts' or 'have tos', no maps, of course, so they never took the wrong path. When they came to a village they sat outside under vines, eating large bowls of pasta and drinking red wine, yet Bacchus never took advantage of them, only let them sleep like babes under large acanthus leaves, hand in hand. At night they would find a decent haystack to sleep in, climbing up to the top and covering themselves with a duvet of hay. They would kiss, like a father and a son, a husband and a wife, a lover and his beloved, and every night they would somehow contrive a position which brought their sleeping bodies, if it were possible, even closer together.

There were the stars, of course. Josiah told Thomas that he'd never actually seen stars before, not a thousand billion of them, not like this. He'd never even known what darkness was like, and how black

| 245 |

it was. Thomas told Josiah how the Romans believed there were sixteen celestial regions, each inhabited by some deity that took an interest in human affairs. They were an immensely superstitious lot, he said, far more interested in the art of astrology than the science of astronomy. Occasionally there was even a celestial marriage. And everything that happened amongst the stars somehow left its mark among men.

'Do you believe in destiny, Josiah? Do you believe that our future is already mapped out for us? Should we even bother to defy it?'

Josiah didn't answer him the first time Thomas asked that question. But as August wore on, and the rhythmical meander of days became a march, and even vast constellations of stars followed their fixed course across the night sky, time began to matter again. No swimming, no reading of poetry, no Latin conversation, in which, incidentally, the two were getting superbly fluent, could compensate for the fact that the end was in sight.

☙

It was the night before their return to Cambridge. They'd been swimming till late, and were now suffering for it, both shivering under blankets with their backs up against the still warm wall of their chapel.

'I think we should stay here,' said Josiah. 'We don't have to go back. No one's making us go back.'

'Life goes on. That's not something we should be afraid of.'

'But I *am* afraid,' said Josiah.

'We'll still have weekends. And the holidays. Nothing's going to change. We're not going to die the moment we set foot in England. And as long as you're not dead, and I'm not dead, how could things ever be different?'

'What if they are? What if they're terribly different?'

'Come closer to me, Jo.'

And all night long, those two shivered into each other; neither could relinquish the stars. Thomas kissed Josiah's cheeks, his mouth, his hair; and he told him that he loved him and would always love him, and that that, at least, would never change.

Chapter Thirteen

THEY WERE WAITING FOR THEM at the airport: four police officers, three social workers. Thomas suffered his fate humbly. Josiah could see his wrists, but not his face. He saw his wrists because Thomas held them up meekly to be handcuffed; but though he hungered for some reassuring glance, some conspiratorial understanding between them which might say, 'These idiots, what do they know about us? What do they know about anything?' Thomas gave him nothing. For even while they were on the plane, the air they were breathing in felt unreal, manufactured and bottled in canisters, a perfect temperature, a perfect pressure, evil stuff. The air separated them from what they had known, and because that knowledge had been transmitted via their skin rather than their intelligence, and because that kind of knowledge can never be written down or even talked about, it is liable to be forgotten, cast aside as a dream, as an illusion, when perhaps in the final counting of things it is as close to truth as we shall ever be.

The police investigation had been a straightforward one. By midday on the morning of Josiah's abrupt departure on the first of August, they knew both the name of the man who had abducted him (there was even a note of it on Josiah's file; June Briggs had always had her suspicions) and the time of their flight to Florence. They had interviewed Thomas Marius' elderly neighbour (whose address Josiah had written in the signing-out book) and she confirmed that the boy whose photograph they showed her had indeed been a regular visitor at his house. She also told them that Dr Marius had had a lodger from the university, though regretted that she had never learnt his name. 'The modern world!' she sighed, as she twisted the corner of a cushion in her arthritic fingers, 'All comes to no good in it! I should have suspected something bad was going on! I'm so sorry, gentlemen!'

By the afternoon, they had traced Greg Wright through the University Lodgings Syndicate; he was a more than happy witness. When the trail ran cold in Florence – after calling over fifty hotels and guest houses in the city – June Briggs hit upon the idea of visiting Josiah's father in hospital. She was adamant that such an interview should be conducted with the utmost sensitivity; Gibson Nelson was not a well man, and had found, according to Daphne Field, the ward sister, his son's visits acutely stressful. Nonetheless, if anyone could throw light on their whereabouts, surely it was Gibson; indeed, his role as their confidant might well have been the trigger for his recent intense bouts of weeping, which were as mysterious and as deep as groans coming out of a mountain. They all said to each other how notoriously difficult such cases were: the rights of a son to see his father, of a father to see his son; and now, should a sick man be protected from such terrible news as his own son's abduction? Or were a child's rights always paramount?

In this case, everyone was keen to see justice done. They needed information. June Briggs assigned two of her most experienced social workers to accompany a police officer to the hospital. The interview was sensitively and professionally conducted, but Gibson was not helpful, and told them nothing. He heaved and rocked, and was often short of breath. Within an hour of their departure he had had an aneurysm, and was admitted to Addenbrookes hospital. Early the following morning he was dead.

Gibson's death was sobering. The police made inquiries at Corpus, but the Fellows there had never even heard of the boy Josiah, and did not know where Dr Marius was spending his summer. So in the end they decided to be patient. After all, there was no one to speak up for the poor boy, no tearful parents parading their loss on TV, and above all, there were no leads. The chances were, the man was a paedophile, not a murderer. They would simply catch him at the airport on their return journey.

The last time Josiah and June Briggs had come face to face was on that fateful morning eight years previously when she had taken him away from his parents and his home. Josiah didn't remember, of course. He had been busy looking forward to his first day at school, not looking at the lady at the steering wheel. Likewise, June had barely registered Josiah: all she knew of that pale, earnest boy was that he had been both neglected and probably abused by his parents. Eve's subsequent disappearance had only served to vindicate her suspicions: what mother could do that to her child? June was unaccustomed to feelings of a personal nature, so she surprised herself when she took Josiah's hand into her own at the airport and gave it a wholesome pat.

'Don't worry, Josiah,' she said to him, while he watched Thomas being taken away by the four policemen. 'Things have a way of coming out all right in the end. The important thing is, you're safe.'

Josiah would have preferred a snake bite and snatched his hand away.

Angela Day said, 'You just don't know how worried we've been about you. We all have. The younger children have been really upset.'

Kevin was Josiah's latest field social worker. They hadn't even met yet. He was sensitive enough not to introduce himself; he just said: 'Right. Let's get out of here.'

These three had previously decided that the most comfortable and appropriate place to debrief Josiah was in Angela Day's private sitting-room at *The Hollies*. The police interviews, they had suggested, could wait until the following day. As he was still a minor, they were legally entitled to record Josiah without his knowledge, and this they fully intended to do. The police could then hear the tape before carrying on with their own interrogation.

The journey back to Cambridge took a mere forty minutes, during which not a word was spoken by any of them. Angela sat in the back of the car with Josiah, but Josiah turned his whole body away from her, and kept his face up against the window, as though the view between Stansted and Cambridge was one of the most fascinating in the world.

No one in *The Hollies* had been told to expect Josiah: so the elder children had gone into the centre of town to 'doss' while the younger ones had been taken on a trip to Linton Zoo. The house felt eerily empty; the windows were all open, and a breeze was blowing crisp packets across the stained carpet.

Angela Day said, 'Come upstairs, let me get you some tea. Josiah, will you have a cup?' Upstairs Angela unlocked the door which said 'Private', and they all went in. On a low table was a bowl of sugar and a box of tissues, ready for Josiah's tears; round it were placed a sofa and two armchairs, in one of which June Briggs had already made herself at home. She was fiddling with the small tape recorder in her bag. Josiah was staring out of the window, his elbows leaning on the sill. Angela was boiling a kettle in the kitchenette, and shouted out to them, 'Does everyone take milk?'

'Thank you,' said Kevin. The other two ignored her, so Angela put a little jug of milk on the tray along with a comforting brown tea-pot of Tetleys and four mugs.

'It's a nice sitting-room they give you,' said June. 'I suppose they've got to give you some perks in this job.'

Angela sat down on the sofa and began pouring the tea.

'I like it here,' she said.

Kevin sat down beside her, and rummaged around in his brief-case: what for, no one ever knew, for he never found it.

'Josiah, come and sit down, love,' said June. To everyone's faint surprise, he did. He took a cup of tea from the tray and added sugar. They all felt encouraged, and smiled benignly. June switched the recorder on.

'The first thing we want you to know,' she said, 'is that we absolutely don't blame you for what happened. You have nothing to fear. Do you understand that?'

'What do you mean, I have nothing to fear? How do you know what I fear?' Josiah spoke easily; Kevin was impressed.

'The small matter of duplicating keys, stealing your passport, absconding… you won't get into trouble for any of it. In fact, we don't even blame you for any of it.'

'Is that what you think I fear?'

'Then what do you fear?'

Josiah said nothing.

'We need your account of what happened, Josiah. How long have you known this man?'

Josiah looked away.

'How did you meet him?'

Silence.

'Then let me tell you. You met him outside your school at the beginning of February. He offered to teach you Latin, and for a while you used to come on Saturday mornings. The lessons turned into days, into weekends, into holidays. Isn't that how it was?'

Josiah looked up. 'Is that so bad?' he said.

'Tell me. I want you to stand back from the situation for a while. You're an intelligent boy. Just look at how this might seem to us. Thomas Marius is a man of thirty-six. He comes from an entirely different background from you. He's mature, educated, for God's sake. You're barely fifteen. What's in it for him, do you think? What could you possibly have in common with one another?'

'A father loves a son. What do they have in common?'

'They have blood in common, Josiah. That is an entirely different thing.'

'Why couldn't he have loved me as a father?'

'Because he isn't your father, that's why!'

'What kind of love do you think he had for me then?'

'Do you acknowledge that he loved you? Can we at least get that straight?'

'Yes, he did,' said Josiah, holding himself high. To have said anything else would have been a betrayal.

June Briggs almost clapped with what she saw as a swift victory. Josiah noticed; he asked her, 'Have you ever been loved?'

'Most people have known that pleasure.'

'So love is a good thing?'

'Of course it is.'

'Is it ever bad?'

'When it's exploitative.'

'But if love's exploitative, it stops being love doesn't it? It becomes something else.' Josiah was sitting bolt upright, his cheeks red, his pulse racing.

'You don't think Dr Marius ever tried to exploit you?'

'Of course not. He would never do that.'

'But he encouraged you to go on holiday with him?'

'Yes, he did,' said Josiah.

June smiled malevolently. 'And why, do you think, would he have wanted your company?'

'He likes teaching. I like learning.'

'Do you really think teachers want to go on holiday with their pupils?'

'If there was a teacher who loved teaching enough and a pupil who loved learning enough, no holiday could be happier.'

'That's an absurd thing to say,' snapped June. 'Do you honestly expect me to believe you read schoolbooks all day? Kevin, do you want to fetch his case? Will we find some history project in there, is that what you're telling me?'

'The word "education" has a Latin root. It means to "lead out", not to "put in".'

'Okay. He's taught you well,' said June sourly. 'Do either of you have any questions?'

Kevin asked, 'So how did you spend your time on holiday?'

And Angela, 'Were you lucky with the weather?'

Both Josiah and June ignored them. 'Tell us what happened,' said June.

'What do you want to know? We went to Siena. We looked around a few churches. Saw a few pictures.'

'Where did you sleep?' asked June.

'We had a… room in the country.'

'Did you share a bed?'

Josiah said nothing.

'Did he try to kiss you?'

Again, nothing.

'What happened between you?'

Josiah shook his head.

'Did he touch you inappropriately?'

'Never,' said Josiah.

'Whatever you tell us now, you understand you will have to submit to a medical examination. The courts need to know if there was anal penetration.'

Josiah stood up as if to go. 'The courts can fuck off,' he said.

'Sit down, Josiah.'

Josiah had no intention of sitting down, but shot June Briggs such a look of rage and loathing that all she could do to retaliate was tell him something that only an hour previously she had been wondering how to break to him.

'All right, stand up then! Stand up! Your father died when you were gone.' The words sprang out of her like a dart. Josiah stood even straighter, eyes staring ahead, unblinking. She relented immediately; Kevin and Angela were looking at her in astonishment.

'I'm sorry to have to break the news like this,' continued Miss Briggs, her voice in gentle mode. 'He didn't know where you were. He was upset. These things happen. Don't blame yourself.'

'I don't,' said Josiah.

And this was how a nice brown tea pot, a jug of milk, a bowl of sugar, one full mug of tea and three empty ones, ended up on June Brigg's lap; this was why the table banged against her shin bone on its way down to the floor, and why June shouted out stuff about his bloody mother that Kevin and Angela were fairly shocked to hear, and why June destroyed the tape afterwards. Josiah, victorious, threw the box of tissues onto June's lap and told her to clean herself up with them. He smiled, took a bow, and left the room.

♣

The police took three days to find him. He had no coat, no food, no money. Both nights he crept back to Thomas' house, but the pile of mail on his doormat made it clear that Thomas was still being questioned by the police. He found a garden shed not so far away and slept between bags of compost; he had his meals at Macdonald's, posing as a customer near tables brimming with children, and eating their leftovers before they were cleared away. If he'd been intent on escaping for good, of course Josiah would have managed it. He could have stowed away on a train to London as easily as any of his 'mates' had, and told as many stories on his return. But Josiah had nothing to escape for. His sense of wretchedness was quickly to smother the rage he felt against *that woman*; and guilt muddied his grief. On the second evening, propped up against a Honda mower, and watching the twilight become night through the small shed window, he remembered Thomas telling him that he loved him for his purity and his strength of character, and how both qualities together amounted to holiness. Josiah had kissed him for that, full-bloodedly on his pursed lips, and had asked him whether his kiss was holy too. And now, mused Josiah, he was neither strong nor pure nor holy. He was a nothingness, he was lower than nothing, he was a contaminated vacuum.

The lady of the house had spotted him pulling carrots from her vegetable patch at half past seven the following morning. The police came to the scene of the crime with their sirens blasting; Josiah lay down between the cabbages and the potatoes and thought of his father as the man he had been. And he thought, how strange it was, that when a man died you no longer remembered him as old and fat and mute and needy, but as vigorous and wise and good and kind; that there was an essence that lived on regardless, an essence of all that had been the best of them.

When the lady of the house heard the commotion outside the door, she was furious, and she ran back to her bedroom window to see whether her trespasser had already run off. But what she saw was Josiah, lying perfectly still on the earth, with tears pouring down his cheeks. She wanted to shout out some warning, and she didn't know who was the more idiotic, the police for their brash announcement of themselves, or the boy for ignoring it. She told the police at the door that she had dropped all charges and wanted nothing more to do with it; but Josiah had other plans. If Thomas wasn't at his house, he was being held in a police cell. This was his chance of joining him there.

'You want me, I think,' said Josiah, meekly, emerging from the garden gate. He introduced himself to a pair of cops who seemed barely older than twenty.

'Josiah Nelson. I absconded from *The Hollies*. I'll be on some list somewhere.'

A cop was on his walkie-talkie in a tick.

'We've apprehended a lad here, uhh, Wilson…' he began.

'No, Nelson. Josiah Nelson. J. Nelson.'

'Nelson. *The Hollies.*'

'But I don't want to prosecute!' insisted the owner of the cabbage patch.

All three gave her a look which said, 'You're irrelevant, darling,' and indeed, within the minute she'd been left, open-mouthed, on her doorstep.

The two cops were proud of their acquisition. They told him he was 'a waste of police time,' when he left clods of mud on their back seat. They presented him at their HQ as happily as a novice angler might a salmon to his family. It was still only eight in the morning, and no one was really interested. He was asked to wait in reception alongside a lugubrious-looking man who'd come to report the theft of his Audi. Josiah had always imagined that goodies and baddies would be separated by at least a screen, but no such luck.

At a quarter to nine a pretty woman of about thirty in jeans and a T-shirt came in to introduce herself. Her name was Margie, she said, she was from the child protection team, and was going to be talking to him quite soon.

'I'm just going to make a few inquiries,' she said to Josiah. 'Will you be alright here just a while longer? I tell you what, do you fancy a hot chocolate?'

'I thought you'd put me in a cell,' said Josiah.

'We're not barbarians here, sweetheart. I'll send in a hot chocolate. Okay?'

'Aren't you going to arrest me for trespass?'

'No one's charging you. We might make a note of it somewhere, in case you make a habit of sleeping in ladies' gardens, but I have a feeling that's a one off, what do you think?'

'What if I want to go into a cell? What if I run away again?'

'Please don't run away till we've had a chat, okay? Is that a deal?'

Josiah stood up to go.

'Look, come upstairs with me, then. Come and meet a few of my colleagues. They'll take good care of you for a few minutes. Come on.'

But the colleagues weren't too interested in meeting him; a couple of police officers sat him on a chair next to the photocopier and went back to their computer screens, and worse, no one mentioned hot chocolate again. By the time Margie summoned him half an hour later Josiah was happy to have any company at all.

The interview took place in a small, internal room which was dominated by the tinny sound of an old air-conditioning system. The evening before a shoplifter had been interviewed there, and she'd insisted on changing the reeking nappy of her baby: modern technology powerless before the oldest dirty protest in the world. So the room smelt of rotting compost. But Margie herself had shoulder-length blonde hair and pink lipstick and even a trace of blue eye-shadow left over from a night out. She was rooting for humanity, she was saying, we humans are all right, you know, once you get to know us.

Margie made a point of moving the desk to one side of the room and moving the chairs closer together, so that their knees were almost touching. Then she said:

'I have two confessions I want to make to you, Josiah. The first, is that I have a tape recorder. I'm putting it right here, on the desk, so that you can see it. But I'm not going to put it on straight away, but you'll be able to see when I do. And the second confession is that I'm getting married next month, and we're going to Italy for our honeymoon. Now, you've just spent a month there. Would you recommend it as a country? Is it beautiful? Did you eat well? Did you eat out, ever? Did you stay in the town or the country? You flew to Florence, I believe. Did you stay there a while?'

Margie had a Yorkshire lilt to her voice, which suited her.

Josiah even smiled when he said, 'I'd recommend it.'

'Where did you stay?'

Josiah was immediately anxious and said nothing.

'Did you stay in Florence at all?'

'No.'

'Siena?'

'We went to Siena. Quite a lot.'

'What's Siena like, then? Do you think we should go to Siena?'

Josiah nodded.

'Where should we go? What do you suggest?'

'The Duomo. On the hill.'

'And what's that, when it's at home?'

'The Duomo. The Cathedral.'

'You went to a Cathedral, did you? Can you tell me about it?'

'It was kind of black and white inside.'

'Were there paintings inside it?'

Josiah shook his head.

'There weren't any paintings?'

'I can't explain it,' mumbled Josiah.

'Where else did you go to?'

Josiah looked blank.

'But you didn't sleep in Siena, did you?'

Josiah closed his eyes and hung his head.

'I'll be honest with you, we know where you stayed. Dr Marius told us.' When Josiah didn't even look up, Margie continued, 'The police were in the chapel yesterday evening. The bed you shared measured thirty-one inches across, or eighty centimetres. That's a narrow bed, Josiah.' When Josiah slumped further, his elbow leaning into his chest, his forehead supported by his knuckles, Margie went on, and as she did so, she switched on the tape recorder.

'Mrs Scroppo told the police there was semen on the sheets.'

Josiah said nothing.

'What happened between you, Josiah?'

Josiah shook his head.

'What happened? Remember, it's not just you we're thinking about here. There are other boys, other holidays. If you heard that Dr Marius was taking a friend of yours from school, what would you say to him? Would you tell him to go, or stay at home?'

'That wouldn't happen,' said Josiah. He didn't look up.

'Why wouldn't it?'

'You wouldn't understand.'

'Why wouldn't I? Try me. You aren't the first, you know.'

'I am the only…' began Josiah, but he couldn't finish what he wanted to tell her.

'You are the only what?'

Josiah shrugged it off.

'You are the only what?'

Josiah shrugged again and sighed. 'You're getting married,' he said, as though that were an explanation.

'Are you telling me you were like a married couple?'

Josiah thought for a moment, but then shook his head.

'You were saying that, weren't you? Did you love him?'

Josiah said, 'I do love him.' Then Josiah cried, silently, profusely, and Margie didn't have a tissue to offer him so he cried on his sleeve.

'Does he love you?' asked Margie. Josiah nodded, and the tears kept flowing. Margie leant forward and put her hand on his knee. 'I understand,' she said. 'I do, I promise. But we need to know… We need to know what happened between you.'

'Nothing did,' said Josiah so quietly that a mouse wouldn't have heard him.

'Are you telling me that he didn't touch you sexually?'

'He didn't touch me.'

'Are you telling me that your bodies were jammed up next to each other all night long, yet you did not touch each other?'

'I know what you're asking me. The answer is no.'

'You'd be happy to say that in a court of law?'

'I would.'

'Why did Dr Marius take you on holiday?'

'I've told you already.'

'I don't think you did.'

'Because… you know why. You know why.'

'Because he loves you.'

Josiah nodded.

'Doesn't it seem strange to you that a man of thirty-six would "love", as you say, a boy of barely fifteen?'

'It's so stupid…' Josiah gave up mid-sentence.

'What is stupid, Josiah?'

'Why are we allowed to love some people and not others?' Josiah managed.

'What do you mean by "love"?' asked Margie. She had a personal interest in it, after all.

'Love is when you give yourself. When you say, "I am at your service. I am yours."'

Margie laughed. 'I shall remember that,' she said. 'But do you think love has anything to do with need? With emotional needs? With sexual needs? Is there not something about love which sees the person you love as the missing link, if you like, the one thing which, if you possess it, will fulfil you forever?'

'Yes,' said Josiah simply.

'Is there anything you'd like to add to that? Do you think you fulfilled Dr Marius' needs? Did he fulfil yours?'

'I didn't fulfil his,' said Josiah.

'So what are you saying?'

'I didn't fulfil either his emotional or sexual needs.'

'You're quite certain of that?'

'I'm fifteen,' said Josiah quietly.

'So why did he take you on holiday with him?'

Josiah began to speak, but Margie couldn't hear him.

'What was in it for him, Josiah?'

Josiah shook his head. 'Nothing,' he whispered.

'Was your relationship sexual?'

'No', said Josiah.

'Josiah, if you submit to an anal examination, and the doctor verifies what you say, the charges against Dr Marius, at least regarding sexual abuse, will be dropped. Do you understand that?'

'Will you take me to see him first?' Josiah looked up now, pleadingly. 'Just for a few minutes?'

'Josiah, he's fifty miles from here. He's in a prison in Lincolnshire. He wouldn't accept the bail conditions.'

'I see,' said Josiah.

'I'm going to drive you to the hospital myself. Is that all right with you?'

Josiah slumped forward. He was bent double, as though he'd been punched in the stomach. Margie switched off the tape recorder.

'It'll all come good in the end. You'll see,' she said gently.

Margie couldn't stay long; just long enough to deliver Josiah safely into the hands of a Dr Hollis and his nurse.

'You were,' explained Margie, 'a delightful emergency. You're a lovely boy Josiah, and I'll do everything I can to help you. But now I've got to be off. Someone from the social services will be taking you back to *The Hollies* in about half an hour, so wait here in the reception till they get here. Okay?'

Josiah nodded and Margie disappeared; he felt strangely on his own again.

♣

Dr Hollis was a thin man with thick black-rimmed glasses, and when he wanted to seem sympathetic he would let his glasses fall down his nose, believing, mistakenly, that his small, piercing blue eyes would somehow comfort his patient.

He looked down at Josiah and said, 'You follow me, young man', and he did so, because his spirit was quite used up. They walked down the corridor together to his consulting room, and on the way he suddenly stopped and said, 'This is my nurse, Liz,' and Liz looked up briefly from her specimen bottles near the sluices and gave Josiah a little wave.

Down came his glasses again when he told Josiah to sit on the couch, and he said, 'I'm going to make you two promises. The first, is that nothing's going to hurt, and the second, is that you're out of here in ten minutes, Now, you can hold me to that, young man. See that clock, it's ten to eleven; and when it's eleven exactly, you'll be walking out of here. Now, Liz is just fetching you a clean gown to put on. Shall we give you three minutes to change into it? I reckon you could change that quickly, what do you think?'

Liz duly came in as though it was a double act they'd been polishing for years, and she said (as she had done countless times before), 'I bet you he could change in two.'

'Let's draw the curtain, shall we, Liz, and give him a bit of privacy,' said Dr Hollis (as he had done countless times before); and so the curtain was drawn and Dr Hollis and his nurse listened very hard. Not a squeak. They caught each other's eye as if to say 'gently does it', and Dr Hollis took his glasses off and popped his head around the curtain.

Josiah was sitting quite still, staring ahead. 'I'm sorry to waste your time,' he said.

Dr Hollis began again. 'There's nothing to fear, you know.'

'I'm not afraid,' said Josiah, and his face, it's true, betrayed not a smidgeon of fear. If anything, he looked bored, listless.

'Perhaps if I told you exactly what the examination entailed. It's not a penetrative....'

'I'm not afraid,' said Josiah. 'I just don't want to be here.'

'No one *wants* to be here,' said Liz.

'You know,' said Dr Hollis, trying a different tack, 'that homosexual acts under the age of sixteen are illegal.'

'No, I didn't know. I thought it was twenty-one.'

'Would you be able to swear in a court of law that a homosexual act has not taken place?'

'I would.'

'You understand that if I examined you and confirmed what you say, your friend wouldn't be in such serious trouble?'

And for a moment Josiah looked more interested; he looked straight into Dr Hollis' blue eyes and was thinking hard.

But then there was a knock at the door. Liz was quick to answer it to send the interloper away, but June Briggs' head had already made its appearance.

'Ah, there you are,' she said to Josiah. 'I didn't know you'd made it here. I'm the last to be kept informed!'

Dr Hollis was irritated. 'Could you please wait in reception,' he demanded, gruffly.

'Of course,' said June Briggs, but she walked into the room with a triumphal smile. Dr Hollis instinctively held up his hands, as if to defend the boy from her.

'Please,' he said.

Meanwhile, Josiah had not spent his minutes on Dr Hollis's couch idly. He had spotted on a nearby shelf a box of syringes already fitted with their needles; even then, when he had no obvious victim, they had seemed an irresistible weapon. Suddenly he leapt up from the couch.

There was a calm before the storm, in which all four seemed to wonder what would happen next; then Josiah moved as fast as a meerkat, and, grabbing hold of the box, shouted gleefully at June Briggs to keep still. Surprisingly, she did, and the dart almost scored a bull's-eye in the middle of her forehead, but at the last moment she used the door to shield her and the needle stuck into the top of her arm. Josiah laughed, and rattled his box; Dr Hollis tried to grab it from him and the syringes spilt over the floor. How wonderful are the laws which make it quite impossible to physically restrain a child! For Dr Hollis was more anxious about breaking medical guidelines and the hollering of June Briggs than about the young and eager Josiah, who was busy picking up the syringes as happily as a toddler might take smarties scattered from a tube.

'You bloody boy! Get hold of him, you idiots! The boy's insane! Just like his bloody parents!' Ms Briggs just couldn't stop herself.

Liz rushed off to get help, and Ms Briggs would have stayed for more had Liz not taken her with her to the nursing station, on the pretext of looking at her arm.

Josiah jumped back onto the couch, clutching a handful of syringes.

'So,' he said coolly to Dr Hollis. 'Do you think I'd make a good doctor?'

Eventually, Angela Day came to fetch him. Dr Hollis, his nurse, and June Briggs all decided not to take the matter further or try to examine him again. It was obvious, they all agreed, that Josiah had been severely traumatized.

'What got into him, do you think?' asked Ms Briggs.

'He's obviously a very distressed boy,' ventured Liz.

'Angry. Frightened,' suggested Dr Hollis. 'I suppose we should ask ourselves, what more can we expect?'

'My sentiments exactly,' said Ms Briggs.

Liz did tell her husband that night that she thought Ms Briggs' rantings were a little out of order, even given the circumstances, but then the matter was sighed over and forgotten.

❧

Angela Day had taken a while to get to the hospital because she wanted moral support. She didn't feel she could face Josiah after that morning when he'd upturned the table and ran off like that. Anyway, she hadn't found anyone to go with her and braved the trip alone.

On their journey back Angela's only remark was to observe at yet another temporary traffic light, 'They seem to be digging up the whole of Cambridge at the moment,' before offering to make Josiah some lunch on their return. Josiah ignored her. Once they were back at *The Hollies*, Josiah ran upstairs to hide away in his bedroom. Not that he knew it then, but this was to be his refuge and prison for the next fifteen months.

Josiah never went back to school. The sight of Thomas' empty house was literally unbearable to him. Everyone thought it was because he was anxious he would be bullied: after all, when the lads called him 'faggot' at *The Hollies*, he could just walk away – after so many years' experience, their words fell away from him as lightly as reverberating air. But school would be different. At school, there would be no escape. They all knew this, and they also knew he had no parents to fine or imprison if he played truant. And when they realised he was impervious to the threat of a secure unit in Peterborough where they could *force* him to receive an education, they gave Josiah a long leash, and a queue of tutors and educational psychologists to try to persuade him that learning was a good thing. He co-operated with none of them; while the five books Thomas had so casually lent him six months before became so precious to him that he took them from their proud, upright pile on his chest of drawers and wrapped them in his clothes and hid them.

One day in the middle of November, about a month before the case came to court, Josiah was lying on his bed as usual in the middle of the afternoon. He was gazing at the ceiling, and indulging in his customary mental occupation of writing a letter to Thomas. An open copy of *The Pilgrim's Progress* lay face down on his chest. He had just read the words, 'I am now a man of despair, and am shut up in it, as in this iron cage', and had been unable to go on. In his head he wrote the words, 'The books you gave me are all I have. The one I'm reading now was your fifth form prize. You were my age when you first held it. Did you once tell me that the only prison worthy of the name was in our own heads? That's where I am now, my dear Thomas. Do you think of me? I would like to think of myself in your head. Then again, I'm frightened that I'm your prison.'

But Josiah's letters never even made it to paper. He reasoned that they'd be intercepted, perhaps they'd even be considered incriminatory. But his heart, more to the point, was afraid. Afraid of what, he did not know. When Angela Day knocked on his door that afternoon, it was a good moment. To be so lonely and yet so driven as to drive all away had often seemed to him a curious paradox. But that particular afternoon he would have befriended a flea, and was pleased when Angela's comfortable figure sat on the end of his bed and said, 'I'm so sorry things have turned out like this.'

Josiah immediately sat up and leant up against the wall.

'It's not your fault. It's not really anyone's fault,' he said.

Angela looked at the book which had fallen to his lap.

'*The Pilgrim's Progress*. Well, I am impressed. I never got beyond the children's version.'

'I don't think you'd like it much.'

'You could try me!' exclaimed Angela, surprised that he could hurt her so much by saying so little. But when Josiah said nothing, she bravely went on, 'The thing is, love, it's so easy to just give up when you've just let things slip a little. Life's like that, you've always got to keep one step ahead or else you start thinking, "I can't cope," or "Why bother?" and then you slip even further down. You're just too special to let that happen to you.'

'It's always control, isn't it? Control yourself, control your life…'

'Before it takes control of you –'

'Before others control it for you,' said Josiah, coldly.

Angela looked hurt. 'People aren't trying to control you. They're concerned for you, Josiah.'

'"Concern" is such an ugly word. It's a clinical word. It's a Latin word, it's a loveless word: from *cernere*, to distinguish, to set apart, to push away.'

'You're setting yourself apart. You and your Latin. It doesn't do, not to belong, Josiah.'

'Why would I even want to belong to you lot?'

'Show some humility. We're all in this together. We're all human beings together.'

'A contradiction!' cried Josiah. '"Human beings together!" We're not, and never will be. That's our curse, don't you get it?'

Angela did not get it. He had hurt her, and she left him.

Then, a fortnight before the case came to court, Joseph received another visitor, Thomas' defence solicitor, young and keen and recommended by the Master of Corpus himself, who had taught him years before when he'd been Headmaster of Eton. David Findlay was a most affable man; handsome, fluent, good-humoured and quite charmed by the young Josiah. It was midday; the dining-room was empty and Angela brought them mugs of tea.

'This is quite the most disgusting tea, isn't it? Don't tell a soul, will you?' and with that he opened a window and threw the stuff onto the grass.

Josiah smiled. It was an auspicious beginning.

'It's good to meet you at last. I'm David Findlay, and I'm representing your friend Thomas in a couple of weeks time. I have to say, he's not told me much about you. He's quite a private man, isn't he?'

Josiah didn't know whether he was a private man or not. He was the first man he had ever known. So he just said, trying to hide quite how much it mattered to him, 'Is he all right?'

'In a word...' began Mr Findlay, and then he looked hard at

Josiah to see if he could bear the truth of the matter, 'In a word, no. But, there's only two weeks left of this to go, and then, if all goes to plan, he'll be free. In fact, I'm angry with him for refusing to accept the bail conditions. His college was happy to put up whatever money was necessary, but he wouldn't hear of it. Is that typical of him, do you think?'

Again, Josiah hadn't a clue. His head was still reeling from that little word 'no', and there was no mental space left to consider Findlay's question.

'Why isn't he all right?' he braved.

'Sexual offenders get a hard time in prison. That means, for his own safety, he's banged up on his own. But he has a few books. Not that he's been reading much. He is extremely preoccupied, Josiah. He didn't want me to see you today. In fact, I very nearly came to see you last week without his permission, but I don't like to betray my clients' trust, if you see what I mean, even if it's in their own best interest. Anyway, he knows I'm here. And he sends you his best wishes.'

'"Best wishes"?' asked Josiah incredulously.

'Well, he could hardly send you more, through me, I mean. But I can give you more myself. In fact, it's his respect and affection for you, I feel, that are holding him back. He's his own worst enemy, as they say.'

Josiah struggled a while, but then looked up and asked, 'Why do you think he'll be let off?'

'Tell me, quietly, here and now, should he be let off? Do you have any reservations whatsoever?'

'He never did anything.'

'He didn't tell you to say that, if anyone asked you?'

'No.'

'It's strange. Only you know and he knows what happened between you. It's your secret. And we have this great formal structure in place to try to make one or other of you divulge your secret.'

'Nothing happened. There is no secret.'

'There are quite a number of people, I believe, who think there is. Though I do know they've decided not to fly the Italian couple over. I fear they suspected you, but they'd already laundered the evidence, I hear, the sheets were hanging out to dry even as the police arrived to question them.'

'What about the hospital's report? I didn't…'

'No, you didn't behave particularly well, by all accounts. But these examinations, between you and me, prove nothing. The courts, of course, have a penchant for concrete evidence, but after that woman, what's-her-name, made such a frightful balls up with her anal dilation hypothesis and took half of the children of Lancashire away from their families, these examinations have rather lost their credibility. So accusations of buggery, of sexual abuse – well, they're all speculation, and I shall tell the court so. But the most awkward charge to dispense with is undoubtedly that of kidnap of a minor, and this is where you come in, Josiah. Now, Thomas doesn't want to be cross-examined under oath, and that's his right, and frankly, I'm not sure that he would do himself any favours in court. But he did tell me, and I believe him, that he thought he did have permission from this place, that he had written a letter to the proprietor or whatever you call her, and had received a letter back from her. Unfortunately, however, we haven't found that letter. I mean, there's no reason why he should keep it. There's a sods' law that crooks have all their documentation perfectly in place because they know they might need it, while the innocent – well, it goes with being innocent, in every sense of the word – they're neither careful nor vigilant.'

'I took the letter,' interjected Josiah.

'You took it?'

And Josiah, who was unaccustomed to blushing, felt his cheeks burn.

'Have you still got the letter?' asked Mr Findlay, eagerly.

'I threw it away.'

'But why would you do that?'

'It wasn't a real letter. I forged it. Thomas didn't get permission. He would never have got it. I know what they're like round here. They wouldn't have let him take me to the zoo.'

Mr Findlay pushed himself away from the table and balanced precariously on the back legs of his chair. 'Ah, I see,' he said. 'Didn't you think you might be getting him into trouble?'

'I just wanted… to go away. I just thought, "I need to get out of here".'

'But the fact that you went to so much trouble… you knew what you were doing was wrong.'

'It's not the first time I've done something wrong. So much is wrong, anyway.' Josiah lay his head down on the table as if it was suddenly too heavy for him to carry any more.

Mr Findlay sighed. 'What you're telling me is serious.'

'I know,' said Josiah, and his words was muffled, because his mouth was buried in his jumper.

'I have a confession to make myself, Josiah.'

Josiah looked up.

'My visit here today isn't strictly professional; there should be witnesses, it should be properly recorded. But I like your friend Thomas. I wanted to meet you first in a relaxed manner, or as relaxed as we can be in the circumstances. In my bones I felt him to be innocent, and now I've met you I know him to be so. We shall do everything we can to prove that. Now, you have to talk to social services, and make a proper statement to them, and tell them you forged the letter.'

Josiah shook his head.

'Or the police if you prefer. These are what they call mitigating circumstances, Josiah, do you understand? Do you know someone by name whom you feel easy with? You really are in a position to help Thomas, you know. Do you want to do that?'

'There's a woman called Margie,' said Josiah.

'Margie Wynter, yes, I know her, good choice. I'll ring her this afternoon to fix an appointment. Just tell her what you've told me, and she'll read your statement in court.'

Josiah sat motionless, crouching over the table, his face buried in his arms; Angela saw him from the doorway and walked in.

'He seems upset,' said Mr Findlay anxiously. He patted Josiah on the back. 'Just two weeks! Trust me, we'll get him off.'

Angela, who was one of those who thought Thomas should be behind bars forever, threw him a furious look.

Mr Findlay ignored it. 'I'm sure you'll take good care of him,' he said, as he brushed past her.

❧

The case lasted three days. Cambridge Crown Court, the full works, the *gravitas*, and an unprepossessing jury, the younger of whom were distinguished by their tattoos and body piercings. How strange, thought David Findlay, that when push comes to shove, that lot will be the most conservative of them, the most eager to convict. He whispered to his barrister words to that effect; and then looked towards the press. There were just three journalists, he had expected there to be more. Even if he was let off, Thomas would never be innocent in their eyes. This would be one of those cases in which justice had not been seen to be done: a paedophile let off on some technical hitch. But justice would be done, that was the important thing.

Josiah's lover was in the dock. He was recognisably Thomas; summer tan had still not completely deserted him. He had lost weight, and he hung his head like a man already convicted.

The prosecution threw down the gauntlet: there were two charges against Thomas, the kidnap and sexual abuse of a minor. The buggery charges were dropped for lack of evidence. A policeman read out a statement from the Scroppos about how it didn't seem to bother the pair that there was only one single bed, about the quantity of dried semen on the sheets, about their suspicions right from the start about the exact nature of their relationship. The policeman then went on to produce his own evidence, which seemed to amount to no more than the exact measurements of the bed in question.

'Would it have been possible *not* to have touched in such a bed?' asked the barrister for the prosecution.

The policeman laughed. 'Not likely, sir.'

But the defence barrister asked him, 'Do we know whose semen it was?'

'No,' the policeman admitted. 'Mrs Scroppo had already washed the sheets by the time we got there.'

'The boy in question is only fifteen. Isn't it possible that he was prone to what we call "wet dreams", that he had ejaculated in his sleep?'

'I suppose so,' said the policeman.

'And one further question. Is it not possible to lie very closely to another human being and not touch them sexually? Because touching *per se* does not imply sexual touching, does it?'

'It doesn't sir, but in this case...'

'What are you implying?'

'I think it's likely there was sexual touching, sir.'

'If there had been two beds, do you think it likely they would have still chosen to share one bed?'

'Yes. I don't know.'

'In other words, you're guessing. In fact everyone here is guessing what went on in that bed. I'm suggesting that there being only one bed in that chapel was a surprise to the defendant; in fact, they would both have preferred two, but they made the best of what there was. There was no other bedding. There was no alternative. Is that possible?'

'Yes, sir.'

Things seemed to be going so well. Even the lodger Greg, with his sly insinuations, his anxieties at finding Josiah sitting at the kitchen table at a quarter to eight in the morning, was unable to meet the barrister's question, 'If you had been so certain that sexual abuse was going on, why didn't you go to the police?'

When June Briggs victoriously declared to a stunned court that Josiah had told her that Dr Marius loved him, the barrister asked her, 'When was love against the law? We're dealing with sexual abuse, aren't we? Sexual abuse is a crime, and rightly so, but if you begin to legislate against love, then God help us.'

To Dr Hollis, who gave an account of Josiah's 'bizarre behaviour' when confronted with an anal examination and his 'violent and unprovoked attack, indicating trauma,' the barrister suggested that to a young boy an anal examination was indeed traumatic, and would have amounted to rape.

And then the defence barrister summoned the Child Protection Officer of the Cambridgeshire Police Force, and Margie Wynter was a brick, now dressed to the nines in her police regalia. She spoke with authority and conviction of her two interviews with Josiah. She said that instinctively she did not feel that Josiah had been the victim of sexual abuse; and she spoke, with great feeling, about the second interview, when Josiah had broken down in tears, declaring that it was 'all his fault that Thomas was in prison'. He also confessed to forging the letter purportedly from Angela Day, which Dr Marius believed had given him permission to take him to Italy. Both defence and prosecution barristers cross-examined her, and she acquitted herself with exemplary professionalism.

But even while the defence team were quietly congratulating themselves on the front bench, even while the chaplain, Justin Phipps, was telling the court how in his thirty years at Corpus he had never met a man of purer principles, Thomas stood up as though he were about to speak, and then sat down again, his eyes darting to left and right and upwards at the ceiling. People had by now stopped listening to an account of his virtues, and were staring at him. Then suddenly Thomas leapt up and shouted, 'It's not true! I am guilty!'

The judge remained judge-like. Barely two seconds' silence had elapsed before he asked the defence team if they would like the opportunity of speaking to their client, and he was happy to adjourn the court for half an hour to that end. But half an hour was too short a time to knock sense into a man who could only plead to be cut in two so that the Court could see for itself how stained he was, how there was no purity in him. In his heart, he told them, he had always realised that the letter was a forgery; but so keen was he to take the child to Italy that he overlooked it. He wanted the Court to know that he loved the boy with his mind, body and soul: and if, therefore, good people considered him to be a pederast, then a pederast was what he was. Thomas did not allow that there was any difference between thought, word and deed in the question of guilt; he said that the divisions were arbitrary and had no bearing on what was true.

Mr Findlay had to tell the judge that he could no longer represent his client, and Thomas Marius took his fate into his own hands. The judge showed leniency, however. He was sent down for three years, with the possibility of parole.

Chapter Fourteen

ON 1ST NOVEMBER 2000, at three o'clock in the afternoon, Elspeth Hardy was watching the sunset from her office window. She was on the top floor of a large, Victorian building, now converted to the premises of the Cambridgeshire Probation Service. The view was good, and her attention was held by the roof of King's College Chapel glistening in the last, low light of the day. There was a two-minute interval between reception ringing through to announce the arrival of a client, and the knock on her door. Elspeth always used that time well: she would gather her thoughts, or, as she was doing now, she would ungather them, thereby creating an empty and welcoming space that a new client (or possible friend, as she liked to think) might occupy.

On this particular afternoon she was about to meet Josiah Nelson for the first time. She vaguely remembered the details from the referral meeting three weeks previously. He was sixteen years old and an arsonist. He was a first time offender and had lived in residential care since he was seven. He'd been involved with a paedophile. She seemed to remember it was a barn he'd set fire to, but Elspeth hadn't read the Social Enquiry Report – not because she was lazy, far from it, but because she always liked to come to her clients with an open mind. She took pride in the fact that she never pre-judged people; she let them explain, in their own time, who they were and what they wanted from this life. Then she did everything in her power to help them get it.

There is one other fact about Elspeth Hardy which set her apart from her fellow probation officers: she was beautiful, and wore her beauty lightly. She had coal-black hair, which she plaited, giving her the air of a seventies American folk singer. Her natural pallor only exaggerated her flawless skin, and her eyes were dark and expressive. She never wore make-up, she didn't need to. The curves of her lips were so perfectly drawn, that they belonged more to an artist's notebook than to a living face. She was tall and slim, and on that particular afternoon, she was wearing a tight-fitting shirt with the top buttons undone, a short skirt and nubuck boots up to her knees. None of this was lost on the young Josiah, who, despite his continued refusal to go to school or apply for a job, had at least succeeded in growing four inches since we last met him, and now used a razor every other day.

Elspeth was still standing by the window when she said, 'Come in.' She was pleased with Josiah. She liked his long blond fringe, and the habit he had of jerking it away from his face. She liked the way he wore an old man's shirt without a collar and with the sleeves rolled up, though it was deeply autumn by now and cold. She liked his trousers, made of grey wool and held up by a belt, also, she decided, bought from a charity shop and part of a suit which might have been cut in 1965. But above all, she liked the way he looked at her. In fact, she enjoyed his appraisal of her quite as much as her own of him.

She said to him, 'Would you like a cigarette?'

Josiah shook his head. There was a 'No Smoking' sign on the wall and Josiah briefly glanced at it.

'Rules are for breaking, aren't they?' said Elspeth, and she sat down briefly at her desk to seek out her ten-pack of French Gitanes. She found it, lit one, and resumed her place at the window to smoke it.

'Do you like Cambridge?' she asked him. 'There's a good view from this window. Would you like to see it?'

Josiah walked towards her, and with a flick of his fringe looked out. They stood next to each other, almost touching, while Elspeth continued to inhale deeply on her cigarette.

'Here, go on,' she said, handing it to him.

Josiah smiled, and put the cigarette in his mouth. Suddenly he began coughing.

Elspeth snatched it back. 'Where, for God's sake, have you been all your life?'

This business with the cigarettes was a ruse Elspeth regularly employed with her young male clients. She'd even put the 'No Smoking' sign up herself. For anyone, she would argue, could put on an act for an hour a week: anyone could appear sensible, hard-done-by, apologetic, and say and do all the right things and then go out, get drunk and slap his girlfriend that same evening. This was Elspeth's first year of her first proper job as a Probation Officer: she was a radical and an idealist. If a youth was unemployed, she would meet them in the Job Centre; if a lad was in custody, she would take his family out for a picnic on the way to visit him. On a Tuesday evening, she would teach 'social skills' to a dozen young people (yes, a couple of girls too) and she used the occasion to give a supper party, designating 'hosts' and 'guests', teaching the hosts how to cook vegetarian meals, for that was another of Elspeth's passions, she was a vegetarian. Of course, her clients loved her: this was par for the course, for why bother to change one's outlook and character for someone one didn't love? And because Elspeth had an affectionate nature, she loved them back, or at least, she said she did.

The fact that Josiah had never smoked a cigarette in his life in some curious way gave him the upper hand. For Elspeth was ever so slightly embarrassed, and it took quite a lot to embarrass this girl. She wanted to rewind, and start the interview again, and in a way, that's what she did.

Elspeth put out her cigarette and laughed. She made a bad joke about not inflicting her smoke on Josiah if he didn't indulge himself; then sat down at her desk and tried to look serious.

'Sit down,' she said.

Josiah obeyed, amused.

Elspeth saw that amusement; and it made her want to confess to him that that whole first scene had been a little trick of hers, which had worked countless times before… and look how much she knew about this boy before he'd even said a word! But wisely she realised that she wouldn't have been able to get her words in the right order, and she was determined to get the interview onto the right track.

'As you can see, Josiah, I know nothing about you. Not even whether you have an occasional cigarette. I know nothing of your character nor your crimes. What are you going to tell me about today?'

Josiah smiled and paused, 'Ask me something easier.'

'Okay, Josiah, how are we going to play this?'

Josiah didn't say anything for a while. He looked first at Elspeth, and then around at her office, the smallness of it, the bareness of it, the floorboards, the cheap desk and bookcase, and the books – *Young Offenders, Criminal Law, The Paradoxical Injunction, The Sociology of Marriage*. And he noticed the mug on Elspeth's desk, on which was written 'Rights For Cows' in large red capital letters. Elspeth was quite relaxed about the silence: there was a trick she'd learnt from the BBC, the longer the pause, the greater the revelation at the end of it.

But then suddenly Josiah said, 'Have you got a car?'

'Why do you ask?'

'I could take you to the scene of the crime, if you like.'

'That would be a start, I suppose,' said Elspeth, wishing at that moment that she hadn't extinguished her cigarette. 'How far away did you commit this crime of yours? I hope conveniently close.'

Josiah considered. 'Twelve, fourteen miles,' he said.

'All right. You're on. Let's go,' announced Elspeth, hell-bent on seizing the initiative.

Elspeth took Josiah down into the basement garage for employees. The garage was very dark: it was hard even to find her keys in her handbag, with the figure of Josiah looming over her. She drove a much-loved Citroen CV, ten years old, and on the panel above the gearbox was stuck a red love-heart with the words underneath, 'I love Gertie.' A client's grateful mother had given her the sticker when she was still a student, because Elspeth had once taken some mothers of young offenders on a day trip to the country (because Elspeth believed in self-help groups, and thought that might be a useful one), and Elspeth had confessed that she sometimes called her car 'Gertie', as in 'My dear Gertie, please start for me this morning! Please ignore the frost, Gertie!' So when the Mum had sent the sticker in the post along with a 'thank you' note, Elspeth had stuck it on her car with pride. Even as she watched Josiah reading it, she would have paid good money for it to self-incinerate.

'Who's Gertie?' asked Josiah, looking at Elspeth and watching her reply.

'Gertie's my car. A friend gave me that sticker. It's a bit silly, I admit.'

'You call your car, "Gertie"?' Josiah was genuinely curious, but Elspeth only saw mockery.

'Well, when you have a car, you never know, you might call it "Fred."'

'I don't suppose I will,' said Josiah. His tone was deadpan.

Negotiating a route out of Cambridge when she wasn't even sure where she was going was hard enough: she couldn't even give Josiah the occasional sideways glance. She suddenly realised quite how idiotic this venture was: in half an hour's time, they'd barely be able to see the scene of the blasted crime.

'Where exactly are you taking me?' asked Elspeth, though what she'd wanted to ask, was 'Where am I taking you?'

'West of here. Beyond Caldicott.'

'Okay,' said Elspeth.

At the traffic lights on Grange Road, Elspeth was finally able to look at her young charge. There was an intensity about him which she felt strangely attracted to. She liked his voice, too: a pure, strong voice, as if he knew something that no one else did, and which set him apart. He seemed more like twenty than sixteen.

Then they were off again. 'You live in residential care. Is that right?'

'Yep,' said Josiah.

'Is that in any way… difficult?'

'I'm probably institutionalised by now.'

'You don't seem institutionalised.'

Josiah shrugged.

'Tell me about it.'

'There's nothing much to tell.'

'What do you do in your free time, then?'

'I don't have… what is the opposite of free?'

'Don't you go to school?'

Josiah shook his head.

'Why not?'

Josiah said nothing.

'Education is a good thing, though you might not think it now.'

'Education is everything,' said Josiah.

'So why aren't you at school, then?'

Josiah simply ignored the question, and looked out of the window. 'I like your car,' he said. 'I see why you've named her.'

'So, if you don't go to school, and if you don't hang out smoking on street corners, what do you do with your life?'

'Three miles beyond Caldicott,' said Josiah.

'How did you find this place you're taking me to?'

'I biked here.'

'You have a bike?'

'Sort of.'

'You mean, you nicked the bike, or you borrowed the bike?'

'Do you have a boyfriend?' Josiah asked her.

'Do you?' Elspeth's question was impulsive; well, he deserved it for being so impertinent.

'No, nor girlfriend. You might say, I'm quite friendless.'

'Ah, that can't be true!' said Elspeth warmly.

'I couldn't even count my friends on one finger,' expanded Josiah.

'Don't you ever get chatted up? You're not bad looking,' said Elspeth, and she thought, 'In fact you're the most good-looking teenager I've ever set eyes on.'

'No one would know how to chat me up.'

'Tell me the secret.'

'There's none to tell.'

'One day you'll fall in love. You shouldn't be so cynical, Josiah.'

'I'm the least cynical person I know,' said Josiah.

'I don't know if I believe you.'

'I'm innocent.'

'I'm not sure I believe that either,' said Elspeth, giving him a sideways glance.

'Why do you think it's good to be innocent and bad to be ignorant?'

'A child is innocent,' suggested Elspeth.

'A child is also ignorant. And both ignorance and innocence need correcting, don't you think?'

'Do you think an innocent child *needs* to be made less innocent? That seems a sad thing to say.'

'It's not sad at all. There is something true about the world which innocent people don't know about. It's important to get access to that truth.'

'What sort of truth is that, Josiah?'

'I don't know because I'm innocent. But I want that truth. It's worth having.'

'Explain.'

'It's not about facts. School knowledge is about facts. Ignorance is about not knowing any facts.'

'So if you're not wanting facts, what is it that you're wanting?'

'Perhaps I'll only recognize it when I have it.'

'I don't understand you.'

'I'm talking about the knowledge of the heart.'

'Meaning, exactly?'

'*Cors non explicanda est*,' said Josiah mysteriously.

'Is that – Latin?'

'Yes,' said Josiah, unapologetically.

'So what are you saying?'

'The heart ought not to be unfolded.'

'"*Ought*" not to be?'

'You can't break it down and analyse it. It is as it is. And you *ought* not to break it down. And the truth is, you won't break it down.'

'What do you mean by "the heart"?'

'There's nothing to be said about it. The heart just is. A description of it can only scrape the surface of it. A description of it can even alter it, that's how sensitive the heart is.'

'Who the hell have you been talking to?'

Josiah didn't answer her, but Elspeth knew. Now she wished she'd read the file.

For the rest of the journey they said nothing to each other. Josiah opened the glove compartment and tried on Elspeth's sunglasses. He looked through her selection of tapes: Billie Holliday, Joni Mitchell, Carly Simon. He pulled out the ashtray. It was crammed full with cigarette butts. Somehow, Elspeth felt ashamed.

They passed a sign to Caldicott. 'It's a couple of miles up from here,' said Josiah.

Elspeth drove on. She looked at her watch. It was five to four. Fuck, she thought.

'Okay, you can park here,' said Josiah suddenly.

'Here? What, in this lay-by? A crime in a lay-by?' Elspeth laughed nervously.

'It's about a ten minute walk from here, perhaps fifteen,' said Josiah.

'It's too dark, Josiah.'

'It's not dark!' insisted Josiah. 'You don't know what dark is! But you're right, we need to get a move on.'

Josiah jumped out of the car and slammed the door. He rolled down the sleeves of his shirt. 'Do you mind if I borrow that blanket on your back seat?'

'If you don't mind dog hairs.'

'Do you have a dog?'

'I walk my neighbour's at weekends.'

'You should come out here sometimes. The last remaining hills near Cambridge.'

'You mean, you managed to find a hill?'

Josiah wrapped the blanket round his shoulders.

'You look like Superman in that,' Elspeth said.

'Then you must trust me. Let's go.'

There was something about Josiah which made her follow him. They walked together, perhaps as far as a mile.

'What exactly was it you set fire to?' asked Elspeth.

'Hay. And the hay set fire to the building containing the hay.'

'Are you disclaiming responsibility, Josiah?'

'Oh no. I had the box of matches. The hay didn't know what it was doing.'

'Why did you set fire to the hay, Josiah?'

'Fire is beautiful and wild and free; the most creative, the most destructive force in the universe. I wanted to sit on the hill and watch it. Of course, the barn's not in such good shape now, but where I'm going to take you is the place I sat down to watch.'

'This is going to be a wild goose chase, I can tell.'

'Far from it. I'm going to take you to the place where I felt... that's all I need to say. Where I felt. Where, if ghosts exist, my ghost would be. I can tell you the date, however. It was the first of August.'

'And why do you remember the date so well?'

'The first of anything is memorable, isn't it?'

'It's getting cold, Josiah.'

'Here, come under the blanket with me.' Josiah didn't put it as a question, but wrapped a half of it round Elspeth's shoulders. There was a moment when Elspeth considered resisting. She could have said, 'Look, it's dark and cold and I don't know who you are and you're frightening me and I want to go back home now.' But she didn't. She let him put the blanket on her, she was even grateful for it. And suddenly she couldn't be bothered to work out quite how dark it would be, and whether they'd be able to find their route back. It was, perhaps, how people feel when they are drowning. Suddenly they no longer need to master their fate, but surrender to it.

The first of anything is memorable. They sat down together on the cold grass and huddled under that blanket together for a long time, as if it were a secret den away from the world. Josiah kissed her cheek and told her she was the most beautiful woman he had ever seen. It was so private, that place. Under that blanket, the gutted structure of the barn faintly visible under a new moon, there were no boundaries, not even the boundaries of words, to separate them. Such was the pleasure of kissing her yielding mouth that a full hour passed before Josiah's hand ventured to her nubuck boot, and upwards to her thigh, and his fingers dared to explore all that was in his possession. He knew he was master of her; Elspeth knew it too.

At nine o'clock that evening they stumbled down the black path together towards the main road and the patient Gertie. On the way back into Cambridge Josiah put on the Billie Holliday tape. They said nothing to each other: the more private a place you share with another, the more private a place you return to. They were at the traffic lights on Lensfield Road.

'So, where shall I take you?' asked Elspeth.

'Your place,' answered Josiah.

Elspeth was rapidly learning how to be obedient. Sometimes, there is no alternative.

☙

Josiah left Elspeth's flat in North Cambridge before she woke up, and the first thing Elspeth did when she saw the empty space beside her was to retch into her loo. She wasn't sick, but if she could have sicked up the whole of the last twenty-hours she would have done. The wine didn't help either; Josiah had refused even a glass of it, while he watched her humiliate herself by drinking a whole bottle of the stuff before midnight. It was 7 am on a Saturday morning: normally it was her favourite moment of the week; she would take a novel and a cup of tea back to bed with her, put on a CD, muse, enjoy. But today she couldn't sit still; she showered, changed her bed linen, mopped the kitchen floor, polished her windows. Then at half past eight she rang her neighbour and told her she's be walking that day, a great marathon walk, she said, and would Rusty like to join her? Rusty would, said the neighbour; but while Elspeth straightened out the blanket on the back seat of her car, she was overcome by that same sickness, and even more to her chagrin, desire.

By the Sunday night she'd walked thirty miles, but her feelings, whatever those feelings were, were stronger than ever. She laid out her clothes for the following morning: no more nubuck boots, her skimpy shirts stayed resolutely on their hangers, and out of her wardrobe came the dark and sombre suit she'd bought from Next for her job interview and had never worn again. She was determined to repent; she considered handing on Josiah's Probation Order to a colleague, with the explanation that her caseload was already too large. She considered writing Josiah a letter of apology. Apology! Sometimes things were too big, apologies were too small. But by the following Friday she had done nothing. The inevitable telephone call happened. Josiah was in reception. He was coming up.

Elspeth stood up to meet him. Even Josiah's act of closing the door was somehow suggestive. The room suddenly became a secret place; Elspeth remembered the sensation of the blanket being thrown over her.

'Hi,' she said.

Josiah looked at her intently, curiously. And you can't read a face that's reading yours. Elspeth couldn't understand how she needed to behave, and there were no clues in Josiah's face to guide her. If this was a game, Josiah won it.

He said, 'You look unhappy.'

'I am,' she said.

'Please don't be,' said Josiah, with feeling.

'Look at me,' said Elspeth, sitting down at her desk, 'I'm having a cigarette.' Her fingers were shaking; she lit it and inhaled deeply. 'Sit down, goddammit,' she said.

Josiah took the chair and moved it so that it was exactly adjacent to hers. He then sat down beside her and put his hand on her knee. When she didn't resist, but carried on smoking as though nothing had happened, he gently pulled up her skirt just a fraction, and began to stroke her.

Then suddenly Elspeth got up and said to Josiah, 'Come on, let's get out of here.'

They quickly learned how to use that three o'clock appointment to their advantage. By the following week, they had both got into their stride. Josiah would come in; Elspeth would say something like, 'So, Josiah, have you been good this week? Confess your sins, boy!'

And Josiah would reply, 'I met a woman. She led me astray.'

'You have to learn self-control!' Elspeth would reprimand.

'But she is so beautiful!' Josiah would insist, gazing at her openly, honestly.

And after this little game, those two would be quiet for a while, and they found, to their surprise, that not touching was quite as erotic as touching.

And then they would drive back to the flat together, leap into bed until supper, and after eating and sharing a bottle of wine, return even more voraciously to their adult play-pen. On Saturdays and Sundays there was more of the same, punctuated by walks with Rusty, and thermos flasks of tea on windy hills. And really, nothing more should have been demanded of those two. The problems come when people try to shift the natural perimeters of a relationship, and when one or other begins to look for more.

That one or other was Elspeth. If her first fear had been too much too soon, and the fear of being caught, of losing her job, or simply, or doing a morally suspect thing in sleeping with her client, this was replaced by a fear that Josiah was hiding something from her, did not fully trust her with the truth. Two months on, not only did Elspeth have no idea why Josiah had set fire to the barn – he had a way of making arson seem quite normal – but he had never spoken to her about his involvement with the paedophile, who was now in prison on account of it, nor had he told her about his parents, or what he remembered about them, or how he had come to be taken into care. She had never wanted to force it, for when her questions were too pressing, he would deflect them. He would say, 'Sometimes, you know, you sound just like a Probation Officer.'

The bottom line was, Josiah could not love her as much as she loved him, and her whole instinct, and indeed training, told her that his behaviour was typical of someone whose emotions had been 'blocked' by some trauma. At first she imagined this was his experience at the hands of 'that man', as she referred to him, but he had calmly told her that he hadn't laid a finger on him and, quite honestly, he shouldn't even be in prison. 'There's nothing more to say about Thomas,' he insisted one Saturday morning as they lay in bed together. 'He was kind, generous, good, the best man I've ever known, really.'

'Then why is he in prison? The courts don't normally fuck up.'

'A thought crime. A crisis of conscience. He confessed to something he didn't even do.'

'I don't believe you.'

'Then you're like ninety-nine percent of the population,' said Josiah.

But Elspeth had one extraordinary advantage over the rest of humanity in her pursuit of the perfect relationship. Namely, she had files. She could legally access files as far back as Josiah's birth.

Josiah's Social Enquiry Report written for his trial had been extremely sympathetic. Josiah's life story had been tragic: his mother had run off when he was barely seven; his father had been a mental patient. After a series of failed foster placements, he had settled well both into his school and *The Hollies*, a residential children's home. Since his involvement with a paedophile, however, things had gone dramatically downhill. He had not been to school or been gainfully employed since July 1999. The offence had taken place a year later. Josiah, the report concluded, should not be given a custodial sentence despite the seriousness of the crime.

'That sheds light on nothing,' thought Elspeth to herself. 'A year is too long a gap. Something else is going on in that boy's head.'

So she found out that the senior social worker involved in Josiah's case had been a Ms June Briggs, and she fixed an appointment to see her. They met in Ms Brigg's office. She explained, at their interview, that she found it difficult to get through to the boy.

June laughed. 'You're not the first who's found that. I knew his mother. I fear genetics are at play here, she was quite impossible too.'

'Do you know what happened to her?'

'I think she ended up in Spain or Italy or somewhere like that.'

'So she's not dead, at least.'

'She might be now, for all I know.'

'So how does anyone know where she went, even approximately? Did anyone ever go out to look for her? Some concerned relation?'

'I'm afraid she didn't even have many of those. Eve's mother was pretty frightful too, as far as I remember.'

'Was she also a client of yours?'

'Thank God, she wasn't.'

'So you really have known Josiah since he was a baby?'

'Only too well.'

Elspeth feigned a professional interest; her love and pity for the boy were overwhelming her.

'So what was Josiah like as a young child? Did you know his father, too?'

'That was what was so strange,' said Ms Briggs. 'Josiah's mother was an extremely vivacious, attractive woman, I'll grant you that, and she married this large silent man, more than thirty years her senior, called Gibson. I mean, he seemed harmless enough – you are staying to read the files, aren't you? You'll see for yourself. I don't think our social workers ever managed to have a single conversation with him. But he was a gentle sort, at least, and more responsible, certainly, than his wife.'

'So tell me about Josiah's mother. Eve, is that her name?'

'Yes, Eve.' Ms Briggs smiled. 'Eve rather lived up to her name. The first woman, she always had to be first, she always had to be right. That might even have been the one reason she married Gibson, to spite her mother. You can imagine quite how much she approved of the match.'

'But are you saying Eve's mother actually cared about who she married? That's a start isn't it?'

'She was an ogre and a half, Eve's mother. She also needed to be in charge. And Josiah does, too, don't you find? None of that family have ever had the… humility to heed advice, or to accept help.'

'So you thrust it upon them.' They were badly chosen words. Elspeth bit her lip, and attempted a look of humility herself. She ignored the expression on Ms Briggs' face which said, 'So are you one of us, or one of them?' and continued, 'So I want to know about Eve.'

'Elspeth, that is your name, Elspeth? You enter deep water when you concern yourself with that family. Luckily, we have only Josiah to contend with, but he's some can of worms, I can tell you. It didn't surprise *me* when he set fire to that barn. It's exactly the kind of thing his mother might have done. In fact, I seem to remember that she did set fire to something. It wasn't serious, it didn't come to court. When you read the file you'll tell me, won't you? In fact, you'll be able to remind *me* of a few things. It's a strange thing, isn't it, DNA. They only lived together seven years. Arson wasn't a learnt behaviour; rather, there's some cluster of genes that say to each other, "Let's destroy!"'

'I'm not sure how much I believe in genetics.'

'There speaks a good student! I suppose you have to believe in people being able to change, otherwise what's the point in being in our trade? But I've been a senior social worker here for twenty years. I'm retiring soon. And every year, I'm afraid, I become increasingly cynical. We can't make people better than they are. We can't make people better parents. We can't make people kinder. Or less self-centred. I simply despair at what humanity is. One huge, self-serving mess, no part of which holds together with any other part. Love your neighbour! That'll be the day, Elspeth.'

They looked at each other for a while, and each surveyed the other with pity.

'How much disillusion lies in store for this young, pretty enthusiast!' thought June Briggs.

'How bitter, how twisted, how unhappy this middle-aged woman is! And she should dye her hair!' thought Elspeth.

Elspeth stood up to go. 'About those files,' she said.

Ms Briggs didn't even look up at her. She was playing with the end of her pen. The spring had broken.

'Ask Marie at reception,' she said. 'She's got them ready for you.'

Elspeth was shown into an empty interview room; she was offered tea, which she accepted, and after a few minutes, a small tray with tea and biscuits arrived, along with three fat files. She didn't even open them for ten minutes, but sat there, catatonic, licking the chocolate off a digestive biscuit as a child might. Then she braced herself.

The first entry was in March 1984. Josiah was still a six-month-old foetus in his mother's womb. They don't miss much, thought Elspeth. Eager beavers, these social workers. It was a photocopy of the minutes of a case conference held at Fulbright Hospital. It had been given the title *Aftercare Proposals for Gibson Nelson and Eve de Selincourt,* and Elspeth scanned the list of people present: Dr Tim Aggs, Dr Michael Fothering, Patricia de Selincourt (presumably Eve's mother, Elspeth surmised), Alison Streetly, Laura Jones (student), Janet Holloway, and June Briggs: there she is, in the story right from the beginning.

Elspeth was not thorough: her curiosity drove her onwards and onwards, faster and faster, and June was right, there was barely any mention of Eve's husband, Gibson. He was featured as this large weight, harmless, hovering in the background. It was Eve that confounded them all, it was Eve that no one could bear.

Again and again, *Eve did not co-operate,* she read. *Eve did not behave appropriately. Josiah walked in half way through the interview. He was covered in mud. Eve didn't respond; she didn't seem to realise he might need her. Eve was dressed in the saffron robes of a Buddhist. It's possible Eve might be acting as a prostitute. Eve is absent again. Gibson doesn't seem to know where she is. Eve had no interest in looking around*

*the local schools for her son. Eve refuses to send her child to school. There
is no evidence that Josiah is receiving an education at home. Eve is
obstructive. Eve is rude. Eve has an irritating laugh. Eve always thinks
she knows best.*

'For God's sake, you control freaks, can't you let that woman
be? Have you ever seen her drunk? Have you ever seen marks on
Josiah's body? Don't you have any serious case against her?' Elspeth
had already skimmed the first file. Eve had been some sort of hippy
manqué, she decided. But nonetheless she was a mother. She was
Josiah's mother.

The second file she barely had the stomach for. By now Eve had
disappeared, but Elspeth couldn't quite grasp the events that had led
up to it. She looked back to the end of the first file, in case she had
missed something. Suddenly Josiah seems to be in a foster placement
because both his parents have gone: Gibson turns up, but Eve never
does. But there is no account of an argument, an ultimatum... no,
there it is, a few pages back, a photocopy of a letter dated August
20th 1991. For God's sake! A letter from June Briggs to Eve, one of
many, yet more hectoring than any of them:

> Josiah has not received an education for a year, nor have you
> made any attempt to educate him at home. If you do not
> enrol your son into the Cherry Hinton Primary School within
> the next fortnight, we will have to take extreme measures.

And they did take extreme measures. Josiah's parents didn't just
walk off, they didn't just desert him. They were as good as taken
away from him. They weren't quite good enough, were they? No,
they didn't quite come up to scratch. They were an itch on the back-
side of the system, they had to be corrected. And no one grieved
when they went. Just the boy. And who was the boy, if he didn't
complain?

By now Elspeth could only read a line or two in every twenty pages. Josiah's unhappiness was too palpable. As each foster placement broke down, a social worker would write about Josiah's incommunicativeness, his wistful look, or even the fact that he was a 'pretty child'. But no one went further than that, no one took responsibility for what they had done to him. Where was the weeping and the gnashing of teeth? Where, for God's sake, was the guilt?

The letter which was to change everything was folded and small, and hidden about a quarter of the way through the third file. It was from Eve Nelson herself, written from an address in Naples. Josiah would have been about eleven years old. In it, she confessed to setting fire to several schools. She said that she missed her son, was sorry for everything she ever did, and wanted to come back home. She needed advice about how she might do so.

Elspeth felt physically sick. She looked for some photocopy of June Briggs' letter back to her, but found none. Was it possible that Eve Nelson was still waiting?

Elspeth's first instinct was to confront the woman, make her remember there and then how she had responded to this pathetic plea from a mother. But she realised she was far, far too angry. So she smuggled the letter into her bag and returned the three files to the reception desk.

Elspeth wrote to Eve Nelson that very afternoon. She introduced herself, made various apologies, hoped she was still at the same address, but quickly got to the heart of the matter. 'We need you here in England,' she wrote, 'Josiah is missing you more than he can say.'

Chapter Fifteen

THE NOTE IN ELSPETH'S TRAY READ, 'Eve Nelson. Tues. 27/2
Duxford airport. Please meet approx. 3 p.m.'

'I didn't know there was an airport at Duxford,' said Elspeth to
the receptionist.

'You learn something every day,' said the receptionist, which was
a phrase she often used, but rarely lived up to.

'Did you take down this message?'

'I did. Have I left out something?

'What did she sound like?'

'She was friendly. Quite a posh voice.'

'She didn't say anything else?'

'Don't think so.'

'Thank you, Margaret,' said Elspeth. She laid the note out on her
desk and had it before her all day long, as though it contained some
secret code. While the recidivist Jason Mulvey was giving Elspeth
an account of his week, and how he'd failed in his quest for a job at
the local chippie, Elspeth was mulling over the word 'Please'. Had
Josiah's mother actually said the word, or was that Margaret's poetic
license? Had she been polite? Had her voice been steady? How she
wished that Margaret had been more perceptive, and could have
given her some clue as to Eve's state of mind!

Elspeth was relieved to find a little aeroplane printed on her Ord-
nance Survey Map. At half past two on Tuesday 27th February (she
had been watching the clock all day) she set out for Duxford Airport.
From her car she spotted a runway and several small aeroplanes

parked near the hangar, and was content to be on course. The signs which directed her to the 'Imperial War Museum' surprised rather than disturbed her. When she was further directed to the car park, she was sufficiently satisfied to be only mildly interested in the signs which pointed the way to the 'Museum Entrance,' which she momentarily considered a charming adjunct to any small airport trying to make ends meet. A further sign, 'Tickets this way,' doubly reassured her, as did the sight of a small plane coming in to land. She presumed that Eve Nelson was both very rich and very eccentric, for she was quite sure that the plane was one of those vintage ones without a roof, and if this was the kind Duxford Airport catered for, even its proximity to Cambridge wouldn't have lured your average businessman.

So, mulling these things over to herself, she walked into the ticket office. It was empty, apart from a couple of bored-looking women behind a till. There were a dozen or so books and leaflets on their counter, mostly on the history of flying, but Elspeth was still oblivious.

'Are you expecting a flight from Naples?' she asked.

Those women didn't quite get was she was saying; one of them asked her, 'So do you want a ticket or not?'

'Oh no, I'm not flying. I'm meeting someone off a plane.'

They both looked at her, nonplussed.

Then suddenly Elspeth almost hugged them in relief. 'It's all right,' she said. 'I think I see her.'

Through the window of the ticket office, Elspeth could make out two figures standing by the plane which had just landed. They were both dressed top to toe in leather, and were taking off their flying goggles; and the shorter and slimmer figure was throwing her arms around her companion, kissing one cheek and then the other.

'That's Eve, all right,' thought Elspeth. She walked through an outside door to reach them. She was barely conscious of the hectoring women behind her, 'You haven't got a ticket! You can't go through there without a ticket!' But hey, it was a bitterly cold February day, and they didn't follow her. Three pounds fifty wasn't worth catching your death for.

Elspeth walked towards the leather-clad duo; the woman began waving at her excitedly. One by one the features of Josiah began to appear, as out of a haze: the long blonde fringe, which she kept in place with a ruby-encrusted hair-grip; the lips, full and beautiful; the eyes, brown, alert and shifting.

'Antonio,' she said, as Elspeth approached, 'this is my saviour, Elspeth Hardy. Elspeth, you're a wonderful woman. And you're exceptionally pretty too. Antonio, you never told me whether you were married or not. If not, darling, this might be your lucky day!'

And when Elspeth found herself at a loss for words, Eve said, 'You are Elspeth Hardy, are you not?'

'I am,' managed Elspeth, just.

'Do you mind, then, if I embrace you, you person of the highest echelons?'

Elspeth stiffened while Eve's arms enfolded her.

'You are lovely. I adore black hair. One always lusts for what one doesn't have, don't you find?'

And then, after the air, and spirit, had been squeezed out of her, Elspeth asked, 'How was your journey?'

'Exhilarating, in a word. A tiger moth is quite new to me, you know. This amazing machine,' Eve said, as she stroked it 'is sixty years old today, isn't it Antonio? *Oggi ha sessanta anni, no? Il aereoplano.*'

'*Si, ha sessenta anni,*' confirmed Antonio, with an equal look of tenderness.

'It's the star performer in an air show on Saturday. And it was by the merest squeak of good luck that I managed to cadge a ride. It's always an advantage to have friends in high places. *E sempre una buona cosa avere i amici in posti elevati, non e vero, Antonio?*'

Antonio smiled. He seemed quite as confounded as Elspeth.

'But now, to business, my dear. Where's your car? Let's get out of here.'

'Don't you have to sign in or anything? Haven't you got any luggage?'

'Darling, I've got four layers of clothes under these leathers, which, incidentally, I'd better return to my dear friend. And somewhere amongst all of this is a toothbrush.'

'But what about your passport?'

'God, that expired years ago. Passports are for ninnies, aren't they, Antonio? *I passaporti sono por gli stupidi, no?* But it does mean you have to be on your toes. Did anyone notice you coming out here?'

'Well, yes,' said Elspeth. 'There are two ladies in the ticket office over there.'

'Well, then, we shall have to find a gap in the perimeter fence.'

'You can't!' pleaded Elspeth.

'Watch me. Antonio, pass me my wire-cutters. *Passame le cesoie, per favore.*'

Antonio did as he was told, removing them from a large pocket on his thigh.

'*Molte grazie, Antonio. Allora, vai alla biglietteria, parla con le due donne la, spiegagli tutto, domanda dell' ingegnere.*'

'What did you say to him?'

'Just to waylay the ladies while we get the hell out of here.'

'But you're breaking the law!'

'The law is for the innocent!'

'What about my job?'

'For God's sake, Elspeth, show some fighting spirit. Just keep your head and follow me. *Arrivederci, Antonio. Grazie per tutto.*'

In the event they didn't even need to cut through any wire. The Amazon found a weak link in a corner post and ushered Elspeth through it. They walked quickly to her car and drove away; Elspeth was shaking.

'I'm sure someone's going to follow us,' she said.

'Rubbish. People only get followed in the movies.'

'Movies are nothing on this,' said Elspeth.

'Relax,' instructed Eve. But then she held out her hands in front of her. They were shaking quite as much as Elspeth's. 'Humph,' she observed, 'We're quite a pair, you and I.'

'You give me the impression you break the law all the time.'

'I do,' said Eve, 'but it's not every day I go to meet my son.'

Eve took off a couple of jumpers and extricated a lipstick from the back pocket of her jeans. She pulled down the passenger mirror and attempted to apply it, but it was an impossible task and she ended up by wiping the whole lot over the back of her hand.

'I look awful,' she said.

'You look pretty good to me,' said Elspeth.

'You don't know how I normally look. Does Josiah live in the middle of Cambridge?'

'I've actually booked you into a B and B. I thought you might want to freshen up. He's not expecting you, you know. I thought we might have a chat on how best to introduce you.'

'A "chat"?' repeated Elspeth contemptuously. 'Good God, I didn't fly back to England for one of *those!*'

'Don't you want me to fill you in at all?'

'You think *you* can fill *me* in? Frankly, if there is a yawning gap within my soul it's not you who can fill it.'

'Is there nothing I can tell you?' pressed Elspeth.

'Listen, my dear. He's either fucked up or he isn't fucked up.' And then suddenly Eve softened her tone and sighed. 'Well, he's bound to be a bit fucked up, I suppose.'

'That's just what I want to talk to you about,' said Elspeth.

'All right, then. Tell me this. Is he healthy? Does he look well?'

'Oh yes!'

'And he's not on drugs? Does he drink?'

'Nope, he doesn't even smoke.'

'Then you can leave the rest to me.'

'He has got a Probation Order you know.'

'Yes, I know. And you're his Probation Officer. You told me.'

'Don't you want to know what he did?'

Eve shrugged. 'I shall ask him what he did.'

'Don't you want to somehow... prepare yourself?'

'Darling,' said Eve, 'I've been preparing myself for this for nine years and a hundred and fifty-two days. I don't need your help.'

'I'll take you straight there, then.' It had taken Elspeth forty minutes to surrender.

♣

Eve stood on the pavement waiting for Elspeth to drive well away, and took in a deep breath. *The Hollies* was already being overrun by children returning from school, but Eve was pleased: the front door was open and she could smuggle herself in. It's so strange, she thought, that even this promising and not unattractive Victorian House can smell like an institution: over-boiled cabbage, stale cooking oil, and bleach-based cleaning fluids. There were boys, even a girl, walking in and out of the kitchen carrying white jam sandwiches and plastic cartons of squash, sucking at them through straws; so intent were they on their consumption that no one seemed to notice her. Finally she approached one of the few who didn't have a straw in his mouth.

'I'm looking for Josiah,' she said.

The boy told her where his bedroom was, and she went upstairs to find him. The landing was large and light, its carpets cheap and frayed. There was a large wicker bin in the corner with a sheet of paper cellotaped to it requesting 'Dirty Laundry Please'; and pasted above it was an old poster of Freddie Mercury singing his heart out.

She knocked at his door. There was no reply. Even a second knock went unanswered. Slowly she opened the door and walked in. Josiah was lying on his bed in the dark, his curtains closed.

'Josiah,' she said, quietly. 'Is that you, Josiah?'

Josiah didn't even move, but let the words wash over him.

'Josiah?'

He wanted the voice again, so he held tight.

'Josiah? It's me.'

Even three times wasn't enough. He needed his name again, just to make sure the tide was finally coming in. So he kept himself still, and his eyes tight shut. Eve closed the door behind her and slowly walked up to his bed. She knelt beside him and stroked his hair.

'Josiah, it's me, Eve. Your mother.'

Josiah's breathing became deeper, and he said not a word, but listened very hard. His mother gently kissed his eyelids, kissed his cheek.

'It's no good, is it, being loved from a very long way away. It's not enough, is it?'

Josiah shook his head, and a tear or two escaped him.

'It's funny,' said Eve, 'to look down on someone else and see my mouth, my lips. It's like we were made in the same factory, you and I.'

Josiah opened his eyes, and when he'd wiped them dry with the backs of his hands he sat up and looked very solemn. Several times he tried to speak, but was like someone who had lost his place in a book, unable to pick up the thread. He stared at his mother and tried to understand.

'My life is yours now, you're the boss. If you hate me and tell me to go, I'll go. I'll do just what you tell me to. Do you want me to go? Shall I just go now?'

Josiah shook his head and began to cry again, more convulsively this time, and he put his arms around his mother and cried into her shoulder. Then Eve gave way too, and all she could utter above her own tears, again and again, was 'I'm so sorry! I'm so sorry!'

Not a word of explanation from the mother, not a word of any sort from the son, and, strange to relate, those two fell asleep together, and despite Josiah now being taller than his mother he somehow shortened himself, curving his back and bringing up his knees, lying his head on his mother's chest as if he were a boy of six; and Eve knew, perhaps for the first time in her life, what it was like to be the protector of some other person, and to commit to that role forever.

The noise of children coming up to bed woke them. They lay there in the dark aware of each others' breathing.

'What happened to your father?' asked Eve.

'He's dead,' said Josiah.

Eve sighed. 'That's no good, is it?'

After a while Eve got up and opened a window. The smell of stale cooking oil greeted her.

'How long have you lived here?'

'Nine years,' said Josiah, flatly.

'Good God.'

'It's okay.'

'How did your father die?'

Josiah paused. 'It was a medical thing.'

'Are you suggesting it might not have been?'

'Sometimes I think…'

'Sometimes you think…?'

'Perhaps he died because of me.'

Eve sat next to her son on the bed, and in the faint, sodium light she looked hard into that beautiful face.

'I tell you what,' she said, 'I killed him before you did.'

They sat close together, hunched over.

'We loved him, didn't we?' said Eve, quietly.

'Yes,' whispered Josiah.

'One day we'll plant a tree for him. You always knew your trees, I remember.'

'Where shall we plant it?'

'In our garden, wherever that might be.'

'I think he'd like an oak tree,' suggested Josiah.

And Eve said, 'Good choice. I think he was probably descended from an oak, don't you?'

'More than likely,' said her son.

And then, after they had both mused on the subject of a garden which was theirs and where an oak stood proud, Eve asked her son why he hadn't gone down to tea with the others.

'I don't have tea with the others. I can take something from the fridge later, if I want it.'

'Aren't they supposed to keep an eye on you? Make sure you're eating, darling?'

'I can do what I like here,' Josiah explained.

'And what do you like to do?'

'I don't go to school,' said Josiah, with a certain pride.

'So do you go out to work?'

Josiah shook his head.

'So what you like to do is coop yourself up here and occasionally go down to the fridge, is that right?'

'I've got a girlfriend.'

'Do you bring her here?'

'I spend weekends with her at her place.'

'Is she pretty? Does she live with her parents?'

'She's got her own flat. It's good.'

'I'm pleased you do something with your time.'

'No, it's good. It really is. And she cooks for me, too.'

'Is she older than you?'

'Yep.'

'And do you love her?'

Josiah paused to consider. 'If you want a Mars Bar I've got some in my top drawer,' he said.

'I don't want a Mars Bar. I want to know if you love your girl-friend. To be able to love someone is a great gift.'

Josiah switched on the light and pulled out the drawer. It was a swift, sudden movement. He looked down on her, and threw the Mars into her lap. The son and the mother, discrete physical entities now, individuated, alone.

'I don't understand what you're doing here,' he said.

His mother looked at him, surprised, hurt.

'I mean, hey Mum! Hey Mum! Why didn't you bother dropping by last year? Or the year before that perhaps? Mum! Does it ring true in your ears, that little word? Who are you to tell me that love is a gift? Who are you to tell me anything, anything about love?'

'I'm so sorry…'

'"Sorry" is what you say when you tread on someone's fucking toe at a bus-stop.'

'I'm going to go now.'

'No!' said Josiah, 'not this time!' At which Josiah bent double on the floor beside his mother and clasped her legs for all he was worth, 'You're not going! You're not going!' he sobbed, 'You're staying here!'

'I am!' said his mother, 'I am!'

Eve got down onto the floor with her son, and they lay together like two seeds in a husk, barely moving. They were joined at their shins, their heads perhaps a foot apart, as though each were looking into a mirror.

'Why did you go?' asked Josiah.

'Because I was a fraud.'

'How were you a fraud?'

'I was untrue to myself, to you and to Gibson.'

'But on that day, at that time? Why didn't you leave years before? Why did you ever marry him? Why did you even bother to give birth to me? Didn't you ever think it might have been easier to have had me aborted?'

'I only wanted to be kind. Gibson loved me. He'd never had a child. And the thing about kindness is that you can will it, you can make it happen.'

'But you yourself were incapable of loving, is that right?'

'I had done with love by then, Josiah.'

'How can you say that?'

'You can only love once in your life. Really, deeply, with all of you. So that not a speck of yourself goes on existing without that other.'

'So who did you love?'

'I loved a teacher of mine. His name was Gilbert.'

'And did he love you back?'

'He did, with all his heart. In the end, with his life. You don't get over that. Ever. You don't give like that again. You can't enter that void again.'

'What did he teach you?'

'He taught me who I was. He showed me what it was like to be human, how to extend every sinew of my body and soul and feel every feeling that was there to be felt. There are some ancient tribes, Josiah, that chew up food before giving it to their young, mouth to mouth. Gilbert gave me his warm, wet, living wisdom to sustain me as it had sustained him. Knowledge is the greatest thing one human being can give another, the greatest blessing one can bestow. When he killed himself, it was as though he had said, 'Fuck knowledge, fuck you.''

'And what happened then?'

'Well I was fucked, well and truly. Forever and ever.'

'And that was why you ended up in a psychiatric hospital.'

'So you know about that, at least.'

'You met my father there.'

'That's right, that dear man.'

'Did you need to be there?'

'Who needs to be anywhere? It's all so random. There's my morsel of wisdom for you. Everything is so random. So tenuous.'

'What can we do about it?'

'We have to pretend to be angels. We have to swoop down from on high and save deserving souls.'

'I can't think of anyone to save.'

'Yes you can, Josiah. There's always someone you can save.'

Now they heard the older boys coming up to bed, deeper voices, angrier. There was a large, ugly belch followed by fucking this and fucking that and why the fuck and you fucking prick.

'Is this what it's like every night?' asked Eve.

Josiah didn't answer her.

'Listen Jo, let's get out of here. I've got money now. I must practise using it. We can go to the Holiday Inn, you and I.'

'No, you must stay here with me.'

'But Josiah, there's an indoor swimming-pool at the Holiday Inn!'

'This is where I've always wanted you.'

'Large white towels!'

'I've always imagined you coming back, you know. I always knew you'd just walk in one day.'

'Can't we just get out of here?'

'I would lie in bed and you would come into the room as though you'd barely been away. And if it was Dad, he'd bring with him a story book, or a book about growing vegetables, and if it was you...'

'*Ritchie's First Steps in Latin.*'

'It was *Ritchie's First Steps in Latin*, yes, that's right. Now mother... no, I can't call you "mother" either. It's no good. But you are her.'

'I am her, yes, Josiah.'

'Now, mater. Perhaps I should call you "mater". Perhaps that should be my name for you. Or perhaps I sound like a Victorian prep-school boy. I want to be lying in this bed in my pyjamas. God, I haven't worn pyjamas for years, but I know I have some somewhere. I want the light to be off. And I want you to come and sit next to me and tell me the story of Jason and the Golden Fleece. And when I'm asleep you've just got to stay there, okay? You can't move.'

'My darling, I need to go to the loo, brush my teeth – see here my Neapolitan toothbrush!'

'There's a small bathroom on the next floor you can use.'

'But what if I bump into someone?'

'Just look glum and weary. No one will notice.'

'What if I'm accosted by a member of staff?'

'I'll go out and make sure the coast is clear. I'll be back in two ticks, okay?'

A snoop around Josiah's room was irresistible. But Eve was so moved by the very first thing she found in the drawer of her son's bedside table that she stopped in her tracks. It was a copy of Lucretius' *De Rerum Natura* and a small Latin dictionary. For Eve had *adored* Lucretius, whom she considered second only to Catullus. She had written essays at Cambridge for a wonderful man called Dr Sedley on the subject of Lucretius and sex, and when she thumbed through Josiah's edition she saw boys' handwriting in the margins and she couldn't believe quite how astute and observant this child was, this child of her womb.

She was sitting on the bed reading it when Josiah came back.

'I know what bedtime story I'm going to be telling you tonight, my darling,' she said. 'Can you read this stuff? I thought you'd given up school.'

'I can get through it,' said Josiah.

'Now, what about Chapter Four? Have you got that far?'

Josiah shook his head and looked embarrassed.

'I'm going to let you get into your pyjamas, dear boy, while I go and freshen up, as they say. Next floor up…'

'Immediately on the left.'

'I'll find it.'

So now it was Josiah's turn to be alone. Immediately he picked up his *Lucretius* to see whether Thomas had signed his name in the front of it, and when he saw that he hadn't he felt a huge surge of relief. He got changed and sat bolt upright in bed, looking guilty.

When Eve came back, squeaky clean, and without having bumped into a single soul, she took one look at him and exclaimed, 'Now, that won't do! Relax, darling! Do you want me to read to you in Latin or attempt some translation?'

'I can't speak Latin,' confessed Josiah.

'Well, we shall have to put that right. But tonight, as a concession, I'll do my best to put it into English. My God, I love you, Jo! My God, I do!'

So Eve sat down on the bed next to him like the mother she never was, and looked for 'the good bits', as she called them. 'Aha,' she said, 'perfect!'

'*Cum primum roborat artus*, when the limbs first grow strong, *namque alias aliud res commovet atque lacessit* ... isn't this just brilliant, Jo? *Alias, aliud*! Another time, another thing, in two words, just like that, to want that other place, that other time, that's what desire is like, isn't it? *Commovere, lacessere*, what verbs! Stirring strong young limbs into violent motion, he says it all, doesn't he, this Lucretius?'

Josiah looked anxious.

'But you've read this, haven't you? Or someone has.' Eve ran a curious finger over the crease of an old earmark.

'No, I haven't got that far,' said Josiah.

'Whoever receives the shafts of Venus, whether it be a boy with girlish limbs who throws him off balance, or a woman ... hey, Josiah, isn't this a wonderful idea, *toto iactans e corpore amorem*, have you ever done that, have you ever known the experience of throwing love out of your whole body? Like it was just too much for your body to cope with?'

Josiah gazed at his mother with a sort of wonder, not entirely appreciative. He said to her, 'Can't you just tell me the story of Jason, like you used to, in the dark?'

'In the dark?'

'Don't you remember how you'd tell me stories, lying next to me in the dark?'

Eve smiled and placed the volume of Lucretius back onto the bedside table. She turned off the light and both sat together for a while in the silence. Then when they lay down what a strange arrangement of bodies it was, Eve's head level with Josiah's waist, and Josiah's hand never letting go of her hair, even in his dreams.

❧

The following morning, Josiah and Eve took pride in the fact they used only one holdall and one large plastic bag to pack all their worldly belongings. Josiah waited until after the school exodus, and then took his mother downstairs to introduce her to a flummoxed Angela Day, explaining to her that the time had come to 'move on', and that he would be leaving *The Hollies* forever.

By ten o'clock they were driving North together in a VW Camper Van advertised in the *Cambridge Evening News* and paid for in cash.

They walked in Wicken Fen; they lunched in Grantham; they took tea in York and bought blankets from charity shops and top notch sleeping bags and torches from Millets. By the time they reached Jervaulx Abbey it was almost dark, and the cold, damp air lent the ruin a gothic, eerie quality. It was the moment in a winter's day when sun and moon glow faintly together, when all existence is luminous. Eve took hold of Josiah's hand and asked him whether he had ever read Wordsworth.

'Do you believe in the sublime?' she asked him.

'What do you mean?' asked Josiah.

'There's a wonderful line in Virgil Book VI, *Tendebantque manus ripae ulterioris amore,* 'And they stretched out their hands in yearning for the other shore.' We all do that, Josiah. Perhaps even people who buy themselves a new TV are *really* doing that. They want to be transported. And the people who built this place, and the people who prayed here, did so in hope of heaven. What is going on in the head of that kestrel, do you think?'

'I don't know,' said Josiah, honestly.

'Why do you think he's chosen to land on the apex of the highest arch?'

'To be close as he can to heaven?'

'I should think so,' said Eve.

They walked on further, skirting round gorse bushes and tripping over dips and large stones, and then they came to the step before the altar and sat down there, and listened to the occasional crow.

Eve said to her son, 'Now, I used to know the whole of this poem off my heart, but hear this, and see if it makes any sense to you:

I have learned
To look on nature, not as in the hour
Of thoughtless youth; but hearing often-times
The still, sad music of humanity,
Not harsh nor grating, though of ample power
To chasten and subdue. And I have felt
A presence which disturbs me with the joy
Of elevated thoughts; a sense sublime
Of something far more deeply interfused,
Whose dwelling is the light of setting suns,
And the round ocean and the living air,
And in the blue sky, and in the mind of man.

There was a pause, and then Eve said, 'It's a shame we missed the sunset.'

'It's okay. The dark is okay,' said Josiah.

'Do you think the music of humanity is sad?'

'I suppose so.'

'Do you think you've ever known the sublime, just for a moment or two?'

'Yes,' said Josiah, 'I have.'

☙

It was nine at night and the two were cosily ensconced in their camper van, up to their necks in blanket after blanket, and quiet as dormice, at least for an hour.

Suddenly Eve said, 'Tell me about Thomas Marius.'

Josiah said nothing.

'The man who lent you, or perhaps even gave you, those fine books. I noticed his name on one or two of the flyleaves. He won a fifth form prize, I noticed. *The Pilgrim's Progress*. Who is he, Josiah?'

And when Josiah still didn't answer her, she said, 'Did he take you to Florence? The tag's still on your holdall.'

Nothing.

'Is he a classicist? I'm sure I know his name.'

'He taught me Latin,' said Josiah.

'I love him already,' said his mother. 'Will you introduce him to me?'

It was only in the middle of the night when, sleepless and shivering, his mother watching him, he found his way to an answer for her. He kept Thomas' letter bound up in a pair of socks, which he retrieved from his bag and handed to his mother with a torch.

'You can read this, if you like,' he said.

She took it. The paper was small, thin and cheap; the address was Bedford Prison. It was dated November 21st 1999.

Dearest Josiah, (she read)

I shall never as long as I live forgive myself for what I have done to you. The month you gave me of your young life was inconceivably precious to me, but moments are moments, they can never be caught again, and I shall never be who I was and you shall never be who you were.

I think of you constantly, dear Josiah. I suddenly realized last week that you'll be in the sixth form now and I don't even know what A-Levels you're taking, nor how you did in your exams in the summer. I so want to know how you're getting on, but don't write if you don't feel like it. In fact, you mustn't write, and nor must I.

We shall probably never see each other again, and I'm convincing myself that it's better that way. I only pray that ultimately, when you're a man, you will look back on our time together with understanding, if not forgiveness.

With love, Thomas

Eve put down the letter.

'Did he hurt you?' she asked her son.

Josiah shook his head. 'He loved me.'

'Then you and I have a mission,' said Eve.

※

At 3 p.m. on Friday 2nd March, Elspeth was sitting in her office smoking, waiting for Josiah. At 3.05 p.m. she balanced a piece of paper over her coffee cup and thrust the stub down into the middle of it, and watched, mesmerized, while the burning edge became a glowing ribbon.

Josiah had never been late before. Even now she looked towards her closed door and felt Josiah on this side of it, his lankiness, his stillness, his power. And then she remembered, she had lost him, and she folded her arms on her desk and lay her head on top of them, as though the softness of her jumper could provide some comfort to her.

Her reverie was broken at 3.15. 'I've got Josiah Nelson on the phone for you,' said the receptionist.

'What, is he here?'

'He's on the phone. I'm putting the call through.'

Elspeth feigned lightness. 'Josiah, why aren't you here? I've been expecting you, you naughty boy.'

'Elspeth, I need you to help me,' said Josiah. 'I want you to find something out for me. I'm going to ring you back in fifteen minutes, is that all right?'

'Where are you speaking from?'

'We're in Yorkshire,' said Josiah.

'How are you getting on with your Mum?'

'It's great, really great, but we need your help.'

That word 'we' was unbearable.

'Fire away,' said Elspeth, and she wished with all her heart she were talking to a firing squad and not her boy.

'When is Thomas Marius going to be released? Do you think you could find that out? I mean, it's normally one of you lot that would pick him up, isn't that right?'

'Yes, that's right,' said Elspeth.

'So when shall I ring you back?'

'Hold on. I can find out right now.'

Elspeth typed Thomas's name into the client box of the Probation Service Portal and the details of his prison sentence and aftercare programme were conjured up before her.

'He's out in five days,' she said. 'Midday'.

'We're going to pick him up,' said Josiah, happily. 'And thank you, Elspeth, thank you for everything you've ever done for me.'

It was, as farewells go, quite a tactful one, thought Elspeth, as her forehead slumped forward onto her desk.

On the very same morning they went to fetch Thomas, Eve and Josiah paid a visit to the gutted barn near Caldecott. It was windy and raining.

'I once set fire to a few schools in Cambridge,' confided Eve, and they walked up the lane from the lay-by.

'You never told me you were an arsonist, too.'

'Oh yes,' said Eve. 'Though I never found out if I was a very good one. Was there some huge commotion after I left, can you remember? I mean, was your school still standing?'

'I think so,' said Josiah.

'I once wrote a letter to this arsehole called June Briggs. She never replied.'

'She is an arsehole, isn't she?' said Josiah, smiling.

'The thing about fire is that it goes on burning in your head. Did you find that?'

'I used to come back here, even before they found out it was me. I wanted to re-imagine it.'

'In my own head the fires burned for days, months. I wasn't left in peace a single night.'

'But my fire gave me peace,' said Josiah.

'Didn't you find, Josiah, that in the one simple gesture of throwing a match everything is contained, every layer of feeling that ever existed, every unacknowledged truth?'

'Mother, I did.'

'Ah!' exclaimed Eve, admiringly, when they reached what was left of the barn. 'It rather reminds me of Jervaulx. These great, black, charred structures are wonderful. Do you think a ruin has a greater soul if it's left to the weather for hundreds of years or created in an instant?'

'Do you really think this old barn has a soul?' asked Josiah.

'Darling,' said his mother, tenderly, 'it has yours.'

❧

Love is, perhaps, the ultimate mystery. Who knows why we love those we do? Who knows what need, what hunger, what hope possesses us when we finally admit to loving another? Love is a kind of stretching out and touching something other, something beyond us, and therefore beyond our comprehension.

Thomas Marius had loved Eve once, not that she knew it; had gazed at her across the table in the University Library and yearned to be noticed by her. Does a mouth, a gesture, an act etch itself forever into our very being, and hold itself there long after any conscious memory of it?

He stood there at the gates of Bedford Prison, thin and hunched and pale, looking out for the Probation Officer who'd been visiting him for the last month or two. He wasn't expecting a camper van. Even when it drew up within yards of him, the blonde hair, the waving, the smiling, took a while to impress themselves upon him.

Those two swooped upon him like angels, and they sat him between them on the front seat, and they said, 'Where to, Thomas? You say.'